WHAT WOULD YOU DO?

ANTICIPATION
DAY

JEFF
MICHELSON

ANTICIPATION DAY
Copyright @2024 OJDM LLC

Editing, design, distribution by Bublish

ISBN: 978-1-647048-36-5 (paperback)
ISBN: 978-1-647048-37-2 (hardcover)
ISBN: 978-1-647048-35-8 (eBook)
ISBN: 978-1-647048-38-9 (audiobook)

*Thank you to my family
for their unwavering support throughout this journey.
You all endured my late nights and countless revisions
with a smile and support.*

*Thank you to Goose the Band,
whose music allowed me to get lost in my imagination.*

*Thank you to cannabis for allowing me to access
the creative side of my brain.*

*Finally, to the readers who embark on this adventure with me,
thank you for giving these characters a home in your imagination.*

CONTENTS

PROLOGUE

CHAPTER 1

THE
SLEEPLESS NIGHT

MARCH 14, 2030

Dr. Joshua Lee rolled onto his back and stared at the ceiling. It was impossible to go back to sleep. He sighed and asked his virtual assistant, Sylvia, what time it was. Her response didn't help: "Good morning, Joshua. It is 4:33 a.m. local time, 6:33 p.m. Sydney time. Would you like me to summarize your upcoming day?"

"God no," Joshua mumbled.

"Alright, Joshua. Please let me know if you need anything," Sylvia replied.

At least he had gotten four hours of sleep. Drinking coffee past 8 p.m. was never a good idea, and having a cup at 9:30 p.m. to help calm his nerves was, in hindsight, an awful decision. With the biggest day of his life staring him in the face, Joshua should have popped some edibles, put on a movie, and gone to bed at a reasonable hour. Oh well, there was nothing he could do about it now.

He pulled off the blanket slowly and stumbled to the bathroom to relieve his bladder. Maybe that would help him relax.

After what felt like a record-breaking piss, he returned to the bedroom and opened the drapes of his suite on the top floor of the St. Regis hotel, staring at the bright lights of Washington, D.C.

He couldn't help but wonder what this day, three and a half *long* years in the making, would bring for him. Joshua had poured his heart and soul into this project, missing first steps, first words and one anniversary with his wife Julie, all for the goal of getting legislation onto President Randolph's desk for signature.

If that happened, and it was still a big if, Julie and Joshua could confidently say it had all been worth it.

As a result of this goal, he had been in Washington, D.C. for the past three painstaking weeks, which were filled with meetings, late-night sessions, and sleepless nights, all to prepare for his speech today to the Special Committee on Artificial Intelligence, a subset of the Senate Judiciary Subcommittee on Privacy, Technology, and the Law.

His colleague, Neil Jergenson, was more than happy to let Joshua handle the speech and was hopefully sleeping in his suite on the second floor. Given his fear of heights, Neil had suggested Joshua take the suite on the higher floor, which was ironic given how high Neil was all the time.

At the relatively young age of 35, even Joshua found himself physically and mentally exhausted by the end of this three-week stretch. As such, everyone on his team agreed that he should take it easy the day before the speech. So, he had done just that by working out in the morning, eating a lean, healthy breakfast, and reading some books he had packed before his trip from Sydney. After a nap, he ordered a late lunch from room service, watched TV, and practiced his speech.

Julie, their seven-year-old son Owen, and two-year-old daughter Olivia had returned to Sydney weeks ago. The kids needed to get back to school, and Joshua and Julie didn't want the kids around the media chaos that could follow his speech.

Joshua already missed his family dearly. And his home city of Sydney. He hadn't spent much time there since they moved to the United States a few years earlier to allow him to perform his research.

He eagerly looked forward to returning home after this exhausting process was over.

Julie had been an absolute angel, supporting him through each failure, redesign, subsequent failure, subsequent redesign, and eventual breakthrough. She was the rock of their family, never complaining about the long nights and weekends required of him and always understanding why it was necessary.

He was grateful she was by his side when he received the call that Neil and he were to present their findings to the panel after the huge success of human trials performed earlier in the year.

As he gazed out at the lit-up buildings of downtown Washington, D.C., tears welled in his eyes. He sighed, turned away from the window, and searched for the remote control to turn on the television so he didn't feel so alone. The local station popped on, with the "really early morning" crew reporting protests in London, which had broken out as a rebuttal to the Church of England's statement that Artificial Intelligence was against the teachings of the Bible and society should eliminate it in lieu of reverence for God.

"*Ah, London,*" he thought, sighing deeper than before.

Though he had been to London only a few times, the city held a special place in his heart. Even as a young boy, reading *Sherlock Holmes*, he had wondered what it would be like to walk the dark and misty streets of London at night.

As a teenager, watching old movies and shows about the Royal Family's history and majesty made him wonder what it would be like to be a royal, surrounded by people who were privileged and wealthy, yet so stuck in their ways. While traveling the world and being adored by millions of people sounded wonderful, the lack of privacy would surely get old after a while.

However, it was his visit to London in June 2026 that he would never forget, as it changed his life forever.

Lying back in bed, he switched off the television, hoping to get a couple more hours of sleep. "Don't get yourself worked up, J-Dog," he muttered out loud, using the nickname he had created when he was very young as a way of fitting in with the cool kids from school. "Stop thinking about London and focus on your breathing. In... out... in... out..."

Yet, breathing didn't help. His mind kept returning to London, to the raw excitement and hope from that phone call in 2026 that brought him to this very bed in Washington, D.C.

▼▼▼

Prior to 2026, Joshua and Julie had been planning a trip to London for many years, starting when they first met in college at the University of Adelaide in 2015. Back then, Joshua was a shy and soft-spoken 20-year-old junior studying computer science on the advanced track, hoped to be part of the generation that took computing technology to the next level.

Growing up as an only child in the middle-class community of Smithfield, in the suburbs of Sydney, he never imagined getting a full scholarship to the university, let alone being accepted into the Australian Institute for Machine Learning program to continue his research into the most advanced computing technologies of the time.

His studies and research took up most of his spare time through the winter holidays of his junior year, when he decided to stay on campus and finalize some of the programs he was working on.

One day in late December 2015, Joshua stopped by his local hangout, the Adelaide Coffee Bar, a few blocks from his apartment. It was there that he first laid eyes on Julie behind the counter.

It was the first time he had seen her there and she was stunning: long blonde hair, crystal blue eyes, and the warmest smile he had ever seen.

When he ordered his coffee and croissant, she greeted him with a friendly, "How are you doing today?" His brain urged him to respond, but his mouth would not follow suit. After several seconds, he managed to say, "I'm good."

As if that bland response wasn't embarrassing enough, he spilled his freshly received coffee across the countertop and onto her apron. He wanted to crawl under the counter and die. It was one of the worst moments of his life.

Fighting the temptation to run out of the coffee shop and back to his apartment, never to set eyes on her again, Joshua, returned to his table with a new coffee and croissant, and escaped into his work.

Thirty minutes later Julie approached him, and asked how he was doing. This time, he replied, "Well, I haven't made a complete ass out of myself in a half hour, so I'd say pretty good." She shook her head and laughed, which led to a huge sigh of relief from Joshua. He proceeded to learn about her studies in Marine and Wildlife Conversation, her part-time job at the coffee shop to save up for a chance to travel the world visiting the most exotic tropical locations, her love of the ocean, music, dogs, and, of course, London.

It was like the heavens had opened up and dropped down the most perfect woman a mere few hundred meters from where he lived.

This conversation eventually led to a first date, subsequent dates, a relationship, a marriage, a family, and a life together that Joshua could never have imagined when he first walked into that coffee shop years earlier.

After college, Joshua landed an entry-level software development role at a fintech upstart in Sydney, making decent money. At the same time, Julie had just landed her dream job working for the Australian Institute of Science, studying the impact of climate change on the coral reefs around Australia.

They got married in late 2019 and planned a honeymoon in London for the summer of 2020, but the COVID-19 pandemic ended any hopes of traveling. Once travel resumed in 2022, they planned another trip to London, only to have it derailed by Julie's pregnancy with Owen.

Finally, in the summer of 2026, when Owen was three, they decided to take the 30-hour trip from Sydney to Heathrow to visit London together, as a family.

It was an exhausting and stressful trip, with stops at most of the major touristy spots. However, it was the phone call Joshua received while sitting in one of the oldest pubs in London, The Seven Stars in Aldwych, that made it an unforgettable trip.

Before they left Sydney, Joshua had told Julie he wanted to grab a proper "pint" in London, preferably at one of its oldest establishments. While he wasn't a huge beer enthusiast, this felt like something he should do. Back then, the relatively few times a year he went all-in on his alcohol consumption, it was usually a nice Australian Shiraz or Pinot Noir. Occasionally, he would dabble in bourbon or scotch, mostly when Julie's parents visited, as her dad had developed a taste for the finer things in life, which included a good bourbon.

On their last day in London, Owen was cranky and tired, so Julie told Joshua to find a pub to have the (hopefully) perfect beer by himself for a few hours.

After some quick research, he saw a pub about a click away called The Seven Stars in Aldwych. According to the website, the pub was built in 1602 and seemed to have all the traditional English pub features: oak floors, wooden beams across the ceiling, and a narrow, steep stairway from the bar area to the second floor. Shakespeare was said to have frequented the bar while working at the Blackfriars Theater, half a mile away.

Funny enough, the owner was Australian and had settled there in the 1970s. It felt like the right place for his perfect beer.

Joshua was feeling down that day as he crossed London Bridge over the River Thames on his way to the pub. The rainy, chilly weather didn't help his mood but he was just in a general malaise.

Sure, he was happy with Julie and adored little Owen, but his career wasn't where he'd hoped it would be. In college, he and his friends had talked about how one of them would change the world by creating the next multi-billion-dollar tech conglomerate. Joshua always believed that he would be the one to do it.

While that hadn't happened yet, Joshua was still regarded as one of Australia's top code developers. He was working on exciting projects in the fintech space that he hoped would receive some investment soon.

On top of his career concerns, he and Julie had also been arguing more recently. He loved her commitment to her research and respected her greatly, but a lot of the day-to-day care for Owen fell on his shoulders since she had to be out of town for her research.

Joshua loved how his relationship with Owen had blossomed, and he loved spending time with his son, but the mental and physical exhaustion was starting to get to him. Owen missed his mom, and with nightmares recently creeping into his nighttime routine, Joshua was not sleeping well and he found himself taking it out on Julie, making her feel guilty for being away so much.

Joshua disliked the person he was becoming and wished his life had more meaning. That's why this trip to London seemed perfectly timed—Julie and he both needed family time together, and he had always wanted to explore London and learn more about its history and lore.

So, while his career wasn't where he ideally wanted it to be, he was enjoying this trip and looking forward to what life had to bring in the coming years. If he only knew how drastically his life was about to change.

When Joshua finally reached the Royal Courts of Justice complex and walked onto tree-lined Carey Street, he was craving a drink. He spotted the small black sign of the Seven Stars bar ahead and headed inside.

It was smaller than he had imagined but cozy, with many old posters and photos on the purple walls. Clearly, the owner was fond of cats, evident from the dominating cat-themed decorations.

The bar area was small, but given it was the middle of the afternoon, it was fairly empty, so he went right up to the bar to place his order. While the beer selection was above average, he went with a traditional Guinness and a beef and potato pie. As he ordered, he felt bad for the hotel room toilet later in the day.

There were stairs to the left of the bar that went up to the second floor, which he decided to quickly check out after clearing it with the bartender.

Upstairs, he found more cat photos, old movie posters, and a small kitchen where something was sizzling in the fryer. It was unlike any bar he had ever been in—the kind he would have likely hung out in if he were a local: quaint, simple, and homely.

Returning downstairs, he sat at a small table by the window with his beer. Looking outside, he thought about the people who frequented this pub throughout the centuries. If only the walls could speak, they would surely have amazing tales to tell.

After a short wait, he received his meal and quickly downed it as he was famished. He ordered another couple of Guinness and checked on Julie and Owen, knowing Owen usually woke up from his nap by late-afternoon.

As he settled his bill, his cellphone lit up with a private number. Normally, he would let such calls go to right to voicemail, but something in him told him to answer. So, he did.

Five minutes later, after a conversation with a gentleman from the United States Division of Health, he knew he needed to get back to the hotel right away to speak to Julie. He had just been scheduled to fly to Washington, D.C., in a week to meet with leaders of something called the Anticipation Day Task Force, which was apparently creating some sort of new simulation experience for citizens of the United States.

Joshua had been selected to join the Task Force by someone within the United States government, although the caller did not say how or why Joshua was chosen. Many questions flooded his mind:

Why him? What would this mean for him and his family's lives? Would they now have to consider moving to the United States? What the fuck was an Anticipation Day Task Force? What would people be anticipating?

He hurried through London's crowded streets, feeling a strong buzz from the combination of the beer and the recent phone call. Passing St. Paul's Cathedral, he stopped on London Bridge to take a few deep breaths and revel in his feelings. The universe seemed to have sensed what was missing from his life and instantly delivered the one absent ingredient: *meaning*.

It felt like his childhood dream had come true, and he was now in a *James Bond* movie.

He returned to the hotel and told Julie they needed to talk. It was a brief conversation, as Owen was begging for Joshua's attention, but Joshua was able to summarize the phone call for her.

While Julie needed time to process the news, as always, she promised to support him, even if it meant finding more help for Owen or working closer to home.

They had no idea what "supporting him" would ultimately entail.

▼▼▼

The sound of police sirens outside Joshua's Washington, D.C., hotel room window interrupted his thoughts. He checked the time with Sylvia: 5:15 a.m. Realizing he needed a couple more hours of sleep, he knew only one thing could relax him enough to put him out.

The one good thing about Julie and the kids leaving was having a huge hotel suite all to himself.

He grabbed his tablet, scrolled to his favorite adult entertainment website, and eight minutes later, he was out like a light.

▼▼▼

The extra 80 minutes of sleep boosted him enough to jump out of bed and into the shower when his alarm went off at 6:45 a.m.

The water pressure was so satisfying that he lingered under the hot stream for a bit, rehearsing the opening lines of his speech. He wanted to ensure he got the speech off to a strong start. While Joshua considered himself a decent public speaker and would have the speech there in front of him, addressing a Senate committee was on a different level. Not many people could prepare for the attention such a meeting would generate.

With the Senators, the media expected in the room, and the audience of hundreds that would be behind him, he half-considered wearing a diaper in case he shit himself. His only goal was to meet the Senators' eyes and project confidence, allowing them to see the intensity in his eyes and hear the passion in his voice, so they knew he truly believed in this technology. Getting the speech off on the right foot was important, so he practiced it until it became ingrained in his memory.

As he finished showering and got dressed, he couldn't help but think of how grateful he was to his family for their support on the long road it took to get to where he was today.

▼▼▼

Once Joshua and Julie realized they would have to move to the United States, Julie's mom decided to accompany them to help with Owen and household chores. The US government also funded a part-time nanny, providing plenty of support for Owen and allowing Julie to secure a research position at the University of Delaware, to advance her own research.

They settled in Rehoboth Beach, Delaware, a quiet and beautiful community situated between Washington, D.C., and Boston. This location allowed Joshua to fly out of Dover Air Force Base, about an hour away.

Joshua needed to split his time between meetings in Washington, D.C., and several leading artificial intelligence research institutions, including MIT, Harvard, Columbia University, Stanford, and the University of California, Berkeley. There, he worked with top researchers and the most advanced technology to expedite the program safely and swiftly.

Consequently, he spent only one week per month at home, which he requested as part of the government deal in order to spend time with his family.

Besides the family support, Joshua appreciated how lucky he was to have been chosen for this position in the first place. As it turned out, Danny Gonzales, a colleague of Dr. Claudine Shanley, the head of the Task Force, was visiting his sister at the University of Adelaide in the spring of 2026 and had happened to sit in on a panel on artificial intelligence that Joshua had led. The panel's topic was how artificial intelligence could lead to the development of simulated worlds, and Joshua had discussed the technological and ethical dilemmas of developing alternate realities.

While it was a great panel, the reality was anyone else with a similar background could have been chosen to be a part of this amazing and life-changing process.

▼ ▼ ▼

Joshua's 7:30 a.m. alarm to meet Neil downstairs jolted him back to his current reality. He checked his appearance in the mirror to make sure his salt-and-pepper hair looked as good as possible, his tie was as straight as could be and no remnants of last night's chicken dinner were stuck in his teeth.

He went downstairs to the hotel lobby, ordered a kale, apple, and carrot concoction to calm his nerves, and popped two prescription scopolamine to control his nausea.

Seated with his drink, waiting, as usual, for his colleague and research partner, Neil Jergenson, to meet him in the lobby for the ride over to the US Capital, he took some more time to reflect, this time on the insane journey the two of them had been on since their first meeting in the fall of 2026.

If they knew the trials, tribulations, failures, and significant graying of their hair it would take to get to this point, Joshua was certain they would still do it all over again.

▼▼▼

Joshua knew Neil was the right man for the job the moment he met him at the Black Sheep bar in Cambridge, Massachusetts, in September 2026. At first, he wondered whether Neil was old enough to drink legally; he had no facial hair, wore glasses, and had a voice that reminded Joshua of Screech from *Saved by the Bell* (Joshua loved cheesy 1990s sitcoms).

Alas, Neil was old enough to order a beer and turned out to be one of the most intelligent people Joshua had ever encountered, even at the tender age of 25.

Neil was an up-and-coming computer scientist who had recently graduated from the Schwarzman College of Computing at MIT. He was in his second year of research at the Computer Science and Artificial Intelligence Laboratory (CSAIL), focusing on visual computing.

They spent hours at the bar discussing the government's request. Neil was intrigued by the technological aspect, bringing up concepts like mind interfaces and implants, duplicating neural connections in the brain, downloading consciousness onto silicon-based devices to arrive at a theoretical Simulation Point, and running ancestral simulations.

Neil mentioned that CSAIL was already working on a smaller-scale project whereby humans could experience a full-scale simulation experience of a specific era within a pod. However, the simulation was limited to a made-up world, with an inability to fully engage all five senses. He was also aware of some private companies that had developed in-home gadgets to create a simulated world, but he hadn't personally tried them as they were costly.

With recent advances in quantum and neuromorphic computing, time dilation technology, reinforcement learning, and generative adversarial networks, they agreed that this could be accomplished relatively quickly with proper financial and regulatory support.

So, Neil came on board with an enthusiasm that was tough to match. Eventually, the Task Force funded hundreds of millions of dollars for securing computer and server equipment, hiring personnel to develop, secure, and test the technology, renting out facilities to administer the experiences, and analyzing the program's impact on the economy and society as a whole.

Over the next six months, Neil and Joshua worked closely with their academic research teams to develop a safe and efficient method for delivering this experience to the public.

While they were involved on the technical side of things, Joshua led all meetings with the Task Force and over 150 government agencies that were involved with the process—an amount he felt was about 50% too many. Unfortunately, this involved many painful and contentious meetings with government officials, lunch and dinner meetings with countless lobbyist groups, late-night meetings with government contractors located in Europe, and 6 a.m. meetings with government contractors in India, Vietnam, and other Asian countries.

The Task Force meetings were much more pleasant, with all the leaders focused on delivering this project as quickly and safely as possible. Joshua led the technological development, which was the most important one, given that if the technology didn't work safely and effectively, the rest of the mission would be rendered useless.

Other leaders on the force were tasked with sourcing data for the simulations, setting regulations around physical and mental health monitoring, sourcing and developing necessary hardware, recruiting test subjects, and overseeing many other changes within the Labor Department, Treasury Department, and the Justice Department, amongst others.

For Joshua and Neil, it was a lot of pressure to deliver something that not only worked, but worked so well that it would leave every participant wanting more. A lot more.

So, they were practically tied to the hip, except during Joshua's meetings with government officials, dinners, or Sundays—their day off. For Joshua, Sundays were dedicated to his family so they could enjoy peaceful walks on the beach, watch movies, or simply spend time together at home. These days were essential for him to help recharge the batteries.

Their hard work paid off in April 2027 when the approval for testing research animals was received, primarily to ensure the chip implants didn't impact brain activity or functions, and confirming there were no immediate issues requiring correction before the use of human subjects.

By late August 2027, as they entered a wait-and-see mode, Joshua and Julie took the family back to Australia to wait for the testing to move the process along. This was a refreshing break to spend time with their families, as they hadn't seen each other in nearly a year.

Unexpectedly, this trip turned out to be quite productive as, in September 2027, Julie discovered she was pregnant again, which certainly threw a wrench into their plans. When they found out it was a girl, Julie expressed happiness since she had always wanted a little girl, leading them both to view it as a blessing.

Julie gave birth to Olivia in June 2028, just as the technology received final approvals for human testing following successful animal trials.

After much discussion, Joshua and Julie decided that he should return to the United States alone. Being away from their extended families with the two little ones would be too difficult, especially since Joshua was going to be traveling so much for work that he wouldn't be home much anyway. It was a tough decision for him, but ultimately the right one.

His first official speech was delivered in August 2028 to the Committee on the Use of Humans as Experimental Subjects (COUHES) at MIT. He summarized the technology, its anticipated use, pre-and post-study monitoring of the human subjects, and the duration of the testing.

He received many questions regarding the potential physical and psychological impacts of this technology on subjects, as well as its ethical implications for society.

Luckily, his team had prepared for these questions and focused the committee on several important points:

1. The human subjects could select the time and location of their simulation, provided sufficient historical information existed for accurate recreation. This allowed subjects to mentally prepare for the world they were being transported to and what physical and emotional challenges they would expect. One of the key theories of this program was that the subjects' experience with their simulation would positively impact the subjects' emotional and mental well-being, even if the simulation itself was a stressful or negative experience.

2. Subjects had the option to change their simulation every year, so they would have the ability to learn and experience various simulations throughout their natural lifetime.

3. The human subjects would be constantly monitored, and they could terminate the simulation at any time, particularly if they felt emotionally unstable or uncomfortable, or if real-word events required their immediate withdrawal from the simulation.

4. The chip implant technology used as a link from the computers simulating the subjects' neuropathways used materials with minimal long-term health risks, validated through prior testing on animal subjects. Similarly, the ring device being utilized during the simulation posed no significant long-term risks to the patient.

5. The subjects would be monitored post-experience, both physically and mentally, to ensure any negative impacts are fully documented and addressed with appropriate medical attention.

Fortunately, the committee agreed, and human research proceeded in the fall of 2028. Forty machines were set up across MIT to conduct over 5,000 simulations, which were expected to take three to four months to complete.

For these tests, each subject would have two simulations run. The first would have the participant choose a historical period from three options provided. In the second simulation, they would choose a specific day from their lives to relive, requiring a separate download of their memories onto a secure drive stored on double-encrypted servers in a government-secured facility.

By January 2029, after completing their final test run and reviewing the favorable survey results, they knew they had accomplished nothing short of staggering.

While Joshua and Neil knew the next step was to convince governmental regulators that this would benefit society, they believed the data was unmistakable and irrefutable.

Over the following year, they monitored the subjects for any long-term negative side effects; with fewer than 1% reporting any such effects.

During this period, the Task Force nominated Neil and Joshua to present the results of this test to the newly formed Senate Committee on Artificial Intelligence, which comprised several influential senators. Approval by this committee almost guaranteed bill passage in the Senate. With Republicans leading the House of Representatives and a centrist Republican in the White House, there was not much to stop the bill from becoming law if this committee approved it.

In February 2030, Joshua and Neil were ready to present to the committee, which brought them to Washington for this morning's presentation.

▼▼▼

As Joshua took a final drink of his juice, he heard Neil's voice behind him say, "Good morning, fine sir. Are you ready for this?"

Joshua snapped out of his third trip down memory lane this morning, stood up, and shook Neil's hand. "As ready as I'll ever be. I slept like shit, but I don't think I was expecting anything else."

Neil quickly replied, "You and me both, but for different reasons. I had to kick that waitress from that Italian restaurant down the street out of my hotel room around midnight, but man, what a ride, if you know what I mean." He winked at Joshua.

Neil had gotten divorced a few months ago and seemed to be enjoying the single life.

"I don't know what you mean, but yeah, she was cute. Glad you enjoyed your night," Joshua said with a smile.

"Well, Bob at Rosenfarb and Craven called. He tried reaching you, but you must have been in the shower or jerking off or something. He wanted you to know that if today's hearing goes well, Claudine and other Task Force members believe we'll have enough support in the Senate to push this through quickly. Boom baby!

There's likely still going to be pushback from religious conservatives, but even some of them can be convinced, given they can go back in time to see Jesus or Abraham or whatever. He also wanted to relay the message, and I quote: 'Do not fuck this up!'"

Joshua chuckled and looked up before closing his eyes and taking a deep breath. As if he didn't have enough pressure to get this speech right, now he knew that this really had a chance of continuing to move forward. He felt both excitement and nausea; not only would there be a lot of eyes on his performance today in the room, but half the country was expected to watch this session live. Soon, he would be the face of Anticipation Day, whether he liked it or not.

Neil broke his train of thought, pointing out that their team was waiting outside with the van that would take them to the Capitol.

"Let's go get 'em, tiger!" Joshua heard Neil say before they exited the lobby into the cool, sunny day, climbed into the car, and headed toward the Capitol building.

CHAPTER 2

THE TESTIMONY

MARCH 14, 2030
- CAPITAL BUILDING 8:15 A.M.

Neil, Joshua, and their assistants, Magda and Omar, arrived at the Russell Senate Building 45 minutes before the 9 a.m. scheduled start time. As Joshua got out of the car and looked around, he remembered the riots of 2028 that had destroyed some sections of the Capitol area, including parts of the Russell building, requiring renovations and additional security measures both inside and outside the building.

As such, it took them about 15 minutes to fully get through security and enter the Russell Rotunda, where Joshua saw multiple white archways and columns extending from floor to ceiling, the coffered dome looming above, and doorways leading in multiple directions.

For anyone seeing it for the first time, the entryway was imposing.

The team walked upstairs to the Caucus Room, which featured a richly detailed ceiling highlighted with gold leaves, twelve giant Corinthian columns, and a multitude of pilasters that had to be over two stories high. There were mahogany benches scattered throughout the room and one large chandelier in the center, which was surrounded by four smaller chandeliers, providing ample lighting.

The room appeared to be about half full, with a few people putting the final touches on the seating and refreshments. A small table was set up in front of an elevated platform that housed a larger table to seat the eleven senators who made up the Special Committee on Artificial Intelligence, along with seats for aids and assistants.

Between the elevated platform and the smaller table, the members of the press attending the hearing were mulling about.

On the floor, there had to be a couple of hundred seats arranged for other attendees, including family, friends, and colleagues of Joshua and Neil, as well as assistants and other guests invited by the subcommittee. Two microphones and a pitcher with glasses, likely filled with water but which Joshua secretly hoped would be tequila to calm his nerves, were on the table.

Neil commented that he was going for a bathroom break. Joshua thought he should too, but before he could turn around to head to the restroom, he heard a familiar voice: "Hey Josh!"

He wheeled around and saw his old classmate, Chris Harbinger, from the University of Adelaide, walking toward him.

"Chris! What on earth brings you here, mate?" Joshua exclaimed, hugging his old junior-year friend.

"Hey man, I wouldn't miss this—you know that! I'm close to Marily Vazquez, and she invited me. She said you were awesome to work with. Looks like this process has grayed you a bit, huh?" Chris said, grinning.

Joshua smiled back. "Yeah, mate. It's been a few long years working on this. How the hell are you?"

"Yeah, the wife and I decided to get out of Sydney a few years ago. She got an opportunity to work for American University, so I applied for contracting work with the Department of Defense. I've been there ever since, doing cybersecurity work. Gotta keep the bastards in the US government honest on some level. But I'm loving it here. We moved to northern Virginia last year so the kids could have a bigger backyard." Chris paused, looking at Joshua. "Crikey, man, it's been so long; it's great to see you! I heard you were doing this presentation and had to find you to congratulate you on whatever world-changing invention you've created."

Joshua felt his Australian slang returning after just these few minutes with Chris. "Goodonya, mate, I'm really happy for you. I had no idea you were here. We lived up in Delaware for a bit before Julie got pregnant with Olivia. She stayed back in Sydney while I finished this roadshow. I wish I'd known you were here, but honestly, I was so busy that it would have been tough to get together. Now that I know, let's catch up after this meeting, okay? You were always a larrikin, but having you here with me means a lot. I gotta take a piss and get ready for this thing. Good seeing you. Find me after the hearing, won't ya?"

"Reckon, mate, good luck with this speech... come here!" Chris pulled Joshua in for another tight hug. "Go piss and give 'em hell!"

"Thanks, Chris. Good seeing you." Joshua turned and headed to the restrooms outside. Chris was a fun time back in college, and their brief conversation calmed Joshua down a bit.

After taking care of business and ensuring he looked presentable, Joshua returned to the room, which was now mostly full. He recognized some familiar faces—colleagues of Neil and other folks he had met at MIT, Harvard, and other colleges during their travails over the past couple of years.

He saw Danny Gonzales, whose recommendation to Claudine Shanley started this process years earlier. Joshua went over to say hello, shook his hand, and then sat at the table to review his speech for what felt like the 4,721st time. Unfortunately, Claudine wasn't at the meeting as she was recovering from back surgery a few weeks earlier. However, they had spoken the day before, and she had wished him good luck and told him how proud she was.

He spent the next ten minutes scanning the speech to ensure he could recite most of the beginning by heart.

Finally, around 9:00 a.m., an announcement was made: "The meeting of the Special Committee on Artificial Intelligence will commence in ten minutes."

Joshua stood, stretched, and saw Neil, Omar and Magda walking towards him, all engaging in small talk with one of his old colleagues. Eventually, Omar and Magda took their seats behind Joshua while Neil sat next to him at the table, giving him a slight nod that said: *You got this.*

At exactly 9:10 a.m., the rear doors closed, and everyone was asked to take their seats. Doors on the side of the room opened, and the eleven senators and their aides began to enter.

The cameras flashed rapidly as the Senators walked in. Joshua recognized their faces immediately from preparation meetings with his team. There was:

Senator Marsha Johnson (R) from New York, Chairwoman
Senator Alberto Guiterrez (R) from Florida, Ranking Member
Senator Harlan Connelly (R) from South Carolina
Senator Chris Donogue (D) from Massachusetts
Senator Kyle Drummond (R) from Colorado
Senator Diane Fielding (R) from Wyoming
Senator Jane French (D) from New Jersey
Senator Jack Hughes (D) from Florida
Senator Robert Mulligan (R) from Arizona
Senator Michael Smith (D) from Minnesota
Senator Robin Tuttle (D) from Virginia

As they sat down in their seats, Senator Johnson took a sip of water, adjusted her microphone, shuffled some papers in front of her, and prepared to give her welcoming remarks.

"Good morning. The hearing will come to order.

I want to thank everyone for being here, especially those of you who traveled a great distance to attend this 22nd meeting of the Special Committee on Artificial Intelligence. Thanks to the Ranking Member and his team for working with us to organize this hearing.

Artificial intelligence is one of the key issues of our time. Its development and implementation is causing, and will continue to cause, significant changes in healthcare, entertainment, the environment, the economy and the way we interact with each other. The very concept of artificial intelligence will challenge our definition of what it means to be 'human.'

Over the past few years, technological advances have increased fivefold due to breakthroughs in computing power and chip technologies. These advances raise concerns about the impact of this technology on everything from privacy and surveillance bias and discrimination to our physical and mental well-being. The questions of regulation and compliance are something this committee has taken very seriously throughout its three and a half years of existence.

However, we have never faced a proposal like the one before us today. If this proposal becomes law, it will result in a full transformation of American society. Therefore, no one on this panel, whether Republican or Democrat, should take this responsibility lightly.

As Stan Lee once said, 'With great power comes great responsibility.' Our task is to ensure that if the government grants the power of a full-scale simulation to each eligible citizen, it is delivered safely, securely, and methodically, and monitored in a responsible and consistent way. This will ensure the long-term implications are properly understood and addressed.

As Shakespeare said, 'We know what we are, but know not what we may be.' All the members of this panel aim to ensure that what we may become in these simulations does not impact what we are as human beings in the real world.

Today, we are here to discuss the results of the technology developed over the past several years to support Bill S1042, sponsored by Senators Mary Childs and Tom Barrows. This bill, introduced last year, proposes to legalize an annual simulated experience for eligible citizens of the United States. The Chairman of the Senate Judiciary Subcommittee on Privacy, Technology, and the Law assigned this bill to the current committee.

I welcome the insights of Doctors Joshua Lee and Neil Jergenson, who have led the development of this technology. They are here to present their findings to this panel. With that, I turn to the Ranking Member, Senator Guiterrez."

Joshua's eyes drifted to his right, where Senator Guiterrez was sitting.

"Thank you, Senator Johnson, and to the expert witnesses for being here with us today.

I cannot think of a more important issue for this panel to discuss than what appears to be a full-scale government-backed takeover of the human mind, for what you say will lead to a happier society. While that sounds idealistic in theory, my Republican colleagues and I have significant concerns about the security, practicality, and moral implications of this rollout.

How can we honestly guarantee positive outcomes for everyone entering these simulations? The mere suggestion to let human beings choose another world to live in for a predetermined period, experience the realness and intensity of that world, and even possibly die in that world leads me to believe this technology is not ready for real-world deployment. We lack a full understanding of this technology's long-term implications for the average American's psyche.

I want to ensure this does not fall into the same category as other failed social experiments like Winthrop Kellogg's Ape, or the Stanford Prison Experiment. Far too many lives are on the line here.

While I appreciate the longing to lead a different life—trust me, I, too, would love to be an astronaut on Mars for a month—the reality is that my real life lies here on Earth. I owe it to the people of Florida and throughout the country, to fully vet and challenge this initiative before I vote to move it forward for consideration.

I hope this committee can maintain a balanced approach, ensuring this technology is secure, safe, and monitorable before making it available to the American public. I look forward to hearing from our witnesses today. Thank you, Chairman, for scheduling this committee."

Chairman Johnson cleared her throat and continued, "Thank you, Ranking Member Guiterrez. Let's begin with our witness introductions.

Our first witness today is Joshua Lee, lead scientist and researcher for the Anticipation Day Task Force. He is a graduate of the University of Adelaide and a recognized affiliate of the Massachusetts Institute of Technology, Harvard University, and Brown University.

We'll start with Mr. Lee's statement. Please aim to stay within 30 minutes; we will not use the gavel for a slight overrun, but if you exceed five minutes, I will have to remind you of the limit. Thank you for your cooperation. Mr. Lee, over to you." Chairman Johnson set down her microphone, and the room fell silent.

Joshua took a deep breath, quickly sipped some water, and resisted an urge to release a huge fart. After glancing at Neil beside him and checking his notes for the last time, he looked back up at the eleven senators. "*Here goes nothing,*" he thought.

"Chairman Johnson, Ranking Member Gutierrez, distinguished Committee members, and staff members who made today possible, thank you for the opportunity to discuss the findings of our Task Force. We believe that these results hold far-reaching implications for our society going forward. I extend my gratitude to the Task Force for giving me the honor of being here today, especially Dr. Claudine Shanley, who has been both a mentor and friend.

My name is Joshua Lee, lead researcher on this project, which has been the passion of both my colleague and friend, Neil Jergenson, and myself for the past three and a half years.

I vividly recall the day in London in the summer of 2026 when I received a call from a man I had never spoken to before who told me that I had been handpicked to join a new task force which had been created to develop a transformative simulation experience for every eligible American citizen.

As soon as I hung up, I knew my life was about to change, but I could not have imagined how much.

With the support of my family, we moved to America to begin a three and a half year journey that has led us here today. From the beginning, the primary goal of my team and the rest of the Task Force was to ensure the technology we developed was applied safely and securely. Secondarily, we aimed to develop an experience so lifelike that it would transform the lives of whomever experienced it.

Neil and I tirelessly worked on developing, testing, and securing this technology to interface with our neurological and nervous systems to facilitate a seamless and safe transition between the real and simulated worlds.

We have conducted over 10,000 simulations, with results that speak for themselves, as I will discuss shortly.

But before I do this, I have a simple request for each member of the Committee: please indulge me for a moment." Joshua paused for a second before continuing.

"Close your eyes and try to tune out any noise in this room. I promise I won't pelt you with anything, but I can't vouch for other folks here." Laughter broke out in the room as Joshua grinned at the line he had incorporated the previous night.

After exchanging brief glances, the Committee members smiled and eventually closed their eyes, relaxing.

"Thank you for indulging me. Now with your eyes closed, take a few deep breaths, relax and calm yourself."

He waited a moment. "I hope everyone is there. Now, I want you to picture a place. It could be a town, a city, a house, a beach, a lake, a national park you've been to, or any other place that lives in your mind's eye. This place doesn't necessarily need to hold special meaning for you, but it should bring you some level of peace and happiness. Have you found your place?

Now that you've found your place, pick a year. Any year—it doesn't matter. It can be this year, or you can go back millions of years, even to the time of the dinosaurs. Okay? Have your year?"

The room was mostly silent.

"Good. Now, picture yourself in this time and place and think about what you see: Are there people? What are they wearing? Do people even exist yet? Is this a natural setting? What surrounds you? Trees, oceans, mountains, forests? Are there animals? If so, what are they doing? Take a moment to truly see and feel this place."

Joshua glanced up at the Senators, who appeared deep in thought and, importantly, calm.

"Think about what you can hear. If people are nearby, are they talking? What are they talking about? Are there cars or other vehicles? Are there natural sounds, like the wind, rain, or animals? Take a moment to imagine the sounds in this place.

Now, think about what you can smell. Are there people who smell? What do they smell like? Are the smells pleasant? Foul? A mix of both? Are there smells from cars, trucks, or other man-made objects? If you're outside, what do you smell from the natural world around you? Perhaps the salty air near the ocean or the sweet, fruity, or musky fragrance of flowers. Take your time to breathe in the various scents of your chosen place."

Joshua paused for effect.

"Next, think about what you can touch. Are you indoors, where you can feel objects like tables or chairs? Are you in a city with cars or buildings that you can touch? Or are you outside in the wilderness, able to touch trees, water, or grass? Can you feel a person's skin? Think about what and who you can touch in this place.

Finally, think about what you can taste. Think about the local cuisine, if there is one. Is it something you have eaten before? What is the texture of the food and the drinks? Imagine those flavors on your tongue. I sense some of you are hungry; I can hear your stomachs growling."

A few chuckles arose from the crowd. Joshua quieted his voice.

"Keep your eyes closed for a moment and picture yourself exploring this place in your mind—whether for a day, a week, a month, or a year. What things would you find? What people would you meet? What sights would you see? What food would you eat? What thoughts and emotions would you have about being in this time and place? Hold those thoughts for a moment, please."

There was complete silence in the room, interrupted by the occasional click of a camera shutter or the shuffle of shoes on the marble floors.

He counted to ten.

"Thank you. Please open your eyes." The Senators opened their eyes looking relaxed.

"Think about what you are feeling right now. Happiness? Positivity? Peace? If I offered you the chance to visit this place once a year, or any other place of your choice, what would you feel? Hopeful? Less stressed?"

He took a moment before saying the next word.

"*Anticipation?*

Think about that word: anticipation. Are you anticipating being able to experience this time and place one day? To live whatever life you desire? To experience a whole new world free from the stress, drama, and repercussions of your current life? Forget, just for a moment, your political affiliation, race, sex, religion, or lack thereof, or the people you represent.

Each one of us knows the pleasure of anticipating something. Whether it is a favorite restaurant meal, knowing you and your partner are about to make love, or seeing a live performance of your favorite sports team or artist, that feeling of anticipation is one of the most powerful emotions we can have as humans. It makes us appreciate being alive and everything life has to offer.

Would it surprise you to learn that anticipation releases dopamine, resulting in a decrease in negative or painful feelings along with increased arousal and excitement?

What if you could harness that sense of anticipation for the entire year?" Joshua emphasized the word "entire."

"Imagine anticipating a positive, uplifting event every day for the rest of your life. After experiencing this technology, we believe every human being will anticipate these experiences every year for the rest of their lives and will strongly incentivize them to meet the program's eligibility requirements around physical and mental well-being, criminal activity, citizenship, and more. It is why this program was named Anticipation Day.

As I mentioned, our simulations will allow participants to revisit any historical period supported by recorded facts and figures. The technology will develop an entire world, which will be loaded onto dissolvable chips implanted safely and painlessly in human subjects. These chips store multiple petabytes of data sourced from over three trillion historical records—governmental, academic, and others. These data sources allow us to recreate how a Great Pyramids builder would have lived their life or what a Mt. Everest climber would go through second by second.

Any period in recorded or scientific history is available for every citizen to choose from. However, spiritual texts such as the Bible, Torah, and Quran require separate consideration and agreement on how certain historical religious events would be portrayed in the simulation. For example, there is no scientific proof of Jesus' resurrection and walking on water, but it could be recreated in a simulation based on the descriptions in the Bible.

Theoretically, we can simulate any purported historical event, regardless of scientific backing. Who's to say we can restrict people's curiosity to see how Noah built his ark, even if there is no proof it happened as depicted in the Bible?

We understand these are sensitive areas requiring further consideration and we look forward to those conversations."

Joshua turned a page of his report and took a quick sip of water. He should have worn a damn diaper.

"One exciting area of development in the field of neuroscience technology that Neil and I are most proud of is its ability to recreate a specific day from a person's life.

These simulations will be based on a download of memories obtained from the human subject in order to recreate any chosen day that is supported by actual memories. Yes, we can do this.

Think about the ability to relive a day with a loved one who has passed away or revisit an amazing trip with your best friend after college. Senator Mulligan, you could even go back and experience that high school football championship game again," he said, prompting a few chuckles around the room. Senator Mulligan smiled at him, nodding subtly.

"*I've got 'em,*" Joshua thought.

"We feel this option will greatly benefit individuals who may want a more familiar and personalized experience.

Our technology is powered by a network of supercomputers with 1 million petaflops of computing speed. A petaflop can perform one quadrillion, which is ten to the 15th power floating point operations per second. This speed allows us to replicate the human brain's activities and support approximately 1 million daily simulations.

Due to the amount of energy these servers will demand, more renewable energy sources must be prioritized to avoid overloading current systems. This bill will provide the largest investment in renewable energy in history, with nuclear, hydrogen, geothermal, fusion, wind, solar, and hydropower leading the charge. This bill will also continue our investment in carbon sequestration technology to offset any increase in carbon dioxide emissions due to the program's rollout.

Our technology will benefit from top-tier cybersecurity programs, with the backing and experience of the most talented cybersecurity experts in the world.

In conclusion, we believe the development of this technology is a remarkable achievement that was unimaginable, even just five years ago. We are immensely grateful to the teams and partners who helped us get to this point. This will transform the life of the average American in ways they can't imagine.

Now, I will proceed to discuss the results from last year's trials. As detailed in the materials submitted to you, we selected 10,210 volunteers from a random pool of over 30,000 eligible volunteers aged 18 to 70, with no restrictions based on race, sexual identification or sexual orientation, religious background, or geography.

These volunteers primarily came from specific subsectors of the population, such as government employees, doctors, scientists, and key academic leaders. Additionally, a small percentage of individuals were from the general population, including social media influencers, leaders of Fortune 1000 organizations, and others we believed could effectively advocate for the implementation of this technology.

Each participant obtained clearance from their primary physician and a trained psychiatrist. Furthermore, all subjects signed waivers acknowledging any potential risks associated with the experience.

There were two parts to the trial.

For the first part, 5,105 subjects were presented with three simulation options:
1. Living in New York City in 1939, during the World's Fair, as the owner of a pizzeria.
2. Living in Rome in 1875 as a day trader.
3. Living in Tibet as a monk in the present time.

Among these, 1,996 chose New York City in 1939, 2,126 chose Rome in 1875, and 983 opted for Tibet as a monk.

The subjects could also choose to be in the simulation for what would feel like one week, one month, or one year. 2,797 chose one week, 1,798 chose one month, and the remaining 510 selected one year. We expected some hesitancy among participants to choose longer times due to the newness of this experience.

To clarify, regardless of the chosen duration, the actual simulation lasted approximately seven hours in real life.

After completing the simulation, the subjects were asked to give detailed feedback on four specific questions about their experience:
1. Was the experience positive or negative?
2. Would they have this experience again?
3. Would they prefer a shorter or longer duration for future simulations?
4. Would they recommend this experience to others?

We also asked a series of questions regarding their physical, emotional, and mental well-being before and after the simulation to ensure it did not impact their capacities.

From the trial's subjects, an astounding 99.6% said they would absolutely or likely want to do the simulation again, with over 92% rating the experience as positive. The 8% who found it negative all ended the simulation early. Most of them mentioned they didn't enjoy the simulation they chose but would try a different scenario again. We believe this issue will be rectified by allowing participants to choose their own time and place upon implementation.

Another interesting finding was that over 93% of the subjects said they would choose a longer period, for example going from a week to a month, or one month to two months, etc. Among the 7% who said they would prefer a shorter time, most had chosen to experience a year and found it too long to feel like they were away from their real lives.

A remarkable 98% of participants recommended others go through this experience, while the remaining 2% were unsure. No one, I repeat, not a single individual suggested others not to experience this. We believe this validates our position that participants felt safe and enjoyed their overall experiences.

For the second part of the experiment, a separate group of 5,105 subjects was chosen to relive a day from their past. This required a download of their memories to find the chosen day.

The subjects were briefed on the simulation and the fact that the day would be relived based on how they remembered it, not necessarily how it actually happened. This simulation, of course, would feel like it lasted 24 hours. In the future, should this legislation be approved, we may look to increase the duration of the simulation, which would require the recall of additional memories.

Again, 96% of the subjects reported it as a positive experience with this part of the trial. This is understandable, given that the day they chose likely brought back warm and happy memories.

73% of the subjects chose a day to see a deceased loved one, while 15% picked a day to relive an accomplishment, such as winning a sports championship or spending a good day with their family. The remaining 12% selected a day to relive an experience with an ex-lover or friend they no longer spoke to.

97% of participants would recommend this experience to others, as even if the day they chose didn't bring back positive emotions, the experience itself was positive.

As you can see, the vast majority of subjects in both experiments had a positive experience, would proceed with the simulation again, and would do so for a longer period."

Joshua quickly looked at Neil, who gave him a thumbs-up.

"Now, on to the participants' physical and mental health. We asked the subjects a series of questions, which you can find in our submitted research papers, about their mental health before and after the simulation.

What emotions did they feel? Did they feel depressed? Did the simulation experience cause any confusion after it was over?

One key component of the simulation is that the memories from the simulation stay with the participant, like a dream. Most participants could remember a good portion of the details of the simulation, but the longer the simulation went on, the fewer specifics they could recall from the entire simulation, similar to real life.

As Dr. Jergenson and I have each done two simulations ourselves, we can confidently say that the detail you see in the simulation is as real as anything you experience daily.

However, we recognize that even if participants report a good experience, they still require monitoring for any potential threat of depression or anger, which could lead to self-harm or harm to others. This would be counterintuitive to what we are trying to achieve. Therefore, we steadfastly support continuous physical and mental monitoring post-simulation to identify and rectify any significant negative side effects immediately.

From a physical well-being standpoint, we monitored significant vital signs during the simulation, such as body temperature, heart rate, respiratory rate, blood pressure, and oxygen levels. We also tracked brain activity during the simulation to ensure it remained within normal levels. The simulation mimics the third stage of the sleep cycle, the deepest stage, where heart rate and respiratory rates are at their lowest and muscles are fully relaxed. This allowed subjects to wake up feeling rested and refreshed, allowing them to recall their simulations as much as possible afterward.

Of the 10,210 subjects, only 98 developed negative physical conditions post-simulation. These included 30 heart-related issues, 22 cancer diagnoses, and the remaining cases of various other illnesses. All the cases were eventually determined to be unrelated to anything from the simulation. Currently, 21 of the cancer patients are either receiving treatment or are in remission. Unfortunately, one individual developed pancreatic cancer and passed away earlier this year, but this was not related to the simulation experience.

From a mental well-being standpoint, we required monthly check-ups for every participant to monitor their mental health post-simulation. When negative mental conditions arose —conditions that would normally require medical or psychological follow-up with a trained professional—we conducted full follow-ups with the subject's primary physician or a certified psychiatrist to ensure the root cause was identified and treated.

Of the 10,210 subjects, 224, or 2.2%, had negative mental conditions post-simulation with 128 related to depression, 68 to anxiety, and 28 to other non-life-threatening mental conditions.

Among the 128 depression cases, we spent significant time with the subjects to determine whether they had a history of depression prior to entering the simulation. Medical records and subsequent interviews revealed that 84 of these subjects had a family history of depression, while the remaining 44 did not. Of these 44 without family history, 32 did not believe the simulation caused their depression, whereas 12 believed the simulation was a factor. That equates to 0.12% of the total subjects for the trial.

Of these 12 cases that believed the simulation was a factor in their depression, eight had symptoms alleviated within 12 weeks after the simulation, and the remaining four within 24 weeks.

Notably, 72% of the depression cases were related to the second experiment, where the participants relived a day in their lives, which we attributed to the fact that it evoked memories of someone from their past, such as a relative or friend that had passed or an ex-lover that got away, for example.

The remaining 28% who experienced depression from the first experiment attributed their symptoms to the overall sad environment they witnessed or other miscellaneous reasons.

The Task Force worked very closely with all cases of negative mental conditions to ascertain whether the simulation may have caused or led to the condition and to ensure ongoing monitoring of these subjects. We have not found any direct link between the simulation experience and any long-term mental issues. To repeat, we have *not* found any direct link between the simulation experience and any long-term mental issues.

This conclusion was verified by the International Psychotherapy Institute and the American Psychiatric Association. The Task Force has teamed up with these and other organizations to accurately and consistently monitor the subjects post-simulation, especially those at higher risk of depression, anxiety, or other negative mental conditions.

We have received opinion letters from the American Psychiatric Association, the American Academy of Child and Adolescent Psychiatry, the Depression and Bipolar Alliance, the American Mental Health Counselors Association, and others. These letters support our position that the simulations do not appear to pose a mental health risk to the average American. They recommend that monthly or quarterly check-ups be a required part of this legislation.

You will find these opinion letters in your materials.

The Task Force expects a reduction in negative mental conditions after proper preparation and guidance. Our analysis shows that the percentage of subjects that had a negative mental condition post-simulation is consistent with the overall population, confirming our believe that the simulations would not result in any uptick in the overall depression rate nationwide.

With all that said, we do understand that the intensity of the experience may cause emotions the subjects are not used to feeling. Consequently, we will continue working with public and private institutions to ensure that future subjects are properly monitored and update guidance accordingly.

The Task Force is also proposing a two-to-three-hour monitoring period directly after the simulation, overseen by trained doctors and psychiatrists, to ensure each patient is tracked for potential negative conditions.

All subjects underwent at least two hours of monitoring post-experiment. Only 114 subjects were kept longer than the required two-hour 'cool down' period, with 28 of them hospitalized overnight and 14 admitted for a longer period of time for further observation.

All those kept longer were discharged within two weeks, only after receiving clearance from certified physicians and mental health experts who reviewed their reports and determined they posed no harm to themselves or others.

Once individuals could see someone familiar, like a relative, significant other, or friend, their symptoms notably diminished or ceased altogether, so the doctors were comfortable with their conclusions.

The Task Force is also recommending monthly or quarterly mental and physical checkups as a requirement for Anticipation Day to ensure all individuals are healthy enough to go through this experience.

Based on an internal analysis provided to you in the submitted materials, we believe that a decrease in overall healthcare costs will significantly outweigh the cost of these periodic checkups, emphasizing preventative healthcare over reactive healthcare.

To conclude, the Task Force believes that these simulations will allow the average American to have something to look forward to in their life. We hope that every law-abiding citizen will be able to experience this.

We firmly believe this will be a transformative experience for society and eagerly look forward to working with the committee and Congress to finalize this once-in-a-lifetime legislation."

Joshua took a sip of water before continuing.

"Senators, please recall the time and place at the beginning of my speech and the feeling you had when you had your eyes closed, imagining this place of your choosing.

Our hope today is for you to hold on to that feeling. That feeling of happiness. That feeling of peace. That feeling of anticipation. We want to ensure every American can have that same feeling. We believe this will be a positive, transformative, and life-changing experience.

Thank you for your time and we welcome any questions you may have."

Applause erupted from those seated in the back. Joshua felt a sense of relief wash over him. He had nailed the speech and gotten through it within the allotted time.

He looked to his right at Neil, who patted him on the back, smiled, and said, "You're the man. Good job."

Joshua returned Neil's smile, bracing himself for the question-and-answer portion of the session, which would turn out to be the longest 90 minutes of his life.

CHAPTER 3

THE DECISION

JANUARY 15, 2031

Joshua knew he should have worn something lighter. A black shirt and dark brown shorts were not the best choice on a bright sunny day with temperatures already at 33 degrees Celsius by 11 a.m. Sydney time.

"*Oh well,*" he thought, taking a sip of water and continuing the never-ending task of stripping weeds from his garden. Unfortunately, the past several months after the committee presentation had been filled with meetings with government officials in Washington and New York, meetings with Neil and his team discussing tweaks they would like to make to the software, and a hundred other meetings that he could barely recall. As a result, everything at his home in Australia had taken a back seat.

With Julie focusing on the kids and schooling and maintaining some semblance of organization inside the house, the outside went by the wayside.

Recent storms had left the yard in a mess. The house needed a power wash, and the garden and landscaping needed a good touchup.

It was a simple house with a beautiful backyard that Joshua loved maintaining, filled with dahlias, roses, and jacaranda bushes mixed with a variety of wildflowers. Bottlebrush, whitegum, and sillyoak trees lined his property, creating a stunning spring bloom. Bushes and flowers surrounded the house, extending all around the sides to the front.

Unfortunately, all of this just created a mess on the ground.

Joshua could have hired someone to do this cleanup, but if he was being honest with himself, he found this work zen-like. After the stress and chaos of the past few years, gardening gave him a sense of peace he hadn't felt in a long time. The sounds of cockatoos and lorikeets whistling in the morning sun relaxed him, and the feeling of the sun on his skin warmed him. Given he was usually stuck inside most days, getting some natural vitamin D felt rejuvenating.

The buzz of the insects around him brought him back to his childhood and his fascination with bees. It made him feel connected to Mother Nature, even if Mother Nature was an absolute bitch sometimes.

So, after returning to Sydney for the holidays in December and finally spending time with his family through the New Year, Joshua was tasked with the unenviable clean-up that awaited outside of his house.

He was up on a ladder, pruning one of the large sillyoak trees while listening to his favorite band, Audiozine, when his virtual assistant, Sylvia, alerted him to an incoming call.

"Joshua, Claudine Shanley is calling. Would you like to answer it?" Sylvia asked in a deadpan voice that sounded like his mom's.

"Yes, Sylvia," Joshua replied as his heart started racing.

"Hi, Claudine. How are you doing today?" He asked as the call went through.

"I'm good, Joshua. Dealing with a snowstorm here in D.C. today," Claudine said from halfway around the globe. Luckily, technology had improved so much that her voice was as clear as if she were sitting next to him in his yard. "How are you?" She asked.

"Oh, I'm okay—just trying to clean up my yard, which looks like the friggin' Amazon. The one downfall of traveling the world for the past few years is that I haven't been able to spend much time with my garden. It's slightly depressing. I'll get it cleaned up, but it's going to take a Herculean effort at this point. Anyway, I'm sure you didn't call to talk about gardening. What's the good word? What is it, 9 p.m. in Washington?" Joshua asked, wiping his brow and grabbing shade beneath one of his larger acacia trees.

"Yeah, it's late, but I just got some news I figured you'd want to hear. I hope you're sitting down in your garden." Claudine paused, as if waiting for Joshua to confirm.

"I'm not, but should I be?" Joshua's voice seemed hesitant.

"You definitely should be. So, I just heard from Bob that we have the votes in the Senate, and they're voting on it on Monday. Barring a nuclear bomb going off in Washington, this should head to the President next week for his *signature!*" Claudine's voice was filled with delight, making Joshua smile instantly.

"Holy shit... I do need to sit down," he slowly replied. "That's amazing! Does Bob know what the final bill will look like?"

Claudine took a moment to reply, sounding distracted: "Well, from what I heard, after a ton of back-and-forth, it has about 90% of what we were looking for. Over 21 years of age, unless enrolled in the military, have no recent criminal record, a valid government ID, and no psychiatric conditions in the past five years.

The government will cover 50% of the cost of a subject's memory recall. I think the goal is to keep the fee under $1,000, which should be doable based on what the new vendor is telling us. So, in total, the participants will be responsible for up to $500. It's not perfect, but that will be a decision they will have to consider themselves.

They agreed to allow people to skip a year if they desired, but two consecutive skips would require them to reapply to join the program.

They were fine with allowing up to a year of simulated time. There was some pushback from a few senators, but based on our results, they were able to get over the hurdle.

Unfortunately, we lost the privacy battle; all simulations will now be recorded and stored. Republicans were adamant about tracking any potential threats as they popped up. It's Big Brother at its finest, I guess, but we figured that would happen.

They were also persistent about having an emergency cancellation option, but supported our opinion that participants should be able to redo the simulation if a personal emergency requires them to cancel the simulation.

I agreed. We can't afford any heart attacks or stress-induced issues coming out of the simulations. And all that other stuff you suggested? Yeah, they went for it." Claudine paused.

"All of it?" Joshua asked, shocked.

"Well, most of it. There were some tweaks, but the core was yours. So, congratulations. This should become law in the next month or so. I'll pause there—are you still with me?"

Joshua took a deep breath, trying to process Claudine's words. "I'm sorry, I'm just speechless."

"Total win," Claudine said firmly. "Bob told me your mini-simulation speech at the subcommittee meeting back in March greatly affected the Senators, and they managed to convince their party leadership to at least work with their colleagues to get something done here. Who knew you had a calling as a speechwriter?"

"Ha." That was all Joshua could muster for a few seconds. "Well, whatever the reason, I'll take it! So, is that it, then? Is this a done deal?"

"According to Bob, it is," Claudine answered. "I wanted to be the first to call you and say what an honor it has been to work through this with you. When I first brought this to the Department of Health years ago, I never imagined in my wildest dreams that we would reach the point where it's ready to become a law in the United States! It's insane! I couldn't have asked for a better partner and friend to work with. Your dedication—and Neil's too—is why we're here today. Thank you for trusting me and letting me guide you through this process as best I could"

Joshua felt tears welling in his eyes. It was amazing how quickly humans could go from smiling to tears rolling down their cheeks. All the emotions of the past few years since his trip to London seemed to come out simultaneously, and he couldn't stop them.

"I'm sorry—I just can't help but cry right now," he managed amidst the crying and sniffling. Good thing Julie was inside; she would have started crying too, which would have made it worse for him. "Thank you for those kind words, and it has been my pleasure to go through this journey with you."

He paused briefly and added, "I will tell Julie and the kids. Can I call you on Monday?"

"Of course, Joshua. Enjoy this with your family; you deserve it."

That was the last thing he heard before the line went dead.

Joshua stood there for what seemed like an hour, gazing up at the sky and thinking about the past few years of his life and what the next chapter of his life would be like. The ups, the downs and the moments of doubt that this program would never come to fruition combined with the sleepless nights and the time away from his family.

All offset by the moments of joy when the team had a breakthrough that worked and the pure elation when they reviewed the survey results together after the initial testing was done.

He was truly part of an amazing team and all of the rollercoasters of emotion they all went through felt worth it at this moment.

Knowing that he was a key part of something that could change the world for the better made him feel a sense of peace and calm that he had never felt before. It was like whatever happened in his life from this point on was icing on the cake. A big, delicious piece of Lamington cake.

While Joshua was excited to see how the deployment of this program would go, he couldn't help but wonder if everything would go exactly as him and his team thought it would.

As Joshua got to the house, he took a deep breath, composed himself and smiled as he walked inside to share the news with Julie.

CHAPTER 4

THE ROSE GARDEN CEREMONY

FEBRUARY 18, 2031

Dr. Claudine Shanley sat in her chair in the White House Rose Garden on a cool but sunny February afternoon, wrapped in a warm jacket, a wool hat snug over her head, and gloves covering her hands.

This was a day that was a long time coming, and Claudine felt proud and honored to be among the many powerful and influential figures gathered, waiting for the President's speech. Today's ceremony followed the official signing of the Anticipation Day bill, formally known as the *Advancement of Society and Healthcare Spending Reduction Act (ASHSRA)*. The name was apropos, though she didn't really care for it.

Claudine was confident this day would go down in history as a monumental change in the arc of human society. While it was hard to fathom that her work was the reason all of this started, at the end of the day, she was just doing her job. If she hadn't discovered the initial unusual patterns, someone else would have. Yet, as the saying goes, "Things don't turn up in this world until somebody turns them up."

"I guess I'm the somebody," she thought, staring into the empty space in front of her.

Glancing at her family sitting all around her, their faces beaming with excitement, Claudine's heart warmed. However, her thoughts kept drifting back to early January 2026, when this journey began.

▼ ▼ ▼

On January 12, 2026, Claudine sat in her Rockville, Maryland, office completing her normal Monday morning routine: reviewing datasets and summaries from state mental health agencies in order to prepare for weekly debriefs with her team.

Given the data was from right before the holidays, she had expected to see some data that looked unusual. The holidays were often stressful and depressing for many, either from overspending on presents or from spending the holidays alone.

Either way, the diagnosis of depression and anxiety disorders usually spiked in November and December. Claudine would typically contact the relevant states to get their view on the anomalies, scheduling calls for the following week. The issues were typically resolved quickly and the datasets returned to normal.

This time, however, something was off—several data sets were not making sense to her. To boot, the data that was off was in random parts of the country, which, from her experience, was rare.

As Director of the Behavioral Health Crisis Coordinating Office for the Substance Abuse and Mental Health Services Administration, Ms. Shanley had seen it all during her 30+ years in the field. From the drug wars of the 1990s to the various mental health issues that confronted the United States after 9/11, she had witnessed almost everything imaginable before her promotion to Director in 2019.

Shortly after taking on this role, the COVID-19 pandemic and the subsequent societal shutdown, coupled with the rise in social media use among the youth, caused a rise in anxiety and depression rates across the country that had never been seen before.

Most recently, she had been dealing with the growing opioid and fentanyl addiction crisis and its related impact on mental health.

There was never a dull moment in her line of work.

Part of the reason for her promotion to Director was that she and her team were able to identify trends in reported mental health cases across the United States that warranted further investigation, research them to quickly identify the root cause, and develop systematic solutions to prevent further spread.

Most trends they investigated involved periodic spikes attributed to seasonal affective disorder, binge drinking, opioid use disorder, or bipolar disorder.

However, the datasets her team saw in January 2026 involving reports of increases in schizophreniform disorder appeared to be something that she had never encountered before.

In her experience, schizophreniform disorder was typically diagnosed when symptoms of schizophrenia—such as delusions, difficulty concentrating, and decreased participation in daily activities—presented themselves for a period of one to six months. After six months, the diagnosis generally shifted to schizophrenia.

So, when she read the monthly summary from several states noting a tenfold increase in schizophreniform disorder cases compared to the same month the previous year, she paid close attention.

Claudine took further notice when she saw that the average diagnosis period for the reported cases was around three weeks, which contradicted the typical length of time for this diagnosis. The patients were snapping out of exhibiting schizophrenia symptoms and presenting normal behaviors to both doctors and their families within weeks, not months, baffling the entire team.

Historically, when there is both a change in trend data and a fact that goes against current understanding, it indicates something new that requires further investigation. As she followed up on the impacted counties to obtain information about the demographic characteristics of those impacted, blood results, and other tests performed at medical facilities, her antennae raised even more.

From her initial reachout, it was determined that the new cases of this short-term schizophrenia were primarily affecting men and women, mostly over 40, from various wealthy clusters across the United States: New York City, Boston, Austin, Texas, and Silicon Valley, amongst others.

Historically, when she observed wealthy people impacted by mental health issues, it involved some sort of illegal drug: cocaine, acid, LSD, fentanyl, or whatever new drug of the month was causing rich people to lose their minds. However, drug tests for these initial cases did not support this theory, as most patients tested negative for any known substances.

She and her team were initially stumped. Although much about schizophrenia was still unknown, some general trends were widely agreed upon:

1. Females had a higher prevalence of mental illness than males.
2. 18–25-year-olds had the highest prevalence of mental illness, with the prevalence decreasing with age.
3. Mixed-race individuals had the highest prevalence of mental illness, followed by American Indians and Caucasians. Individuals identifying as Asian had the lowest prevalence of mental illness.
4. Higher-income individuals had lower rates of schizophrenia than poor individuals.

Essentially, while older, rich individuals had some risk of developing schizophrenia, they were not generally considered high-risk. So, everything her team was seeing went against the known patterns of the disorder at the time.

Initially, there were theories thrown out suggesting some sort of early-onset dementia or Alzheimer's disease. However, the percentage of patients with a family history of these conditions was in line with averages for the United States. Additionally, CT or MRI scans showed no brain lesions or brain damage, though a few people did have small tumors that were discovered incidentally.

Other theories involved previously unknown drugs or viruses that were undetectable when the patients presented themselves for testing, but the virologists Claudine contacted dismissed this theory.

So, again, Dr. Shanley and her team were stumped. Personally, she was frustrated, as she prided herself on quickly picking up on a trend and identifying potential causes.

By February 2026, similar schizophrenia episodes were reported in 15 states, with over 2,500 individuals affected. She then received clearance to conduct a full investigation to determine what was driving this increase. The summary findings she reviewed were perplexing.

The night she read the summary in early March 2026, sitting in her bed with a glass of Cabernet by her side, she was overwhelmed by the magnitude of its implications.

That report, now engrained deep in her memory, was presented to the late President Logan later that month.

Though the investigative process eventually uncovered the root cause, she couldn't shake the thought that if her team had identified it sooner, they could have helped more people. By the time corrective actions could be taken, over 500,000 people had been diagnosed with schizophrenic disorder.

She hoped the long-term impacts of these cases would be minimal, though it was hard to say. Despite doing everything "by the book" and informing department leadership as quickly as possible, she still felt it wasn't fast enough.

Regardless of how she felt, her journey to the Rose Garden ceremony was long and personal. A journey that eventually led to President Randolph signing the legislation this afternoon.

▼ ▼ ▼

A police siren brought Claudine back into the present. She turned to her boyfriend, Charles, who was sitting beside her, and smiled. Behind her, her two daughters, Eva and Monica, chatted with their husbands and children about where they wanted to go eat after the ceremony.

Claudine was so happy to have her family with her today. They were the reason she did everything and they fully supported her journey to get here today, even with all of the scrutiny on her and her team's work over the past several months.

As she turned back and looked at Charles, she smiled and once again got lost in her thoughts.

▼▼▼

Claudine had lost her husband to cancer three years ago, in the middle of this entire process. After a long period of mourning, she finally got up the courage, with her daughter's insistence, to join a popular dating app called *Higher Connections*, where all of the people on the app were cannabis users. One of the dates through this app resulted in her meeting Charles, a widower who had lost his wife to a car accident 18 months ago.

They bonded over their shared grief, and eventually, their friendship became romantic. Six months later, they were still together, and she was happy he was here. She needed a rock today, and he was it.

Her work to finalize the Anticipation Day bill led to much public attention for Claudine, which, given her introverted nature, was difficult for her. Claudine's family supported her as best they could, but there was only so much they could do. The committee presentations available to the public plastered her face on every news channel and media outlet across the country. Calls flooded in: TV show bookings, media spots, speaking engagements, and even a book deal. Forced to hire a publicist and not see her family for weeks, she worked tirelessly with House of Representatives and Senate members to finalize key parts of the legislation.

While not as popular as Michael Jackson in the 1980s, Michael Jordan in the 1990s, or Taylor Swift a decade earlier, she was still a face people recognized in public.

It was one of the reasons she had asked Dr. Joshua Lee to deliver one of the final presentations to the Special Committee on Artificial Intelligence a year ago. She needed a break from the limelight, and he was up to the task. She appreciated Joshua for stepping up to give that speech.

Some days, she still wondered how this could happen to a girl from Asheville, North Carolina.

Meeting the late President Logan back in 2026 was one of the most nerve-racking, yet coolest, experiences of her life. It was rare for a federal agency director to interact directly with a President, at least in one-on-one meetings.

Though most of that day was a blur, the 60-minute conversation with President Logan was fully engrained in her memory. He was genuinely interested in getting her thoughts on the situation, strategies to confront the root cause, and the level of support she needed to develop an alternative solution. Despite his reputation as a selfish and narcissistic guy who didn't care about the average American, her interactions with him suggested otherwise.

President Logan had always supported the foundation of this bill, even if it was tough to discern his true motives. While she believed he supported the program to benefit the average American, a small part of her suspected that he wanted to take credit for the program himself.

Nevertheless, his administration consistently provided support and funding, so he deserved all the credit for getting the bill to this point today.

Unfortunately, President Logan was assassinated in February 2027 and was quickly replaced by Vice President Randolph, a new-generation Republican leader who had been elected to the office of Vice President just a month earlier after former Vice President Ruff's forced resignation due to a bribery scandal that ended his political career.

Before his vice presidency, President Randolph had served as the head of the Environmental Protection Agency, and was known for his tireless work to help shift the country to nuclear and other renewables as part of President Logan's push for a zero-net-carbon society by 2045.

Even though President Randolph was a Republican, he was able to win favor with some Democrats due to his scientific background and general respect for science to guide proper policy.

In a short span, President Randolph had gone from head of the EPA to the most powerful man in the world. His first huge task was taking over President Logan's work on the Anticipation Day Bill.

The assassination, unexpectedly, seemed to finally bring the country together. Extremists on both sides turned down the heat enough to cool temperatures, allowing politicians to work together again. Talking heads on both sides of the aisles stressed unity and compromise rather than division. It was a strange yet productive time in Washington, D.C.

For his own Vice President, President Randolph chose someone with experience and relationships on both sides of the aisle: former Vice President Paul Hughes, who had served under President Bush in the late 2000s.

This was a solid choice, as Mr. Hughes brought key relationships and experience to the administration and was instrumental in nailing down the key economic provisions of the bill.

Claudine did not envy President Randolph or Vice President Hughes, as this bill's impact would fall squarely on their shoulders, for better or worse. Sure, she was its architect, but people don't remember the architects; they remember the administration in place when bills are implemented.

▼▼▼

The sound of trumpets broke her train of thought. She immediately refocused on the podium in front of her. Once the trumpets ceased, a booming voice projected from the speakers across the Rose Garden: "Ladies and gentlemen, the President of the United States, accompanied by the First Lady, and the Vice President of the United States, accompanied by the Second Lady."

"Hail to the Chief" played as President Randolph, Vice President Hughes, and the first and second ladies walked out and greeted the crowd.

President Randolph waved for thirty seconds or so before gesturing for everyone to sit. He singled out Claudine in the front, and she waved back shyly. Over the past several months, they had grown close. She felt very close to him and his family—his wife, Sandra, and their two little daughters, Haley and Ella. They were his world; Claudine knew President Randolph wanted this program to go well for their sake.

After the crowd sat in their chairs and quieted down, the President began his speech in a loud and confident tone.

"Thank you. Ladies and gentlemen, thank you for joining us on this beautiful, historic afternoon in Washington, D.C. This is a treat for Sandra and me, as well as Suzanne and Paul, to share the signing of this bill with you in the Rose Garden. This Rose Garden has been the site of many historical legislation signing ceremonies, from the establishment of Martin Luther King Day as a federal holiday in November 1983 to the signing of the Protect Act in April 2003 to the signing of the Bipartisan Safer Communities Act in June 2022. We believe today's legislation will add to this amazing list of legislation.

When I joined the EPA in 2018, I vowed to be open to all ideas that crossed my desk, regardless of how preposterous they seemed. I have succeeded throughout my career by hearing all viewpoints before deciding on a course of action. So, when I assumed the late President Logan's responsibilities, my first task was to think about how the concept of Anticipation Day would change the lives of qualified Americans and their families. The question I had to ask myself was simple: Would this legislation improve their lives, or would it make it worse? Was this concept too unusual to proceed with?

However, when you look back on the history of science and civilization, ideas that have elevated society were often considered unusual at one point or another:

1. The 3500 B.C. invention of the wheel, which helped to revolutionize agriculture and commerce.

2. Johannes Gutenberg's 15th-century printing press, which allowed for the mass production of books, making knowledge more accessible worldwide.

3. Thomas Edison's light bulb, invented in the 1800s, which brought electricity into homes and eliminated the dependence on natural light.

4. The 1960s creation of the internet by a team of computer scientists working for the U.S. Department of Defense's Advanced Research Projects Agency, which connected people globally and enabled unprecedented information exchange and access.

5. Artificial intelligence, which is already reshaping every aspect of human society, from healthcare to the economy to how we consume information and interact with the world.

So, after discussions with members of several Departments, my Cabinet members, and my family, I decided that I wholeheartedly believe that what we do with this legislation will improve the average lives of every eligible American citizen and their families.

We fully believe this bill will lead to a healthier society, both physically and mentally, by providing people with something to look forward to and implementing preventative healthcare measures rather than our current reactive healthcare system.

As President, I believe that every American can and must be better, both to each other and to this planet. I hope that giving people access to this technology will create a more advanced and harmonious society—one grounded by core principles like family, well-being, and taking care of the world around them for future generations. A society where peaceful coexistence is expected to participate in the experience of Anticipation Day.

This experience will be unlike any other. It will change you in ways you didn't know were possible. It will transport you from your everyday life to a world of your choosing—a world that is yours for the taking—to accomplish whatever you want, experience whatever you desire, and find peace again with your mind, body, and soul. The kind of peace that is difficult to achieve with the everyday worries about work, money, health, and countless other stressors the average American has. Believe me, as President, I understand that my stressors may be different than yours, but they *are* stressors nonetheless.

Now, to everyone here in the Rose Garden, watching on television, listening in your self-driving cars, aboard trains or planes, or at home, I have a simple request. It's going to sound silly, but please humor me.

All I ask is that you close your eyes. If you don't have a self-driving car, please do not close your eyes, but wait to try this at home. Everyone else, please close your eyes and tune out the world for a moment. I'll wait ten seconds."

There was silence in the Rose Garden as Claudine glanced around at the attendees closing their eyes. She joined them, hoping not to fall asleep in the process.

The President continued, "Now, imagine you could go anywhere in the world. Anywhere at all. No restrictions. Where would you go? Are you on a beach in the Caribbean by yourself, listening to the crashing waves? Are you at the base camp of Mt. Everest, attempting a summit you have always dreamed of? Are you visiting Tuscany and sampling wine among the beautiful local vineyards? Or, are you back with a loved one who passed away a few years ago, reliving a wonderful day you had together while they were alive? You can choose any place you want. Go ahead and imagine that place. I'll give you a few seconds."

Once again, there was absolute silence in the Rose Garden. Claudine wondered if other places were as silent as here.

"Now, imagine the time period you wish to be in. Do you want to return to World War II, fighting for the United States against the

Germans? You can. Do you want to witness the birth of Jesus? Go ahead. Do you want to live alongside dinosaurs like the T-Rex and Brontosaurus? Sounds fun to me! Any year that can be recreated by our supercomputers is possible.

Again, I will give you a moment to imagine the time you want to visit your chosen place. Although, maybe you have changed your mind given what I just said," the President added with a chuckle.

"Focus on the place you have chosen. This place is yours and yours alone. Ask yourself: Would you like to fully experience what it's like to live in this time and place for what will feel like a week, a month, all the way up to one year?"

Now, please open your eyes." The President paused as the crowd open their eyes before he continued.

"Be honest with yourself. If your answer is 'yes,' welcome aboard. You are signing up for an adventure of a lifetime—one that will be life-changing for all involved.

If you find yourself saying 'no,' that is okay. You can still opt out of this program. I can understand the hesitancy in allowing the government to lead this kind of initiative.

However, I have three things to say to you:

First, once you hear from your family, your friends, your colleagues, and others about how amazing and easy this experience is, you will change your mind. Word-of-mouth will be our biggest advertisement. That's how confident my administration is in this program.

Second, my administration will crack down hard on unregulated and underground simulations attempting to mirror this program. Anyone caught manufacturing, distributing, or participating in these underground simulations will face fines and jail time. We want this program to be administered safely and securely so that all participants can be properly monitored by certified professionals.

Third, as you will hear in a little bit, there will be a financial incentive to participate in this program. A rather large financial incentive.

Before I continue, I wanted to inform everyone that Vice President Hughes, First Lady Sandra, Second Lady Suzanne, and I have *all* participated in our individual Anticipation Day experiences.

My experience was in December 2030. Due to security protocols, the Vice President and I had to schedule our experiences at different times, so Paul took his in November 2030. As I joked with him before I did my own experience, I said I was going to simulate being him to see what it was like to work under me. That would have been a good test of how good the supercomputers really were."

The President looked back at Vice President Hughes, who was laughing, as were some of the members of the crowd behind him.

"I'm just kidding, of course. While I cannot divulge my experience, I promise you that it was utterly surreal and life-changing. Sandra, Paul, and Suzanne would all agree with me when I say it is safe, realistic, and helped all of us appreciate our real lives a hell of a lot more.

I can only speak for myself when I say that the feeling in this simulated world is indescribable. At first, you're scared and nervous, trying to understand how such a world could be created. Once you get used to that concept, slowly but surely, you become your simulated character. You have their memories, you see yourself in a reflection and somehow accept that you are this different person, and this is your real life for however long you are in the simulation.

Eventually, you just become that person. And that feeling of becoming someone else is so freeing and uplifting that it's almost hard to put into words.

However, I will stay that the strangest part was not using the bathroom, which you don't need to do while in the simulation. I have to say I got used to not needing to use the facilities for a month, or at least what felt like a month.

President Randolph laughed as he said that last part, and the crowd in the Rose Garden joined him in light laughter.

"But on a serious note, what I want to stress to the American people tonight is that in my heart, in my soul, and in everything true and dear to me, I knew by the end of this experience that I was a changed person. For the better. I appreciated everything I had in my life more, and I learned to see the world from someone else's point of view.

And that's what we want. We want people to be better. We need people to be better. We want and need people to have more empathy and understanding of other Americans. We want that feeling of anticipation to dominate everyone's life going forward.

Think about the last time you anticipated something. Maybe it was going on a vacation for the first time in a year. Or maybe it was your first date with someone you have had a crush on for months. Maybe it was seeing your favorite band live for the first time in ten years. Maybe it was just taking a day off work to do nothing but sleep and watch TV.

Stop and think about how that made you feel. I bet it made you feel damn good, didn't it? You can't look me in the eye and say that's not a feeling you want every day of every year. That is the feeling we want you to have with this program. We want each of you to have something to look forward to, so that, even on your darkest day, you have something to escape to, something to keep living a healthy and happy life for.

If that feeling is escaping to another life or another world, even for a while, then so be it. After going through what I have, I would understand. Who doesn't need time away from their life occasionally? I tell you who did—this guy!"

President Randolph raised his arms and pointed at himself with his thumbs. The crowd laughed and applauded.

"I understand everyone listening could probably use a break from their lives. Kids, school, work, money, illness, stress, divorce, marriage, births, deaths—life is a constant barrage of stress-inducing events that make us lose focus on what truly makes us happy. Whether it's being outside in nature by yourself, playing basketball every day, traveling to new places, or reading a good book by the pool, we, as a society, have forgotten how to be happy. And we want to fix that.

Before I go on, I want to thank a few people involved in crafting this legislation. Dylan, where are you? There you are—I like that shirt. Purple is definitely your color. Ha. Dylan Hatch, thank you for your dedication over the past few months. We wouldn't be here without your security expertise. Monica Henry? Monica, where are you? Oh, there you are. Monica has been instrumental in sourcing materials for the technology and collaborating with partners worldwide to ensure the core of the operation were in place. Robert Hirsch? Robert? There you are. We wouldn't be here without your continuous encouragement and wisdom. Thank you for being my shoulder on which to bounce ideas off of.

Dr. Joshua Lee and Neil Jergenson, I know you are listening somewhere in the world with your friends and family. Thank you for your dedication, your devotion, your sacrifices, and your creativity in making this technology what it is today. Dr. Joshua Lee's speech nearly a year ago was a huge inspiration for my thoughts today, and I cannot thank them enough for their role in getting here today.

While I can't thank everyone individually, as thousands of dedicated people from nearly every government department were involved in crafting this legislation, you know who you were. Leadership within the Department of Labor, the Department of Human Services, the Department of Justice, the Department of Defense, the Department of Education, and many others, I thank you for your passion, dedication, and willingness to meet in the middle so often. Although we didn't always agree with each other, we all knew what this bill could achieve and worked toward a common goal to get it across the finish line.

With this level of involvement, the rollout of this bill will be done as efficiently and with as much communication as possible, minimizing any major disruptions to our everyday lives.

However, there is one person I am especially grateful for, and she knows who she is. For those who don't know Claudine Shanley, you must have been living under a rock, as her face has been on television for quite a long time." The crowd laughed again as Claudine felt herself blushing.

"For those of you that truly don't know, Claudine Shanley was the woman who has been on the ground since the beginning, poring through the data and analysis that led to the initial crackdown on unregulated and unmonitored simulation technologies back in 2026. These technologies, primarily sold to wealthy individuals, promised experiences of a lifetime without considering the psychological aftermath for the individuals that took them.

When I was first briefed on this program upon becoming Vice President in January 2027, Claudine's initial report to President Logan was part of the materials I reviewed. President Logan and I met to talk about his desire to keep the program well-funded and to ensure that these simulators developed, and I quote: 'One hell of a fucking experience.' Pardon my French there, but President Logan certainly knew how to deliver a message."

The President paused as the crowd roared.

Claudine looked around in amazement. Even years later, President Logan was still admired and respected by many within the Republican party.

President Randolph calmed the crowd down before continuing:

"When the unfortunate events of February 13, 2027 unfolded and I was installed as President, one of my first tasks was to meet with Ms. Shanley to review the findings of this report and for her to brief me on the status of the Anticipation Day Task Force.

I will read her report in a moment, and I apologize in advance for the detailed statistics it contains, but I want every American to see the level of thought put into these types of analyses and how potential causes were ruled out before further investigation was pursued.

I know there has been some discussion of this topic among those who opposed this bill, but please ask yourself what any President would have done if presented with this situation. Also, it's important to understand what the hell I had to get my head around in short order—it was a lot.

I truly believe that if Ms. Shanley had not acted as quickly as she did, many more people would have gone through this without the proper help and monitoring.

So, without further ado, I will read Ms. Shanley's report to President Logan, dated May 30, 2026. Again, I apologize for the detail.

'Dear President Logan,

On behalf of the Department of Health, the Substance Abuse and Mental Health Services Administration, and the Behavioral Health Crisis Coordinating Office for Substance Abuse, I write to you today to alert you to a disturbing trend in cases of schizophrenia and schizophreniform disorders over the past several months. First noted in November 2025, with 19 cases reported, the number of cases increased to 282 in December 2025, 721 in January 2026, 1,525 in February 2026, 126,000 in March 2026, and 252,000 in April 2026. As of the writing of this letter, nearly 316,000 cases have been reported in May 2026.

Initially, when we began looking at the data, there was no clear link between the rise in cases and any other historically associated factors, such as drugs, viruses, or a mass physical trauma event. Consequently, protocol called for an initial investigation into medical records as well as interviews with patients and their families to determine the potential causes.

Below are the findings from the three-week investigation of 2,265 cases diagnosed through February 25, 2026:

- Of the total cases, 74% involved male patients, and 25% involved female patients (1% identified as "other").

- 53% of the cases involved individuals who identified as Caucasian, 19% as Asian, 8% as African American, and 7% as Indian, with the remainder being Hispanic or other.

- The median age of the patients was 51.5, with 45 under the age of 20, 318 individuals between 20 and 30, 334 individuals between 30 and 40, 576 individuals between 40 and 50, 632 individuals between 50 and 60, and another 360 over the age of 60.

- The youngest patient was 16, and the oldest was 84.

- Of the total cases, 829 were in the Silicon Valley region of California, 615 were in the New York City metropolitan area (including Manhattan, the five boroughs, New Jersey, and Connecticut), 221 were in Boston and the surrounding areas, 252 were in Travis, Hays, and Williamson counties (which make up the city of Austin and surrounding areas), and 348 cases were in other locations throughout the United States.

- The average reported household income for the patients was over $625,000. Even adjusting for geography, this is significantly above the median household income for the United States, presenting a distinct profile for a typical schizophrenia case.

- Approximately 12% of patients had prior mental health issues, identified by themselves or by a family member. Of these, 92% of the issues were related to depression or anxiety and had previously been treated with medication, with the remaining 8% related to diagnosed bipolar disorder, opioid use disorder, or other. None noted any previous schizophrenia diagnoses.

- About 28% of the patients reported a history of dementia or Alzheimer's in their immediate family (generally in line with the overall percentages for the US population).

- Only 1.5% of patients reported a history of any schizophrenia in their immediate family, again in line with overall US population percentages.

- Approximately 8% of the patients had severe stress in their lives before their diagnosis, with divorce being the most common stressor, followed by job loss and the loss of a close friend or relative.

Medical tests were run, with the results summarized below:

- 14% of the patients tested positive for having drugs in their system, with the most common being: 1) cocaine (194 people); 2) THC or CBD (99 people); and 3) LSD/other (24 people). Please note that cocaine has not historically been associated with the development of schizophrenic symptoms.

My team researched cannabis use and discussed it with the leading cannabis researchers. While cannabis use has been linked to schizophrenia symptoms, these individuals had not been diagnosed with any similar symptoms previously, and the symptoms presented themselves long after any cannabis effects would have worn off. This limits the likelihood that cannabis was the sole contributing factor for these diagnoses.

However, only 99 people, or 4.4% of the cases, involved THC or CBD, so we did not consider this a main contributing factor.

- 38% of the patients tested positive for alcohol, with the most common types being: 1) wine (329 people), 2) liquor

(309 people), and 3) beer (221 people). To be clear, Mr. President, at this time, no significant association between alcohol consumption and schizophrenia has previously been established.

Additionally, none of the patients had been diagnosed with alcohol use disorder before. These appeared to be casual consumers of alcohol, making it unlikely that alcohol was the cause of these cases.

- No unknown viruses or diseases were detected in any of the patients. However, approximately 8% of the patients tested positive for: 1) influenza (96 people), 2) COVID-25 (62 people), and 3) respiratory syncytial virus or other virus (23 people).

Mr. President, while influenza is known to cause fevers, which may cause hallucinations, no known link between influenza and schizophrenia has previously been established.

Additionally, while the long-term impacts of COVID-25 are still being researched to determine if this virus is similar to COVID-19, which many leading virologists currently believe, there is a risk of a long-term impact on the central nervous system, potentially causing schizophrenic symptoms.

However, these symptoms would likely only present themselves many months after the initial diagnosis. Given the newness of COVID-24, we do not believe this is the case here. Additionally, since this has only affected approximately 3% of the cases, we do not believe this is a main factor.

- MRI and CT scans revealed no signs of brain trauma, although approximately nine patients were diagnosed with

Stage 1 brain cancer. Thus, we do not believe this is a primary factor.

Mr. President, here are some additional findings from the investigation:

- The medium length of the official diagnosis by certified medical professionals was 17.4 days, with the shortest diagnosis being 14 days and the longest being 32 days. These averages include a required 7-day holding period between the latest symptoms and the patient's release to a family member.

- In all but one case, the diagnosis was schizophreniform disorder, typically diagnosed when schizophrenic symptoms are present for one to six months.

- In all cases, individuals were required to return to the mental health provider for monthly follow-ups. Of the 1,008 cases with follow-up visits as of our investigation date, 15 individuals were diagnosed with depression, but none were diagnosed with any continued schizophrenic symptoms.

To step back, Mr. President, schizophrenia is a severe neuropsychiatric disease that remains poorly understood and treated. Its onset typically occurs in adolescence or early adulthood, but its underlying causes are thought to involve neurodevelopmental abnormalities. However, historical research suggests the most common causes of schizophrenia involve genetics, everyday stresses such as losing a job or getting divorced, and drug use.

Given the diverse demographics of the cases, we did not believe they were due to any known genetic issue. Additionally, we found nothing unusual in the patient responses to whether stress-related issues could have caused their experience. Although some patients tested positive for alcohol or drug use, the percentages were consistent with overall averages in the United States. As such, we did not believe this was a major factor.

As we were unable to identify any initial cause, we elevated our findings to Dr. Keenan, head of the Department of Health and Human Services, on March 8, 2026. In the subsequent days, our team met with members from the National Institute of Health, the Centers for Disease Control, and the Office of the National Coordinator for Health Information Technology. The purpose of these meetings was to determine if additional resources were required to identify the cause of the cases.

As part of these meetings, Dr. Keegan and I stressed that these trends were abnormal due to: 1) the diverse demographic profile of the patients, 2) the economic profile being so narrow, and 3) the short-term duration of the schizophrenia symptoms.

In mid-April 2026, approvals were granted to utilize law enforcement and the Federal Bureau of Investigation to conduct searches of the patients' homes and internet browsing histories. The results were staggering: in 93% of the cases we investigated, the individual had purchased a new form of simulation technology that used artificial intelligence called NSM (Nine Sense Modalities) to recreate a simulated world. These products, marketed as life-like and life-changing, were available in the comfort of people's homes. Most of this technology was marketed on the dark web and was known only to well-connected individuals in the tech sector.

This technology was not cheap—the average cost was approximately $145,000 for the equipment, sensors, and *software. The systems were primarily manufactured by two main suppliers in China and Japan, with the technology originating in India and the Philippines.*

As you are aware, the FBI is continuing its investigation and, in conjunction with the Federal Trade Commission, the Department of Commerce, and the Department of Homeland Security, is working to stop the sale of this technology to US consumers and identify the buyers of this software to ensure they receive proper treatment and support.

However, based on initial estimates, hundreds of thousands of additional people undertook this experience before these enforcement provisions began.

Upon further investigation and discussions with the patients, it was discovered that, while the simulation appeared to function properly, when the patient ceased the simulation and came back to their real life, they were not properly integrated "back to reality" by someone familiar to them, such as a family member, spouse, or friend. Most individuals appear to have had this experience while alone, either because they lived alone or because they did not want their spouse to know they purchased this technology. For those who did have families or lived with someone, the family member was unaware of the purchase and thus could not provide details to medical personnel or our team on what may have caused the symptoms to appear.

Essentially, while the technology appeared to function as designed, when the simulation ended, the perception of reality was lost for these individuals. Without proper monitoring and assistance, they ended up detached from reality and exhibited schizophrenic symptoms.

These symptoms eventually passed with proper medical treatment, allowing them to recall normal memories. However, once back to normal, they were hesitant to provide information to medical personnel or our investigation team, likely because they wanted to avoid getting in trouble for purchasing unregulated technology.

It wasn't until the detailed bank account activity was searched that the vendors were identified and our conclusions reached.

The recommendation was then made to summarize our findings for presentation to you, Mr. President, and to discuss the next steps.

All of this to say, I am not here to set policy or suggest what the government's response should be. Our team has concluded the cause of these cases and now looks to others to decide what should be done going forward. Given advancements in artificial intelligence and the capability of private companies to design and manufacture these products that can allow citizens to experience a distorted reality, this issue is not going away anytime soon.

Mr. President, I look forward to working with you and your team to create a realistic plan going forward to ensure our citizenry is protected from these types of products and limit the resulting mental health issues.

I look forward to your questions and thank you for your time.

Respectfully,
Claudine Shanley.'"

The crowd stood and clapped for Claudine. Five seconds, ten seconds, twenty seconds. Overwhelmed with emotion, her eyes started tearing up.

"What a report, huh? Ms. Shanley is here with us tonight. Claudine, please stand up."

Claudine instantly turned red but eventually stood, slowly turning to the crowd behind her. Camera flashes went off in the distance as she waved before sitting back down. She had been in the spotlight for a long time, but hearing her report read to the crowd and millions of people watching and listening was a lot to take in.

The President continued, "Again, I apologize for the length of that summary, but I wanted you to appreciate how Ms. Shanley and her team stuck with the facts and let science guide her hypothesis and decisions. From that letter stemmed the process of working with foreign governments to limit the sale of these products to US consumers and clamping down on any new, unregulated technology entering the market.

At the same time, we realized this was a short-term solution. With advancements in artificial intelligence, we were likely fighting a losing battle and needed to make this experience part of our society moving forward.

So, with members from every major department within my government, including the newly created Department of Artificial Intelligence, and with direct involvement from Ms. Shanley and the Anticipation Day Task Force, we began crafting the legislation that sits before us today.

So, what does this legislation do? Starting early next year, it establishes an annual day for law-abiding US citizens over 18 (or 21, as I will describe later) to participate in a government-run and government-regulated simulation. Each participant will enter a world of their choosing for a period of up to what will feel like one year. There will be some parameters; for instance, murder will be prohibited unless the participant is recreating a historical event. Other parameters will be announced at a future date.

Our simulations draw from over 5 trillion historical data sources and records to create a simulated world as realistic as the one you reside in today. These simulations are then loaded onto supercomputers, downloaded onto dissolvable chips capable of holding multiple petabytes of data, and implanted safely and painlessly within each human subject. These chips are then synchronized to a device attached to your head that will allow you to enter the world you created.

In addition to this, you will have the option of going back to relive a day from your own life based on downloads from your memories. Our administration is currently reviewing this technology but I am expecting its release and approval later this year."

Cheers and applause broke out from the crowd, then subsided.

"Now, we understand there will be concerns over security and safety. We have employed a network of supercomputers with the power of 10,000 petaflops, sufficient to power the entire superstation on the Moon. Our cybersecurity programs are the most advanced, with the backing and experience of top cybersecurity experts worldwide. We constantly monitor these networks and promise the utmost security around the software and the simulations themselves.

All simulations will be stored for one year post-simulation. Under this law, these simulations will only be able to be retrieved under lawful circumstances that may require these simulation experiences as court-ordered proof of evidence. I understand some will have privacy concerns, but I give you my word that no government personnel will review a simulation unless court-ordered. And again, we have deployed the best cybersecurity measures that prevent hackers from accessing any stored simulation.

Now, let me explain the measures we are implementing to ensure the mental and physical safety of all citizens who undergo this process.

First, before the simulation, we will provide guidance and counseling on what the experience will be like during an intake process, which will explain some nuances of the experience. This will allow individuals to enjoy their experience from the beginning and understand what to expect while in the simulation.

Second, all citizens must undergo an initial mental and physical checkup to be eligible for this program. Anyone deemed unable to participate in this program will receive instructions and guidance on the conditions necessary to move forward with the experience. To be clear, these diagnoses will be made by certified physicians, who must justify why there would be a risk to the patient from proceeding.

Third, each individual will be assigned a medical practitioner and a certified and trained psychiatrist to monitor the patient for any potential issues, both during and after the simulation. Any issues identified post-simulation will result in a subsequent review period in a certified medical facility. This stay will be free, and the government will reimburse any lost wages because of this review period.

Finally, and this will be the most game-changing part of this legislation, in my opinion, the government will provide free mental and physical checkups once a quarter to any individual in the Anticipation Day program. Everyone must complete these quarterly checkups to stay eligible each year. Additional terms and conditions involving eligibility, potential charges for this program, and other details will be rolled out later.

I want to reiterate that as part of this program, every eligible individual will receive complimentary healthcare and mental health services once a quarter throughout their participation in the program."

A roar erupted from the crowd, lasting about 15 seconds before the President gestured to calm them.

"I know—it's crazy, right? How is that possible, you ask? Well, in the grand scheme of things, it's quite simple. Healthcare costs in the United States exceeded $8.5 trillion last year, which represented over 24.5% of our Gross Domestic Product. Essentially, out of every dollar the United States government spends, approximately 24.5 cents go to health care costs.

This figure doesn't even include the impact of lost productivity because of physical and mental health issues, estimated by my administration at an additional $1.5 trillion per year. The bottom line is that we are not a healthy country.

With a focus on preventative healthcare, we estimate we will be able to take close to 90% of that $9.0 trillion of healthcare spending and lost productivity and put that to other uses, including education, infrastructure, the environment, and, yes, providing free healthcare to all who are enrolled.

Yes, there will still be a need for some government spending on healthcare costs, especially as the US population continues to live longer and longer. However, our society has accepted a culture where we do not take care of our bodies and our minds for too long, and this must change.

There will be further details on how our healthcare system will be changed in the coming months. My administration is beginning to work with respective government agencies and private and public insurers to effectively communicate these changes to you going forward."

The crowd applauded again behind Claudine. Claudine was in awe of how composed the President was. He was announcing a complete change in the United States healthcare system, and he was doing it with confidence and poise.

"That is our part of the deal. Now, you may ask. What is your part of the deal? Well, thank you for asking!

One: Stay healthy, mentally and physically. You will want to experience this, and once you do, you will want to experience it again and again. The best way to ensure you are eligible for this program is to stay healthy. Eat well, exercise regularly, and if you aren't feeling like yourself, consult a doctor for proper treatment.

Two: Serve. This program will be eligible for individuals aged 18 and older who enlist in military service at the end of their high school graduation. Not serving means you will be eligible only after turning 21. Military enrollment will still be voluntary, and we will leave it up to every American family to decide. This may sound extreme, but several countries, including our good friend Israel, require military service after high school graduation. While not mandatory, we believe that our young men and women will benefit from service long-term and will be able to participate in this program upon enrollment.

Three: Stay out of prison. Anyone in prison will be ineligible for this program. It is that simple. The bill has limited exceptions for good behavior after a certain number of years of incarceration. This will be coordinated with state officials going forward.

Four: Stay away from illegal activities. Anyone under investigation by any federal or state agency will be ineligible for this program until the investigation is cleared. Cheating on your taxes or threatening other individuals are no-gos. Basically, don't do anything illegal, and you will be eligible. For those of you wondering, traffic and other minor violations will not count, and we will release a full list of these ineligible activities in the coming months.

Five: Get a job. You'll see why in a second.

Six: Learn how to invest. Why do you ask? Well, let me tell you. As part of this bill, we believe we can significantly reduce healthcare costs, pay down our debt, and move money to other government areas. In addition to all of that, we will also be paying *you*."

The crowd cheered when he said that. Money really did rule the world.

"That's right. As part of this legislation, every eligible citizen participating in Anticipation Day will receive an annual payment, taxed at current individual tax rates, starting at age 21 and continuing until you turn 65. These payments will be eligible to be paid on your birthday, either as a lump sum or an annuity spread over the next year.

To be clear, these payments should not replace a career. If you want to go to college, go to college. When you leave, you will have money waiting for you instead of piles of debt. If you don't want to attend college, you can invest in the stock market or create a new business. Either way, you will have seed money to create financial security for you and your family. These payments will increase each year based on several characteristics, including the number of dependents you claim, the zip code of your current residence, and other factors. The best part is the freedom to decide how to use your money to fund the lifestyle you want, whether it is getting a minimum-wage job, or going to college to be a successful partner at a law firm. We encourage that, as our society still needs workers of all kinds.

Want to know how much we currently estimate you will be getting from the government? It's not chump change, folks. While these estimates are subject to change based on growth rates, underlying economic conditions, and population changes, we currently estimate that, by age 25, you will receive a gross payment of $55,000, increasing to $100,000 by age 35, $167,000 by the time you are 45, and $225,000 by the time you are 65.

We feel these are conservative numbers, but they may increase or decrease depending on how much healthcare costs decrease going forward, inflationary risk factors, government revenue taken in, and other factors that will dictate the budget for these payments.

Your annual payments will only increase if you are fully employed, or a contractor, for at least eight months of the year. Otherwise, your wage will remain at the same level as the prior year. So, to earn more of our money, you must go out and find employment. If you do not hold a job for two or more years, we will reduce your contribution to a minimum annual amount of $45,000.

If you want, you can stay home playing video games all day, but our contribution will not increase from that base rate. We want people working, and we want to reward you for continuing to contribute to society. You can choose not to work, that is your decision, but you will only receive the minimum annual payment from the government.

My administration will continue to monitor inflation and overall prices to ensure they do not spiral out of control.

At age 65, payments will begin through a new social security plan, boosted by our ability to invest in private markets and high-growth initiatives. At 65, the requirement to hold a job will cease, and you will receive the same employment benefits as everyone else in your age group.

This is why I say: learn to invest. Investing will allow you to funnel your payments into the stock market, real estate, a business you choose, or even government bonds. Seek advice from a financial professional about what you can start doing now.

Get smart about your money and learn how to make the most of it.

That's your part. We realize this bill will change how we act and function as a society. However, the change in your everyday life will be minimal. You are still free to attend school, get an education, find a job, and contribute to society.

If you are turning 18 soon and want to join the military, start those conversations with your parents now. If you don't, that's okay too. Go to college, get a traditional education, and start your Anticipation Day experience when you are 21. We want you to be happy, live your life, and make the best decisions for yourself and your family.

We expect to begin implementing this program early next year and anticipate, no pun intended, performing one million simulations a day once fully ramped up."

The crowd rose to their feet and applauded for several minutes. Finally, the President beckoned them to sit down.

"I know there will be questions and concerns, as this bill will reshape how we view our country, ourselves, and society. I promise you this decision wasn't taken lightly. For the first time in a long time, we had the support of both parties in the Senate and the House of Representatives. This will be a net positive for our society, and we hope that other countries will adopt similar initiatives.

The United States should, and will, set the gold standard for how society can function, and how the government can lead that change through this technology's implementation. In the future, we might consider privatizing some aspects of this rollout, but for now, the government will take the lead.

As Teddy Roosevelt once said, 'Believe you can, and you're halfway there.' That means taking action and beginning to move forces in the universe. We are doing that, and I ask you to join us on this journey. With all of us on the same journey, I know this country can achieve amazing things.

So, on behalf of myself, First Lady Sandra, Vice President Hughes, Second Lady Suzanne and my entire administration, we thank you for your time this afternoon and I wish you all a good evening from the Rose Garden. God bless you and God bless the United States of America."

President Randolph stepped back from the podium, waving as the crowd roared in a standing ovation. The First Lady, Vice President Hughes, and his wife joined him in a warm embrace by the podium. Confetti sprayed down from above, and cameras flashed while reporters shouted questions.

Claudine turned to kiss Charles, then her children and grandchildren. Tears filled her eyes as she hugged Charles again and, for the first time ever, told him "I love you."

PART 1

CHAPTER 1

GETTING READY

- MARCH 7, 2032
4 P.M.

It was just four words that formed a simple question: "Where are my shoes?"

For most people, this question would have elicited a simple response like "In your closet." or "I have no idea." However, it wasn't the question itself, but the tone accompanying these four words that came out of Eric's mouth, that enraged Alexandra.

What was the phrase? "It's not what you say, but how you say it?" That couldn't be more appropriate here. As if it were her responsibility to keep track of his goddamn shoes.

She wanted to take one of her high heels she had just put on and ram it through his thick skull. Alexandra was sure she wouldn't do it, but the thought made her smile a bit. What was the worst that could happen? Sure, she might end up in jail, but the boys were practically old enough to take care of themselves. Sophia had just turned five and had Anya and Alexandra's parents to help take care of her until Alexandra plea-bargained down to some sort of self-defense or insanity plea.

"I think I saw them by the washing machine," she replied, snapping out of her mini-daydream, hoping he would use his two fucking legs to find them himself.

Alexandra opened her closet door and surveyed her options for the evening's dinner. There were a few options but the new green Honeycomb Knit V-Neck Mini Sweater Dress caught her eye. Slightly low in the front and loose enough to cover her recent weight gain, it was her favorite. It looked and felt great and seemed perfect for a night with friends.

As she undressed and looked in the mirror, she was somewhat unhappy with what she saw. Her breasts were starting to droop more, her belly had gotten a little bigger, and everything just felt *heavier*. Whenever she tried focusing on going to the gym, running, or biking, something at work or with the kids always took priority.

At 40, Alexandra knew she could do better. She swore she would exercise more going forward—it would help if Eric stepped up and helped more around the house and with the kids' activities.

As she put her shirt and pants on and started to do her makeup, she thought about how rough the past few weeks had been for her. The kids had been sick and not sleeping, and the continued stress of both their jobs had left them both on edge, leading to constant fights, bickering, and Eric drinking more.

While their relationship had seen its share of ups and downs, this felt like a big down. Neither one wanted to admit their unhappiness, but she believed they both sensed it right beneath the surface.

It was something she needed to confront him about after their experience tomorrow. However, they were both in a good mood today, as the excitement of having dinner with friends and sharing their Anticipation Day experiences tomorrow seemed to outweigh anything else going on in their lives right now. At least for one day, they seemed happy.

Alexandra's close friend, MaryAnne, had gone through the program a couple of years ago as she worked for the National Security Agency and was part of the "Guinea Pig Population," as they eventually became known. She was one of the first humans to go through the simulation experience to ensure there were no negative side effects that warranted further refinement of the technology or process.

MaryAnne had shared minimal details about her experience, and Alexandra didn't want to pry at the time given MaryAnne was recovering from a bad divorce and was still trying to get her life back in order at the age of 40. However, what little she did share gave Alexandra the impression that this experience would be amazing and life-changing.

With that in mind, Alexandra clung to the hope that tomorrow would be good for both Eric and herself. She hoped it would help get their marriage on track, or at least give them the clarity and motivation to change things, if only to stop the constant arguing and bickering in front of the kids.

"Found them!" Eric shouted from the laundry room.

"You're an idiot," Alexandra muttered, just loud enough for him to hear but not to understand.

"What?" Eric replied, sounding confused.

"I said, 'Are you ready to go in 10?'" Alexandra replied, a bit louder, pleased she could quickly make something up.

"I was kinda hoping to take a quick dump, but I can probably hold it until after dinner," Eric announced proudly as he approached their bedroom door.

▼▼▼

Standing in the doorway, Alexandra couldn't help but think that, while still handsome at 44, he appeared older and sadder than she remembered. The past year's stresses had caught up to him, with more gray creeping into the sides of his brown hair and stubble, and his hazel eyes seeming sadder these days, with fairly pronounced bags under them due to lack of sleep. His hairline had also started receding drastically, which she knew bothered him. She had suggested medical alternatives, but he had not gone for them yet.

He no longer worked out as much as he used to and while they still had sex, she was not as physically attracted to him as she used to be. Alexandra wasn't a bikini model by any stretch, but she had started getting back into shape, more for her mental well-being than anything else.

She felt bad for Eric in some ways—the pressure at his job was intense. His life as a partner of an accounting firm kept him busy with clients, and the threat of artificial intelligence taking over the industry kept him up at night.

Certainly, the financial benefits of being a partner were not something she was complaining about, but the stress was wearing on him. They had a conversation months ago when the financial incentives as part of the Anticipation Day program were released, and he was thinking about taking a package offered to some partners to leave the firm.

While getting paid not to work was enticing, Eric took pride in his career and wanted it to continue as it was.

The daycare Alexandra owned and ran was still doing well. She learned years ago that if there was one thing that stood the test of time, it was that parents would *always* need a break from their young kids and would pay *well* to have someone else watch them, even for just a few hours a day.

While robotic nannies like Anya were becoming more popular, many people still didn't trust them enough to leave their young kids alone with them for hours. So Alexandra didn't see anything that would cause her business to decline, at least in the near future. As such, her business was still doing okay and would have been enough to support them if Eric had taken the severance package.

She had considered selling the business and living off the government incentive for a bit, but she wanted to see how Eric and she would react to the experience tomorrow before making any decisions.

Either way, while she felt bad for him; he needed to address his drinking, and she hoped tomorrow would give him the clarity he needed, one way or the other.

▼▼▼

"Lovely," she replied dryly while snapping back to reality. "Well, let me know your decision so I can ensure the kids are good before we leave."

"Fuck it—I'll be quick. Wait for me downstairs," Eric said as he walked towards the bathroom, already beginning to take his belt off.

"I'm a lucky woman," Alexandra said quietly, rolling her eyes. She applied the final touches of eyeliner and blush, then headed downstairs to check on the kids.

As she walked downstairs, the projection TV was on, and she caught a snippet of the news: "Coming up, are depression and suicide rates on the rise because of Anticipation Day? Our own Scott Stevens has some more details after the break."

"*Great*," Alexandra thought as she was quickly interrupted by Sophia running up to her with some sort of paint emergency.

Sophia was a blessing to her and Eric. Years earlier, they had a lost pregnancy, causing her and Eric to go through a rough patch and split up for a few months. Eventually, they got back together to try to work through things, and, with Eric's "super-sperm," she ended up getting pregnant with Sophia. Even though she never told Eric directly, she had always wanted a daughter, and the day she found out it would be a girl was one of the happiest days of her life.

Sophia ran the house; there was no other way to say it. She was the perfect mix of Eric and Alexandra, and knew she could get away with anything by pouting her lips and saying the only two words in the English dictionary that seemed to work on Eric: "Please, dada."

Corey, the oldest at 13, loved playing chess with friends across the country. He was such a damn competitor—whatever he did, he had to win, which she loved, as she was the same way. She always had a special connection with her firstborn; hell, he had slept in the bed with her and Eric until he was almost six years old and still liked cuddling with her, even though he would never admit it. Looking at Corey, she saw a miniature version of Eric with his lean body, hazel eyes, and warm smile.

At 11, Noah was more into sports and war simulations. He was always a goofball and had an amazing personality. Even though he looked like her, he had his dad's personality and always wanted to impress him with his achievements at school or on the baseball field. It was cute to see.

"Noah! Corey! Come up, please, and watch your sister for two minutes," she called out to them from the top of the basement door as she checked her virtual glasses to see tonight's weather: a 50% chance of snow and temperatures in the mid-30s. It was colder than normal as snow had become rare in March due to climate change, which had reduced Denver's wintry season over the past decade.

"Oh, but we're playing Webster's World," they both chimed in unison. Webster's World was the new "hip" game of the year, where kids could create a character from scratch and make life choices to help them live as long as possible. They could also interact with other virtual characters, which usually ended up being their friends.

Alexandra tried to encourage them to hang out with their friends in person, but it was challenging. Sports were their biggest interactions with their classmates, primarily baseball, hockey, and karate. Still, she hoped that would change as they got older and could use self-driving cars independently.

"I don't care—pause the game and come watch your sister for a few minutes while Anya finishes charging!" she yelled downstairs. She hated screaming, but it seemed like the only way they would listen sometimes.

As Eric returned from completing his business, he went to the closet to get a coat. "You about good?" Eric asked as he grabbed a coat and a sock hat.

"As I'll ever be, I guess. You feel better?" She asked, pretending to smell something.

"I feel like a new man, ready to tackle whatever challenges come my way," he replied with a grin.

"Alright, let me check on Anya, and then we can go. Don't want to be late for the extravaganza," she said, heading to the back room. Anya was charged at 92%, which would be more than enough until tomorrow. She pressed the "Wake" button and then the "Babysitter" button.

At first, Alexandra was not entirely comfortable with having a robotic nanny in the house, but she eventually gave in after several of her friends tried them and couldn't stop raving about them. Now, she couldn't imagine her life without Anya. The robot helped with laundry, dishes, cleaning the house, and ensuring the kids were alive. Anything beyond that required an updated model, which was too expensive to justify. She was comfortable leaving Anya with the kids for a few of hours; anything longer required human supervision.

Her thoughts were interrupted by a loud fart from Eric, causing the kids to laugh hysterically. All she could do was roll her eyes, grab her glasses, and look at Eric. "Really? You still have more gas in you? Let's go before I throw up."

Eric laughed and said, "You know you love me. Bye, kids!"

"Bye, Dad!" All three exclaimed in unison and returned to whatever was on TV that was entertaining them. "*Ah, to be a kid again,*" she thought as she kissed each child, walked outside, and headed to their car.

▼ ▼ ▼

The drive to David and Clarise's house took only about 15 minutes through the Denver suburbs.

Clarise, Alexandra's good friend from college, had moved to New York to become a powerhouse lawyer but eventually moved back to the Denver area with her husband, David, to support her parents, whose health was heading in the wrong direction.

David was a stock trader in New York when he met Clarise through a mutual friend, and together they had done very well for themselves.

As they drove away from their house, Alexandra's thoughts drifted to how lucky she was to have her kids. Everything she did was to ensure they were happy and taken care of. She wanted them to have a better childhood than she had and was grateful that, so far, she had succeeded.

The government money would be an added benefit to them, allowing them to save, invest, and hopefully provide more opportunities to find happiness in the future.

While Corey was only 13, they would eventually have to talk to him about whether he would serve in the military; fortunately, they had a little time before that discussion. Alexandra was strongly against it, but Eric seemed more open to letting him and all the kids decide what they wanted to do for themselves.

She felt especially fortunate after what Clarise and David endured three months earlier, losing their youngest son, Charlie, to cancer at age 8. Although David and Clarise seemed to be processing their grief as best as they could, P.J., their 11-year-old son, was taking it hard. He and Charlie were best buds, and they did almost everything together before his death.

The moment the doctor gave them the horrific news that Charlie's brain tumor was too large and deep to operate on effectively, David and Clarise knew the situation was dire. They could try therapies to reduce the size of the tumor, but the side effects would be severe, and the risk of permanent brain damage was high.

After much reflection, David and Clarise decided to focus on giving Charlie the best life possible for however long they had left. That time turned out to be about 15 months, with Charlie passing away on the morning of December 8, 2031.

David and Clarise took the loss hard, as one would expect any parent to. The timing of his death, right before the holidays, caused them more grief than normal, leading them to retreat from those closest to them for several weeks.

When Alexandra finally saw Clarise in early February, she seemed more at peace than Alexandra had expected. Clarise explained that she had inquired with the Department of Anticipation Day (DAD) about reliving a day from their past instead of the original experiences they had chosen.

Alexandra remembered Clarise's joy when she shared that the proposed changes had been accepted. "We'll be able to see Charlie once a year and always remember the happy type of boy he was," she had kept saying.

Unfortunately, the date for downloading their memories wouldn't open until May 2032, so they would need to wait a few more months and hopefully reschedule their experience for later in the spring or summer.

Before Clarise and Alexandra departed that February afternoon, Clarise suggested hosting a dinner the night before the Anticipation Day experience for their little group. It sounded like David and Clarise could use the company, and they wanted to wish everyone else a pleasant experience.

So the wheels were set in motion and arrangements were made for the dinner tonight.

▼▼▼

Alexandra decided to break the silence a few minutes into the ride. "So, are you excited for tomorrow?"

Eric, also lost in thought, took a moment to acknowledge he had even heard the question but finally responded, "I think so. It should be fun."

"Are you seriously not going to tell me what it is?" Alexandra asked.

"What do you mean? We agreed to see how it went and decide afterward whether we wanted to share, assuming we're still together." A small smile formed on his lips. Alexandra couldn't tell if he was joking or genuinely smiling about the thought of not being together with her.

"Yeah, that makes sense. Lord knows I don't need you making fun of my simulation. You'll probably call it 'stupid' or a 'waste of time', so we're probably better off keeping it a secret and revisiting it afterward."

"Well, knowing you, I'm sure you picked somewhere where you can hang out on a beach and fuck Rico Suave," Eric replied, laughing to himself.

Alexandra laughed too but didn't reply. Eric still knew her so well. Even after all these years, he knew how to make her laugh, which was why she still loved him. Come to think about it, besides her sister, no one had ever known her so deeply.

That's why their past year's struggles were so hard on her. Despite his quirks and issues, he was still the love of her life, and she wanted to try to work things out with him.

She hoped whatever simulation he chose would help him find meaning and happiness in his life and that he would come out of the other side a stronger and happier person.

"Damn, can I go back and change my simulation?" She paused before adding, "Hey, by the way, try to be nice to MaryAnne. I know you two don't get along, but she's still struggling with what happened with Kevin. What do they say? It takes you six months to get over someone for every year you were together?"

"They were together for, what, 15 years?" Eric said. "So, it'll take her seven and a half years to get over him? Please. We both know she was 'over' someone else a few weeks after she found out. She'll be fine. Didn't she do her trial simulation a couple of years ago? I guarantee she fucked a hundred people in whatever simulation she did. She's fine."

"You're such an asshole. I am sure she did not 'fuck a hundred people' in her simulation. She took it hard, and while she's had sex since the breakup, it still affected her a lot. Kevin was cheating on her for years before she found out," Alexandra replied, feeling the anger coming back.

"Fine, fine. I'll be nice to her. I just get annoyed because she never hangs out with us. She spends time with you, but when did she last see me or the kids?" Eric asked.

Alexandra thought about his question. It had been a while since she had seen Eric or the kids. Although she and MaryAnne had met for coffee, drinks, and dinner numerous times over the past couple of years since the divorce, it was always just the two of them. She knew MaryAnne was sad about not having children; despite advances in reproductive technology, she and Kevin were never able to conceive. They had talked about adopting, but the cheating and subsequent divorce had put a solid end to those plans.

"I know," she finally replied. "She's been dealing with a lot, but I know she wants to see the kids. I'll ask her to see everyone after we finish this tomorrow. Either way, please be aware of what you say around her."

"Okay, okay," Eric said with a heavy sigh. "By the way, do you know when Clarise and David will find out when they are doing their simulations?"

"Clarise mentioned something about the summer, but honestly, I didn't get into many details with her. I'm sure she'll divulge more tonight." Alexandra responded, unsure how much Clarise wanted her to disclose to Eric.

"Really? Interesting. Will P.J. be at the house?" Eric asked as Alexandra looked out the window.

▼ ▼ ▼

Alexandra ignored the question as her mind was still focused on Clarise. She missed hanging out with Clarise greatly. Before Charlie's death, they would hang out weekly, going to their usual coffee spot every Friday morning to catch-up on what was going on in their lives. The two couples would try to go to dinner at least once a month, which was always a good time.

However, since Charlie's death, Clarise had retreated and they had only seen each other a few times since December as Alexandra wanted to respect Clarise's need for time and space.

She had never told Eric, but she and Clarise had a "thing" in college. They attributed it to experimentation, which lasted a few months, but they still maintained a close friendship. After a few drinks, some flirtatiousness always came out in private, but they had never taken it further since college.

Was Alexandra bisexual? Possibly, but she had never fully explored those feelings. At her age, she wasn't inclined to go down that path without a good reason.

Maybe in her simulation.

Eric and David had become close since David and Clarise moved back from New York, mostly because Eric and David were both finance professionals and gravitated toward the same network. Alexandra was relieved Eric had found someone to hang out with, especially since some of his closer friends had left the area after the COVID-19 pandemic.

While he had some local colleagues, along with his college friend, Patrick, a recent divorcé, and his high school friend Mike, whom he saw as much as possible, Eric needed someone with whom he could talk about drinking, sports, and wife problems.

Eric and David were cute when they were together, although since Charlie's death, they hadn't seen much of each other, mostly communicating through text. This would be the first time the four of them had gathered since the funeral.

▼▼▼

"Yoohoo! Wakey, wakey!" Eric snapped his fingers at Alexandra. "You okay? Where did you just go?"

Alexandra jolted back to the present. "Oh, sorry—I was trying to remember if Clarise said P.J. would be there tonight. I am pretty sure they shopped him to a friend's house for the night."

Eric sighed. "That poor kid… I can't imagine explaining to an 11-year-old that their brother is gone forever. It's just so fucking heartbreaking. I hope David hasn't been drinking too much. I know it had gotten worse once Charlie was diagnosed. Has Clarise mentioned anything to you?"

Alexandra looked at him before responding matter-of-factly, "Yeah, we talk about everything, Eric. So, yeah, she's mentioned his drinking. I figured that was what you guys had most in common."

"Ouch." Eric fell quiet for a few seconds. "Look, I know I've been drinking more lately, and I know when I drink, I get a little stupid. Work has been super stressful, and I want to cut back, but it's the only thing that calms me down. I know you want me to try weed or mushrooms or whatever, but I just don't feel comfortable with that. I promise, I'll work on cutting back. Let's talk after our experiences and see what makes sense regarding my job and the business. Maybe neither of us needs to work going forward. Okay?"

"Okay, well, thank you for being so honest. Yes, the drinking hasn't helped. I know you're stressed with work, but whatever happens, we'll be here for you, and we can work through it together. I just don't want what happened to MaryAnne and Kevin to happen to us. They seemed genuinely happy, but it shows that you never know what's happening beneath the surface in a relationship." Alexandra grabbed Eric's hand and leaned over to kiss him. "Thank you for telling me that. Let's enjoy dinner, get through tomorrow, and take it one day at a time, okay?"

"Okay, deal. Wanna get a quickie in before we get there?" Eric asked, massaging her inner thigh.

"In your dreams, buddy. Don't think you're getting lucky just because you say some nice things to me." After a few seconds of silence, she added, "Maybe on the way back."

CHAPTER 2

THE DINNER

MARCH 7, 2032 - 5 P.M.

Alexandra and Eric finally arrived at Clarise and David's palatial mansion as the sun dipped lower in the sky. The house comprised five bedrooms, six baths, and 5,500 square feet set on two acres on the outskirts of Denver. It also included an outdoor heated pool, hot tub, gym, wine cellar, and tennis court—not too shabby.

Not that Eric and Alexandra's house was anything to sneeze at, because it wasn't, but this house was a step above. Alexandra wondered if Clarise and David would stay in the house, given the memories with Charlie here. She hadn't broached that question yet with Clarise, but this place was just too big for three people.

It was, however, a beautiful setting to get the group of friends together for a nice "home-cooked meal" catered by one of the nicest restaurants in the area.

The instructions for Anticipation Day were to avoid eating or drinking anything for 12 hours before your simulation began, mostly so you wouldn't soil your pants. So, as most of the group had the simulations scheduled between 7:30 a.m. and 8:30 a.m. the next morning, they wanted to have their meals wrapped up by 7:30 p.m.

As they approached the door, it opened automatically, allowing them entry into the lit-up grand foyer. The floors were black-and-white marbled tiles, and the walls were covered with beautiful paintings David and Clarise had collected over the years. Hanging from the ceiling was a large, golden chandelier.

Their robotic nanny, Rebecca, rolled up from the back of the house and said, in her mechanical voice, "Greetings, Mr. and Mrs. Right. May I take your jackets? Clarise is in the kitchen if you wish to make her acquaintance."

"Thank you, Rebecca," Alexandra replied, noting how formal Rebecca was. An upgraded model over Anya, Rebecca was programmed to resemble a traditional 1960s English butler. Alexandra made a mental note to splurge for one next year.

They walked through the foyer, past the staircase leading upstairs, and turned right into the spacious kitchen, where Clarise was putting something in the oven. Seeing Eric and Alexandra, she turned with a big smile, took off her oven mitts, and ran to give Alexandra a long hug and then followed up with a shorter hug for Eric.

"Hi, guys! You're always on time! David is finishing getting ready upstairs, but he'll be down here soon. Can I get you anything?" She pointed to Rebecca, who was parked near a small table outside the kitchen stocked with various bottles of wine, scotch, bourbon, tequila, vodka, gin, and a selection of beers. "I also have some joints and gummies in the den, if that's more your style," she added.

"Wow. Thank you, Clarise," Eric responded as he walked towards Rebecca. "What a selection! So…" Eric hesitated, seeming tentative about how to say the next words.

"I guess I'll just come out and ask. How are you both doing?" Eric paused. "Alexandra and I wanted to give you time to process everything after what happened. I haven't reached out too much to David as I wanted to let him be after the funeral. I, well, *we*, were so sorry for what happened—it's awful. How have you been since the funeral?"

Clarise smiled sweetly, taking a moment to compose herself.

"Thank you, Eric, seriously." She cleared her throat. "We're doing okay. We miss Charlie every second of every day, but we had to accept early on that we might lose him at some point. We did everything possible to give him a wonderful life with the little time he had left. And I think we did, you know? We took that trip to California last summer, where we went to Disney World, saw the coast, and took him to Mendocino to see whales, which he had always wanted to do. It was a blessing to be able to do that with him and P.J. It was such a fun time. He was such a happy little boy, and that's how we wanted to remember him."

Clarise pressed her hand to her upper lip, unable to hold back her emotions. Alexandra walked over and wrapped her arms around Clarise's shoulders.

"We just didn't want to see him suffering with medication that might have prolonged his life but would have made his quality of life so much worse. You know?" Clarise continued softly. "I think you both know that David and I were at peace with that decision, so when he passed, we turned all our love and attention to P.J. to ensure he understood that he was not alone."

Clarise began tearing up, making Alexandra hand her a tissue. Clarise briefly paused to wipe her eyes.

"Sorry, sometimes I just can't help it. I thought I had run out of tears, but I guess not. Anyway, the holidays were god-awful, I'm not going to lie. Spending time together as a family didn't make sense without him there, you know? So, we went to the mountains to get out of the house. We all agreed that being home without Charlie's laughter during the holidays was too tough. But every day, it gets a little easier.

Don't get me wrong; there are still moments when I can't help but cry for hours because I miss him so much. Usually, it's when I walk past his room and expect him to run out laughing or chasing a ball, but it just never happens. Sometimes, I think it's just a bad dream, and I'll wake up to find Charlie lying on my chest, snoring. I'll kiss his little head and tell him that I love him." She stopped again to wipe away her tears.

Alexandra stepped forward, crying too. "Oh, honey, I know. Come here." She pulled Clarise in for a comforting hug. "You guys did everything you could for him, and he was such a happy little boy. Sometimes, there are no answers, regardless of how much you want them. We are here for you in whatever way you need us, okay?"

Clarise needed a second to calm herself. "I know Alexandra. Thank you. You both have been supportive throughout this process, watching P.J. and helping with the funeral arrangements. You've been a godsend. I'm so grateful for you both, and we're happy to have you here for dinner tonight."

After a few seconds, Clarise took a deep breath and continued. "Okay, no more crying tonight—at least, I hope so. I do have some good news. As I mentioned to Alexandra when I last saw her, we were waiting to confirm the date for the simulation where David and I can go back and relive a day with Charlie. We just heard back that the download will be at the end of May, and we should be ready by the end of June or July to do our experience. We both decided to relive a trip to California we took a few years ago, before he was sick.

Honestly, the thought of seeing him again, even if just from my memories, is the only thing keeping me going right now. I have mixed emotions about it, but I'm ready to do it. I miss him so much." A large smile broke through her tears.

"That's great, Clarise," Alexandra said, smiling back while rubbing Clarise's arm. "I can't even imagine how much you miss him. This is what you wanted, though, right? To see him again?"

"We did. We wanted to try it and see how it made us feel. It might turn out to be a bad idea if it leaves us feeling worse, but we want to find out." Clarise took a deep breath, clearly getting emotional again. "Okay, seriously, Eric, go grab a drink."

"I will, thank you," Eric responded, turning towards Rebecca. "I think this bottle of Jefferson's Ocean is calling my name; what do you want?" He glanced at Alexandra.

"I'll just take a chardonnay for now," Alexandra answered. "I'll probably dabble with some gummies before dinner. I have a feeling I'm going to need it tonight."

"One chardonnay coming up," Eric said as Rebecca handed him a Jefferson's and a glass of chardonnay.

He passed Alexandra her glass as Clarise turned back to check something in the oven. "How are you, honey?" She asked Alexandra.

"I'm fine. Thank you, dear," Eric interjected before Alexandra could finish her sip of wine.

"Very funny, you goofball," Alexandra finally said.

Clarise chuckled in agreement. "Hilarious, Eric. Are you guys ready for this thing tomorrow? Are you excited, nervous, scared, or somewhere in between?" She continued removing dish trays from the oven.

"Well, I feel like I should be more nervous than I am, but I've heard good things about the experience from MaryAnne," Alexandra responded. "I trust the process and hope I don't end up with three boobs or missing brain cells. I think we're both ready." She looked at Eric, who raised his glass as if to say: *Cheers to that.*

Alexandra rolled her eyes before turning back to Clarise. "I've gotta ask: are you going to reveal what you're doing with your simulation to everyone else?"

"I probably will. I don't have any shame in it. As I mentioned before, I started looking into this early on since the option became available. So, I don't see any reason to be ashamed of it. David and I both agreed that it was the right thing to do for us. We'll just have to see how dinner goes I guess."

A voice called from behind them. "Did I hear my name?"

Alexandra and Eric turned to see David standing in the kitchen's entryway, holding a glass of brown liquid—probably bourbon, if Alexandra had to guess. Tall, dark and handsome with slicked back hair, David was wearing a sweater vest with slacks and nice dress shoes. He was the typical banker and while he wasn't Alexandra's type, she certainly understood why Clarise was initially attracted to him.

"Hey buddy!" Eric said, moving in for a hug and patting him on the back. "How are you doing, man? It's been too long. We were just catching up with Clarise on how you guys have been."

"Well, I'm sure she filled you in properly," David responded as Alexandra approached and hugged him before stepping back.

"Every day is a challenge, that's for sure. We're doing the best we can I guess. The only thing I know is that I miss the kid every goddamn day. I miss his laughter. I miss his smell. I miss his snoring on my chest when he fell asleep. I miss all of him. That will never go away but I imagine it'll lessen over time. Right now, it feels as real as the day he passed. All Clarise and I can do is focus on P.J. and make sure he is alright and getting the help he needs to cope."

David's voice cracked with emotion, so Clarise walked over to hold his hand.

"So, yeah, we're doing. That's the best way to put it. We appreciate you guys coming here, and we're sorry we can't do this experience tomorrow with you all, but when we heard that there was an option to relive a day from our lives, we had to see if that was something we could do this year. I'm not sure if it's the right decision, but we agreed it was something we wanted to do.

At least we have Rebecca, right? She's been a constant in our lives to help manage the day-to-day shit that probably would have fallen by the wayside. You've been a godsend, haven't you, Rebecca?" David turned to Rebecca standing behind him.

"I am not programmed to believe in a traditional God, Mr. David. But your viewpoints on God fascinate me, and I enjoy listening to them."

"Thank you, Rebecca!" David exclaimed, apparently proud that a robot cared to know his thoughts on God. "Sometimes, when I'm alone at night, I wake Rebecca up and talk to her for no apparent reason. She's like a therapist who doesn't know a thing about what she's talking about, yet she somehow proves helpful. Anyway, are you guys excited about tomorrow?"

Clarise took the cue to respond. "Alexandra and I were just talking about it. She's feeling a mix of nerves, excitement, and fear. Am I right?"

Alexandra shrugged slightly. "I don't know. It's scary, going into a simulation—a whole new world to live in for however many weeks or months. It's just a little unnerving, I guess. Don't get me wrong, I'm excited to try this, but I'm worried they might inject too many chemicals into my brain or that I'll freak out and demand they get me out too early. I know I'm probably being paranoid, but that's all I can think about."

"You paranoid? Nooo." Eric laughed, taking a sip of his drink.

"You're telling me you're not even a little bit nervous?" Alexandra asked Eric sweetly, with an undertone of "fuck you" attached to the question.

Eric stared at her for a moment before responding, "I mean, I don't know. Millions of people have done this and survived. We're not hearing anything about people having issues afterward, so I'm ready to see what this thing can do."

"*Actually*, I think I heard on the news as we were leaving that there are more cases of suicide and depression linked to this," Alexandra replied quickly.

"Really?" David asked, sounding genuinely curious.

"Yeah, that was the headline, but I didn't catch the full story because Sophia spilled paint all over herself, so I had to deal with that." Alexandra took a sip of her wine.

"Oh, I'm sure it's just the typical media bullshit. They probably manipulated some study from some partisan group to grab eyeballs," Eric said matter-of-factly.

"Well, who knows?" Clarise interjected. "I'm sure you guys will be just fine. I'm curious if you'll share your experiences with everyone tonight. She looked at Alexandra and Eric as if saying: *Well?*

Eric took the lead this time as Alexandra was taking a sip of her wine. "We talked about it, and I don't think we'll share what we're doing this year. We want to see how it goes and decide later how much to reveal. But knowing Alexandra, I'm sure she picked something fun and exciting." He paused to take a drink.

"Oh, I'm sure you did too, honey. I figured you'd be living the single life somewhere like you did in your 20s," Alexandra said sarcastically.

"Ah, those were the days. I guess I will see tomorrow." Eric winked with a smirk.

"Well, either way, I agree. We both decided not to share this year. Clarise mentioned you might share what you're doing with the others…?" Alexandra asked, looking at David.

"Great question," David said. "Clarise and I talked a lot about this, and we're happy to share tonight if people want to know. I'm pretty sure everyone knows what happened, so there's nothing to hide. We want to see him and remember him the way he was before the cancer. So yeah, we'll tell people if we think it's appropriate."

Rebecca chimed in from across the room, "Sir and madam, you have guests arriving."

"Thank you, Rebecca," Clarise responded. "Let's see who is here." She headed toward the front door.

"*Hellooo!*" came a voice from the kitchen, and Alexandra knew MaryAnne had arrived. She looked at Eric and mouthed, "be nice," to which he responded with a middle finger. Lovely.

"Hello everyone!" bellowed another voice. Alexandra instantly recognized it as Patrick's.

Eric had met Patrick at Penn State as they hung around the same circle of friends and grew closer once they learned they were both from the Denver area. They spent several spring breaks together, and eventually, they were best men at each other's weddings.

Recently, however, they had grown a little distant. Patrick had decided to view his recent divorce as a sign to travel the world, apparently to see how many foreign women he could sleep with, or so Alexandra gathered from what Eric had told her.

Patrick claimed that his engineering firm wanted him to spend more time with international clients, so this was a good time for him to meet with them.

Alexandra was never really a fan of Patrick and thought his decision to travel was selfish, especially with seven-year-old, Joey, and five-year-old, Anna, at home.

However, given she had just asked Eric to be pleasant with MaryAnne, Alexandra would be pleasant with Patrick this evening.

"Hey, folks!" Alexandra exclaimed as they entered the kitchen area. After everyone exchanged hugs and kisses, Clarise proclaimed, "Why don't we all head to the sunroom and sit by the fire to continue the conversations? MaryAnne and Patrick, grab some drinks, and Rebecca will serve the appetizers in a few minutes."

"Sounds good, this way, everyone," David added, walking across the kitchen, past the foyer entrance, and turning right into the large sunroom/den that overlooked the Rocky Mountains in the distance. The late afternoon sun was setting as clouds were rolling in, casting an array of beautiful colors across the sky. Outside the sunroom, a large patio featured a pool, hot tub, and tennis courts towards the back right of the property. It was truly a beautiful view.

The sunroom had a cozy fireplace and enough seating for everyone. Alexandra settled onto a loveseat next to Eric, and moments later, MaryAnne and Patrick joined them, drinks in hand, plopping down on an adjacent couch. David took the chair nearest to the fireplace.

"Ah," David sighed as he relaxed in his chair. "The older you get, the better sitting down feels and the harder it is to get back up," he continued, taking a sip of his bourbon.

Eric chimed in, "Tell me about it. I think I separated a disk getting out of bed this morning. Does anyone know a good rehab doctor? Holy hell." He laughed briefly, shifting in his seat. "Speaking of rehab, did you see Smith from the Avalanche get absolutely crushed when the goalie fell on him? I have to ask Mike if that ever happened to him when he played in high school—I know it never happened to me."

David interrupted, "I did see that! Fucking nuts. With all that gear those guys have on, that's gotta be 250 pounds falling onto you, right? Damn, that poor guy. Hope he didn't shit his pants!"

Patrick, David, and Eric laughed while the girls gagged in disgust.

David continued, as the laughter subsided. "Speaking of Mike—he's still coming, right?"

Eric took the question: "Yeah, he's got a history of being the last to anything. He messaged me 15 minutes ago to say he's on his way, so he should be here soon."

Mike was Eric's close friend and ice hockey teammate from high school. He was a great high school player before tearing his ACL twice, which essentially ended his hockey career. Although Eric and Mike drifted apart for some time, they reconnected once Mike returned to the Denver area.

Mike had struggled with drugs and alcohol in the past, battling depression through the years. After his hockey career derailed, he bounced around in various sales positions in companies across different cities, but that never really went anywhere. Ultimately, after a near-death experience, he ended up back in Denver to get his life together.

Mike was a nice guy, but he and Alexandra had never gotten close to each other, which she was fine with. Eric had asked him to do this experience with the rest of the group, and he accepted, so it was natural that he joined them for dinner tonight.

From what Eric had told her, Mike had been sober for a couple of years and was seeing a girl, but they had recently broken up.

As David, Patrick, and Eric discussed sports and fantasy football, Alexandra smiled at MaryAnne, "Thanks for coming; it means a lot to Clarise and David for you to be here for them. So, how was the date last weekend? You didn't message me about it."

MaryAnne had been going on a streak recently with men: a golfer, an investment banker, a female bartender, and most recently, a software developer named Opie. From what she divulged, this guy seemed to have money and was somehow involved in the development of Anticipation Day, though she hadn't shared all the details yet.

"No, no, of course. I just feel awful for them. I can't imagine what they're going through. I hope our presence helps them a little, you know? I appreciate you guys organizing this; it's great to go through it together. Two years ago when I did this, I was alone, which was tough because I couldn't talk to anyone about my experience. We had to sign all this non-disclosure shit, so I never really got to share my experience. I think this is good timing for all of us."

MaryAnne sipped her drink before answering Alexandra's second question.

"So yeah, 'Mr. AI,' as I'm calling him now. The date was *really* nice. We went bowling and then had dinner. He's a down-to-earth and normal guy, which is weird for someone in software, but he's brilliant. And he's funny, too. He kept telling me jokes about Artificial Intelligence. There was one that got me: 'What do you call a blonde who dyes her hair brown? Artificial Intelligence.' It was stupid, but it cracked me up.

I'm playing it by ear and taking it slow. As you know, I've had a good run of 'bad boys' for a while, so I'm fine with getting to know someone first before opening up. I can't handle any more pain at the moment." MaryAnne took another sip.

"I know, sweetie, it's been a shit couple of years for you, so I'm glad to hear you're taking it slow. Sounds like this guy is cool, though. Have you seen his, you know, supercomputer?" Alexandra snickered at this one, proud of herself.

MaryAnne nearly spat out her wine. "His supercomputer? Seriously? You're such a dweeb. What are we, in fourth grade? No, we have not slept together, but thanks for your concern about my vagina."

Alexandra laughed right back. "I'm very concerned about your vagina. It has seen a lot of action over the past year, darling. But seriously, I'm glad you haven't. Hopefully, this guy is long-term for you. Speaking of long-term guys, how is your dad?"

MaryAnne gathered her thoughts before responding.

"Thank you for asking. He's still 'okay,' but my mom says he needs to go into hospice at this point. The Alzheimer's medication isn't working the way the doctors expected it to. Just the other day, he swung a golf club at my mom because he thought she was a burglar, so she's understandably scared. He doesn't recognize her anymore, and if he's trying to harm her, there's just no way we can leave them alone anymore.

It's fucking heartbreaking. He was doing okay until a few months ago, and then things seemed to go downhill fairly quickly. I'm planning to visit her next weekend to look at some options for care. We have a day nurse to make sure he behaves and doesn't try to hit my mom with a nine-iron again." She paused for another sip of her drink, and Alexandra followed suit.

After a few seconds, MaryAnne leaned in closer and whispered, "I wasn't planning to tell anyone, but you're my best friend, so you might as well know."

Alexandra was generally curious as to what she was about to hear. Is MaryAnne pregnant? Is she moving across the country? Is she attracted to her?

MaryAnne finally revealed the mystery: "I ended up paying extra to have my memories downloaded so I can relive a day with my dad. You know, before he was sick. My first simulation was just to clear my head after the shit with Kevin. And it helped, for sure; we've talked about it. But this year, I chose my parents' 50th-anniversary cruise to Bermuda a few years ago. I picked the best day from that trip—the last one. Everyone was happy, and I was in a good spot. This was obviously before I found out Kevin was cheating. When I asked the download center if I could throw Kevin overboard or at least stab him, the nurses laughed."

Alexandra could easily picture MaryAnne during her experience, trying to toss Kevin off the boat. Friggin' hilarious.

"Yeah, but basically, they said I'd be reliving that day as I remember it, not how I'd want to relive it. That's fine, though. I don't want to waste my time focusing on Kevin. I want to remember how I felt with my family on that trip when we were all healthy and happy together! I don't need much excitement this year; I just want to feel good mentally. I'm hoping remembering my family like that will be a good start. But yeah, *that's* my secret."

Alexandra replied quietly, "Wow, that's great. You didn't tell me much about your simulation two years ago other than that it was 'freeing' and 'eye-opening', but I hope this experience is what you need right now. I know how close you and your dad are, so if you want to do this, I fully support it and hope it's amazing."

"What are you two hens whispering about over there?" David interrupted with a laugh.

"Hey!" Clarise yelled as she walked into the room, balancing two trays of something that smelled delicious. "You do not refer to us as 'hens'!"

"Sorry, darling, just trying to see what secrets they're hiding over there," David said, grabbing what appeared to be a crab cake and standing to take one of the trays from Clarise. He walked the food trays to everyone else. "Here you go, folks. Crab cakes and risotto balls, right?"

"Yep! The chef highly recommended these, and they smell fucking incredible, so dig in. There are also some dipping sauces, if you want. Rebecca is warming up the main courses, and they should be ready in about 30 minutes." Clarise turned to Eric. "Mike is coming, right?"

"Yeah, he texted me and should be here soon. He's always running late," Eric responded before eating his appetizers.

"Perfect," Clarise noted as she sat in a chair near David. She took a deep breath, exhaled, and raised her wine glass. "Well! Welcome everyone! I appreciate you all coming by; this means a lot to us. As I told Eric and Alexandra earlier, we've really missed being around adults. We took the time to think about what Charlie would want us to do with our lives and realized he'd want us to be happy. Or, at least, try to be happy. We knew what happened to him was an eventuality, and we did our best to give him the best life while he could still enjoy it. He'll always be our little boy, and that will never change. But we both realized that we needed to be around people again—it's part of the healing process. So, thank you again for coming and hanging out with us." She was getting emotional again.

"Cheers to that," David said, grabbing Clarise's hand. "And cheers to you all!" He clinked his glass against Clarisse's, then stood to clink everyone else's glass as they all said, "Cheers!"

After sipping her drink, Clarise asked, "But, seriously, what were you 'hens' chatting about over there?" She chuckled and reached for her appetizers.

MaryAnne laughed as well, took a bite of her food, sipped her drink, and replied, "Well, first off, thank you for hosting us. I am so sorry about what happened with Charlie and if you need anything going forward, you know all you need to do is ask. We're always here for both of you."

Clarise held her drink up in acknowledgment.

MaryAnne continued, "If you must know, I was telling Alexandra about my simulation experience this year. I know I haven't been around much these past two years, but after what happened with Kevin, I needed time to focus on myself and get my head right. Luckily, my first Anticipation Day experience was right after I found out he was cheating on me, which allowed me to refocus on myself and what made me happy: traveling.

I won't bore you with the details, but it involved me traveling to Europe for three months—mostly through Spain, Amsterdam, Austria, France, Greece, and Italy—with a few detours here and there. I had never really been able to spend time in these places, so I figured, why not?

When I tell you it was real, I think that would be an understatement. It felt more than real—it just felt perfect, you know? Like, they knew everything you wanted to get out of the simulation. It was an amazing experience, and I've spent the past year and a half focusing on myself, which has been healing, if not somewhat boring.

Anyway, for this year's experience, I've chosen to relive a day with my family from my memories. Clarise, you may know this, but my dad is getting worse from Alzheimer's, and we're not sure how much time he has left. In fact, I'm going to see my mom next weekend to help find

a care facility for him; it's just too much for her. It's sad, you know…"
Her eyes were welling up with tears, so she took a second to breathe.

Alexandra stood, taking MaryAnne's hand. "It's okay. We're here for you."

MaryAnne laughed, nodding gratefully, before taking another sip of her wine. "So, yeah, I was telling Alexandra that I had them download my memories so I can do this. I figured this would be more meaningful now than trying to create another life I wanted to lead. So, I chose my parents' 50th-anniversary cruise a few years back that we took to Bermuda with my brothers and their families, my aunt and uncle, Kevin, and my parents. Even though I was blissfully unaware of Kevin's infidelity, I actually had a great time on the cruise, even with Kevin.

The creepy thing, which I didn't mention to Alexandra, is that you can't control anything in the simulation. Essentially, you're just along for the ride based on your recollections of that day. You can't change anything that is already in your memory bank. Honestly, I kind of like that because if I could change something, I would probably stab Kevin a few hundred times and throw his lifeless body overboard."

Everyone chuckled as MaryAnne mimicked stabbing someone with an imaginary knife.

After the laughter died down, she continued, "So, that's what us 'hens' were talking about since you *had* to know." MaryAnne finished the last of her wine, and everyone else laughed.

Clarise stood up to hug MaryAnne, then released her and said, "I'm so sorry—I didn't know your dad was that bad. I've been so wrapped up in my own world after what happened with Charlie that I barely checked how others have been doing. I'm really sorry for that." She hugged MaryAnne again.

MaryAnne started crying. "Goddamn, this is turning into a cheesy made-for-TV movie". She laughed before wiping away her tears and continuing. "I appreciate it, but there's no need to apologize after what you guys went through. I've been tight-lipped about my life recently anyway, especially about my dad, so you couldn't have known." She paused. "It just sucks because he was so smart and creative. Seeing him like this really, really sucks. I don't have another word for it. So, I hope this experience helps me remember who he was and what made him 'him,' you know?"

"That's great, MaryAnne," Patrick chimed in. "I'm happy for you. It's amazing they can do that. It's scary, really. I don't know if I want my memories floating in some government database. I was reading that, in a few years, they might allow people to go into the future and do some 'Star Wars' shit, like find far-away planets and galaxies or whatever. I guess they want to see how people react to these simulations first. Either way, I hope it helps you find peace with your dad.

My mom went through Alzheimer's too before she passed eight years ago, and it was awful to see that decline. You couldn't believe it was the same person you'd known all your life—she just seemed like a shell of her past self, and by the time she died, she was a different person. Hell, if you're comfortable sharing how it went afterward, I know I'd be curious to hear about it in case I want to do something like that next year. How much was it if you don't mind me asking?"

"I think there are different tiers you can pay for," MaryAnne responded. "I got the package that includes the past ten years of memories for $1,000. You can go back farther, but it costs more, as I assume it takes more computing power to pull from more distant memories. The guy explained it, but it went over my head. I am sure there's information on the government's website." She picked up a rice ball and stuffed it in her mouth.

Patrick asked, "I assume they can do any day?"

MaryAnne thought for a moment before replying. After finishing her rice ball, she said, "That's what they told me: as long as they can recall enough of the day to get you through the full 24 hours. The guy said it has something to do with the health of your neurons and neural connections in the brain. Apparently, computers can take the memory recalls and piece together the sequence of the day based on factors like the surroundings, people, clothing, lighting, and any time indications from memory.

They also asked some basic questions about what I could recall from the day and if I needed help recollecting any parts. They offer hypnosis sessions in case you need help with recollection. Since this was only a few years ago, I could remember most of the details pretty well—maybe just forgetting specifics about what I ate or wore—but I think they're able to piece that together from the downloads they did. It's amazing shit when you think about it."

"It *is* amazing stuff," Clarise agreed. "If you're comfortable, David and I would love to hear how it goes the next time we see each other. But, in line with that, we have some news to share." She finished her glass of wine as she looked at David, who nodded at her gently.

"This may or may not be a surprise, but David and I won't be doing our Anticipation Day experiences tomorrow. Soon after Charlie's diagnosis, I reached out to the DAD to apply for a change in our experiences after sharing what we were going through. They eventually agreed to let us relive a day from our past. It wasn't easy—they were a bit disorganized—but we recently got an appointment in May to do our downloads, and we hope to do our simulation in June or July. David and I talked through it, and we will both relive a day from when Charlie was happy and healthy. We both chose a trip to California to visit his brother a few years back." Clarise took a deep breath to steady herself.

"We don't know what we will feel before or after the experience, but we feel good about it now. MaryAnne, I'm sure we'll want to pick your brain, no pun intended, about what it was like and how you felt afterward. I can't wait to go through this, and I believe David feels the same, right?" She looked at David.

"Yeah, it's going to be weird and emotional to see Charlie again. I have no idea what it will look or feel like. MaryAnne, it would be great if we can chat after you do yours to see what you experienced, but, yeah, I feel the same way. I'm grateful to have this opportunity, and I want to go in with an open mind to see if it helps." David said, sipping his drink.

"That's amazing news, you two," MaryAnne responded. "I'd be happy to talk about my experience if it helps you guys. I may need a little time to gather my thoughts, especially after seeing my dad again next weekend, but I'll definitely let you know."

"Thank you," Clarise and David said in unison.

"Yeah, that's cool, guys," Patrick said after a few moments of silence. "I hope you find some peace with the experiences and that it helps you all."

MaryAnne took another sip of her wine. "I think it will be weird to watch ourselves go through a day." She glanced at David and Clarise. "I hope they don't pull in memories of me taking a shit or something." Everyone laughed, which was much needed. "It's going to be trippy to see yourself reliving a day and having all these thoughts while watching it play out in a simulation."

She finished the rest of her drink and said, "I'm going to grab another drink. Anyone want anything?"

"I'll take one," Patrick said, standing up and offering his hand to help MaryAnne off the couch.

"Me too." Clarise handed her glass to MaryAnne.

David turned to Eric and Alexandra. "So Eric, you said you guys aren't going to share what's in store for you tomorrow, right?" He looked at him expectantly.

Alexandra and I decided to wait a bit before sharing our journeys. We'll go into it at some point. If I had to guess what Alexandra is going to do, it would involve traveling and a beach. Am I close?" He smiled at Alexandra as he grabbed a few more risotto balls.

"I don't know what you are talking about," Alexandra said, taking the last few sips of her wine with a smile. "Look, I've had a long year. The kids have been sick constantly, your job has been stressful, and the daycare is always a pain in the ass. If you don't take me to the beach, I might just go alone!"

"We were supposed to do the cruise last year, but it got called off because of that virus running rampant on the cruise ships," Eric replied, referring to the Muskrat Pox outbreak that impacted several cruise lines last year and caused their Panama Canal cruise to be rescheduled until next year.

"I could have used another vacation besides that!" Alexandra exclaimed, giving Eric a fake death stare. "Maybe we can plan something with you all for next year?" Alexandra asked the group. "What do you think?"

"Yeah, we'd love that," Clarise answered, apparently speaking for herself and David.

"Sure, guys," David added. "What were you thinking? Antarctic? The South Pole? Europe? I haven't been to South America in a few years. Wanna do that? It's so damn hot, but the new ships have some radiation-deflecting technology to keep things cooler, so hopefully we're not hanging out in 110-degree weather."

"Maybe we should get through our Anticipation Day experience and then start thinking about an actual trip." Clarise chuckled.

"I agree. Let's get through tomorrow," Eric noted, taking a sip of his drink.

Patrick laughed as he started to leave the room with MaryAnne. "From my personal experience, there's nothing more freeing and uplifting than traveling the world and seeing what and who is out there. Expand those horizons."

"Oh yeah? Tell me more about the 'who' part," MaryAnne said with a wink at Alexandra before disappearing with Patrick around the corner toward the kitchen.

Alexandra had tried setting Patrick and MaryAnne up for a date after Patrick's divorce, but Patrick wasn't interested in dating anyone then—at least not in the United States. She was sure they had hooked up a couple of times anyway, though she never got confirmation. They were both attractive and physically active, so why the hell shouldn't they? They deserved to be happy, at least in that department.

Rebecca appeared and announced to Clarise, "Ms. Clarise, you have a visitor."

"Ooh, I guess Mike is here," Clarise said, getting up to meet him at the foyer.

"Let me go find him so he knows he's in the right place," Eric groaned as he slowly lifted himself off the loveseat and followed Clarise.

"I'll grab another drink," David declared, turning to Alexandra. "Do you want anything while I'm up?"

"Sure, I'll take a refill. Thank you," she responded as she handed him her glass of wine.

"I will be right back." David smiled and left the room.

She smiled back and said, "Thank you."

Alexandra took a breath and realized she was now alone in the sunroom. She closed her eyes, taking in in the warmth of the fire as she breathed deeply. She would never admit it to Eric, but she was nervous about tomorrow. Given her natural paranoia and a history of not making rash decisions before doing her research, she had spent countless hours looking up the potential risks of Anticipation Day.

Most of the articles she found indicated that the majority of Americans were not experiencing any noticeable side effects. However, a few sources noted there was some concern about the potential mental health risks associated with the experiences, which were mainly symptoms of psychosis and schizophrenia, although these seemed rare.

Similar to the news story she briefly heard, there were also mentions of the need to review suicides and suicide attempts to determine if they were linked to Anticipation Day. So far, no proven correlation has been found.

She hoped tonight's dinner and hearing about how others felt would calm her nerves. Plus, she planned on taking Clarise up on the edibles she kindly offered.

As everyone, including Mike, slowly drifted back into the den, she got up and hugged Mike, kissing him on the cheek. She hadn't seen him in a long time, but he looked good and happy. He had a warm, friendly smile that definitely drew the ladies in.

"How are you doing, Mike?" Alexandra asked.

"Good, good. I'm good, thanks. It's been too long. Work is good, you know? This cool weather snap is causing some chaos at a few of my sites, but overall, I'm doing well. I picked up a couple of new contracts for the city, so I've been busy getting those up and running. More importantly, how are you guys? How are the kids? I gotta swing by one of these weekends," he said to Eric and Alexandra.

"The kids are good, man. It's amazing how quickly they grow up on you," Eric replied, looking down at his glass. "All three were sick pretty much all winter, but they seem to be coming out of it now. Work has been a pain in the ass, but what else is new? Trying to stave off these robots for as long as possible." Eric laughed as he raised his brow at Rebecca. "At this point, maybe I should just quit, live off the government stipend, and find something less stressful."

"I hear you. I can't imagine what the accounting profession must be like with these damn computers calculating everything instantly. Didn't they put you in charge of figuring out what the hell to do with AI and how it would impact the firm?" Mike asked.

"Yeah, AI has changed everything. It's almost made us accountants obsolete. If a computer can review data and determine if something is accounted for correctly, what the hell do they need a human for? I mean, shit, computers can analyze financial information or tax returns at the lowest level of detail available and see if things look weird in a fraction of the time it takes a human. And computers, in theory, aren't trying to be fraudulent, but the real risk is the potential for being hacked, you know?

So, all these firms are trying to work with the government to ensure that humans still have a role in the accounting and legal processes. Humans will always be needed to some extent, but right now, it's just about figuring out what that extent is. So, yeah, it's been a bit stressful, which is why I am looking forward to this fucking thing tomorrow." Eric took a sip of his drink.

"Damn man—I'm sorry it's come to this. You should take the government money, take some time off, and figure out what you want to do," Mike suggested.

"Yeah, I've been thinking about it. Just makes me feel like I gave up if I did that. Still, I'm considering it. Anyway, it's good to see you! It's been way too long. So, did you work things out with your girlfriend? I know you told me you were on a break or something."

"Oh man, we need to catch up. Let me grab a soda or something." Mike turned toward the kitchen, then looked back at Eric. "It's good to see you too buddy. It's been way too long."

As he walked away, Eric asked Alexandra, "Does he seem happier than normal to you? Wonder what he's got going on now."

"Well, I've only seen him a dozen or so times, but I'm sure he's excited about tomorrow, as we all are. But he said you needed to catch up, so maybe there's more. I guess we'll find out soon. Wow, something smells so good. I'm starving!"

Just as Alexandra said that, Clarise appeared in the foyer and announced that dinner would be ready soon. Everyone got up from their seats, left the sunroom and headed to the large open dining room. A beautiful chandelier hung over a wooden table that could easily seat 16 people. There were seven place settings, each with the finest plates, wine glasses, and cutlery. A few candles in the middle of the table warmed the room. It was a beautiful setting for dinner.

Alexandra walked over to Clarise and said, "Thank you again for hosting us all tonight. This is so beautiful! And the food smells really good—I can't wait."

Clarise briefly leaned her head on Alexandra's shoulder before responding: "Aww, thank you.

I'm so glad you could come. It means the world to us. And yes, please sit!"

"Before I do, do you have some of those gummies you mentioned earlier?" Alexandra asked.

"Oh, they're on the table, silly," Clarise responded. "There's a bowl in the middle with a cover on it. Just open it and enjoy. Five milligrams each."

"Well, that's easy enough," Alexandra said. She found the bowl and opened it to reveal about 15-20 colorful gummies. She took a couple for herself and asked if anyone else wanted one. Patrick, MaryAnne, and Clarise said yes, and David added, "Fuck yes!" She knew Mike was sober, and Eric didn't touch the stuff.

All the participants held the gummies up in the air, said "cheers," and consumed them. They were tasty. At ten milligrams, Alexandra would be fine as long as she didn't have any more wine, which might cause her to sleep right through her 6 a.m. alarm tomorrow. She had been consuming cannabis for many years, given that Colorado legalized it nearly 20 years ago.

While she didn't consume every week, multiple times a month had become the norm as a way to take the edge off a long workday or when the kids were driving her nuts.

Clarise walked into the room, carrying a couple of bottles of wine, followed by Rebecca with more bourbon and scotch bottles. They placed the bottles on a small table next to the dining room table.

"Alright, folks—everyone comfortable? Anyone need a drink or a gummy?" Clarise asked.

"We're good with the edibles," David answered. "Patrick looks like he needs a refill, as he downed that drink pretty quickly. Anyone else?"

"I'll take one more," Eric said.

Alexandra shot him a look and mouthed "slow down" so no one else could see. She hated when he drank too much; it turned him into a different person—angry and depressed. She wished he enjoyed cannabis instead, but he never seemed interested since he got sick after each try. She had suggested using cannabis without alcohol to see if it helped, but so far, he hadn't taken her up on that.

"Remember we have a 6 a.m. wake-up call tomorrow, darling," she reminded Eric, clearing her throat.

"Yeah, yeah, I'll be fine once I get some food in me. It smells delicious," Eric said, inhaling deeply.

"I hope you enjoy it," Clarise responded cheerfully. "This place is one of our favorites. The chef was a client of mine a couple of years ago, so he's always happy to help. He recommended the lamb chops, glazed salmon, and chicken milanese for the mains. I also got some rigatoni vodka, which I know Eric loves, along with mashed potatoes, string beans, sweet carrots, and truffle fries—because why the hell not? There's dessert too, so save some room. It's to die for. Just let Rebecca know what you want."

Everyone placed their order with Rebecca. As Clarise finally sat down, David stood up, raised his glass, and smiled. "I wanted to take this opportunity to thank you all again for joining us tonight on 'Anticipation Day Eve'—that sounds like a fucking horror flick." He chuckled. "We appreciate you all doing this together with us, especially after the circumstances of the past several months. Initially, when Clarise and I were discussing whether we wanted to do the download process, we were on the fence about whether to do it or not; it's a bit nerve-wracking to know the government can monitor your thoughts and feelings. But we realized they track every other goddamn thing in our lives, so what's one more? Each of us is on a different path on this ridiculous journey we call life. Except for MaryAnne here, who had the fortune to do this two years ago and survive, Clarise and I hope that your initial Anticipation Day experiences tomorrow, and ours a couple months later, are as rewarding, uplifting, and eye-opening as promised. Maybe MaryAnne can share some tips while we eat. Either way, cheers to all of you! Let's enjoy some good food, drink, edibles, and great company this evening."

Glasses clinked together, and a chorus of "cheers" and "salut" erupted from the group as Rebecca served the mains to the group.

Alexandra got the salmon, while Eric chose the Lamb chop and rigatoni vodka. The sides smelled heavenly, so everyone piled their plates high with a bit of everything.

"So, I never got to hear why yours will be in a few months," Mike asked Clarise and David between bites.

"Sorry, Mike," David said, cutting up his chicken dish. "You walked in right after we broke the news. We deferred our Anticipation Day to get some memories downloaded so we could do a day with our son, Charlie, who passed away in December. We were initially set for tomorrow, but now it looks like it will be later in the spring or summer."

"Oh my god, I'm so sorry. Eric had mentioned it to me, but I wasn't sure if we were talking about it," Mike said, nearly choking on his food. "My condolences to both of you. I didn't know your son, but when Eric told me, it was really upsetting. I feel like such an idiot now."

"Oh no, Mike, please don't worry." Clarise responded. "You had no way of knowing. But yes, we will hopefully be able to do ours in a few months after our downloads are complete. Thank you for your kind words, though.

Originally, we had planned other experiences in case Charlie was still with us on our chosen day. David, do you want to tell everyone what you would have done? I think it was great!"

"Sure, why not?" David replied, setting down his silverware, taking a quick drink of water, and swallowing his food.

"I've always admired great comedians—George Carlin, Eddie Murphy, Jerry Seinfeld, Jim Norton, Bill Burr, and, hell, even Rich Vos, who was one of the quickest guys I've seen live. Watching them do crowd work so easily was amazing. I always thought it must be so cool to stand on stage every night, sharing funny stories and anecdotes and making people laugh. Years ago, when I just got to New York, I dabbled with a few spots on open mic night but never really went anywhere with it.

So, for my experience, I was going to be a comedian for a few months. The idea was to live the life of a working comedian in smaller clubs, building up to a big one-hour special at a major venue.

As you all know, my sense of humor won Clarise over, and I think I'm a funny dude, but I figured even if I bombed in the simulation, only I, and whomever in the government was watching, would remember it.

So that is what I wanted to do initially." David stopped to take a bite of his food.

"I think that's awesome, man," Patrick said. "Would you have written your own jokes or had them written for you?"

"I thought about that. I asked them to prepare about 20 minutes of material for me, and I would work on the other 40 minutes for the special. I did want to write some of my own jokes while in the simulation. They said I'd think like a comedian, so producing material wouldn't be too difficult."

"That's so cool, man," Eric added between bites. "When and where would you have been?"

As David finished a bite of the side dishes, he replied, "Well, I asked to be placed in New York City in 2001 or 2002, so I would have worked at some cool clubs while making simulated people laugh. I wanted to go back to a time when cell phones weren't distracting and people still actually paid attention when they went out."

"Very nice," Eric chimed in. "That would have been fun. I imagine traveling on the road would have been a blast—maybe you'd even have roadies. Hah!" He laughed at his own joke.

David chuckled too. "That would be funny if I did. I told them to surprise me with my road gigs, but I'm sure I would have done a couple of sets in New York City and then been on the road for a few weekends. I wanted the excitement of not knowing where I was headed next, and I'm sure a few roadies would have tagged along." He raised his eyebrows suggestively at Clarise, implying those roadies would be female.

"If you wanted to sleep with a couple of roadies, go for it. As long as you didn't bring any genital warts back from the simulation, I wouldn't have cared." Clarise lifted her glass of wine in the air as if to say: *More power to you.*

"Can you have sex in the simulation?" Alexandra questioned, turning her gaze to MaryAnne across the table.

MaryAnne set her knife and fork down, finished chewing her piece of salmon, and slowly said, "Without divulging too many details here, yes, you can have sex, and before you ask, yes, it feels as real as fucking in real life."

Alexandra looked around, and saw large grins spread across the faces of David, Eric, Mike, and Patrick. "Look at you, dolts. I should have known this was possible, given that mostly dudes created this. I'm sure that's the most lifelike part of the entire experience."

"I don't know about that," MaryAnne interjected. "Don't get me wrong, it did the trick, but I certainly prefer real-life sex to whatever I may or may not have experienced in my simulation last year."

"Okay, since you are blushing, why don't you share your experience, MaryAnne?" David asked, grinning widely.

"Not yet. I want to hear about what Clarise had planned first," she quipped, turning to Clarise, who was sitting to her right.

"Fine. I've had a few glasses, and I think the edible I took is starting to hit, so why not?" After taking a final sip, she put her glass of wine down. "I am sure Alexandra will get a kick out of this, but I wanted to do something *fun*, you know? I, well, we haven't traveled much the past few years, especially with everything that happened with Charlie, and being in Denver, it's always a little harder to get to Europe than it was in New York. I used to love traveling. Alexandra, remember when we used to go all over the world together before we had kids?"

"Of course", Alexandra replied. "We had a blast together."

"Yes we did," Clarise chuckled before continuing. "So, when I was deciding what to do for my first simulation, it was an easy choice: I wanted to travel. I started thinking about what I could do that would be fun and interesting beyond just vacationing in Europe. Eventually, I came up with the idea of traveling as a social media influencer for a major fashion design company to the biggest fashion shows worldwide.

David knows I've always been passionate about fashion and dreamed of attending major fashion shows in New York, London, Paris, Milan, and Brazil. Hell, I minored in fashion and design in college.

So, I figured I would do that for my first simulation - travel to major fashion shows across the world, explore amazing cities, wine and dine with the elite, and live the life of a social media influencer. I think it would have been fun!" Clarise waited to see everyone's reactions.

Alexandra finished a bite of french fries before exclaiming, "That would have been amazing! I know you had your heart set on fashion when you graduated. Not that law isn't exciting, but I always knew that wasn't your passion. 'A passion for fashion,' you always said!

So, what would your role have been in the simulation? Would you just sit and watch the shows, or would you be 'on the clock'?"

Clarise swallowed her food before responding. "Well, I initially told the folks that arranged this that I wanted to be a semi-successful woman in her 30s who started a line of handbags made from hemp in her parents' garage."

Everyone chuckled.

"The theory was that I eventually gained millions of followers on social media and got contracted by a major handbag designer to go over to the different shows and promote their product lines on my accounts. My job would involve mingling with stylists, celebrities, VIPs, and brand leaders, encouraging them to take pictures and videos of the products. Talk about an easy gig!

You get to travel the world, stay at the best hotels, enjoy amazing food and wine, and all you have to do is convince people to take pictures. It's insane—where has this been all my life?" Everyone laughed again, including Alexandra, who was definitely going to consider doing the same thing in her simulation next year.

"That's amazing, darling," MaryAnne acknowledged. "I did something similar last year, which I can get into, but traveling to places you normally can't reach is, in my opinion, the coolest part of all this. You can see whatever you want in the cities you are visiting."

"I'm sure I would have loved it," Clarise conceded. "I thought about skydiving or going back in time to be a princess, or something like that, but for my initial experience, I wanted to do something close to my heart—something I could relate to. Maybe next year. We'll see!"

There was a brief silence before Patrick spoke with a smile. "Okay, MaryAnne, I think you are up now."

"Fuck that. I wanna hear what you're up to, Patrick," MaryAnne said with a grin. "And if Mike is willing to share, I wanna hear his plan before I spill mine."

"I don't think I want to share my simulation, but I do have some exciting news," Mike replied. "But first, let's hear from Patrick. I'm still finishing this lambchop—it's friggin' delicious, Clarise. Compliments to the chef, please."

"Agreed." Patrick nodded. "Thank you all for having us and for this delightful food."

"Here, here," Eric said, finishing his glass of Jefferson's.

"One more, Eric?" David asked.

"Sure, but this is the last one. Alexandra is right, and we have to be up early tomorrow. The last thing I need is Anya dumping water on my face to wake me up, something she may or may not have done in the past."

David laughed. "Okay, my man, one more coming up for you." He poured Eric another glass before putting it in front of him. "Cheers!" They clinked glasses.

"Alright, Patrick, you're next," said Eric. "I can't wait to hear what this one is. It feels like you've already been living in a simulation with all your travels over these past six months, so I am curious what you decided to do with this experience."

Patrick took a sip of his drink and finished his mashed potatoes. "As Eric knows pretty much everything about me, this one shouldn't surprise him."

"We'll see," Eric interrupted, chucking and taking another sip of his bourbon.

"I'm sure most of you know the past six months have been interesting for me. Between the divorce and flying all around the world to meet with clients—and yes, I was actually meeting with clients," he said with a laugh of his own. "But, honestly, in reality, it's been a hard 18 months or so. Courtney and I were having issues, really since Anna was born. The pregnancy did a number on Courtney, both mentally and physically, and we struggled for a while after Anna's birth. We tried working on it, you know, mostly for Brin and Anna's sake.

But after *many* therapy sessions and countless fucking arguments, we decided early last year to split up. Honestly, it was a painful and emotional process, but we tried to keep things civil for the kids' sake and not argue or bicker in front of them. Behind the scenes though, we were both struggling and resentful towards each other. So, I took some time to travel— honestly, it was needed for all of our sakes, not just mine. The kids are adjusting, and I see them almost every weekend, but it's been a rough period of my life.

But, for my experience, I wanted to do something near and dear to my heart. Something that I had always had a passion for, but never worked out.

Eric knows that I majored in meteorology at Penn State for a couple of years before failing miserably and making that natural switch to sales and marketing as a major." He paused to let the chuckles die down.

"One of the things I wanted to do with a meteorology degree was study tornadoes and do field research with the government or some private university. Living on the front range, I have seen a few tornadoes from a distance, but I never saw one up close.

Even now, I am still interested in climate change and weather, and I try to follow what is happening with the planet. The size and power of tornados have always intrigued me. They are so indiscriminate and unpredictable, you know?

Either way, it has fascinated me for most of my life, so I figured, why not do a tornado-chasing experience for my simulation? I'm guaranteed to not actually die in one and can still feel the awesome power and awe of seeing one up close.

So, I am returning to 2001 to chase tornadoes for ten days. It should be pretty cool—driving around in some beat-up van with whatever tornado-chasing technology they had back then, living out of cheap hotels, and eating crappy food while hopefully intercepting some cool tornadoes. I hope it will be a cool experience and something that intrigues me enough to take my kids on a tornado-chasing vacation one day.

Who knows, though? It's nothing scandalous or crazy, like traveling to Europe or being a comedian. Still, I think I'll enjoy it!" Patrick sipped water and finished a few more fries.

"Sounds cool, man," Eric acknowledged. "I know switching majors was tough for you. I remember how much time you spent struggling with those awful fucking calculus classes we had freshman year and how frustrating it was. How will this work, though? Do they guarantee you'll see a tornado, or is it just totally random?"

"I told them I wanted it to be as realistic as possible but I wanted to experience good days, boring days, and even days where you see the destruction from these things. We've all heard stories of people in eastern Colorado or western Kansas losing everything. It's fucking awful what tornadoes can do to a community. I didn't want to be blinded by that and just witness the perfect tornado from afar without understanding its impact on people's lives, you know? So, I told them to throw it all at me and see how it goes. I'll probably be the first person in the history of the simulations to get blown away by a tornado," Patrick quipped, laughing to himself.

"No thank you," both Clarise and MaryAnne chimed in unison, sharing a laugh.

MaryAnne added, "But I think that's pretty cool! If you don't get crushed by a cow during your simulation, I hope you come out of it reinvigorated. I'd love to hear how it goes. But why 2001?"

"Well, that's when I started getting into weather. When I was home sick from school, I'd watch the weather channel on television and eventually started tracking severe weather and tornadoes. So I don't know. I guess that year always held a special place in my heart, especially with 9/11 happening," Patrick explained matter-of-factly.

"That makes sense, man. Maybe one of my gigs will be in Kansas or Oklahoma, and I can come visit you." David laughed.

"True! It's funny we chose the same year for our simulations. I can't imagine there will be many comedy clubs where I'm going, but you never know!" Patrick chuckled.

"Okay, Mike, you're done with your lambchop, man," Eric said with a laugh. "What's this 'exciting' news you have to share with us?"

"Yeah, please, what is this news?" Alexandra asked, her voice piqued with curiosity as the edible was kicking in. "Is there a special lady in the picture? Do tell if that's the case—I love gossip!"

"Haha, hilarious," Mike replied with a big smile. "Yes, I'm done with this lambchop. Not sure I'll have room for dessert, but man, it was good. I hope I don't sleep through my alarm from being too full!" He remarked. "Alright, alright. I was just going to tell Eric, but I guess I'll share with everyone. I know you all don't know me well, but, as some of you know, Eric and I go way back, so he knows my life story. I was a hockey player in high school—I was pretty damn good, if I say so myself—until I tore both my ACLs in consecutive seasons. It derailed my hockey career at the prime age of 18 years old. It sucked balls, pardon my French, and I was depressed for a long time. I *really* wanted to play professionally, even if it was in Europe or Canada. Something where I could play at a competitive level for as long as possible.

But, hey, that's life. It kicks you in the balls, pardon my French again, and you recover as best you can. I've also had a small history with drugs and alcohol," he said, pinching his thumb and index finger together closely and chuckling.

"Hell, who am I kidding? I had some pretty bad issues with painkillers and alcohol after I tore my ACLs, and, unfortunately, it did negatively impact my life. I had trouble staying in relationships, and my relationship with my family soured a bit, which made me drink more and do drugs more. There were times I ended up in the hospital and didn't think I'd make it.

But I guess someone had a plan for me, you know? That's the way I have to look at it.

I got sober and have been sober for two and a half years now. When my mom died, I came into some money and invested in a construction company, which I've been running for the past two years." He smiled.

"While I've never been married, I've had some committed relationships over the years—some more committed than others," he said, making everyone laugh. "Anyways, Stacy, this recent girl I'd been dating for the past year or so was a cool chick. Sorry—woman.

She worked in marketing for a tech start-up in downtown Denver and had a good head on her shoulders. We met through a mutual friend and got along well. I liked her, I really did.

She was a few years younger than me and was ready to settle down and have kids. Unfortunately, I wasn't. I never wanted kids, as Eric has known for a while. It wasn't an issue for her… until it was. Of course, we were having unprotected sex, as she claimed to be on the pill, which is supposed to be 99.7% effective, or whatever.

We broke up around Halloween because she wanted to be with someone who wanted kids, which I understood. She could have done it artificially, but she wanted to have kids naturally while she was still physically able.

I cared about her, so while it hurt, I understood and wished her the best moving forward.

I didn't hear from her until about two months ago, and you can probably guess where this is going, but she called me and told me she was five months pregnant, and it was mine. Naturally, I questioned that claim and asked her for a paternity test…I mean, she had told me she was on the pill. She agreed eventually, and after a little delay in getting the results, I got confirmation a few weeks ago that it was mine.

At first, I was pissed and told her she should have told me. It wasn't fair for her to make this decision without me."

Mike paused momentarily, collecting his thoughts as he became emotional, then continued, "But, after thinking about it and reflecting on it, I came to the realization that this pregnancy was meant to be, and I wanted to be a part of this kid's life." He took a sip of water.

"I know the relationship between Stacy and me won't be perfect, and we'll have to figure it out, but I want to try to give this kid a normal upbringing. So, that's the news—I'm going to be a dad!"

Mike couldn't contain his excitement. "And…it's a girl. I'm having a little girl!" He was tearing up at this point.

"Oh my god, man, that's amazing. Congratulations!" Eric exclaimed, walking around the table. "You are going to be a dad—who would have thought?" He smiled as he bear-hugged Mike. "That is absolutely amazing news, man."

"Seriously, congratulations, Mike," Alexandra added as she stood up to hug and kiss him. "No wonder you seem like you're on cloud nine!"

"Yeah, it's the craziest shit. She's due on July 7th. We already have some names picked out, but we want the middle name to honor my mom, Megan. We'll see how the rest of it turns out. But yeah, I am over the moon right now. I don't know how this can compare to my simulation tomorrow, but I can't imagine it's close. I never imagined having a kid would make me feel this way, but here I am.

Stacy and I will try to work things out to see if we can be in a long-term relationship, so who knows where that will go? But either way, I'm going to be a dad! So, that's the news! Surprise!"

Mike laughed as he sat back down, wiping away a few tears from his eyes.

David, Clarise, MaryAnne, and Patrick all offered their congratulations and said how happy they were for him.

"I know you guys don't know me that well," Mike pointed out after seeing their faces. "But Eric knows I was *never* looking to have kids. I'm a pretty selfish dude, and I never wanted them. I just didn't. So, this is probably a surprise for him, especially with me being 43 years old." Mike nodded towards Eric next to him.

"Hey man, most pregnancies are a surprise. I've had three surprises myself, and I'm sure Clarise, David, and Patrick have too," Eric responded. "You're never really ready, but I am sure any of us can give you some tips and horror stories. You do the best you can and hope you don't fuck up your kids as much as you were fucked up by your parents."

David and Patrick raised their glasses and said, "Cheers to that."

"I wasn't going to bring this up, especially with what you and Clarise were going through, and I'm sorry if this brings up anything bad on your end." Mike looked at David and Clarise.

"No, we're happy you shared," Clarise said quietly. "I think we all needed some good news tonight."

"Thanks, Clarise," Mike continued. "Well, hell, I wasn't going to say anything, but real quick, so for my simulation this year, I decided to play in Game 7 of the Stanley Cup Finals as the Rangers against the Oilers. I figured if I can't play professionally in real life, I'll play in this fucking thing!"

Everyone laughed at that.

"That's awesome, man!" Eric said, raising his hands in the air. "I was going to do something like that for mine. It would be awesome to play in the Super Bowl, the World Series, or something like that. Bet half my workforce is doing that for their simulations." He chuckled.

"Yeah, I never thought of that," Patrick said. "Playing in front of millions of people watching your every move? I'd probably shit my pants under that much pressure."

"Cheers to that," David chimed in.

"Ha, yeah, I know. That's kind of why I wanted to do it. To see what it's like playing in that environment, you know? Under the lights of MSG? With millions of people watching on television? That has got to be some crazy shit, right?" Mike laughed, glancing at the other guys.

"Offense or defense?" Eric asked.

"Offense, of course! I wanna score the winning goal, not get scored on!" Mike laughed again. "Yeah, man, offense. You know I always loved scoring goals. I was damn good at it, too. So, yeah, I want to play offense, and who knows? Maybe I will score that winning goal this time." Mike quieted down after saying that.

Sensing the mood change, Eric said, "I'm sure you will, man. I know you'll do everything in your power to get it, too."

"Cheers to that," MaryAnne added. "Maybe this is the edible kicking in, but you seem like a chill dude. I'm sure you'll be a great dad. Unfortunately, I was never blessed with little ones, but I've come to terms with that. I know you can never say never, but it's great that you have been given a chance to be a dad. Just don't fuck it up." She laughed and looked at Mike.

"I'm kidding, dude—you'll be fine. If Alexandra and Eric can do it, you can too. Maybe that will be my simulation next year—having a flock of youngins and seeing how I'd be as a mom. You can fuck them up as much as you want in a simulation, right?"

"Speaking of your simulation," Clarise interrupted. "I think we all wanna hear about your experience, MaryAnne, and what we can expect tomorrow. Let me get Rebecca in here with some dessert and coffee while you regale us with your experience from two years ago." She got up to go to the kitchen.

"Yeah, I wanna hear all about this too," Patrick added. "I didn't know you had already done it until Eric mentioned it a few weeks back. I knew government employees were allowed early access, but I never knew anyone who did it. It'd be pretty cool to hear about it straight from the horse's mouth." Patrick paused. "Sorry, I wasn't calling you a horse; you're much more attractive than a horse." He paused again, turning red. "Shit—these edibles are kicking in, sorry. I should shut up now."

MaryAnne laughed. "You're good, Patrick. I know Kevin didn't cheat on me because he wasn't attracted to me. He was just attracted to many, many other women as well, and unfortunately, his dick was always stronger than his brain. It's funny—we tried to have kids for so long, but it never worked. We could've gotten help to conceive, but Kevin was always adamant about doing it naturally.

I don't think I told you this, Alexandra, but I found out last month he had a kid with one of his *lovers* that he was fucking during our marriage." MaryAnne emphasized "lovers" as if it were some sort of romantic description of the woman he was cheating with.

"So I guess in the end, it wasn't him that was the problem—it was me. I had some tests done, and it looks like my ovaries are 'no bueno,' as they say."

"Oh, I'm sorry, MaryAnne. I had no idea," Alexandra said, rubbing Maryanne's arm to comfort her.

"It's okay. As I mentioned, I think I'm okay with having kids in a simulation. It's so real—so lifelike—that I think it can be almost as good as having them in real life. I will likely never know the difference, but I think I'm okay with that." Her eyes got teary. "Plus, I look at it this way: I don't have to go through the hell of childbirth." She laughed as she looked at Alexandra, tears running down her face.

"Ah, fuck it, there's been enough emotional shit here tonight," MaryAnne said as Clarise rejoined the table with Rebecca in tow with a tray of lovely-looking desserts and some coffee.

"Damn, this looks good," David chimed in. "What do we have here?"

"So, the chef recommended the eclairs, tiramisu, chocolate lava cake, and the cookies he makes on-site. We will all have to visit the gym next week, but I've had his phenomenal desserts. Please dig in and enjoy. Hopefully, those edibles are hitting right now, and everyone has a sweet tooth because I need these desserts eaten and away from me after today, or else I will have to be in the gym for a week straight." Clarise laughed.

"MaryAnne, you okay?" She asked, looking up from the desserts to see MaryAnne teary-eyed.

"Yeah, sorry, I was just giving everyone an update on my failed reproductive system. Nothing major," MaryAnne responded, trying to laugh off the tears.

"Oh no! I'm so sorry," Clarise responded.

"Thank you. I've accepted it, and as I was saying to everyone else, I'm okay if I just end up being able to have kids in some future simulation," MaryAnne replied, reaching for an eclair. "I think stuffing my face with delicious desserts will help anyway."

Everyone laughed at that statement.

"Well, if you're going to stuff your face, I might as well join you," Patrick said, grabbing a piece of lava cake. "My dad bod has been lacking recently, and this edible certainly isn't helping."

"Me too," Mike added, also reaching for a piece of lava cake.

"Ah, hell, I'll go for an extra 20-minute run next weekend," Alexandra said, taking some tiramisu along with Eric.

"Great minds speak alike." Eric responded, slurring slightly.

"*Oh, great,*" Alexandra thought, looking at Eric. He was officially drunk. At this point, one of two things would happen: he would either get sleepy and pass out when they got home, or he would get angry, start a fight about something ridiculously stupid, slam doors, wake the kids, and end up on the couch all night.

She hoped being around people and having a good time would calm him down and make him sleepy. Time would tell.

As everyone grabbed dessert and coffee, Rebecca left the room, and Clarise sat back in her chair.

"Okay, first off, this is just delicious, so thank you for all this," MaryAnne said as she chewed on her eclair. "Second, let me give some insight into what you can expect tomorrow by relating to what is happening right now."

MaryAnne put her fork down and cleared her throat.

"So, take a moment to look around. Think really hard about everything you can see, hear, touch, smell, and taste, like these delicious desserts. Just take it all in. Now, in the simulation, everything will be *exactly* the same. The color of that wall will be the same. The cushion under your ass will feel the same. The birds outside will sound the same. These desserts will taste the same. Everyone sitting around this table interacting with you will be the same. *Everything* will be the same.

Except...you'll be someone else.

Your skin, hair, height, and weight will be different. Everything physical about you will change. But you will still be you. You'll remember everything from your real life, yet somehow, you will be this other person in the simulation.

People will ask you questions about your simulated character's life, and you'll know the answers. You will just know, instinctively. It's honestly the creepiest thing at first, but eventually you get used to it.

You're groggy when you first wake up, which they said was normal. It's like your real-life mind needs time to combine with your mind in the simulation to form some sort of 'super mind,' and it takes a few minutes to adjust to that.

Before you enter the simulation, you'll chat with your simulation coach. They'll confirm the details of the simulation, its length, some of the ground rules for the simulation, what to expect when you wake up, and what happens if you need to leave early. Make sure you ask any questions then because you want to be as comfortable and ready for this as possible." She stopped to eat more of her eclair.

"When I woke up in my simulation, I was on a lounge chair on a rocky beach somewhere in Italy, and it looked like sunset. I had my clothes on and a bag with me. It took me a few minutes to sit up and shake the cobwebs off, but once I did and took in my surroundings, it was like I was really on a beach in Italy.

I could hear the ocean in the distance, with the waves crashing on the shore. I could feel the coolness of the rocks against my feet. I could feel the breeze on my skin, or whatever it was in the simulation. I could hear people around me speaking German, English, and Spanish. I could hear cars and trucks driving on the road above the beach, with horns honking occasionally.

I saw seagulls flying all over, probably looking for the last scraps of food. And speaking of food, I could smell it from the beach vendors— garlic, meat, fish, oils—it all came through the breeze and right to my nose.

And then the sunset. My god, the sunset. It was as if every color on the spectrum was forming in the sky above me. It took me back to my childhood, sitting outside with my dad, watching sunsets from our porch. I felt instantly calm. Maybe they set it up that way to ensure you entered calmly. Who knows?

Either way, it was a fantastic way to start. But then, I just kind of knew things about my simulation. I knew where my hotel was, what I had done the day before, and that I was on the trip alone. I just felt it and knew it.

It was as if memories were implanted in me, and I could recall them instantly. It was wild.

You generally knew everything about the simulated character. If someone asked me what I had for breakfast 17 years ago, I'd struggle; but I would also struggle in real life. But if someone asked me who my favorite cousin was, I could answer that. They give you enough knowledge to get through what any conversation in real life would be like, you know?" MaryAnne took another bite of her delicious eclair while others did the same.

Alexandra looked around, noticing how everyone was hanging on her every word. It was truly amazing and something she had never seen before from this group. Everyone was silent, waiting for her to continue.

"It just got more amazing from there. The sites I saw. The food I ate. The people I met. The smells I smelled. It all felt as real as real life. It was like I had the freedom to do whatever the *fuck* I wanted.

I told the simulation team I wanted to travel around Europe for a year. They gave me free reign to explore any European country, but if I tried to go anywhere else, the simulation would end.

Obviously, I was fine with that—I wasn't planning to return to the US in my simulation. For what?" She seemed to ask herself the question, but no one responded.

"So, I traveled. I visited Italy: Rome, Florence, the Amalfi Coast, Tuscany, and Sicily. I took a boat to Greece and saw the ancient ruins in Athens, the coast of the Aegean, and then traveled up through Bulgaria, Serbia, Romania, and eventually to what is left of Ukraine. I headed west through Hungary and Austria, finally reaching Switzerland to see the Swiss Alps—amazing and stunning. It was one of many places on my trip that just took my breath away.

I think I went to the Netherlands or Germany from Switzerland. I can't remember. But in Germany, I toured Munich, Berlin, and Hamburg, which were phenomenal, and the people there, at least in the simulation, were amazing. From there, I think I went west through the Netherlands, Belgium, and Luxembourg, which I had always dreamed of seeing.

The food in that region was unbelievable! Everything was so delicious and fresh and different. It was honestly the best food I had ever had.

Finally, I went south through my dream city of all dream cities, Paris, and spent what I think was three weeks there, seeing everything I could before heading to the south of France and eventually to Spain and Portugal before my time ran out.

The amount of detail in the simulation was mind-blowing. I remember looking at a blade of grass in France and seeing a colony of ants running up it. I thought, '*How the fuck did they do that?*' Every detail of every place was meticulously thought of by whatever supercomputer created this thing.

It felt like a year of my life went by—a year! But it had only been seven hours when I woke up.

The experience was not comparable to anything else in my life. I felt re-energized and reinvigorated, and it felt like I was alive again. After the divorce, it was exactly what I needed." She paused to take the final bite of her dessert. Again, no one said a word.

She continued, "The weirdest thing by far is not needing to use the bathroom. And, yes, the sex. You do get tired if you physically exert yourself. If you pass out, you wake up seven hours later or something, feeling either good or bad, depending on what you did the night before. There were certainly times I drank too much, passed out, and woke up at 11 a.m. with a hangover. They sure got that part right if they're trying to simulate real life. But essentially, if it's nighttime and you're bored, you just tell them to skip ahead to the next morning, and they do. It's crazy.

The lack of having to use the bathroom is a little weird, but you get used to it. Honestly, it frees you up to do other things. It's funny because you're wearing an adult diaper in real life, in case you do piss or shit yourself during the seven hours you're under.

Now, the sex. At first, I was hesitant because I wasn't sure who was watching, either back in the facility or elsewhere. But eventually, your hormones take over. I mean, I was a 20-something chick who was good-looking, so I had my pick of the litter when it came to men. And let me tell you, there were some attractive men in this simulation. And yes, I took advantage. And yes, I felt... everything." MaryAnne smiled.

"Whew, I'm going to need a shower pretty soon," Clarise said, and everyone laughed.

MaryAnne laughed before continuing. "I think that's all I need to say there. I felt pain when I hurt something, felt my stomach growl when I was hungry, laughed when I wanted to, cried when I wanted to, even though no tears fell, and felt every other emotion imaginable during my time there.

You're just free. You can do whatever you want without worrying about what awaits you at home. You know everyone you know is safe, and you're only in this simulation for a day or whatever, and then you're back home.

So, that's pretty much it. All I can say is that we're fucking lucky to be living in an age where you can do this. I can't imagine what they'll have for us ten years from now, but I'm certainly looking forward to doing this again, and I'm sure you all will say the same thing after tomorrow. Any questions?" She smiled, pausing for questions.

After a few seconds, Alexandra finally asked, "Were you ever scared? Like, did anything scary happen during your trip where you thought you were going to get hurt or die?"

"I mean, there were a couple of times where I was hiking, and the weather got pretty hairy, and I retreated to higher ground to avoid being swept away or struck by lightning.

And one time, I almost choked on food, which was fun. Luckily, I had a gentleman with me who could dislodge whatever I was eating. But no, I never felt scared. You have to constantly remind yourself that it's not real and that, even if something bad were to happen, you wouldn't get hurt or killed. If you stepped in front of a bus and got run over, the simulation would end, so yeah, please don't try to commit suicide in the simulation." MaryAnne chuckled.

"Obviously, it depends on what you're doing in your simulation, but when I did it, it ended if you died. I understand they have tweaked that to allow you to continue the simulation if you die somehow—I'm not quite sure how it works. But no, I was never truly scared. If you keep reminding yourself that it's not real, you'll be fine."

"So, you had sex, huh?" Patrick asked, smiling at her. "How was it? Do you… you know… orgasm?"

"How did I know you would focus on that?" MaryAnne replied with a wry smile. "Yes, you do orgasm. Or at least I did. It was pretty fucking real, I'll tell you that much. I think I finally understand how a guy thinks! Apparently, my goal was to have sex in every country I visited.

I had no idea what I was doing in real life while in the simulation room, but I didn't care. I am sure it wasn't the first time someone had sex in a simulation, and it won't be the last. Guaranteed, one of you fine folks will be getting some ass tomorrow, one way or another." Everyone laughed.

"Changing subjects," Clarise said, also smiling. "Did it really feel like a year in the simulation? How the hell do they do that?"

"I dunno, darling," MaryAnne responded. "That's above my pay grade, but it certainly felt like a year. It was 365 'days' of adventure, which is amazing to me.

That's why they say it takes time to recover when it's over. It does take some time to get your senses back and remember that it was just a simulation and you're back in your real life.

Think about how you feel when you return from a two-week vacation, and then multiply that by whatever number gets you to 52. Sorry, this edible is fully kicking in, so I can't do math."

"Was there anything that bothered you about the simulation?" Mike asked, having just finished his piece of the lava cake. "It sounds amazing, but I'm sure it had a downside, right?"

"Look, nothing's perfect, but this was as close as it gets." MaryAnne took her time to think through her answer. "The only thing I'd say is that I can see people getting attached to the simulation, either to the lifestyle or the people they meet in the simulation." She air-quoted the word "people."

"I certainly met some fascinating characters in the simulation, but I had to keep reminding myself they weren't real. That is very important for whatever you're doing. The people you meet aren't real, and they won't be there when you wake up.

I guess you could continue the simulation next year with the same people if you want. That's part of the draw and the 'anticipation' part of the equation, I guess. But remember, whomever you meet in the simulation won't be there forever, so be careful not to get too attached.

I'm sure people fall in love in the simulation—the question is how that transfers to your real life, especially if you're married. So, be careful, please, is all I can say. Other than that, I didn't have any downsides."

"Wow, thank you for sharing that," Mike responded. "I think the biggest question that no one has asked is: Do you get constipated? I don't want to spend my simulation playing a game constipated the entire time. If I do, they better have some serious laxatives available." He laughed, and everyone joined in.

"You know what?" MaryAnne exclaimed. "That's probably the best question I've gotten! The answer is no—you don't have to worry about that."

As laughter erupted again, Rebecca told Clarise it was 7:15 p.m. and everyone needed to head home shortly.

"Oh my god, I thought it was way later," Clarise said, glancing at her watch and chuckling. "Thanks, Rebecca! They say time flies when you're having fun, but when you're having fun and high, it goes by *really fucking slowly*."

Everyone burst into laughter.

"Before you all leave, I gotta know what everyone is doing with the government's stipend. Who could have imagined a day when nearly everyone agreed with how their government spent their tax dollars?" Clarise laughed again.

"I've got baby expenses coming up, so I know where my cash is going," Mike said, shaking his head with a grin. "Baby shit is fucking expensive!"

"Yeah, I remember those days," Eric replied, his eyelids heavy. "Strollers, cribs, car seats, diapers, bottles, milk, daycare, gym classes, karate, swimming, sports equipment, doctor visits, birthday parties, clothes—shit, man, it adds up fast. Save up!"

"It's not that bad, Jesus," Alexandra said, acting surprised. "You'll be fine, Mike. As for the stipend, I'm not sure what we'll do with the cash yet. We want to see how we feel afterward and then decide. We might go on a long vacation or invest in real estate. We'll see how we feel about our jobs first."

"You guys should definitely travel," MaryAnne chimed in. "You both deserve it—shit, you work harder than anyone I know! Take some time off; you can always open another daycare later."

"I know. We'll see," Alexandra responded. "What about you? You should go relive your simulation from last year!"

"I know—I wish," MaryAnne said, rolling her eyes. "No, I need to save up a bit since I'll probably take some time away from work to help care for my dad. I can't do both, and I want to be there for as long as possible until the end. And staying alone with my mom? We'd kill each other. I'll probably find a short-term rental up there and save for now, then see how much I have left to travel."

"That's great—good for you," Clarise replied.

"Yeah, we'll see how long he has left, but it isn't expected to be long. What about you guys?" MaryAnne looked at David and Clarise. "Have you even had time to think about it?"

"Great question—not quite sure of the answer right now," David said slowly. "We want to finalize our downloads first, then focus on the simulation. I imagine we'll be pretty emotional afterward, so we'll just have to see where our heads are. I had the idea of visiting every Major League Baseball stadium in America. Charlie loved baseball, and we had always toyed with the idea of taking him to different cities to watch baseball games. Honestly, I don't know right now." David paused, collecting himself.

"He would have loved that," Clarise said slowly, looking down at the table, also seeming to get emotional.

"I did that with my dad growing up," Patrick noted. "We went to a few different baseball stadiums from the age of 10 through 16, right before he passed. I'm sure we would have continued that tradition, and I plan to do it with my kids someday, so I think it's a great idea."

"Oh, Patrick, I had no idea. That's so sweet. I'm so sorry about your dad. I think David mentioned it a while back, but I forgot," Clarise said, looking over at Patrick.

"It's okay. I appreciate that, Clarise, really."

"So, what are you going to do with the money, Patrick?" David asked.

"Hah, well, I kinda already spent it. All that traveling overseas was mostly covered by my company; the rest was on my dime. I figured with this bonus from the government, why not give that right back to foreign governments?" Everyone laughed.

"No, but seriously, I spent a lot of money over there, so I'll be waiting for next year to hopefully start saving for the kids' college funds."

"That's really funny—I hope you enjoyed," Clarise said, raising her wine glass. "Again, thank you all for coming, and I wish you the best of luck tomorrow. May your experiences be everything MaryAnne said they would be, and may you come out of them different but better. Cheers."

"Cheers!" The group echoed.

As they all said their goodbyes and prepared to head home, they exchanged hugs and kisses, thanking Clarise and David for hosting. Eric and Alexandra offered to host this dinner again next year.

Fifteen minutes later, as they were in their car heading home, Alexandra looked back at the huge mansion they were just in, wondering if they would all be together again next year for another dinner on the eve of Anticipation Day.

As Eric took her hand, a feeling started building up inside her. She knew that after tonight, things might never be the same again. Whether that was good or bad, she couldn't tell.

PART 2

CHAPTER 1

– PATRICK – THE
TORNADO CHASER

MARCH 8, 2032
7:30 A.M.

"It's been a long three years," was all Patrick could think as he sat in the back of his car service, driving through the streets of Denver. Leaving his apartment at 6:45 a.m. to arrive at the facility by 7:30 a.m. for final paperwork was rough. He had chosen the earliest time slot available, as he had an early morning call for work tomorrow and wanted to get home at a reasonable hour. Maybe he should have asked for the day off tomorrow if what MaryAnne said was true, and it did take some time to settle back into "reality."

He remembered the guidelines suggested by the Department of Anticipation Day involved taking a day or two off of work to unwind from the simulation, but he had ignored that suggestion.

"Oh well," he thought.

As the cab drove through the empty streets of Denver, he couldn't help but feel that the scene unfolding before him mimicked his life at the moment. Empty.

▼▼▼

It had been a little over six months since his divorce was finalized and over 18 months since everything went south with Courtney.

On his way to a sales meeting in Boulder, Patrick had caught Courtney cheating with an ex-boyfriend. Watching them stumble out of a bar together, drunk, filled him with nothing but rage. He was left confused, hurt, and in jail overnight for knocking the ex-boyfriend out cold.

Courtney bailed him out the next morning, and they talked calmly, deciding it was best to start the process of splitting up. Two weeks later, she called to tell him she was pregnant. He demanded a paternity test, as he couldn't believe it was his.

When the test results came back positive for Patrick, he was *shocked*. What the fuck was he supposed to do? His ex-girlfriend, who had been cheating on him with her ex-boyfriend for six months, was now pregnant with Patrick's second baby.

Every instinct told him to divorce her and raise the kids separately. How could he stay with a woman he couldn't trust?

Courtney said all the right things—how sorry she was and how lonely she felt with Patrick always away for work. She blamed her connection with her ex and kept apologizing for taking it too far.

She swore on their firstborn, Brin, that she had ended the affair, was committed to their family, and would try to work things out with Patrick.

Patrick decided to leave while he contemplated what to do next. After working with a therapist and having many discussions with his friends and family, he eventually decided to give her another chance. If only to say he tried to provide his kids with two parents as they grew up.

Patrick had grown up without both parents, and it sucked. He wished his parents stayed together or at least tried to after their divorce when he was nine. As he got older, he swore he would do whatever he could to give his kids a two-parent upbringing.

So, he put his faith in his heart and tried to work it out with Courtney. It was awkward and uncomfortable at times. They were barely intimate and certainly weren't having sex. Patrick was cordial through the pregnancy and they both attended therapy to work through their issues, with an overall improvement in their relationship by the end of the pregnancy.

Anna was born in June 2031, a beautiful little girl full of life and always smiling. She immediately brought Courtney and Patrick closer again.

Unfortunately, postpartum depression set in after Anna's birth. While they continued therapy for a while, between Patrick's resounding distrust of Courtney and her depression and anxiety from fearing he was cheating on her as retribution, he finally decided to initiate divorce proceedings in September 2031.

They both agreed it was better to do it while the kids were young and had no real memory of their parents being together.

After the divorce in October, his partner at their engineering firm suggested Patrick take some time overseas to meet with some of their international clients and take some downtime to get his head right. Initially, Patrick was hesitant. However, after speaking with Courtney, she assured him it would be fine since her mom would be coming to help with the baby and she assumed time apart would be good for both of them.

Plus, the extra cash from the government for Anticipation Day would allow him to take some personal time away on the company's dime and visit places he had always wanted to see in the Far East and Middle East.

So, he traveled, spending a few months in the United Arab Emirates, Dubai, the Philippines, and Tokyo. The trips were extraordinary, with beautiful and amazing places to see in each country. However, they were long trips, and because he had promised to visit the kids every other weekend, his time on airplanes racked up quickly.

Being away from the kids was tough, but he knew it was temporary. Besides, the sight of Courtney still made him sick, so he figured it was better to take some time away rather than say or do something he would regret.

His time overseas was interesting. Patrick did what any newly divorced and handsome man would do—he took advantage of his freedom. A lot.

Despite all the female companionship, he felt alone and disconnected from the world. Being cheated on was not something he had ever prepared mentally for. He always assumed that if anyone cheated, it would be him. However, he had loved Courtney deeply for a long time.

During the trip, he did a lot of introspective thinking and couldn't help but blame himself for putting his career before his family.

The fact of the matter was that Patrick was good at what he did. He was *damn* good. He was Salesman of the Year three years in a row in a company that employed over 80 sales personnel, enough to earn him the partner position. He loved the rush of securing a win. It was better than having sex—well, bad sex. He could always sense the moment he sealed a win, often after a long process, which could include meetings, calls, dinners, drinks, and sometimes strip clubs.

While he was never proud of the strip club events, unfortunately, going to strip clubs with male clients, especially drunk male clients, was the best way to earn their trust. And their dollars. Patrick never did anything inappropriate, except for that one time in Austin when he was really drunk.

There was a famous sales quote: "How you sell is more important than what you sell." So, he sold and sold and sold.

This success meant being on the road two to three weeks a month, leaving Courtney home alone with a baby and little help.

While he had to come to grips with this in the months since the divorce, he was now yearning for a connection to someone or something bigger than himself—something that gave him meaning again.

He hoped the experience today would reawaken that feeling and help him move on from the past year and a half. He needed that.

▼▼▼

So, he truly was full of anticipation as he pulled up to the massive facility, the remnants of a giant mall that used to be well-known in the Denver area. The government had bought these large spaces to facilitate the provision of these simulations to as many people as possible daily.

It was turning into a beautiful morning as he stepped out of the car. In a short while, he would hopefully be in the middle of some nasty, made-up thunderstorms, finally seeing a tornado up close and personal.

He entered the facility, found the waiting room, and checked in. The waiting area was a little chilly; they had said to bring some warm clothes since the facility was kept at a balmy 68 degrees. The computing power needed on-site required a significant amount of energy, which meant they needed to keep the facility cooler than most locations.

Patrick was comfortable in jeans, a long-sleeve shirt, and a light jacket, though others around him seemed cold.

His adult diaper was bothering him, but he assumed it was better than going home with piss-stained pants.

After about 15 minutes, an attractive female blonde nurse called his name and led him through two large steel doors into a larger area with multiple hallways.

Noticing her nametag, Patrick smiled. "So, Emily, how many rooms do you have here for these simulations?" He couldn't help himself.

"We have about 550 rooms available, but not all the rooms are active. The rings undergo regular maintenance programs every two weeks, so they try to schedule about 10-20 of them to be under maintenance at a time," Emily replied without smiling.

"Wow. 530 simulations at the same time? I bet you've seen some crazy shit," Patrick said, hoping for a better response.

"Sorry, sir, we are not allowed to discuss any details from the simulations due to privacy laws. Still, yes, we have approximately 530-540 simulations at this facility each day, which keeps us busy for sure," Emily responded, still unsmiling.

Realizing the conversation wasn't going anywhere, Patrick kept his mouth shut as they walked down a hallway through another set of double steel doors and arrived at room 112. She opened the door and invited him in.

Inside, there were shockingly no massive supercomputers, but he did see a skinny chair that appeared to recline, a long table against the wall with essential equipment, including two computer monitors, a first aid kit, a blood pressure monitor, resuscitation equipment with a defibrillator, and some other liquids that were part of the kit. On the floor was an IV cart with liquid bags attached to the hooks, and above it was a monitor that he assumed would be used to monitor his vitals. On another smaller table was a closed box with a computer screen setup with Patrick's picture and vitals already loaded on it.

"Ever had to use that thing?" He asked Emily, pointing to the resuscitation equipment.

"I have not, sir, but it's there for your safety in case of a medical emergency," Emily noted while sitting at one of the desks.

A robotic assistant rolled in through a side door, announcing itself as "Alice." Patrick always wondered who came up with the names of these robots; he would have come up with something more creative than Alice.

"Alice will assist with monitoring your vitals during the simulation and alert us if anything seems off," Emily said, noticing the confusion on Patrick's face.

"Oh, no worries. I assume she knows what she's doing." Patrick chuckled lightly.

"Why don't you take your shoes off, put your items in that locker, and have a seat in the chair? We'll go through a few ground rules and confirm your simulation with you."

Patrick took his personal effects out of his pockets and placed them in the locker. He remembered a day not too long ago when he would walk around with his wallet, phone, car keys, house keys, and a dozen other things in his pockets. The development of contact lens technology, which scanned everything automatically through sensors, had eliminated many of these daily items, making it much lighter to get around.

"Please have a seat, and let's confirm your simulation first," Emily said, holding her tablet as Patrick relaxed in the chair. "Your simulation will be a tornado-chasing vacation in April 2001. Is that correct?"

"Yes, ma'am," Patrick replied.

"And we have that this simulation will originate in Denver, Colorado, starting on April 14, 2001, and last through April 24, 2001. Is that correct?" Emily asked, her eyes on the tablet.

"Yep, that sounds about right," Patrick said quietly, thinking she must be an absolute blast outside of this place.

Thinking back to his intake last November, the personnel had given him the option of either recreating an actual historical and documented tornado in the time and city of his choosing or letting the simulation create a completely new story. Patrick had thought about it for a while but eventually chose the latter for two main reasons:

First, he didn't want to ruin the suspense by researching the actual tornado he was recreating because, knowing his personality, he would analyze the thing to death. He wanted the experience to be unpredictable.

Secondly, he wanted to see what this technology could do. So, he figured, let it ride and see what the technology was capable of. Maybe next year, he would try to recreate some historical event to see how it would differ.

"Perfect, thank you," Emily noted. "We have you as a 22-year-old college graduate whose parents paid for a trip after graduation. Is that correct?"

"Yeah, sounds good. Just make me as attractive as possible, please," Patrick replied, chuckling. Emily remained as stoic as ever. He wondered if she was a robot too.

"Can you confirm if you have had any changes in medicines, health conditions, physical or mental, or significant trauma in your life since your interview in November?"

"Nothing that I can think of other than dealing with my ex-wife." He paused for a laugh, which never came.

"So, is that a no?" Emily asked, still staring at her tablet.

"No, no trauma," Patrick responded, wanting to just get this over with.

"Perfect, thank you." Emily tapped a few things on her tablet. "Okay, now that that's confirmed, let's review what happens next. We'll lay you down on the chair and attach the ring that goes over your head while you're sedated. The ring has approximately 1.5 billion sensors, allowing it to interact with your brain and your implanted chip to interpret everything you are experiencing within the simulation as 'real.'

The ring will essentially take over the sensations of your eyes, nose, ears, skin, and tongue. Due to this, we need to give you a sedative—a mixture of Midazolam and Propofol—that will allow your brain activity to slow down while the ring takes over. Any questions?" Emily asked, though she seemed uninterested in answering any.

"The only question, I guess, is how safe the sedatives are. Like, I'm going to wake up again, right?" Patrick asked, having given up trying to make Emily laugh.

"Yes," she responded, finally chuckling. "I promise you will wake up. We have administered these sedatives millions of times, and I'm not aware of any issues with them. Based on your height, weight, body mass index, and genetic disposition, we calculate the appropriate dose that will last for the 6.5-hour simulation.

Alice will be here monitoring your vitals and I will check on you every 30 minutes and review your vitals while in the simulation. It is safe, I promise."

Emily waited for Patrick to confirm he understood. He nodded.

"Now, once you wake up in the simulation, you may feel confused for a few minutes as the ring adapts to the environment and learns your neural pathways. Don't be nervous; this should pass as you get acclimated to your new surroundings, okay?"

"Okay, sounds cool to me," Patrick said quickly. He wanted to get started at this point.

"Great. A few points to note before we begin. These were covered during your initial intake, but we want to reinforce them. Please hold off on questions until the end.

One: You will have your normal memories during the simulation. Even though you're sedated, you'll know who you are and remember your real life. You'll also have memories of your character that will come to you automatically—details like their name, job, family, and why they're there. The characters will engage you in conversation, resulting in you recalling information that would otherwise be foreign to you. It will come to you automatically, which is expected and normal. If a character asks you something that doesn't trigger a recall of memory, feel free to improvise or say you don't know. We've loaded certain pre-conditioned memories, but it's normal to be asked something outside those parameters.

Two: You will have real emotions in the simulation. Everything you feel will be as if you were actually living through these experiences—love, fear, humor, anger, sadness, surprise, and disgust. Again, perfectly normal.

Three: You won't be able to cry, urinate, defecate, or ejaculate while in the simulation, and better yet, you won't feel the need to use the bathroom. Liquids will exist in the simulation, but none will originate from you. You may have sex and may experience the sensation of an orgasm, but again, there will be no ejaculation."

Patrick felt a stir in his pants. Great, just what he needed—to get all horned up before going into the simulation.

"Four: While you may eat in the simulation and experience the taste of food, eating will not affect your weight in any way during the simulation. You can eat as much as you like, though. It won't satisfy your real-life hunger, and you'll likely wake up hungry. We'll provide a small meal during your mandatory two-hour recovery period after the simulation. I'm unsure what they are serving today, but it's usually pasta and something sweet to wake your brain up.

Five: To replicate sleeping, there are two options: If you do not feel tired, you can skip ahead seven hours every night to simulate the passage of a normal sleep cycle. After 10 p.m., you may ask to advance to the next day. Alternatively, if you're tired, you can simulate falling asleep by closing your eyes for 30 seconds after 10 p.m., and we'll automatically advance you seven hours. So, if you decide to skip ahead at 3 a.m., you will advance to 10 a.m. to continue the simulation. Note that you won't dream within the simulation.

Six: You can skip ahead up to fifty times, but only up to 50% of your remaining simulation. For example, if you have six days left, you can skip up to three days ahead. If you have one day left, you can skip up to twelve hours. Everyone gets a different number of skips, but you've been given more skips than most, probably because it might get boring driving around for all that time.

Seven: Given your tornado journey, this may apply to you: If you die in the simulation, you will skip ahead one hour as if you hadn't died. You may feel a little bit of pain before the simulation skips ahead—it will be brief and will feel like getting hit in the head lightly. But please be prepared for that if you do end up dying in the simulation. You are limited to three deaths per simulation. After three deaths, your simulation will end. So, please be careful and avoid circumstances that may lead to your simulated death. Rest assured, a death in the simulation does not lead to a real-life death. Also, if you try to self-harm while in the simulation, the simulation will automatically end.

Eight: If you feel uncomfortable or need to ask a question, say 'Alice' and then ask your question. Alice will be able to communicate with you as needed. For example, if something doesn't feel right or you feel nauseous, have a headache, or don't feel right, just say, 'Alice, I have a bad headache,' and she will review your vitals and make necessary adjustments. Situations in the simulation that would normally cause a headache, like a branch falling on your head, are not the time to reach out to Alice. However, if you're just sitting somewhere and something feels off, we have a team of doctors on call who will come and take a look. Please don't worry; we rarely have anyone that needs our intervention, but we're here for you if you do.

Nine: If, at any point, you want to be extracted from the simulation, say, 'Emergency, please extract.' We will stop the sedation immediately, remove the ring, and work to understand what the issue is on your end. We'll have a 30-minute window to either continue the simulation or end it permanently. We'll allow you to wake up for five minutes and then try to understand what happened. If you want to be reinstated into the simulation at that point, we will do so with your verbal consent. If not, you'll have to confirm that you want to cancel the simulation.

Ten: You may end the simulation without penalty when 80% of the planned simulation is completed. For example, you can end on day eight of your ten-day simulation. Just say, 'Alice, please end my simulation,' and we'll take care of the rest.

Eleven: If we need to cancel the simulation due to a real-life emergency, you will hear Alice's voice saying that the simulation will end. After ten seconds, the sedation will end, and you'll wake up. We'll explain the situation, and you can determine if you need time to recover or leave the facility. Hopefully, that won't be necessary, and you'll complete the simulation fully.

Okay, any questions?" Emily finally paused.

"Wow, no, I don't think so. That was a lot. I guess if I have any questions during the simulation, I'll just ask! I'm glad I can eat whatever the hell I want without gaining a pound. I wish that were true here..." Patrick chuckled, patting his stomach.

"Based on your BMI, you're doing just fine." Emily smiled.

"*Better late than never*," Patrick thought as Emily put down the tablet.

"One last thing, sir. Do you plan on deviating from the planned simulation? For example, if you decide to run off to another country to see what it was like in 2001, we don't have that loaded. If you feel like that's something you would do, please let me know now. Otherwise, we're good to go.

Also, so that you know, we do allow you to purchase one add-on parameter to the simulation once you begin. For instance, if you want to visit another part of the country, you can stop the simulation and buy the add-on, and then we can continue. Please note that this will take additional time to prepare and process, so you'll need to make arrangements for any responsibilities, like childcare. I just wanted to make sure you understood that."

"Okay, I'll see how I feel once I'm in there, but that is pretty cool to know." Patrick considered it. "How long would it take to add this on, and how much is it?" He didn't have the kids this weekend, so he could stay a little longer if he decided to do this.

"Well, every process is different, sir. Most people are happy with their planned experience, but for the few add-ons I've handled, it takes about 2-3 hours, depending on how much data is needed to process. The pricing is dependent on the data required, and I can review that with you at the appropriate time."

Patrick took a deep breath. "Got it. I think I'm ready to get going then."

"You're ready to start?" Emily asked as she walked over to the table and opened the box to reveal a blue and white cylindrical ring, similar to something the Elf Lord wore in *The Lord of the Rings*. She placed the ring on his head and adjusted it to fit comfortably.

"Just lay back while we sync the ring to the computer and your chip and ensure the simulation is properly loaded. That should take a few minutes, and then we'll start the sedation." Emily returned to the computer screen to do some computer-screeny things with it.

As he lay there, Patrick felt a mix of nervousness, excitement, and anxiety. He wondered what this experience was going to be like. He had seen a tornado or two in his day, but he *really* wanted to see one up close. Hopefully, whoever created this simulation made it easy to find one. It wasn't easy to track them in real life, but this wouldn't be real life.

"Okay, Patrick, we are ready to begin," Emily stated, interrupting his thoughts. "We'll start the sedation drip shortly. You'll hear a low hum as the ring powers on and feel some tingling in your head, fingers, and toes as it interacts and maps out your neural network; this is completely normal, so please don't worry. As the sedation starts, you'll likely feel warmth in your arms and chest, which is also normal. You'll drift off shortly after that, and we'll see you again in 6.5 hours. You good?" Patrick noticed she wasn't wearing a ring on either ring finger.

"I'm good—just happy your face is the last I'll see," Patrick said, throwing everything he had at Emily.

"That's very sweet of you. I'll check on you 30 minutes after you're out." She rubbed his hand quickly before heading back towards the computer. "I wish you an awesome trip."

The last thing he heard before he went under was, "I'll be back in 30, Alice, okay?" Then, darkness overtook him.

APRIL 14, 2001

Patrick was blinded by sudden brightness. It was much brighter than the facility he had just been in—so intense that he had to raise an arm to shield his eyes.

Was he standing? He could feel his feet, which felt solid beneath him, so he was indeed standing.

Birds. He heard birds and cars and thought he heard a man talking, but his ears felt clogged as if stuffed with five Q-tips. His mouth was dry, and his armpits felt sweaty.

Patrick reached up and touched his face—mouth, nose, and eyes— all were there. Above them, he felt the brim of a hat and what appeared to be sunglasses. He took the hat off and put the sunglasses over his eyes. Much better.

There were maybe a dozen or so figures he could make out that were standing around two bright white vans. Looking down, he saw the outline of his feet, confirming he was in fact standing on dirt. Looking up, he saw a bright blue sky mixed in with scattered high-level cirrus clouds. Judging by the sun's angle to his left, it appeared to be early-to-mid morning.

Patrick felt his hair, which was way longer than he normally had, which was weird. He took a deep breath, inhaling a mixture of fuel and dust. Not a great combination, but it woke him up.

As he worked to unclog his ears, he finally heard two engines running, a man talking, and cars driving off to his left. He seemed to be in a dirt area next to a two-lane road, standing alongside two vans and a group of people—likely the tour guests for the tornado-chasing excursion he was about to join.

After a couple of minutes, his senses seemed to be fully functioning.

"*Wow, this is fucking weird,*" was his first thought. While he couldn't see his face, he examined his arms and fingers. They looked different. Fewer freckles, less hair, but darker than normal. He wiggled his fingers, looked down at his shoes, and moved them around. Everything seemed to be functioning fine.

He strolled over to one of the van windows and took off his sunglasses to see his reflection: a young man with longer hair slicked back and some facial hair that looked like it hadn't been shaved in about 48 hours. He appeared tan, although it was hard to tell in the reflection from the van window. Based on the van's height, he seemed to be about 6 feet tall, plus or minus an inch. Not a bad-looking dude.

"Sir, are you okay over there?" A man called out from behind him.

Patrick cleared his throat. "Yes, sorry. I'm fine. Thank you." His voice sounded weird; lighter and cleaner than usual.

"Okay, why don't you come back over here with the rest of the group while I go over some basic information?" The man replied in an accent that made it clear he was from the deep south somewhere. Patrick walked back over to the group, which now appeared to be around 15 to 20 people.

"So, as I was saying, my name is Dale, and I'm originally from Alabama. I majored in meteorology and climate studies at the University of Alabama, and after working for the National Oceanic and Atmospheric Administration for 15 years, my family and I moved out to the Fort Collins area, and I got a job with Colorado State University studying tornado formation. After six years of field research, my colleague Mitch and I decided to start this tour company 11 years ago, allowing us to continue researching tornadoes while having fun with folks like you interested in seeing tornadoes up close.

Mitch started his own company last year, but I'm lucky to be joined by my fellow research associates, Katy and Billy, who are here with us for the next ten days or so. I'll let them introduce themselves in a second. Katy has done this for a few years now, and Billy is joining us for the first time right out of graduate school at the University of Colorado.

I'm delighted that you folks put your trust in me and my team to guide you through this journey as safely and happily as possible. I know there are many ways you can spend your vacation and a lot of companies to choose from, so I appreciate you taking the time to join us here.

Before we go over the rules and details of our journey, let's introduce ourselves so we can associate names with faces. Let's start with Katy and Billy. Guys, please introduce yourselves."

Dale looked to his left at a young man and woman who appeared to be in their mid-20s.

"Hi everyone," the woman kicked off. "My name is Katy Smith, and, as Dale mentioned, I'm one of the research assistants joining you. I'll be driving Van #1 and promise to do my best not to drive you directly into a tornado." That got a few chuckles from the crowd. "I'm originally from New Jersey but have loved weather, thunderstorms, and tornadoes since I was very young. I'm thrilled to join Dale and Billy on these trips, and I'm eager to learn as much as I can each time we go out.

The data we gather on these trips will help scientists and our fellow researchers to understand tornado formation, duration, and strength so they can predict them more accurately in the future. Anyway, that's my short speech. I look forward to getting to know you all and hopefully seeing some awesome tornadoes together."

The guests responded with light applause. Patrick joined in, clapping to ensure his hands were working properly. He was still getting used to this. His mind was still tripping a bit. If it was still *his* mind.

The gentleman next to Katy was up next. "Thanks, Katy. I'm Billy Clinton. Yes, I know—no relation. I've checked it out, believe me." Billy chuckled, and the caravan members laughed alongside him.

"I'm originally from Texas." A cheer rang up from a couple standing to Patrick's left. "Oh, y'all from Texas, huh? Where from?"

"Austin," the lady from the couple replied.

"Very cool. I'm from Ft. Worth, but I have family in Austin. We'll try to find some good BBQ joints along the way. For dinner, though, you don't want that stuff sitting in you while we're driving. Trust me."

The caravan laughed again. This guy was a real hoot.

"Anyway, welcome, folks. Like Katy, I've loved hurricanes, tornados, flooding, hail, lightning, and locusts since I was young. Growing up in Texas, we would get some awesome thunderstorms, you know? There were some scary storms too. But when my family would run like heck to escape the storm, I would run outside to my front porch to watch it.

Those nighttime storms were the best. The lightning would flash, lighting up the night sky so bright, and the thunder, man—y'all know that thunder I'm talking about, the type that makes you flinch?

If it was during the day, you could see the clouds moving across the sky in all directions and when that rain started softly falling on porch roof, you knew what was coming. In just three minutes, or maybe thirty, all hell could break loose, and at some point, your life may be in danger.

Luckily, we had a storm shelter, which we used a few times when I was growing up. I remember sitting down there as an eight- or nine-year-old, wondering what it would be like to see one of those storms from the other side of the door.

When I was 15, a tornado hit our house at night. Though the entire house wasn't destroyed, my parents' room was and they were both crushed by the roof collapsing on them. My brother and I... were spared. Somehow. It was like there was some sort of invisible barrier between our room and the tornado that protected us from dying." Billy swallowed hard, unable to speak for a few seconds as he was tearing up.

"I'm sorry, y'all. When I told this story to Dale the first time I met him, I did the same damn thing." He lifted his shirt and wiped his eyes before continuing.

"But, you know, surviving that, I felt like that was a sign that I had to do *something* to help others so no other kid ever loses his parents to a tornado. Or, God forbid, a parent loses their child. No one should ever go through that.

So, I dedicated my life to helping figure out how these damn things form and why they go where they go. There is nothing we can do to prevent tornados from being as strong as they are, but if we can predict their paths with accuracy, maybe we can save lives. You know?

Honestly, starting my career off doing this is something I could never have imagined. I'm so thankful to Katy and Dale for giving me this opportunity to work with them and drive y'all around looking for some darn amazing tornadoes!

I'll be driving Van #2, and unlike Katy, I'll do my best to drive you all directly into a tornado."

Billy stopped as a few folks laughed. "Just kidding—safety is first and foremost for all of us, but we look forward to being with you over the next ten days or so. That's it, y'all. Thanks." He gave a small wave to the crowd who clapped back.

"Thank you, guys," Dale continued. "And Billy's story is why we do this folks. His story is sad, yet inspiring. He took a tragedy and turned it into something positive. We all have a reason for doing this, but I promise you, Billy, Katy, and I have all put our lives into tornado research. We have a passion for it, certainly for the research, but also because we are amazed by the raw power of these storms. But we also have to respect them very much—their strength, unpredictability, and speed.

I want you to always know that we have your safety in mind, because your safety means ours as well. These are our lives too; we also have friends and family who may or may not miss us if we get caught in one of these things."

Dale chuckled to himself. Some in the crowd did as well, although a little less enthusiastically.

"*Damn, these simulators get you going early with your emotions, huh?*" Patrick thought. One thing was for sure: being in Billy's van would likely be livelier than being in Katy's van.

Dale continued, "We welcome Billy and thank Katy for joining us on this adventure once again. Alright, folks, let me go down my list here and see who you all are. The Wards?"

A couple to Patrick's right said, "Here." They were the middle-aged couple from Texas who noted they were married and left the kids with grandma and grandpa. "*Cute,*" Patrick thought.

"The Center family?" Dale continued. That was a Minnesota family of six—three brothers with their wives from Minneapolis, again leaving the kids at home. It seemed to be a theme here, but it made sense, given the age restrictions on these tours.

"Mary Childs?" Dale called. "Over here!" A young female voice replied behind Patrick. He turned around to see an attractive, athletic brunette who didn't appear to be more than 22, wearing short jean shorts and a low-cut shirt, revealing an ample amount of cleavage. Her tan wasn't too dark, so she clearly didn't spend all day working on her bikini lines. Her beautiful hazel eyes were full of life and passion.

"How are you doing, young lady? Tell us a little about yourself," Dale asked.

"Hi, everyone. I'm Mary, and I'm so stoked to get going here," Mary replied. Patrick cringed at the word "stoked," but his character didn't seem to mind much as he realized something was moving in his pants.

"I'm originally from Kentucky but graduated from USC in December with a Bachelor of Science in meteorology. I'm currently applying to the graduate program with the Department of Atmospheric and Oceanic Sciences at the University of Washington. But I wanted to have a little adventure first. While I originally considered trying to be on TV, I found research and fieldwork more exciting. So here I am! I'm so happy to be going on this adventure with y'all!"

Patrick was in awe. Mary Childs was not only extremely attractive but also smart and well-spoken. *"Is this heaven? Have I died and gone to heaven?"* Patrick thought, looking at the sky and mouthing, "Thank you."

"Welcome, Mary! We love that excitement here!" Dale replied before moving on to the Benjamins, an older couple from Vermont; the Bradfords, a foursome from Florida; and finally, the Collins, a younger couple from California who were spending their honeymoon on this trip.

"Yikes," Patrick thought. Who would spend a honeymoon chasing tornados?

Finally, Dale called out, "Jack Mercer?" and Patrick replied instantly, "Here!" Wow, that was fucking weird. He instantly knew that was his name. That's what Emily said would happen. Still creepy.

Jack Mercer? His name sounded like a serial killer or a hockey player on the Avalanche, his favorite hockey team. He didn't love it, but he didn't hate it either.

"Hi Jack, welcome. Why don't you tell us a little about yourself?" Dale asked.

"Sure," Patrick continued, now as Jack. "I'm Jack, originally from New Mexico. I went to school at Penn State University, as they had a great meteorology program, and I loved the campus there. I graduated last December with a Bachelor of Science in meteorology, like Mary."

He glanced at Mary and smiled. She half-smiled back. *"Ouch, rough,"* Patrick thought, then continued as Jack.

"I have a job with the NOAA starting in September, but my parents got me this trip as a graduation gift. I've never seen a tornado up close, so it'd be cool to see one and learn more about your experiences doing this. And if I had to choose, I'd love to drive *into* a tornado, so hopefully I can drive in Billy's van." Laughter broke out in the group. Nothing from Mary though.

He had forgotten he told the simulators he wanted his character to be from Penn State. At least he could say "We Are!" in the simulation and not deviate from his character's background.

"I think we can make that happen." Dale laughed. "Alright, folks, that's everyone for our journey. Let's review some basic rules and regulations before we get going:

One: We have two vans, Dorothy and Toto—very original, we know—but those are the names we came up with. Billy will drive Toto, and Katy will drive Dorothy. These are state-of-the-art vans with radar technology, GPS positioning, fortified glass windows, a reinforced steel frame, and top-notch transmission, engine, brakes, and tires. We've invested heavily in upgrading and maintaining these vehicles. Now, with that said, these vans are subject to the elements as we drive and may break down. Hail, tire issues, and engine busts are the biggest threats to our vehicles that may require downtime to fix. We have arrangements with major car repair companies across the country, so if we break down, help should never be far. We ask for your patience if we need to stop for repairs.

Two: Tornadoes are never guaranteed. We do our best to intercept severe weather outbreaks where we believe they will occur. However, this is Mother Nature, and she is unpredictable. In my 11 years of doing this, we've had a tornado intercept on all but a handful of excursions. There's never a guarantee on the number or quality of the tornadoes we'll see. We'll get you as close as is reasonably and safely possible. However, there may be days when we're driving through blue skies and sunshine. That's part of the process, but it doesn't mean we won't eventually see a tornado. Remember, the more sun, the more unstable the atmosphere, which can produce some amazing tornadoes later in the day. We've been checking the forecasts for this upcoming week, and there should be plenty of opportunities for severe weather outbreaks that could potentially spawn tornadoes, including today.

Three: Safety is our top priority. If the three of us determine we need to back away from a situation, that will be the final call, regardless of what you fine folks think. Your safety comes first on this trip.

Four: You will all get to know each other well over the next ten days. We'll be in enclosed spaces for many, many hours, staying at cheap motels, and having truck-stop dinners. Please prepare yourself emotionally and physically. Bathroom breaks are usually scattered every few hours, but if you need to stop, we will accommodate you as best we can. Tempers may flare, and we may have disagreements, but please remember that our ultimate goal is to see a tornado as safely as possible. If anything gets out of hand, we can rearrange the vans, but please try to control your behavior so we don't have to.

Five: Have fun! This is a vacation, a honeymoon, and an adventure for most of you. This is supposed to be fun and, hopefully, an adventure of a lifetime. So, please remember that when we've been in the car for six hours with no tornadoes on the horizon, you haven't eaten a proper meal in two days, we all smell, and you haven't slept in a comfortable bed for three nights."

The caravan members laughed.

Dale continued, "Any questions before we start loading up? We will head southeast from here and hope to be in an area of potential convection later today in northern Oklahoma. We are still analyzing the forecasts and the data, but we may see a tornado later today if conditions are good."

He answered a few questions about where the team would eat and when each day would start and end. Someone even asked whether they could smoke weed in the van. The answer was, "Preferably no, but what folks do on their downtime is up to them." Interesting.

"*They were still in Colorado*," Patrick thought with a laugh.

Finally, Dale was ready to load the vans.

"Okay, let's divide the vans as follows: The Center family, you will go with Billy in Toto, and Jack and Mary will join you. The rest of you will join Katy in Dorothy. I will alternate vehicles each day, but I will start with Billy in Toto. Why don't you all grab your luggage and start loading it up?"

Patrick looked down at a small piece of blue luggage and a backpack labeled Jack Mercer. He was still trying to wrap his head around how real everything was.

Even though he knew it was a simulation, it felt real enough at this point—the people he just spoke with, the sounds he was hearing, the smells he was smelling, and everything he was seeing felt... real. How was this possible?

▼ ▼ ▼

Patrick was excited about the next week and a half as he loaded his luggage into the back of Toto and brought his backpack into the main van cabin.

The Center family took the first two rows, leaving Mary and Patrick to sit together in the back. "*Thank you, simulators,*" Patrick thought as he settled beside Mary.

After loading the luggage and a quick discussion between Dale, Billy, and Katy, Dale and Billy took the driver and passenger seats, respectively, and the van headed onto the highway, with Katy right behind them in Dorothy.

A few minutes into the drive, Dale picked up a small microphone and pressed a button to broadcast his voice through the van's speakers.

"Alright, folks. Welcome onboard, Toto. She's small but feisty, like in *The Wizard of Oz*," Dale said with a smile. "Here's the plan for today. We'll follow Route 70 from Watkins, east out of Colorado, and into Kansas, close to Hays, and then follow Route 183 south into northern Oklahoma, around Buffalo or Freedom. This should take us seven to eight hours. It's now 9 a.m. local, so we should arrive between 5 and 6 p.m. central time, considering we'll move forward an hour as we head into Kansas. We'll also stop for food, fuel, and bathroom breaks.

We expect a line of storms to develop in northern Texas, and with the prevailing winds, these storms will likely move northeast into Oklahoma. Where exactly they develop during the day will dictate how far east we need to drive, but we'll monitor the radar as we get closer. For now, sit back and relax. We'll aim to stop for food in Kansas in about three hours. Any questions?"

Patrick wanted to ask sarcastically, "What is fuel?" given that cars were mostly electric or hydrogen-powered back in 2032. Still, he held off, fearing confused looks from the simulated characters. If they only knew.

He continued as Jack, "Good thing I shot-gunned three beers before getting onboard." Mary laughed next to him, which made him feel good. He could get used to being 22 again.

"Maybe we should stop for adult diapers for you before we get going?" Dale quipped. "I'm sure we'll have some time for drinking later tonight, depending on how the chase goes."

"Party time! Excellent!" Mary exclaimed, throwing her hands up in the air. Somehow, Patrick recognized the *Wayne's World* reference, even though he'd only seen parts of the movie once on the Classic Comedy channel on WAT (We All Together), the entertainment platform launched in 2029 that revolutionized how entertainment was consumed.

Mary turned to Patrick and asked, "So, Jack, what are you all about? Penn State, huh? One of my exes from high school went there. I followed him on MySpace for a while, but we lost touch. He was a good lacrosse player, so he ended up getting a scholarship there. Knowing him, he slept with most of the women's field hockey, volleyball, and swim teams, so I'm sure he enjoyed it there. How did you do?"

"Ha, well, I couldn't compete with that. Maybe just half of the women's fencing team, but that's about it." Jack smiled, taking a good look at Mary. She reminded him of an ex-girlfriend Patrick had in high school—Jackie, with her long brown hair, hazel eyes, tanned complexion, and amazing smile. Did the simulators somehow know that and put her into this simulation?

As the inside of his pants shifted again, he couldn't help but wonder if he was having an erection in real life and if Emily was back in the facility secretly admiring it.

Since his divorce, Patrick had been with a few women, including a secret fling with MaryAnne that no one knew about, not even Eric or Alexandra. He did fine for himself in that department, but this felt different. It was as if he knew he could sleep with her without any consequences and there was nothing to stop him from trying. If he got an STD, so what? If he got her pregnant, so what? If he got rejected, so what? None of this mattered, so he knew where this would likely go.

Patrick decided to continue the conversation as the van continued down the highway. "What's your story? You said you grew up in Kentucky. Did I hear that right?"

"That's right!" Mary replied, perhaps too enthusiastically. "Wow, most guys our age don't listen like they should. You're a special man, Jack." Mary smiled and laughed.

Patrick was still getting used to hearing his name as "Jack." He half-expected to meet a girl named Rose who wanted him to help her find the Heart of the Ocean.

"Well, my mom always told me that listening was the secret to finding happiness," Jack responded, though it could have been Patrick, as he remembered his mom actually saying that in real life. Jack continued, "I've only been to Kentucky once in my life—Louisville for a baseball tournament when I was in high school."

That was funny, as Patrick had also been to Kentucky once for a baseball tournament. Seeing that the simulators seemed to incorporate parts of Patrick's life into Jack's character made it feel more real. Although the fact that they seemed to know his mom said that happiness quote was creepy.

"I grew up just outside of Louisville, in a town called Shelbyville," Mary said. "Not much going on there, but it's known as the Saddlebred Capital of the World, so, of course, I grew up riding horses when I was younger. They have this annual horse show that all these celebrities attend. I remember seeing them and thinking, '*I want to move to Hollywood one day and make it big as a movie star.*'

So, that's what I tried to do at USC—be a weather girl on TV—but there was a ton of competition with all these fake female models pretending they knew anything about the fucking weather. They were dumb bimbos who could read and knew who to suck up to and who to suck off. I'm generalizing, but I just didn't like it there.

I figured, rather than fighting a losing battle to be on TV, I'd do something meaningful and helpful to people, you know? So, I turned my focus to research into severe weather and tornadoes. I love thunderstorms; they're powerful, magical, and terrifying at the same time. I could watch them for hours.

My friend suggested I do this before my master's program started, so here I am!"

Patrick enjoyed hearing Mary talk. Courtney was from Indiana and had a similar "twang" as Mary. He wondered if the simulators somehow knew this.

"What about you, Jack? Why did you want to become a meteorologist?"

"You mean, besides meeting attractive young women from Kentucky?" Patrick responded as Mary smiled and blushed. Boy, he was throwing it all at her now.

"I guess it goes back to when I was a kid. I was sick… a lot. I had mono like three times in high school—so I was home a lot during the winter. Where I grew up in the mountains of New Mexico, we had a lot of snow and storms in the winter, so I would always turn the television to the Weather Channel and watch their coverage of whatever blizzard was heading our way.

Eventually, I became more interested in the weather and spent hours watching the Weather Channel. The monsoon season was always fun because we would have these awesome thunderstorms that I would just watch for hours trying to see how they would predict where storms would form and how powerful they would become. When I was applying for college, I looked for schools with great meteorology programs, and it came down to Penn State and the University of North Carolina. But I was really into football, so I went to Penn State, and I haven't looked back since. I'm definitely looking forward to working with the NOAA, though, as a field researcher. It should be pretty cool—at least I hope it is! Hopefully, this trip will give me a taste of what it takes to do this type of research."

Patrick was amazed at how smoothly and naturally those sentences spilled out of him. Even though the Penn State part was comparable to his real life, the rest wasn't. However, it was true for Jack, and Patrick could just say it seamlessly as if Jack's life were his.

"That's awesome. I am happy for you," Mary said with a smile, her hazel eyes gazing deep into his.

"*Oh boy,*" Patrick thought. This could get interesting quickly, and he was perfectly fine with it.

▼▼▼

For the next 30 minutes, Jack and Mary chatted about random nonsense while the Center family conversed among themselves in front of them.

Finally, Dale interrupted to see if anyone had questions about tornado chasing.

Mrs. Center was the first to ask a question: "What was the biggest tornado you have ever seen?"

"Great question," Dale replied. "Before I answer, it may make sense for me to give y'all some background on the types of tornadoes we may encounter as it will be helpful to answer your question. So, there are generally four categories that we break tornadoes up into.

First, we have rope tornadoes. These are the most common, and, as the name suggests, they resemble a long, curved piece of rope. Most tornadoes start and end as rope tornadoes, either growing larger or dissipating into thin air. While most rope tornadoes don't inflict much damage, some can be dangerous, especially as they narrow and tighten. We will likely see a few of these during our journey together.

Next are cone tornadoes. These are probably what you picture when you think of the tornadoes you've seen on television or in movies. As you can probably tell, they get their name from their shape, which resembles a cone. They are narrower at the bottom, closer to the ground, and wider at the top, where it meets the storm. Generally, these tornadoes are more destructive than rope tornadoes due to their wider paths. We may encounter some of these, but hopefully they won't cause much damage.

The third type is wedge tornadoes. Now, if we see a wedge tornado, there will likely be significant damage, as these are the most destructive and are typically a half-mile wide or greater in diameter. Anything in their path will likely be damaged. They are generally classified as EF-3 or greater on the Fujita scale. Are you all familiar with the Fujita scale?"

Dale waited for their response. Patrick, both in real life and as Jack in the simulation, knew about it. Mary nodded, and four out of the six Centers said yes, but of course, two didn't, so Patrick knew an explanation was coming.

"For Luisa and Jessica," Dale said, addressing the two. "The Fujita scale is a rating system for tornadoes developed in the 1970s by Ted Fujita, a meteorologist at the University of Chicago. He wanted to create categories that could separate weak tornadoes from strong ones. He really wanted to be able to rate historical and future tornadoes according to the same standards. Mr. Fujita linked wind speeds to the Beaufort Wind Scale and the damage they caused. The Beaufort Wind Scale was developed back in the early 1800's by a British Navy Admiral to measure wind speeds.

The Fujita scale has five categories:

F0 has wind speeds less than 73 miles per hour and causes minimal damage. It's like a bad thunderstorm—maybe some downed trees, a few shingles blown off roofs, and lawn chairs scattered, but nothing more.

F1 has wind speeds between 73 and 112 miles per hour with moderate damage to houses, cars, and farming fields. It's not terrible, but people will have to clean up afterward. This is the most common type of tornado, making up 30% to 40% of all tornadoes.

F2 is where you start getting into some bad stuff. An F2 has wind speeds between 113 and 157 miles per hour. This will cause significant damage to houses, cars, and anything else the tornado comes across. With those wind speeds, you may see houses and barns destroyed, cars overturned, and loss of life. It can be pretty bad.

An F3 is categorized as 'severe,' with winds between 158 and 206 miles per hour. If you are in an F3, you better be somewhere safe because anything can be damaged or destroyed in this type of tornado. This is where wedge tornadoes may lie, which is why they are so dangerous.

Above F3, you're talking about F4 and F5, which cause catastrophic damage with wind speeds up to over 300 miles per hour. The peak of the Fujita scale is 318 miles per hour. In these types of tornadoes, not much survives. You better have a tornado shelter because anything in the path of an F4 or F5 will likely be completely destroyed. Luckily, F4s and F5s only make up around 1% of all tornadoes.

If we see an F3, F4, or F5, please be prepared for significant property damage and, potentially, loss of life, depending on where it hits. If one hits, we may have to assist with recovery efforts, so please be mentally prepared to see damage and suffering. While seeing one of these tornadoes is rare and awesome, please know that for those in its path, it is certainly not awesome. Let's hope we don't have to deal with that.

Okay, so going back to the original point, those are wedge tornadoes." Dale took a sip of water.

"Does anyone know the fourth type of tornado we may see?" He asked, smiling at Mary and Patrick in the back row. "I'm looking at you two meteorology geeks back there," he added with a chuckle. "Jack, Mary, from your studies, can you tell us what it is?"

Mary gave Patrick a look that said: *I got this.*

"Is it satellite tornadoes?" She said.

"Yes! Good job!" Dale exclaimed. "They are called multi-vortex tornadoes, but I'll accept that answer. A multi-vortex tornado is where a supercell spins off more than one tornado at a time that rotates around the supercell's main circulation. They are generally rope tornadoes but can evolve into larger cone tornadoes. They're rare, but we see them occasionally, and they are spectacular to watch. Again, remember that when we see two tornadoes simultaneously, more damage can occur on the ground.

Is everyone good with the types of tornadoes and the Fujita scale? Now, to answer Ellen's question about the largest tornado I've ever witnessed—in May 1999, almost two years ago, my ex-partner and I were tracking a line of supercells heading northeast in southern Oklahoma. In the late afternoon, we spotted a tornado touching down in Grady County, about 45 minutes southwest of Oklahoma City.

At first, it appeared to be a normal-looking tornado, but it quickly exploded into a massive wedge tornado nearly a mile wide as it headed northeast. It struck Bridge Creek, Oklahoma, as an F5 tornado with wind speeds exceeding 300 miles per hour. We later found out that 12 people died in Bridge Creek. The tornado continued through southern Oklahoma City, weakening and then re-strengthening before hitting Moore as another F4 or F5 tornado, causing dozens and dozens of casualties. All in all, almost 150 people died from the tornado, which spanned about 40 miles and lasted nearly an hour and a half.

It was the most remarkable yet devastating thing we had ever witnessed. While we learned a lot about the nature of tornadoes that day, we spent the following days assisting with search and rescue operations and providing aid to the injured. It was a sharp reminder that, while it can be exciting to chase tornadoes, people's livelihoods are impacted. Let's hope we see nothing like this on this trip."

Everyone generally fell silent after that story and didn't have any more questions for Dale, allowing Patrick to focus on the view outside the van. He was still wrapping his head around the level of detail this simulation could produce. As they drove through eastern Colorado, closing on the Kansas border, Patrick watched the corn and wheat fields roll past his simulated window. He noticed birds flying in the distance, cirrus clouds above, and the occasional roadkill along the highway. He felt as though, if he squinted enough, he might see anthills in the fields, beehives in the trees, and grains of dirt along the side of the road.

It was simply unbelievable and his mind drifted to one of the final trips he had taken with his dad before his passing.

▼▼▼

They had taken a family trip to the Great Canyon when Patrick was 16, accompanied by his brother Rob, his dad's sister and brother-in-law, and his dad's parents. They camped out on the rim of the Grand Canyon, went rafting on the Colorado River and just enjoyed being together as a family.

It was also the first time Patrick was allowed to drive, and he remembered the thrill of driving on the open road, adhering strictly to the speed limit the entire time, while his dad instructed him on what to look for, how to use cruise control, and other tricks of the trade to drive on the highway.

He always loved being with his dad's family and it was one of the warmest memories he had growing up. It was also the last time their entire family was together before his father died of a heart attack the following winter.

His dad had been a warm, loving man who encouraged Patrick to do what made him happy in life, whatever that might be. Patrick missed him deeply.

Thinking about MaryAnne's story from the previous night, he realized that he might want to do a simulation next year where he relived a day with his family when his father was alive. Perhaps a day from that Grand Canyon trip made sense. It was certainly something to consider.

▼▼▼

As they reached the Kansas border a couple of hours later, Dale noted to the group that a small line of storms had formed in the Oklahoma panhandle and they were going to track them for potential development. For now, the caravan would continue heading east for a bit before turning south near WaKeeney, Kansas, and aiming to stop near Dodge City to assess the storm situation.

Patrick considered using Alice to skip ahead to avoid the ride but decided against it, wanting to get to know Mary better. Why he was interested in getting to know a simulated character was beyond him, but he figured it would be good practice for flirting in the real world.

"So, do you have any siblings?" Patrick asked as he turned his attention back to her.

"I do! I have an older brother, Andrew, who's 27 and a doctor in Florida, and a younger sister, Stephanie, who's 17 and still in high school. We call her the 'whoopsie' of the family since we're pretty sure my parents only intended to have two kids. I just took her to the airport in Denver; she was going to Cancun for spring break. It was her first trip alone, so I walked her to the gate to make sure she was ready. She was nervous about flying, but I told her if I could chase tornadoes for a week, she could get on an airplane by herself." Mary laughed.

Patrick remembered that 9/11, the defining event of the decades to come, hadn't occurred yet. Oh god! He wanted to warn everyone in the van about the tragedy just five months away, but he reminded himself that these people weren't real and wouldn't be impacted by it. Still, it was interesting to recall how different the world was before 9/11, when it was still possible to walk someone to an airport gate.

"That's pretty funny," Patrick replied. "I'm sure she'll be just fine. Maybe you should have given her an Ambien before she left."

"She called me once she landed to tell me she was fine. She ended up sleeping most of the way anyway. What about you? Any brothers or sisters?" Mary asked.

"Yeah, I have three younger sisters," Patrick answered as Jack. "21, 19, and 14. My parents were quite active, I guess. It wasn't so bad, especially with my oldest sister, Elizabeth; it was always nice to have all her friends come over, especially when they went swimming in the pool. I may or may not have hooked up with a few." Patrick threw his hands up as if to say: *What was I supposed to do?*

Mary smiled. "I'm sure you did. You're a cutie, so I can see that happening. I may or may not have made out with my brother's friends when he was in college. Just saying." She lightly punched him in the left shoulder.

"Well, I'm sure we'll see some studs in Kansas, Oklahoma, or wherever else we end up," Patrick said, laughing. "I hear they love southern belles down here in Tornado Alley. You better watch out."

"Good thing I have you to protect me then." She smiled and punched him again. He wanted to kiss her but decided to save that for later.

"I will do what I can", Patrick replied with a smile and stared back out the window watching the beautiful day pass by.

▼ ▼ ▼

The rest of the ride through Kansas was filled with more back-and-forth between the two. Patrick eventually started to chat with the Center family, learning that all the simulated siblings took vacations annually. The oldest brother, James, had always wanted to chase tornadoes, so he convinced his youngest brothers to join him with their wives. James was a failed meteorologist, much like Patrick himself, though he couldn't share that.

The family seemed nice enough, but he didn't envision interacting with them much, as they were reticent and reserved. Patrick was fine with this, as he was focusing on Mary anyway.

They had reached WaKeeney and began their march south on State Rt. 283. As they arrived on the outskirts of Dodge City a couple of hours later, the weather had begun to turn cloudy and windy. They could see storms in the distance to the south. It was around 3 p.m., and the day's heat was almost at its peak. They stopped at a gas station to refuel, stretch their legs, get snacks, and assess the situation.

While the others ventured off to the bathrooms to do whatever simulated characters did there, Patrick closed his eyes, taking in the wind and the smells around him. The smells weren't great—mostly truck exhaust and cow manure—but they reminded him of Wellington, the town in Colorado where he grew up, where it was mostly farms mixed with trucks bringing agricultural products south toward Denver.

At night, when it was quiet, he and his dad would sit on their porch and talk about the most random things, from aliens to school to what Patrick wanted to be when he grew up—a professional baseball player, of course. He yearned for those talks with his dad, which always held a special place in his heart.

Opening his eyes, he saw the other passengers, including Mary, returning to where Dale, Katy, and Billy were discussing the plan for the rest of the day near one of the vans.

Finally, Dale announced to the group, "We're heading east towards Wichita. The storms currently in Oklahoma are moving northeast, and we're hoping to intercept them. So gather your belongings and let's load up so we can get on our way."

Patrick turned to Mary. "I've never been to Wichita before. This should be fun!"

"I went there for a cheerleading competition in high school. Honestly, there's not much there," Mary replied, pretending to cheer with imaginary pom-poms.

"Maybe you can reenact your cheer for me when we get there," Patrick implied, as he climbed into the back seat of Toto.

"I'll see what I remember. I didn't bring a proper outfit, but maybe we can figure something out," Mary replied quietly with a smile.

"Everyone good to go?" Billy asked from the front seat. Dale was now traveling in the Dorothy van, leaving Billy alone up front to continue telling his life story. He was born in Wisconsin, and his family moved to Texas for his dad's work when he was young. He eventually went to Colorado State to study meteorology. There, he met Dale the year before and expressed interest in helping Dale with these tours, as the previous graduate student who was helping had graduated.

He was single, loved racing cars, and eventually wanted to move to Alaska.

"So, Jack, are you excited to start working for the NOAA? What will they have you doing?" Billy shouted over the Center family talking.

It took Patrick a moment to remember that he was, in fact, Jack and needed to respond to the question. "Yeah, man, I'm excited. It's a dream job for me. I was fortunate that my dad had a connection there that helped me get an interview. It's a competitive time now with all the new radar technology—many people want to be part of this research. I'm lucky and honored to have this opportunity. I should know more in a few months once I start, but they mentioned I'm going to be researching wind shear and how it impacts tornado development. I'm excited."

"That's awesome, man!" Billy shouted back. "I hope you come back in a couple of years and teach us old folks about what you've learned. We're always looking into new technology for the vans and tapping into the NOAA radar and GPS, so maybe you can hook us up with the latest equipment at a nice discount!"

"I'll see what I can do," Patrick replied but his mind was elsewhere.

Patrick had just realized that Jack had a dad in this simulation. Since Patrick's own father had died suddenly of a heart attack, he'd always wished he could tell his dad how much he loved him just one more time. Patrick really just wished he could hear his dad's voice again. Sure, Patrick went to visit his gravestone as much as he could and he swore he actually did hear his dad's voice one night in his house soon after he died, but it just wasn't the same.

So, while he couldn't talk to his dad in real life, he knew what he had to do in this simulation.

Since he hadn't yet looked through his backpack, he reached down and opened it up where he found a few items: a poncho, an umbrella, a map of the midwestern states, a notepad, a camera, and—bam!—a cell phone.

Patrick had heard of how awful early cell phones were, mostly from his older relatives. He had never seen one, as by the time he got his first phone, they were on the "smarter" side of the spectrum. This thing he pulled from his backpack looked like a clunky piece of metal. Lord, how did anyone use this? He pressed the power button on the small NoW-branded phone, and it turned on excruciatingly slowly.

After what felt like an eternity but was probably only five simulated seconds, a "Welcome" screen popped up, but the phone was locked. Somehow, Patrick knew the password: 6969. Even in his simulation, he was a child.

A small menu appeared: Calls, Contacts, and Settings. He selected Contacts and pressed the numerical buttons to spell "Dad."

Bingo. There he was: his simulated father.

Patrick decided to wait to make the call until they stopped somewhere and he was alone. He didn't want to start bawling in front of a van full of simulated strangers.

What would he even say? How would it feel to call somebody "Dad" who wasn't even his real father? It was freaking him out, but he'd decide whether to call him or not later.

For now, Billy was explaining how Wichita began as a trading post on the Chisholm Trail in the 1860s and had become known as the Air Capital of the World. This kid could talk.

Patrick shifted his focus back to Mary. "So, do you have a boyfriend back home?"

Mary laughed. "No, why are you interested in the position?"

"Uh, well, no, sorry, I was just striking up a conversation." Patrick was surprised at his own stuttering. He should have said yes and moved on. Why did it matter?

"Relax, silly. I'm just messing with you. I had a boyfriend for a few years, but we broke up about six months ago. We wanted different things in life, so it's for the best. I'm still young, and I wasn't ready to settle down. For now, I want to focus on my career, and he wanted a housewife. I wasn't up for that. I've played the field for a few months, but nothing serious. How about you?"

"Nah, my boyfriend and I broke up a year ago," Patrick responded, hoping she'd catch the sarcasm. "He wanted to bring a girl into the relationship, and I couldn't handle that. Men only for me."

"Wait—serious?" Mary asked, her expression slightly confused.

Patrick looked at her for a few seconds but couldn't drag it on anymore. "Ha! Got you! You should see the look on your face! I'm totally straight. Not that there's anything wrong with homosexuality. Hell, I once kissed my friend at a gay bar in college. We were drunk, and we wanted to make sure we weren't hit on, so we pretended to be a couple. It was pretty fucking hilarious. But no, staunch heterosexual here. I also ended a relationship recently. She cheated on me with someone I thought was my friend. That ended things right then and there."

Patrick wasn't sure why he just said that last part. He had a nagging feeling that this wasn't true for Jack. He had no memory of a girlfriend who cheated on Jack and this wasn't entirely true for Patrick. Maybe he was subconsciously rehashing memories of Courtney. At this point, he gave up trying to sort out which brain was in charge here.

"Oh, you poor thing," Mary said, frowning as she placed her hand on his arm. "Being cheated on is awful. It has happened to me, too. I know how much it hurts."

Patrick decided to go along with it. "Yeah, it still stings. Every day, I ask myself, 'Was it something I did?', 'Was she not attracted to me anymore?', 'Was I not good in bed?' The last part isn't true, in case you were wondering." He chuckled.

"Maybe I was, maybe I wasn't. Get a few drinks in me, and I'll let you know," Mary said with a smile, turning to look out the window as the rain started.

Patrick resisted the urge to shout to Billy to stop the van so they could find a local bar.

▼▼▼

The late afternoon weather was now turning stormy, with rain pounding the van. They passed a sign that noted they were passing Kingman, Kansas. Billy was up front on the radio, with Dale in the van ahead of them. Dale was responsible for monitoring the radar and communications from local weather stations to note if there were severe storm or tornado watches or warnings that were issued by the National Weather Service.

A tornado watch had been issued for an area just south and east of Wichita, which was likely where they were heading. They decided to make another stop at a gas station to get their bearings before deciding where to head.

About 15 minutes later, they pulled into a small gas station in Kingman to use the facilities and decide the plan. Patrick rinsed his face and freshened up in the bathroom. He could get used to having no bladder.

By the time he ran back to the van, the rain had intensified, with possible hail, though it was tough to tell.

Dale stood outside Dorothy under the gas station's covered canopy. "Alright folks, the plan is to head southeast to catch what we believe is a supercell moving toward Arkansas City. We might be approaching it at a difficult angle due to the heavy rain associated with this storm, so we'll have to reassess the situation as we get closer. We want to be careful not to get caught up in a rain-wrapped tornado; they're harder to spot and therefore can be dangerous.

We'll also be losing daylight in a couple of hours, so we don't want to be caught up in a cell at night, which can also be dangerous. So, point being, we are going to try to head in that direction and see how it develops but just giving you a heads up that we might need to stop if conditions become too dangerous or it gets too dark. Any questions?"

After a few seconds of silence, he continued, "Okay, let's load up."

Patrick felt a combination of nervousness and excitement build for the first time in the simulation. It was reminiscent of the feeling when Brin was about to be born—he was eager but anxious at the same time.

As he got into the van, he thought, "*It's not real. What's the worst that could happen?*"

He had no idea what he was in for.

▼▼▼

As they made their way south on Interstate 35 toward Arkansas City, not much was visible due to the rain. Dale was still with Dorothy, so

Billy explained that most tornadoes seemed to form at the rear of a thunderstorm.

"In northeast-moving storms, which is the most common motion of storms in the United States, the rear portion is at the southwest point of the storm," Billy said. "For y'all newbies, a thunderstorm consists of an updraft, where you have warm, moist air rising up with water vapor condensing at the storm's rear, and a forward downdraft, where cool air descends and forms rain.

Warm air usually goes into and rises through this updraft. However, in some thunderstorms, the warm air spirals inward and ascends in a corkscrew pattern through a rotating updraft. This is generally where tornadoes form." He demonstrated the spiraling motion with his fingers. "*Hands on the wheel, big guy,*" Patrick thought.

"That's why we try to position ourselves at the rear end of these storms. It's the safest spot and is generally where the most tornadoes form." Billy paused to focus on driving as the rain fell hard.

"Everyone, make sure your seatbelts are fastened, please. We're pumping up the speed to catch this line. Mary, Jack, you guys good back there?" He swiveled his head a bit to try to take a look.

Mary gave a thumbs up, and Patrick replied, "We're good, man. Just keep your eyes on the road."

"10-4, Captain Jack. Hold onto your butts," Billy said. He was a funny dude, but Patrick hoped his driving skills were top-notch, as he felt they'd likely need them.

▼ ▼ ▼

As they neared Wellington, Kansas, Dale's voice crackled over the radio: "Billy, we're detecting rotation on our radar here about two miles east of Arkansas City. Let's get off on Route 160 and head east to try to intercept. Copy?"

"Copy Dale. I'm right on your tale. Lead the way!" Billy exclaimed, excitement building in his voice. "Alright, group. It looks like we have a live one. As we get closer, please keep an eye out for any rotating clouds or any debris in the air—a dark mass of clouds or swirling dirt. If there's anything that you think could be a tornado, please call it out immediately.

I'm not sure if this rain or hail will lighten up; it depends on how the storm is developing, but if it is raining, it may be tough to see. Again, we should be coming up from behind the storm, so we shouldn't be in danger, but these storms are unpredictable. We need everyone's help to spot a potential tornado. Cool?"

Everyone responded with a tepid "cool," but there was a nervousness in their voices. Patrick's anxiety was amplified now. Even though he knew this wasn't real, it certainly felt like it.

As they got off Route 160 and headed east, the rain did lighten up a bit. Patrick could see the sky brightening behind him, which he assumed meant the storm was dying. However, Billy chimed in that they were now at the rear portion of the storm, which was good news for spotting a tornado.

The lightning ahead of them was intense as they passed farms and silos that looked like they'd just had a good soaking from the rain but showed no damage.

After 20 minutes of continuous light rain, one of the Center uncles shouted from the left window seat in the second row: "I think I see something off to the left! Maybe 10 o'clock? Do you see it? It seems to be rotating, but it's hard to tell through the rain."

Everyone strained their eyes. Patrick, who was sitting in the far back row on the right, moved closer to Mary on the left to get a better view. She smelled nice, but he tried to ignore that and focus on the distance.

Then he saw it.

A tornado, maybe a mile or two away. It was a definite cone tornado, with a wider funnel toward the top and a narrower one toward the ground.

The distance, along with the rain still coming down, made it a little hard to gauge its rotation speed or movement but it seemed to be heading in the same direction as they were. Thankfully, it didn't appear to be moving toward them.

Billy radioed Dale and Katy in Dorothy to confirm they saw it, which they did. Dale wanted to keep driving east past Winfield to get ahead of it from the southeast.

They decided to keep driving east on Route 160 to track the tornado, as long as it stayed on the ground. Everyone was staring at it—it was big and seemed to be getting even bigger, though it was hard to tell from where they were. Given they were in open country now, there wasn't much blocking their view other than the occasional building or patch of woods. As they got closer, that seemed less of an issue.

After 30 minutes, they reached a road in Moline, Kansas and turned left, heading north. The muddy roads, due to the rain, sprayed mud onto the windows, making it even harder to see the tornado, which was closer now and heading past them towards the west.

Finally, after about 20 minutes heading north and passing Route 400, Mary asked, "Are we going to stop to get outside and see it for a few minutes?"

Billy waited before responding, focusing on not crashing. "Yeah, we wanted to get closer to hear it better. We should reach Route 54 in about 10 or 15 minutes, and we'll try to stop there, depending on which way it passes."

The daylight was beginning to fade, so when they got to Route 54, they turned right to head east and drove about 100 yards, before Dale and Katy pulled off into a grassy area, with Billy right behind them.

"Okay, everyone, we'll get out of the van. If you have a camera, feel free to bring it. Remember, there's lightning in the area, so please stay close to the van if possible. The tornado is going to pass to the northwest of us, so we should be okay. However, tornadoes can shift without notice, so if we tell you to get back in, please do so immediately. This is a big one, so if we need to move, it's for everyone's safety. Please follow our instructions. Let's go!" Billy opened his door and jumped out. Everyone else did the same.

The Centers got out first, then Mary, and finally Patrick. As Patrick walked around the parked van, the first thing he felt was the wind. It was definitely blowing around 40 to 50 mph. Enough to blow the street signs back and forth but not strong enough where it was blowing the group members over. The wind actually felt good after being couped up in the van for most of the day.

The next thing he noticed was the roar. Some horses in a nearby field were neighing occasionally, but the roar was loud enough to mostly drown them out.

People often compared the sound of a tornado to a freight train, but to Patrick, it sounded more like a mix of a jet engine and a waterfall. It was louder than he expected, as sound traveled far over open ground. With the energy this tornado generated, Patrick wasn't surprised they could hear it from where they stood.

The sound was scary yet… peaceful at the same time, as if Mother Nature was literally singing "Hear Me Roar" to anyone who would listen.

Everything else was silent around him, except for the sounds of the others shuffling their feet and taking out their cameras. There were no cars on the road at this point.

He looked up and saw an absolutely massive, rotating wedge tornado moving in a northeastern direction, maybe a half-mile away. The rain had mostly stopped near them, which offered a clear view of the tornado, and one could even see the entire supercell spawning it. The sun setting in the west made the clouds a unique blend of orange, gray, and black.

A huge dark area of cloud, dust, and dirt swirled around the center of the tornado in a counterclockwise direction. Luckily, the tornado seemed to be in the middle of nowhere, so the only things that seemed to be impacted were fields, trees, and probably the occasional cow.

However, this was a dangerous-looking tornado, powerful and large and if this did hit a populated area, it would likely cause major damage.

Patrick closed his eyes and spent a few seconds taking it all in. Just hearing it brought him a sense of calm he hadn't felt in a long time. The wind blew against his face, and the light rain hit his jacket. Every negative emotion or bad feeling he had carried for years seemed to be sucked up by this simulated tornado.

He kept his eyes closed for a few more seconds until Dale called the group over to explain something.

Patrick got close enough to hear him: "If you look closely at the eastern part of the storm, where the rain is, you can see the downdraft occurring. What we look for when chasing is the 'wall cloud,' essentially the area of the strongest updraft in a storm and where tornadoes are likely to form. You can see a very well-defined wall cloud right here." He pointed up toward the sky.

"Also, if you look to the left of the tornado, you'll see what we call the 'rear flank downdraft.' This is where dry air wraps around the back of the supercell, where it descends. We're still trying to understand why it's essential in producing many tornadoes, but these areas form a 'hook echo' on radars, which we chasers use to identify where a tornado has formed.

Looking to the right, you'll see a long line of dark clouds extending east to west. This is a condensation cloud formed by air cooling as it's pulled into a thunderstorm's updraft. As chasers, we sometimes look for these as a sign of a tornado forming."

Dale stopped to let everyone take it all in before continuing briefly.

"As tornadoes go, this one seems to have all the classic traits of a strong wedge tornado. Luckily, we're not near any cities right now, but we need to keep tracking this to ensure it's not heading towards any population centers."

After about six or seven minutes of watching the tornado, Patrick approached Mary, standing a few feet away. "This is amazing," he said, staring at the tornado moving away from them after crossing State Route 99 to the northeast.

"I always imagined it would be amazing," Mary said softly, making her hard to hear. Patrick leaned in and asked her to repeat herself.

"Sorry," she said, a little louder now. "I always imagined it would be amazing, but I just don't have the words to describe my feelings. You know how powerful nature can be but seeing it this close is just… awesome. I'm scared, happy, nervous, in awe, amazed, enthralled… I'm sure there are a few more I can come up with if I think about it some more."

She laughed before shouting, "This is by far the coolest thing I have ever seen!"

Dale turned to her and replied, "Remember, young lady, it may be cool to you, but these things can destroy livelihoods. However, they are amazing to see and help remind us of how small and fragile we all are in the grand scheme of things."

Patrick let those words sink in and infiltrate his soul. Seeing how large and powerful this tornado was really did make him realize how small and insignificant his life was in comparison. Sure, his job was important and gave him some meaning, but his kids were the most important thing in his life and needed to be his focus going forward. They had to be.

A lightning bolt struck a few hundred yards away, followed by booming thunder that echoed through the simulated Kansas sky. Dale quickly said, "Okay folks, let's get back in the van and keep tracking this thing. It looks like it may have some staying power."

▼▼▼

As everyone settled back into the van, there was a ton of excitement and chatter about how amazing an experience that was. The emotional impact of what they had witnessed was overwhelming for everyone but the sheer size and power of the tornado was just amazing.

And the sound; Lenore Center framed it perfectly: "It was as if the Devil himself was speaking."

"You got a good one y'all!" Billy exclaimed from the front seat as the caravan continued east on Route 54 for about 30 minutes before turning left and heading north toward Burlington, Kansas. The tornado was still ahead of them to the left, about a couple of miles away from them at this point

Somehow, it seemed to be getting larger and better organized. It was dusk now, which made it harder to see. Billy sensed some folks were getting nervous about the darkness and reassured them that Dale and Katy were monitoring the radar and they'd maintain a safe enough distance to minimize any risk.

Billy explained that most tornadoes stay on the same general path once they hit the ground, and this one was heading northeast, so they should be safe following behind it.

They headed north for another 45 minutes. By this time, it was completely dark, and the ambiance in the caravan was tense. No one said a word, except for Billy's occasional check-ins to Dale and Katy in Dorothy.

They passed Burlington, a cute farming town with a small downtown and various local shops. Luckily, the tornado seemed to pass around the city without causing any visible damage.

They continued north on Route 75. Dale radioed that the tornado looked like it was passing east over Route 75 and heading northeast. He noted they would continue north until they reached Interstate 35, which connected Wichita to Kansas City, Missouri. The tornado would likely be southeast of them at that point.

The trip continued for another 15 minutes before they got to the Interstate and headed east toward Kansas City. Nothing could be seen outside the window now.

Dale informed the group that they had called in the tornado to the local authorities so people could find shelter. Hopefully, with the warnings they called in, people would be listening to their radios or watching television and were informed of the tornado outbreak.

Patrick realized that 2001 was before any cell phone technology existed to alert people to weather warnings on a real-time basis. With how addicted humans were to their virtual glasses in 2032, most people knew within seconds if a severe storm warning or tornado warning was issued in their area.

Back in the early 2000's, no one had this technology and had to be either watching television or listening to the radio to be informed of the details of these warnings. Several towns in the Midwest had tornado sirens which were loud enough for most people to hear, but even they took a few minutes to sound, which, when dealing with tornados, could mean the difference between life and death.

This tornado was still south of I-35, heading northeast toward Ottawa now, about 20 miles to the northeast. From the radio chatter, Dale explained that tornado warnings were now in place for the entire area east of them.

As they continued driving, there was chatter that the town of Ottawa was now in the tornado's direct path, and on the radio, people were being directed to seek shelter immediately. Patrick felt the tension in the air as they continued driving east.

Finally, after ten minutes of silence, Dale came on the line, "It looks like Ottawa has taken a direct hit. We'll be getting off to see if we can help in any way, as there appears to be significant damage being reported by the local authorities."

They left the Interstate a few minutes later and headed slowly north toward Ottawa. As they drove back into civilization, they initially saw houses and businesses with lights on, allowing them to see some trees and branches down on the road around them, which Billy and Katy tried their best to navigate around.

Eventually, the lights went out as they approached the small town of Ottawa.

Patrick was stunned as he looked out the window. It looked like a bomb had gone off---cars were flipped over as if they'd been tossed on their roofs by some supernatural force. Trees were uprooted, and power lines were down everywhere.

Ahead, they saw fires rising into the night. A few police cars and fire trucks were trying to navigate the damaged streets with little success. Dale radioed, "Let's stop to see how we can help."

As they pulled up to where a group of firetrucks and police cars had gathered, the group's mood had changed significantly. Any smiles or laughter from before were gone, replaced with looks of concern and a few tears. Dale asked everyone to stay put while he spoke to the local authorities to see how they could assist.

After five minutes, he was back and gathered everyone around.

"Okay folks, this town has taken a direct hit. We're being asked to help with search and rescue. They need all hands on deck. This means we are tagging along with local fire, police, and ambulance crews to assist in locating anyone who may be injured or missing.

There may be things that are difficult to see, so if you're uncomfortable with this or need a moment to decide, I understand. Please take a moment to think about it, but I'll need a confirmation quickly if you can help.

If not, no one will hold it against you or look negatively at your decision. This isn't for everyone, but please decide in the next couple of minutes, okay?" Dale walked away to grab something from the other van.

Mary looked at Patrick with a concerned face, tears welling up. "Can we go together? I'm scared, but I want to help these people. Will you come with me?"

"Of course," Patrick responded as Jack. Although he didn't expect this and understood this was a simulation, everything in him told him he would be needed here. "Let's see what Dale says, but we'll stick together and do what we can to help, okay? Here, have some water and take deep breaths." That seemed to do the trick, as she calmed down a bit.

Dale returned with a flashlight, rope, a few jugs of water, and some sort of bullhorn. "Okay, so what does everyone think?" He asked nervously.

"We're in to help, except Marsha," Joe Center of the Center family said. "She has a bad back and won't be of much use here, but if she can help assist in any other way, please let us know."

"Marsha, please go over to that firetruck and ask that gentleman over there how you can assist, okay? You can help people get blankets or find food and water. Just ask them what you can do while we head out. Anyone else?"

The older couple from Vermont said they'd like to join Marsha to see how else they could help. Marsha and the couple said her goodbyes to the rest of the group and headed towards the firetruck, 25 yards away.

Dale quickly turned to the rest of the group. "Okay, the rest of you, we'll split up now. Mary and Jack, why don't you join Billy and myself? The rest of you, please go with Katy. The local police force will also join us. We are heading north as that area seems to be hit the hardest to help with search and rescue efforts." Dale paused.

"I'm sorry, folks. I know this is difficult, but we have moved from storm chasers to first responders here. Please stay strong and remember that there may be parents, siblings, friends, and children who are missing or injured. Okay, let's go!"

Jack, Mary, Billy, and Dale headed out to the north joining a group of first responders, while Katy the rest of the caravan and other first responders moved northwest into the eerie darkness of the night.

▼▼▼

As Patricks' group headed out, it was still drizzling. Other than that, there was an unsettling silence around them that felt like they were in the eye of a hurricane.

The first responders accompanying the group were all talking into their radios to see if there had been any county or federal assistance requested and discuss which areas they were searching, amongst other topics. It sounded like unorganized chaos.

Walking together a couple of blocks north, they came upon their first fire at a small supermarket. The smell of gas made the fire department instruct everyone else to walk away while a few firefighters approached the fire.

Some local residents had ventured out of their houses to assess damage, check on others and seek help. Paramedics attended to the injured as best they could.

Soon, only the storm chasers and the police force were left, as most of the firefighters and paramedics were attending to the initial wave of injured people. A few local residents had now joined the search and rescue efforts with them.

With no one taking charge, Dale turned toward a young police officer named Wade and yelled, "Alright, let's break into groups of two or three and start door-to-door searches of the surrounding blocks. I can already see significant damage to most of the houses in this area. If people were home for dinner and didn't hear the warnings in time to get to their basements or tornado shelters, they could be trapped and need medical assistance."

"Okay, that sounds good," Wade responded as he started to organize the remaining group into small teams to do door-to-door searches.

Dale, Mary, and Jack would head east along 11th Street and zig-zag the streets to the east of Main Street. Dale had a radio to communicate with paramedics about who was found and in what condition.

Mary turned to Patrick. "Please don't leave me alone, Jack. I'm nervous about what we're going to see—some of these houses are completely destroyed. Whoever was inside couldn't have survived."

She was right. Patrick hadn't considered that he might see a dead person, albeit a simulated one, for the first time.

Patrick had dealt with dead rabbits, cats, and guinea pigs before and had seen dead people in videos online but this seemed...different. Maybe the simulation wouldn't replicate death realistically, but based on everything else he had experienced so far, he expected it to be pretty damn close.

He felt bad for Dale and Mary, even if they were simulated. At least Patrick could remind himself that none of this was real.

They proceeded toward the east along 11th Street with rope, flashlights, and walkie-talkies provided by the local fire department.

Some residents stood outside their houses, shocked at what they were looking at. Others cried or stared in disbelief. Dale was asking if people were okay as they continued east.

Eventually, they turned north toward 12th Street, where they made a left and began their zig-zag pattern. As they went another 100 yards on 12th street, they heard a woman screaming at the top of her lungs: "Suzie! Suzie! Suzie, where are you? Can you hear me? Suzie!!"

The three of them ran over to the woman, who was racing around what was left of her house and screaming for Suzie. Dale approached her. "Ma'am, who is Suzie? Is she your daughter?"

"Yes! She's only five years old. She was upstairs taking a bath while I was making dinner when I heard the tornado siren. I didn't even have time to get upstairs before the house exploded. I was thrown to the ground but I was fine. Now I can't find her! Please help me!"

"Okay, ma'am. If she was in the bathtub, it might have broken her fall. What side of the house was the bathtub on? Let's start there," Dale said, trying to keep her calm.

"It was in the back left corner!" She exclaimed, running towards the far side of the house. When everyone arrived, she screamed, "It would be on this side, but it's entirely collapsed!"

"Let's look for water or soap leaking on the ground—that part of the house would have been covered and the ground should be relatively dry given there hasn't been much rain since the tornado passed. If you see pooling water or soap, start shouting. Let's go!"

Patrick was impressed by how quickly and easily Dale stepped into a leadership position. He got the sense that Dale had done this before.

Patrick, Mary, and Dale started climbing onto what was left of the poor lady's house. Debris was everywhere: wood, sheetrock, remnants of insulation, broken pictures, plates, glasses, and other materials that couldn't be identified.

They all called out, "Suzie, Suzie, can you hear us?" but received no response.

Patrick frantically lifted up as many objects as he could, looking under them and searching for anything resembling a bathtub. Mary and Dale followed suit.

A minute or so passed without success. Finally, as Patrick moved toward the center of the house, he noticed what looked like the bottom of a tub sticking out from the rubble, surrounded by soap and water. He raced over, screaming for Mary and Dale. When he reached the area, he could only see part of the bathtub; the rest was buried under several layers of rubble, including a plasma television that probably weighed 200 pounds.

He began removing things as quickly as he could when Dale shouted from behind, "Jack! Wait! Don't move things so quickly! We need to make sure she isn't buried beneath anything before we move it. We don't know where she ended up, so please be careful."

Patrick stopped, breathing heavily. "Okay, sorry, sorry. I think this is the bathtub, but it looks upside down. What do we do? Just start taking stuff off?"

"Yes, but be careful. Make sure you don't see any body parts that might be Suzie's. If she's alive, we don't want to make things worse. If she's dead…" Dale hesitated. "Just be careful, please, and take things off individually."

"Understood," Patrick said, slowly removing wood and sheetrock. He had to stand on the television to reach some of the upper levels of debris. Slowly, they cleared that and started to work around the tub in case they had to flip it over. This involved moving sharp objects, wood with nails, and other areas. Patrick's hands were cut, though there was no blood, which was weird. Either way, he was sure Dale and Mary were dealing with the same thing, and since they weren't complaining, he wouldn't either.

Patrick reminded himself that Jack was a solid 22-year-old kid who wasn't real. If he had to get a few cuts on his hands to help this lady get her daughter back, simulated or not, so be it.

After some digging, they cleared enough to see most of the tub, which was facing the ground. Patrick leaned down to a dent in the tub's rim that was open enough to look inside.

"Give me your flashlight," he asked Dale, gesturing impatiently. Dale handed it to him, and Patrick shone it inside the tub.

"I see her! I see her hand! It's not moving!" Patrick screamed. "We gotta get this tub flipped over."

"The television is still on top; we gotta move that first," Mary said with a hint of trepidation in her voice. "Let's both climb up there and push it off."

"Ok - good idea." Patrick said, jumping onto the bottom of the tub. He grabbed Mary's hand and pulled her up, making sure she didn't fly off the other side before steadying her. "Okay, on three, we need to push this off the other end." Patrick paused, gauging how much they had to push before they hit the tub's edge. It looked at least a foot away, maybe two. "This sucker is heavy. Watch your footing, okay? It's pretty slippery. Ready? On three. One… Two… Three… *Push!*"

Patrick and Mary pushed with all their strength. Jack was apparently stronger than he looked in the mirror, and they quickly moved the television closer to the edge. One more heave, and it was almost there.

"Heave!" Patrick shouted. With one last push, the television toppled off the tub's edge, landing with a thud. Mary slipped and fell onto some pieces of wood and sheetrock on the ground below. "Ow!"

"You okay?" Dale asked, running to grab her up.

"I think I twisted my ankle, but I'm okay." Mary flinched as she stood. "Don't worry about me. I'm fine."

"My baby! Where is my baby?" The mother was now in full panic mode, screaming.

Patrick knew they had to ask fast. He quickly thought about the situation and shouted, "Can we get a piece of wood or something through that dent to create a fulcrum and lift it? The tub is too heavy, and there's still too much crap on the other side. But maybe we can lift it by getting something through that hole.

"Good idea, Jack," Dale said, looking around for something that would fit. It had to be thin but strong enough to lift the metal tub. After a few seconds, he returned with a steel rod. "Here, let's try this."

Dale ran to the hole in the tub, stuck the rod in, and said, "Ok, I'll push as hard as I can here; you both get ready to grab the kid down there."

Patrick turned to Mary and said, "I'll help lift the tub once Dale starts—you grab her as soon as there is room, okay?"

"Okay, I'll do my best," Mary replied, wincing from her fall.

"Please hurry!" The mom shouted, which wasn't helping, but there was nothing he could do about it at the moment.

"On three, ready?" Dale said, positioning the rod at the open area of the tub.

"One... Two... Three!" Dale pushed the pole down, lifting the tub, but it slipped from his hands and crashed back down. "Dammit! Ah! Fuck!" He screamed in pain, clutching his hand.

"You okay, Dale?" Patrick asked. "Here, let me take it, and you lift the tub once I get it high enough."

"Okay, got it," he answered quickly, realizing he probably wasn't strong enough to do this.

Patrick grabbed the rod while Dale got settled next to the tub, ready to lift it. With all his might, Patrick pushed down on the metal pole, gripping it tightly to avoid it slipping out of his hands as well. It burned in his hands, which were already hurting from the previous 20 cuts. Still, no blood, though.

He continued to push as Mary exclaimed, "A little more! I can almost grab her hand! Keep pushing, Jack!"

Patrick dug in and pushed harder. The pain was real, even if this was a simulation. He would definitely need a good dose of Tylenol later.

"Get her out!" Dale screamed as he helped lift the tub. Mary reached in, grabbed Suzie's hand, then the other, and pulled her out next to the tub.

"I got her!" Mary exclaimed as Patrick and Dale let go of the steel pole and tub, respectively, screaming in both pain and relief. Patrick was winded and needed to sit against the tub to catch his breath. "Is she breathing?" He asked, gasping for air.

"My baby, my baby!" The woman screamed as she quickly ran to her daughter, grabbed her by the head, and pulled her close. "She isn't breathing! Does anyone know CPR?"

"I do," Patrick said, still recovering his breath. "Put her down, and I'll start chest compressions." Patrick didn't think Jack knew CPR, but Patrick did from his years as a lifeguard during high school. He found it interesting that a real-life skill would now translate into the simulation to impact how the story played out.

Patrick kneeled over Suzie's body and began the process of 30 chest compressions, followed by two breaths, followed by 30 chest compressions. Given Suzie's age, he had to be careful not to press too hard, but he continued for two minutes.

"*Come on, Suzie!*" Patrick thought as he continued CPR. He wondered if someone watching the simulation could step in and press a button to get Suzie to breathe. That would be nice right about now.

Whether his wish was granted or some other higher power intervened, Suzie began to move after the last series of breaths. Soon, she opened her mouth to cough, which could've been the best sound Patrick had ever heard.

"Oh my god!" The mother exclaimed. "Suzie, wake up, honey. It's mommy. I'm here. Breathe, baby, breathe. That's right. In… and out… I'm here. I'm right here." She kept repeating that as she hugged Suzie.

Still recovering from the past ten minutes, Patrick said slowly, "Ma'am, we must get her to the paramedics. We don't know how long she's been without oxygen. The longer she goes without help, the greater the risk. Let me take her over to the paramedics, okay? You can follow me to the ambulance, but we need to go now."

Crying, the mom reluctantly released Suzie, and Patrick lifted her. He knew what it was like to carry kids this age and weight.

Seeing a five-year-old in pain, simulated or not, was awful. Even though he knew Suzie was not real, everything in his soul told him he needed to get her to the nearest ambulance.

As he carried her away from the house, he realized how much he missed his own kids. Brin, his four-year-old, was the apple of his eye and was smart and funny, just like him. Anna, almost nine months old, was also smart and already close to walking.

He hadn't seen them much the past few months and he absolutely knew his recent decision to spend more time at home and less time traveling for work was the right one. They needed to be his focus now, more than ever.

Patrick, as Jack, stepped onto 12th Street and headed west toward where help was gathered. It was about a ten-minute sprint, and he was completely out of breath when he arrived. He found an ambulance along Main Street and ran Suzie over to the paramedics.

"Folks, we have a five-year-old girl who was buried under a bathtub. We found her unresponsive. I gave her CPR and resuscitated her after about a minute and a half. Her mom is right behind me. Please help her."

"Okay, son, let's place her on here," the older paramedic said, bringing up a wheeled stretcher. Patrick carefully laid her down and quickly ran back about a quarter of the block to find her mom and guide her to the ambulance.

As Suzie was transferred into the ambulance with her mom and the doors were shut, Patrick looked up, breathed deeply, and saw the mom turn toward him inside the ambulance window.

Even though she didn't say anything, her tearful eyes told Patrick: *Thank you.*

▼ ▼ ▼

It was after 10:30 p.m. when the storm-chasing group was all finally back together. They had been searching for over two and a half hours and they were tired, hungry, wet, and getting somewhat cold as the front that had pushed through the area started to bring some cooler air in with it. After all, it was still April.

Patrick and Jack were both exhausted. It was hard to believe that less than about twelve simulated hours earlier, he had been sitting in a facility, flirting with Emily. He could only hope she'd been watching the events unfold and was planning a vacation for the two of them to Bermuda when he returned to reality.

Being 22 in the simulation did help a little, but even a 22-year-old would get winded from what he just did.

Everyone in the group had a story to tell. The Center family had helped a family locate some elderly family members who had gone missing, and they found several residents of homes that were destroyed who were now deceased and covered with blankets and sheets to keep their bodies protected from the elements.

Many were crying and emotional based on what they had witnessed. After helping find Suzie, Dale and Patrick continued for another hour and a half, guiding people to ambulances and fire trucks for medical assistance or directing them to other assistance.

They had also seen deceased people, including children, which ranked among the worst things Patrick had ever seen, simulated or not. The tears and emotions of the characters in this simulation felt real enough to cut him to his core.

He knew that many people had endured these exact scenes in real life, and it must be heart-wrenching for anyone to see this.

Patrick considered skipping ahead to get through the night but held off.

The Red Cross and National Guard had arrived an hour ago, setting up medical tents as well as handing out food and water to anyone who needed them.

Mary had her ankle looked at by a paramedic, who said it appeared to be a bad sprain. She had it wrapped up but refused any further treatment.

Billy and Katy were talking quietly near Toto, waiting for the go-signal from Dale. Both looked stunned and tired, but they seemed okay.

Dale walked over to Patrick, who was sitting on the curb along Main Street, and sat beside him. "How are you doing, kid? That was some swift thinking with that little girl. That fulcrum idea was smart; she probably didn't have much time left under that tub. I'm not sure the three of us could have lifted it ourselves. I asked the paramedic to call me if he heard anything about her. Hopefully, she'll be okay. At least you gave her a chance to live, and that's all we can do." He looked at the ground. "Hell of a first day to chase, huh?"

Patrick thought briefly and then asked, "Have you ever seen anything like this, other than the Bridge Creek tornado? This loss of life and damage?"

"A few times, Jack. It happens, unfortunately, during our season. People living out there on the coasts don't realize that these small towns in the Midwest get hit year after year. Our work is to help prevent these disasters in the future by giving people enough warning to get to safety. The size, strength, and timing of this one likely didn't give people enough time to find shelter, especially since it was dinner time for many. We do our best to report these tornadoes to the local authorities so they can handle them appropriately. We called this one in pretty quickly, but, unfortunately, it depends on people paying attention to their TVs or radios or hearing those sirens.

This area wasn't in the bullseye of the expected tornado zone today; it was forecast to be about 50 miles farther south, closer to Oklahoma. It's an unfortunate part of the business son and something we don't like seeing.

But if you want to help people, like *really* help them, keep researching these fucking things. We're learning a lot, but there's a lot more to go, and I hope you're a part of that, even after today."

Dale took a deep breath. "Everyone is pretty beat—are you ready to head to the hotel?"

"Yeah, I could use a good meal and a shower," Patrick said slowly.

Dale chuckled lightly. "Well, a shower I can guarantee. A good meal? We'll have to see what we can find. Deal?"

"Deal," Patrick responded, standing up to head over to the van. He saw Mary leaning against a tree and walked over to her.

"Hey, how are you feeling?" He asked her, already knowing the answer given her pained expression.

"Not gonna lie, it hurts like hell." Mary grimaced. "I twisted it bad back there, but I hope it was worth it. Did you hear anything about Suzie?"

"Dale said he gave a paramedic his number and asked them to call if there was any update, so we'll see. We did our best and gave her a chance, at least."

Patrick slowly looked around at the damage and chaos. Ambulances, fire trucks, and police cars were still everywhere, now joined by National Guard and Red Cross vehicles. The wind was picking up, ushering in chillier air. Blankets and kerosene lamps were being handed out to residents, and tents were being set up in the park along Main Street for people to stay overnight.

"These poor people," Mary said, looking around. "One moment, you're having dinner with your family, and the next, your life is completely turned upside down. I saw dozens of people with sheets over them, and that was only on this side of town. We didn't even see the other side, which that family said was hit hard. I can't even imagine how many people lost their lives tonight, including kids."

As Mary started crying, Patrick wrapped his arms around her, holding her close. He felt her tears soaking his shirt, but he didn't mind one bit. She clung to his lower back, and they stood in an embrace for what felt like an hour but was probably only 45 seconds until Dale came over and asked everyone to get back into the vans.

Once back in Toto, with Dale in the front passenger seat again, everyone was dead silent as Billy pulled out, heading south towards the highway and Kansas City.

Sensing the mood, Dale turned around and quietly said, "Look, folks, this was a horrible first day. I know all of you were significantly affected by what you saw and experienced. We can take some time tomorrow to regroup. It looks like the weather is supposed to be fairly calm over the next couple of days, which, normally, I would say is a bummer. However, after today, it might be just what we need.

Thank you all for helping. I'm sure the residents would say the same. As I told Jack a little bit ago, this is why we do what we do: by understanding tornadoes better, we can understand where they will likely form and head once on the ground, giving more advanced warnings so people can get to safety. Every tornado, including the one tonight, is analyzed and researched to better understand future tornadoes.

This was a tough day, so we'll find a decent hotel on the outskirts of Kansas City, check everyone in, and regroup in the morning to figure out a game plan, okay?"

The group nodded, exhausted from the day. The next 30 minutes were mostly a blur—some folks dozed off, others stared out the window silently.

Patrick was one of those who stared outside the van, wishing he could give his kids a big hug.

▼▼▼

By the time they arrived at the hotel, it was nearly 11:15 p.m. Everyone was exhausted, so most of the group dispersed straight to their rooms.

Patrick entered his room, undressed, and jumped in the shower. He felt grimy, but it could have been worse. There was no sweat on his body, no blood from where there should have been, and he didn't shit his pants because, well, he couldn't.

The shower felt good and helped him regroup mentally. Even if he was in a simulation, he didn't like feeling dirty.

Next to the hotel was a convenience store where Dale, Katy, and Billy had gone and picked up a few meal options. They went to each of the guests' rooms to offer food. Dale stopped by Patrick's room around 11:45 p.m., and Patrick took a pre-made turkey sandwich, some cookies, and two beers from their selection.

It was better than nothing, although this would've been a great time to have the instant drone food delivery of 2032. Unfortunately, online food delivery did not exist in 2001.

After chowing down his food and beer, Patrick was about to call it a night when he heard a knock on his door. Expecting it to be Dale to discuss tomorrow's game plan, he was surprised to see Billy.

"Hey, man. I know it's late, and you're exhausted. I just wanted to say that it was amazing what you did today—saving that little girl. Losing my parents to that damn tornado… you know, it's why I do this. To honor their memory." Billy paused and looked down for a second. "I just wanted to say thank you." Billy gave him a tight hug before breaking away with tears in his eyes.

Patrick was at a loss for words but tried anyway. "Yeah man, I'm happy I was able to do that. I'm sorry about your parents. That just sucks but what you're doing would make them proud."

"Yeah, thanks, man," Billy said quickly. "Sorry, I don't know why I did that. It's just so emotional hearing about kids getting hurt because I know that easily could've been me and my brother. Fuck man. I'm wiped, so I'm gonna head to bed, but I just wanted to tell you that. See you in the morning."

And just like that, Billy was gone.

Patrick closed the door, feeling wiped as well.

Thirty seconds later, just as Patrick was going to ask to skip ahead to the next day, there was another knock.

Patrick sighed. "What now…" He assumed it was Dale or Katy this time, but when he opened the door, it was definitely *not* either.

Mary stood in the doorway, holding a few beers. She'd changed into her pajamas, which included a t-shirt and shorts.

"Sorry if it's late. I was hoping you were up. I'm still freaked out from earlier." She dangled the beer bottles as if to say: *Whatcha say, pal, can I come in?*

"Sure, I'm tired, but let's do it." Patrick smiled, realizing his brain wasn't speaking for him anymore. He stepped aside to let Mary into his room.

"Man, Jack, you are a total neat freak," she said, plopping down on his bed and opening the beers, handing one to Patrick.

"Yeah, I get it from my dad," Patrick said, responding as Jack now. "He always stressed organization and neatness, so I guess I picked up on that from him."

"Well, I love it. My family is unorganized, so I always appreciate someone neat like me." Mary smiled as she took a few chugs of her beer, and Patrick did the same.

"Ah, the finest shit beer this side of the Mississippi," he said, laughing and sitting on the other side of the bed.

"You were awesome back in that town," Mary said after another swig. "You just jumped into action to clear that tub out. And figuring out that fulcrum was genius! We couldn't have lifted that whole tub without serious help. I hope that girl survives. That poor mom—I could feel her pain and desperation when she spoke, you know? It didn't feel real to me, but I knew it was, and we just had to help her."

"Tell me about it," Patrick said quietly. "Yeah, I just reacted without thinking. We didn't have time. If she was stuck under that tub, she was likely running out of air. I knew we had to move."

Patrick took another sip of beer. "When I was younger, my brother got his arm stuck under a table that had flipped over. I had to create a fulcrum to free him. That memory just popped into my head, and I figured it was the best solution."

Patrick remembered the day his younger brother Rob got his arm pinned under a table that had flipped over outside. Patrick was only ten at the time, but he probably saved Rob's arm from being amputated with his quick thinking.

Patrick glanced at Mary's taped-up ankle. "How's your ankle? Still hurting?"

"It has seen better days, but this helps," Mary said, pointing at the beer and finishing it with a big gulp. She opened another and offered one to Patrick, which he accepted and finished his first one.

"Here, let me rub it a bit; see if that helps." Patrick took her ankle and brought it to the bed. It was swollen through the tape, so he unwrapped it and gently rubbed where it looked the most swollen.

Mary grimaced but said, "Oh man, that feels pretty good." She lay on the bed with her head on the pillow. Her breasts were almost hanging out of her t-shirt, and Patrick felt something in his pants move. Maybe it was a mouse from the motel they were in.

"Okay, I'll keep doing it if you like it," Patrick said slowly, continuing to rub.

"I do like it. You know what I'd like better? If you'd kiss me," Mary said with her eyes closed.

"Uh, yeah, sure. I mean, are you sure you're okay with that?" Patrick asked nervously. This must have been Jack kicking in, as Patrick would never sound that nervous.

"I'm okay with it... I've been thinking about it most of the day, honestly," Mary said quietly, her eyes still closed.

As Patrick leaned down toward her mouth, all he could think was, *"I'm about to have sex in a simulation on the first day—this has got to be some sort of record."*

He pressed his lips against hers, gently at first, then more intensely as her mouth opened and her tongue met his. He had to be careful with her ankle, but he moved his hands to her hair as she kissed him deeply.

He moved down from her mouth to her neck and then to her chest, where she began to moan louder. He took off her shirt and saw a lovely pair of breasts demanding his attention. She was moaning louder now, and her hands worked down to his crotch, meeting a rather impressive erection on Jack's part.

She decided his pants were no longer needed, and neither were hers. Soon, he was ready to enter her.

The only thought in his mind was whether they used protection in 2001. In 2032, most sexually transmitted diseases were treatable, and safe sex was not a thing. Some people still used protection, and Patrick certainly practiced safe sex when traveling to Asia, as he didn't trust anyone there. However, back home, most women didn't care about condoms, which was nice.

Apparently, Mary didn't care either, as she pulled him right into her with a large moan and a skin-tearing scratch down his back from her nails.

She felt wonderful, and she was ready for him. The next 25 minutes were filled with as much raw passion and sensual lovemaking as Patrick had ever experienced. He was sure Jack had never experienced this either. They did positions that Patrick couldn't do in real life; not with his knees, but Jack had no problem performing.

Patrick incorporated a few moves and positions he had learned over the years to help Jack out. Mary was amazing; her body was everything he loved—dark, firm, in proper proportions, and nothing fake about it.

Once he finished, or at least he felt like he finished, and they had each gone to freshen up, they lay in bed, still breathing heavily. Mary's head was on his naked chest, rubbing it slightly. Patrick hadn't felt this good in many months. That sex was just raw and animal-like, like they both had to have it.

"Wow, well, I certainly don't feel my ankle hurting anymore, so thank you for that." Mary chuckled. "I'm certainly glad I stopped by."

"Me too." Patrick laughed as well.

A few minutes later, Mary seemed to pass out while still on him. Patrick didn't mind—it felt good to connect with someone after the day's events.

He also knew he wouldn't be sleeping anyway and was sick of thinking about the day, so he called Alice out to do her thing. What was he supposed to say? Oh yeah. "Alice, advance to tomorrow, please."

In his head, or maybe it wasn't, Alice's voice said, "Confirming you would like to advance to tomorrow. Please say yes or no."

"Yes," Patrick responded.

APRIL 15, 2001

The next thing Patrick saw was a sliver of light coming into the motel room from outside. He looked down next to him and saw that Mary wasn't in his arms or in bed with him.

"*Shit, maybe it was a dream,*" he thought, getting out of bed and going to wash his face in the bathroom.

As he dried off, he heard a ringing noise behind him. He couldn't locate the source of the noise, but it seemed to be coming from his backpack. Opening it, he found his cell phone buzzing. He looked at the screen:

Dad.

He took a second before pressing "Accept."

"Hello," Patrick said quietly.

"Jack? Jack, is that you?" A man's voice asked from the other end.

"Yeah, hi, Dad." Saying "Dad" felt weird. It had been over 20 years since he had last addressed a person that way.

Hearing the man call him "Jack" was a little strange, but he understood why that was.

"Hey, Jack! Oh, son. We were so worried! Your mom is flying to Florida to visit grandma and grandpa, but I'll let her know you're okay when she lands. We saw the news about the tornado in Kansas and how awful it was. I knew you guys were heading in that area. Are you okay?"

"Yeah, Dad, I'm okay. I'll explain everything when I get home." Patrick knew he was lying, but there wasn't anything he could do about it. "It was crazy. We had to help with search and rescue, and there was this little girl trapped. We freed her. It was awful, but I think she'll be okay."

"Oh my god, Jack! Were you hurt? Are you still going to continue with the trip?" Jack's dad asked. He genuinely seemed concerned for his simulated son.

"Yeah, as far as I know, everyone wants to keep going. I haven't seen anyone this morning yet, but I'm in. This is what it's all about, right? The tornado was amazing yet terrifying. It was just so powerful and destructive—more than I ever imagined. We chased it until dark and just saw this town completely destroyed from it. Just damage everywhere. It was surreal but I'm okay. Tired, but I'm okay."

He couldn't tell his fake dad why he was up so late. He wouldn't have told his real dad that part either, so why start now?

"I miss you, Dad," Patrick said suddenly, tearing up.

"I miss you too, son. I'm glad you're safe, and we can't wait to see you when you get home. I know your mother feels the same. Well, I'll let you go now. I'm sure you have a busy day ahead, so please be careful and take care of yourself. We'll see you soon." His dad paused for a second. "I love you, Jack."

Patrick was crying now. He took a second to compose himself.

"I love you too, Dad."

▼▼▼

By the time Patrick showered, dressed, and went outside, the group had gathered by the vans, including Mary. She smiled at him, glowing. Was that from him? Maybe it wasn't a dream after all.

They decided to hold steady in their current location. The front that had blown through had chilled the air significantly, now down in the 40s. Unfortunately (or fortunately), the weather forecast for the next few days showed little thunderstorm activity in the region. Some potential storms were predicted farther southeast, near Louisiana, Mississippi, and Alabama, but Dale didn't want to go too far as the confidence in severe storm development was low, and the farther east they went, the longer it would take to get back home.

Plus, there was guidance that some storms could reappear in their current area in a few days, so Dale preferred not to venture too far.

The group decided they'd had enough action for a while and wanted to relax for a few days. Patrick was fine with this. It would give him more time to spend with Mary and do some fun things in the simulation. And fun things they did.

They watched movies in the local theater, including *Godzilla vs. Kong* and *Mortal Kombat.* He even sat through *Tom & Jerry,* as it was Mary's favorite cartoon growing up. They explored downtown Kansas City, went out to eat and drink, and, of course, had plenty of sex.

Patrick vowed to find the person who created Mary and gave him a nice old bottle of tequila to thank them. She was perfect. She was fun to be with, smart as a whip, had a great sense of humor, was attractive as all hell, and was just chill. They spent hours watching TV in the motel, talking, and ordering crappy food. Patrick didn't care what he ate—he was 22 and in a simulation.

Pizza? Check. Chicken parm? Check. Ice cream? Double check.

His simulated mother called to check on him from Florida, showering him with love and affection from 1,500 miles away. She reminded him of his real mother: very loving on the phone but asking six questions a minute. He was happy to hear from her, but also happy to get her off the phone and return to lying in bed with Mary.

APRIL 16, 2001

On the second day in Kansas City, Mary wanted to go shopping, so they took a taxi to one of the larger malls he had ever been to. In 2032, malls were mostly shuttered, with some remaining but transformed into entertainment venues: restaurants, theaters, virtual reality hubs, small concert venues, comedy clubs, and other attractions. Shopping still existed for high-end stores where paying for rent still made sense. Overall, they were more interactive entertainment venues and less shopping hubs like they were in 2001.

However, the mall Mary and he went to was packed with all sorts of stores designed to stimulate people to buy all sorts of useless crap.

Walking from shop to shop with a girl was something he hadn't done in probably 15 years since he was in college. But that was different from walking an entire mall with Mary.

Patrick had no problem going into the different stores with her; it was fun watching her try out new outfits in Macy's, bras in Victoria Secret, cheap rings in Zales and some perfume in Express.

They went into a pet store and held a little puppy golden retriever, which reminded Patrick of the golden retriever puppy, Zeus, Patrick got for his kids a few months before the divorce.

They got lunch in the food court and played video games in Dave and Busters for a few hours before heading back to the motel.

After walking around the mall for the entire day with heavy pockets full of his wallet, car keys and his phone, it certainly made him appreciate life back in 2032, where he didn't have to carry any of those around. Everything was linked to virtual glasses or contact lenses, and his pockets were generally free and light.

APRIL 17, 2001

The next day, him and Mary rented a car and went hiking in a small wildlife refuge just outside Kansas City called the Tallgrass Prairie National Preserve. It was beautiful and invigorating to see nature like this.

Being from Colorado, Patrick loved being outside and experiencing nature. While this wasn't Colorado, being outside with Mary on a cool day in Kansas was exactly the breath of fresh air he needed in his life. Even if she wasn't real, they were having a blast together, and, in a way, he didn't want this journey to end.

They held hands as they walked among the buffalo grazing in the distance in the vast grasslands of this preserve, enjoying each other's company. For the entirety of the day, he forgot he was in a simulation and made sure he enjoyed every moment with Mary.

On the night of the third day, as they lay in bed mostly naked, watching some awful cheesy movie on television, Mary turned to him and asked, "Jack, where do you see yourself in ten years?"

Patrick thought for a second. In 2011 in real life, he would just be graduating from Penn State. He obviously couldn't tell her that, so he just responded as Jack:

"Jeez, making me think deep here.", he chuckled. "Well, let's see. I guess I would love to continue researching severe storms, maybe become a Dale, and start taking people on storm-chasing trips. Maybe I'll teach. I'm not exactly sure. I love the weather and understanding how different factors like heat, cold, humidity, winds, ocean currents, or whatever dictate how these storms move and grow. It's fascinating to me. Everyone's starting to talk about global warming and how it will worsen and impact storms, so I want to be a part of that discussion, you know?

I also want to have a family and raise some kids with a hot mom by my side." Patrick laughed and hugged Mary.

"What about you?" It was such a weird question to ask a simulated figure, even though she felt as real as anything he had experienced in real life.

"I don't know. Probably the same as you. I want to travel and see the world. Maybe start writing for a magazine about how weather impacts populations in different parts of the world. The weather is just so fascinating because it impacts everything we do: how we live, what we do day-to-day, what we eat, how much things cost, what we wear. It's so ingrained in our lives, yet most humans only care about the weather in their backyard, you know? They don't give a shit about how the weather or climate changes in the Philippines or Zimbabwe impact the local population; that's their problem. It's so fucked up and I just see it getting worse so I want to try to help out, you know?"

Patrick thought, "*Yes, I know. I've been there.*" However, as Jack, he responded, "I think that's amazing and very creative of you. I hope you can do that one day. But if you do, you have to take me with you, okay?"

"I'll take you however I want to take you," Mary said as she mounted him, leaned over, breasts exposed, and kissed him deeply.

"*It's good to be 22 again,*" Patrick thought as he removed her panties and entered her for what was probably the 20th time since they arrived in Kansas City.

▼ ▼ ▼

APRIL 18, 2001

On the fourth day in Kansas City, Dale and the team gathered the troops for breakfast and decided to head northwest into Nebraska, as a system coming out of the Rockies had the potential for supercell development.

"Hey, Jack! Come here for a second, buddy," Dale called out as he threw his gear into the van.

"I just got a call from my contact at the Ottawa Police Department. That little girl that you got out from the tub—she's going to be okay. She had a bad concussion, some broken bones, and internal bleeding, but it sounds like she'll be fine. The mom wanted to personally thank you for saving her and said that anytime you're back in the area, please look her up. Her name is Anna Daniels. What you did was amazing, so I hope that puts a silver lining on what was otherwise a tough day."

Patrick took a moment to think about it. While everything in him knew this world wasn't real, it was the proudest he had ever felt. He wasn't sure whether someone else doing the same simulation would have made the same decisions, but it didn't matter. He/Jack did, and it saved this little girl's life, even if it was just a simulated life.

Patrick felt an overwhelming sense of peace, like something in the world was better because of him. He would remember this moment for the rest of his life.

"Thank you, Dale. That means a lot to me, and I'm so happy to hear she is doing okay. Let's hope that's the last rescue we have to do on this trip!"

"Well, we'll likely have one more shot to see a tornado before going back to Denver, so let's see what we can find." Dale turned to Billy and Katy standing by the vans and asked them to load everyone off.

After a few minutes, they were back on the hunt for a tornado.

▼ ▼ ▼

At some point during the next day of driving through Kansas and Nebraska without any tornado sightings, Patrick made the decision to end his simulation on the eighth day, as permitted without penalty.

He had seen a tornado, rescued a girl, had more sex than he'd had in the past ten years of real life, and talked to his simulated father. Overall, he was satisfied with the simulation.

But the truth was, he missed his kids. Another two days in this simulation wouldn't add much to his journey here. Maybe, in a twisted way, he was meant to save that young girl to reinforce his decision to spend more time with his kids. All he knew was that he wanted to see them and hug them tightly once this was over.

Plus, as strange as it sounded, he didn't want to grow more attached to Mary. He kept trying to remind himself that she wasn't real, but he also knew that, if he wanted to, he could see her again on his next Anticipation Day. He would take time to think about what he wanted, but he was sure this wouldn't be the last time he interacted with Mary. Maybe next time they could go to the Far East together and work on her writing about the local weather.

Back in Kansas, the weather had just not been cooperative as the group was too far north in Nebraska to catch a line of cells that produced a tornado on the Kansas/Nebraska border. That night, they stayed in Medicine Lodge, Kansas, where Patrick learned that a famous treaty was signed between the United States and multiple Native American tribes in 1867.

Who said you can't learn things in a simulation?

The full group had a nice dinner together and finally talked about their thoughts on that terrible night, particularly after Jack shared his story about Suzie. It was an emotional night, with many in the group saying how guilty they felt, going from being excited to see the tornado to being distraught about the death and destruction that it caused. Everyone knew what they had signed up for but seeing it in "real" life was not something anyone knew how to process.

Towards the end of the dinner, Dale stood up with a beer in his hand and started a toast:

"Folks, I know we have a few days left on our journey, but I just wanted to quickly say that I hope you all come out of this trip appreciating both the power and the beauty of Mother Nature. I know from what we have seen the other day, she can absolutely be a bitch at times, but she can also be a beautiful creature too. Full of *magnificent* spectacles and sights. Coming from the field that I am in, I hope that you appreciate that while our ultimate goal is to protect lives, we are also very passionate about protecting the one and only planet we live on.

We see a lot of beautiful places on our drives through the Midwest and the southeast and we want to help keep those places beautiful. With that said, please consider donating to an environmental organization of your choosing to help conserve and protect these places. I'm not asking for much here, but humanity as a whole needs to do a better job of supporting organizations that help protect our planet.

If you do donate, please keep your receipt and you will get a discount off your next trip with us.

Okay folks, that's my commercial for this evening. We should have some good opportunities for a tornado tomorrow, so let's enjoy the rest of this dinner and get some rest tonight. Cheers."

After dinner, everyone seemed to feel lighter and in much better moods, which was good to see.

APRIL 19, 2001

The next morning, Dale and the team headed south through Oklahoma towards the Texas panhandle, which Dale said was primed for supercell formation. The weather had warmed up about 20 degrees within a few hours as a warm front approached from the west.

As Billy drove south on Route 281 through northern Oklahoma in the mid-afternoon, the skies were turning darker. Dale and Billy worked to find the best route to catch some storms running through northern Texas, heading east toward western Oklahoma.

"Alright, gang, we have a decent setup here. We'll have to step on the gas to catch these storms, as they're moving pretty fast. If we time it right, we should catch them on the backside and hopefully see more tornadoes. Everyone okay with that?"

Everyone, including the Centers, nodded, and off they went.

After about 10 minutes, Dale spoke up: "Folks, I don't expect this system to be as destructive as the one from Monday night, so let's hope that we avoid a repeat. If we do have to chip in, I hope I can count on everyone to assist as needed.

The good news is that this system appears to be moving faster than the last one, so the tornadoes might not have time to gather as much steam. However, as you should know by now, many factors impact a tornado's strength. We'll just have to see what forms.

Either way, you've all been amazing this trip. I hope we finish with some strong, beautiful tornadoes that impact only unpopulated areas."

Dale stopped and turned around, and that was the last time he spoke until they reached Frederick, Oklahoma, about 160 miles south.

During those 160 miles, Patrick knew he was likely approaching his final moments with Mary.

As she napped on his shoulder, he felt grateful for having met her. She brought life back to him after the heartache and stress of the past

18 months that had him go from a husband to a divorcé to a world traveler to a tornado chaser.

All while searching for some sort of happiness in his life.

Leave it to a simulated character to find that happiness. *"You know what?"* He thought. *"She's not simulated. She's real. She's real in my heart and mind, and that's what matters to me."* He knew he would miss her.

After another half-hour of driving, Dale broke the silence. "Okay folks, we have a supercell with a hook echo forming about 40 miles southeast of here, near Wichita Falls, Texas, so we're gonna have to step on it. If anyone really needs the bathroom, let us know; otherwise, we're racing to catch this. Anyone need to go?"

Patrick was fine. He'd not used the bathroom in close to eight days, which he could get used to. Mary glanced at him as if to say: *I have to go, but I don't want to be the one to ruin this for everyone else.* Patrick laughed as the silence from everyone else indicated they were fine to go chase their next tornado.

▼ ▼ ▼

When they finally saw it, it was perfect. Just perfect.

It was quiet and calm as they stopped on the side of Route 79, east of Wichita Falls near Dean, to watch the tornado slowly roll towards the east. There was no rain this time, and the winds were blowing gently around the group, allowing them to stand outside and admire the beauty of nature unfolding before them.

Though this tornado was far smaller than the previous one, the way the perfectly formed cone tornado went from the dark sky down through a backdrop of an orange, yellow, and brown, all the way down to the green trees on the ground swaying in the wind, it was a perfect setting to witness a tornado, especially with no major towns nearby.

The Center family captured as many pictures and videos as they could. Dale was explaining something to the Ward couple, while Billy and Katy took measurements from instruments on the van.

Patrick walked over to Mary and took her hand. Why not? A sense of calm and peace overtook him, and he wanted to spend a few quiet moments with her.

She leaned her head on his shoulder and said, "Thank you, Jack."

"For what?" Patrick asked, curious.

"For just being here. I don't know. I've known you for a week, but it feels like I've known you my whole life. This trip would've sucked without you. So thank you for experiencing this with me."

"You're welcome. I was going to say the same thing about you." Patrick laughed softly. "I'm going to miss you. I hope you know that. You've made this trip more enjoyable than I ever imagined. Please don't forget me."

"I could never forget you, Jack. I'll visit you in Boulder, and I'm sure you can get away to wherever I end up. We'll expense the airfare to the schools." She smiled.

"Definitely." Patrick paused. "You know, my close friends called me Patrick when I was younger. I loved Patrick Ewing and Patrick Roy, if you have any idea who they are, so they eventually called me Patrick. I think you should call me Patrick."

"Okay, Jack…weird. I mean, I loved Monica Seles, but my friends never called me Monica." Mary laughed. "Monica is a silly name anyway, so I'm glad they didn't. But, fine, Jack. I'll call you *Patrick* from now on."

She leaned in for a kiss. It was passionate and something he didn't want to end but knew he would remember for a long time, even after his simulation was over. God almighty, would he have to wait a year for this?

As the tornado drifted east, it was about 5 p.m. and Dale decided to call it a day, as there didn't appear to be any new storms forming behind the current line.

He suggested the group head toward the Dallas/Ft. Worth area, which was around two hours away, for a group dinner.

That night, everyone dressed in their best outfits for dinner at a local steakhouse in Ft. Worth, where the food was fantastic. Stories were shared, laughs were had, and Patrick and Mary joined the group for a photo before they all retired for the night.

Patrick thanked Dale, Billy, and Katy for their time and guidance, which confused them since they still had another day of two of chasing ahead of them before heading back to Denver. He didn't bother explaining; they'd probably just assume he was drunk.

Later that night, as Patrick and Mary had finished their 41st romp of the trip, Patrick looked at her as she slept.

"I know you won't understand what I'm about to say, but you have changed me in many ways." Patrick said quietly. "You were just... perfect. Everything I always wanted, you were it. Everything I needed right now, you gave to me. You were exactly what I needed when I needed it. I didn't come into this looking for love; I just wanted to see a tornado. But I love you. I can say that without feeling weird. I hope you loved me too.

I'm not sure what I'm going to do with my life going forward, but this time with you has been incredible. I hope we can do it again next year. Thank you, Mary. I'll see you soon."

Patrick stared at Mary's naked body for several minutes before asking Alice to skip him forward to the next morning.

APRIL 20, 2001

Patrick slowly got out of bed, careful not to wake Mary. He kissed her forehead and stepped outside the hotel in Ft. Worth.

He walked to small pond across the street from the motel, sat on a bench, and watched some ducks swimming in the distance. He didn't know how this simulation might change him in the future, but he knew that after his children's births, this had become the most life-changing experience of his time on Earth so far. He considered himself lucky to be able to experience this.

As Patrick reflected on his time in the simulation, he couldn't believe what he had gone through. It was even more remarkable than in his wildest dreams. He had witnessed death and destruction but also formed a connection to another person, one he hadn't felt in a long time. And it was a real connection to him. It didn't matter what anyone would think in the real world; this was his experience, and it was real.

However, now Patrick needed to focus on finding his happiness, and he fully believed it lay in his kids. He deserved happiness, and this experience made him realize that. Yes, he was scared, but he was also hopeful.

After ten minutes on the bench, he was ready to go back, but he had one more thing to do before he asked Alice to end his simulation.

He needed to say goodbye.

He pulled out his cell phone, scrolled through recent calls to find "Dad," and pressed the green phone button, excited for the voice on the other end to answer.

CHAPTER 2

MIKE – THE NHL PLAYER

MARCH 8, 2032
8:15 A.M.

Mike was glad it was chilly in the facility's waiting room; it would be a good precursor to how cold the playing environment would be in Madison Square Garden, the World's Most Famous Arena.

He was generally excited. He couldn't wait to step onto the ice for the first time, to see the lights of MSG above him, the crowd in the stands, and to be with his teammates who would all be focused on one goal: winning the Stanley Cup, the most cherished trophy in sports. While there was no way this simulation could recreate the actual feeling of playing in the Stanley Cup finals, he couldn't wait to find out how close it did.

During his intake a few months ago, Mike was offered two options: 1) go back in time to recreate being a player in a game of his choosing, or 2) let the simulation create a unique player and game based on some basic parameters set by him.

Both options were intriguing in their own way. Would it be cool to be Marc Messier or Brian Leetch hoisting the Stanley Cup? Of course. Yet he was curious to see how capable the simulation was of creating something entirely new just for him.

Mike had rooted for the Rangers growing up, so this would be a dream come true for him. While being a Ranger's fan hadn't been easy, with some highs and lots of lows, he was still a diehard fan. The 2024 playoffs, where he watched them make their magical run to the Stanley Cup quarterfinals, held a fond memory in his heart and was why he chose that year to go back to for his simulation. Mike had gone to Game 2 of quarterfinals against the Florida Panthers, where the Rangers won in overtime. It was one of the singular greatest memories of Mike's life.

While the Rangers eventually lost to the Panthers, he always remembered that experience back at MSG.

Mike was also excited to prove that he had *it*—something special that would have propelled him to the greatness he believed he had inside him, before his career was cut short by multiple torn ligaments.

During his intake, Mike had asked if they could project his skill level as if he had never been injured. Luckily, they could based on his stats and rankings in high school compared to the quality of the competition and other factors.

So, this simulation was a big deal for him. In real life, he had spent months skating and getting his skills back, just in case it helped somehow.

While the simulation would provide a new body for him, he would still need to adapt to the faster pace of NHL players, who would be moving twice as fast as the high school players he last competed against. His decisions would need to be quick and they would need to be smart.

As Mike stared out the window of the simulation facility, he realized it had been over two decades since he last felt this positive about his life and excited for his future. With all the ups and downs over the years, he felt he was finally in a good place, and it wasn't just because the government was throwing extra cash at him to help him buy diapers.

▼▼▼

Positivity had always been something that was hard to come by. As the leader of Mike's AA group always told him: "There is an island of opportunity in the middle of every difficulty."

He loved that phrase, and he used it when he found out Stacy was pregnant. The old Mike would have stayed angry and broken ties with her. However, the new Mike took time to process his feelings and eventually realized that this was a blessing and that he would be fortunate to be a dad given the way his life had gone. Having a baby felt like he got a second chance at life, and he wanted to take advantage of that. That meant continuing to stay sober and focusing on his mental health so he could be the best dad possible.

Looking back on his life, it was easy to explain why positivity had been hard to come by recently.

When Mike was younger, he dedicated himself to becoming a skilled hockey player, training everyday, dedicating himself to practices four to five times a week and waking up at 5:15 most Saturday mornings to get to a weekend tournament when his friends were still sleeping from partying the night before.

He had done everything he was told to do to achieve his dream of playing in the National Hockey League.

That dream was shattered when he heard the first pop in his left knee during his junior year of high school. Initially, he wasn't sure what it was. He hoped it was just a sprain, but when it was diagnosed as an ACL tear, he tried to remain positive. His doctors assured him that hockey players recover from ACL injuries all the time. Mike was still young, and while rehab would be a bitch, the doctors were all telling him he could make a full recovery and play again.

So, Mike continuously put in hours and hours at the gym to rehab—two hours before school and an hour after—to get better as quickly as possible. Eventually, he was back on the ice skating, which felt incredible. Although he didn't return to games until midway through his senior year, the hard work was worth it to get back to playing the game he loved.

Mike had regained his speed and agility, scoring goals at a rate close to what he was before the injury. It felt like his NHL dream was back on track.

That is, until a freak divot in the ice during the state championship game caught his right knee in the worst possible way. When he heard the pop this time, he knew exactly what it was.

The following weeks were some of the worst of Mike's life. He had multiple doctor visits to get opinions, but at the end of the day, he knew he didn't have it in him to go through the rehab again.

The doctors told him he would likely lose some of his speed and agility, which would make it tough for him to get back to the way he played before the injuries. Even if he did recover, and it was a big if, he would miss nearly two years of exposure to professional scouts. It was a hard decision, but ultimately, Mike chose to end his dream of playing professional hockey.

It was a decision that Mike took hard and unfortunately, alcohol, drugs, and depression followed, derailing any chance of short-term happiness in his life. In fact, they nearly killed him.

▼ ▼ ▼

His stomach growling snapped him out of his daydream. He was hungry, given he hadn't eaten anything since the group dinner.

"Man, I hope I get some good fucking breakfast in my simulation to make up for this. He should be able to afford one," he muttered to himself.

Finally, a male nurse stepped through the double doors and called his name, inviting him back into the larger hallway structure.

After walking in silence down several long corridors and making a few turns, they arrived at room 185. It was a small and chilly room, furnished with tables, a chair, some equipment he didn't recognize, and an IV cart with a monitor and other computer screens scattered throughout the room.

"*Impressive,*" Mike thought.

The nurse broke his silence. "Hello, sir, I'm Charles. I'll be setting you up this morning. Please remove your shoes, put your personal effects in that locker, and sit in the chair. We'll go through a few details and confirm your simulation with you."

"Alrighty," Mike said. This guy was very military-like, so Mike did what he was told, as he just wanted to get to it.

Over the next several minutes, Charles introduced Stuart, the robotic assistant, and went through the questions to confirm the details of the simulation, which was taking place on June 13, 2024 in New York City and would start at 9 am and continue for 24 hours.

Charles explained the rules regarding his and the character's memories, skipping ahead and ending early, the procedure in case of a real-life emergency, and how Mike could continue the simulation even if he died, which seemed a highly unlikely scenario. He also noted that Mike could end the simulation at the end of his game without penalty.

The weirdest thing would be the lack of fluids emanating from his body, which meant no pissing, shitting, or sweating. Weird.

"Okay, any questions?" Charles finally asked.

"Uh, that's a lot, but I think I'm good. Hopefully, I don't get cross-checked into the boards and end up with a concussion. But good to know I can end it early if it gets too painful," Mike said, laughing to himself.

"I'm sure you'll be fine, sir. I need to confirm if you plan to go beyond your experience's parameters, like flying out of New York City to see Las Vegas as a star NHL player. That's something we need to know, as it would be outside of the developed simulation. If you want to do that, it would be an extra add-on you'd need to pay for." Charles paused, noticing Mike's confused expression.

"No, man," Mike said with a laugh. "Why the hell would I want to do that?"

Charles chuckled. "I have no idea, sir. They make me confirm that. I wouldn't do that either." He continued laughing.

"Are you ready to get started?" Charles asked, setting down the tablet and opening a box containing a red and yellow cylindrical ring.

Charles placed the ring around Mike's head and moved to the computer to load it up.

Mike was nervous, excited, and curious about what he was about to experience. He had recently played recreational hockey with guys his age, but this would be a totally different experience.

This would be intensity to the max, with adrenaline and emotions running as high as any professional athlete would ever experience. He hoped that whoever created the simulation was a Rangers' fan too.

"Okay, Mike, we're ready to begin," Charles said, interrupting his thoughts. "We'll start the sedation drip shortly, and you'll hear a low hum as the ring powers on. As the ring interacts and maps out your neural network, you might feel tingling in your head, fingers, and toes—that's normal. You'll also feel warmth in your arms and chest as the sedation takes effect. You'll drift off soon after, and we'll see you when you wake up. You good?"

"All set!" Mike said, excited. "Just ready to score a goal."

"I'm sure you will, man," Charles said, giving him a nod. "Good luck in there. I will stay with you for a few minutes after your simulation begins." He returned to do whatever he did to get this started.

The last thing Mike heard before everything went black was Charles whistling some familiar tune.

▼▼▼

JUNE 13, 2024 - 9 A.M.

The first thing Mike felt was pain—everywhere. Did Charles sit on him? What the fuck?

Ow! His shoulders, back, right foot, and left hand throbbed. Was he dying? Had the simulation started, or had the sedation gone terribly wrong?

Mike wiggled his toes and fingers, then slowly lifted his head. It felt like he was in a bed, which was confirmed when he grabbed a few pillows behind him. It was like waking up from the worst hangover of his life, and he'd had plenty of those to compare to.

Wherever he was, it was dark but there was the sound of a waterfall playing softly to his right, probably from a sound machine.

Mike sat up and let his eyes slowly adjust to the room. A large television, at least 70 inches, was mounted in front of him. To the right, he saw an open door leading to what seemed like a bathroom. To the left, he could make out the shape of a dresser with dark pictures hanging around it. Drapes covered the half-dozen windows lining the entire left side of the bedroom.

God almighty, this pain. He hoped it wouldn't last throughout the experience. "*They better have some good drugs here,*" he thought.

Finally, as his eyes were fully adjusted, he caught a whiff of something. Was that bacon? Eggs? Good lord, he was hungry, and that sure as fuck smelled delicious.

While he was thinking about the food, the bedroom door cracked open. A voice called out, "Honey, you up? You there?" The door opened wider, and a blonde, easily a nine, walked in wearing pajamas that accentuated her ample cleavage and perfect ass. She sat on the bed next to him and kissed his forehead.

Okay, this certainly wasn't the world with Charles. This was a much better world.

"Hi babe. I know you asked me to wake you up around 8:30 a.m., but you seemed to be tossing and turning last night. I wanted to let you sleep a little longer. I can only imagine what was going through your head, but I thought you might need the extra rest. Hope that's okay." The lovely lady smiled warmly.

Mike was speechless. She was beautiful. Breathtaking, really. She had to be a former model or an athlete.

"Oh, that's fine. I wanted to get in the hot tub for a bit," Mike said, noticing his voice sounded younger and deeper. As he became more alert and his "brain" started to fully function, he realized he could have sex with this fine simulated specimen—an opportunity he was *not* going to waste.

If he wasn't going to score in the game later, he was certainly going to score now.

He ran his fingers through her hair and couldn't help but think how real and lifelike it felt. When he pressed his palm against her cheeks, the skin felt like real skin. She even smelled like flowers at this hour of the morning.

"How the fuck did they do this?" Mike asked out loud.

"What do you mean?" She responded, her brows furrowed.

"Ha." Mike chuckled as he had to think quickly on his feet. "How did the gods create such a perfect specimen as you?" Damn, he was good.

Eileen smiled widely.

"*Is her name is Eileen?*" Mike thought to himself. How would he know that? Maybe it was part of the discussion with Charles ten minutes earlier about him knowing his character's memories. Still weird.

He snapped back to "reality" as he felt the warm embrace of her lips on his. They felt amazing.

This was pure passion—like her tongue had nowhere else to be but deep in his mouth. Wow, he could get used to this.

"Robby's still asleep. How about we take your mind off the game tonight?" Eileen asked, nibbling his ear. Mike felt his eyes roll back in pleasure.

"Uh, if you keep this up, I might not make it to the game," Mike murmured.

Mike looked down and saw his boxers pitching a rather large tent. "Well, I guess that works," he said out loud again.

"*This dude must have slayed in college,*" he thought, realizing that if he had more time, he'd dig through this guy's memories to see who he had fucked in the past.

"It better work," Eileen said as she put her hand on his erect penis.

Mike flipped Eileen onto her back on the bed. Given her short shorts, it was fairly easy to slip them off to expose her panties.

As he slid two fingers into her, he kissed her ear right back, making her moan loudly as her head tilted back slightly. God, she was ready for him.

She turned and kissed him deeply, stopping to say, "I want you inside me now..." Well, that was one request he wouldn't say no to.

As he took off his pants, she removed her panties and shirt, revealing the nicest pair of breasts he had ever seen. After his simulation, he made a mental note to write the government a 'thank you' note. She was tan, with a hint of a six-pack under just a little belly—which made sense since he knew they had a newborn in the other room. Her legs were tan and tight, and her toenails were painted a perfect shade of pink.

"*My god,*" Mike thought. He would do this simulation every year if this was what he got to see.

As she lay on the bed, fully naked now, he began kissing the inside of her right thigh, then the left, making his way with his tongue to her vagina and pleasuring her. She let out a loud moan, her hands grabbing the back of his head.

"Oh my god, Nate, don't stop," she managed to say as she moaned more.

"*Who the fuck is Nate?*" Mike thought. "*Has she been cheating on me? What kind of fucked up place is this?*" He paused before realizing that Nate was his simulated name. Jesus, he was slow. He couldn't help but laugh as he stopped pleasuring Eileen.

"What the hell are you laughing at? Why did you stop?" Eileen asked between heavy breaths.

"*Yikes, you better think quick again,*" Mike thought.

"Sorry, hun, I was just remembering the time I was doing this same thing to you at your dad's beach house, and the housekeeper walked in on us as you were spread-eagle on the couch. Sorry, I don't know why that came to me."

"*Wow, that actually happened,*" Mike thought to himself. Good for this guy.

"Oh my god! I forgot about that." Eileen laughed, covering her mouth. "I couldn't look my dad in the eye for most of that trip because I assumed Eva told him. To this day, I have no idea if my dad knows or not." She kept laughing. "You're the worst. Come here." She grabbed his face, bringing it to her mouth, and kissed him deeply.

As he was now fully erect, he spread her legs and entered her, drawing a deep moan from Eileen. He was grateful to be 28 again.

▼ ▼ ▼

9:15 A.M.

Luckily, Nate finished about five minutes before Robby, their now-four-month-old, awoke from his slumber.

Mike was curious to see him, so he excitedly ran to grab him from his crib, noting it could have also been Nate's excitement.

Damn, Robby was adorable—not surprising, given how Nate and Eileen looked.

In the bathroom, shortly after he felt like he had come, Mike had gotten a good look at Nate's naked body, which he was renting for the next 24 hours.

Mike would have sex with Nate. He looked like a GQ model, 5'11" or 6', with a lean, muscular body, veiny arms, a well-defined six-pack, a nice ass, and well endowed. His face wasn't much worse, with light hazel eyes, long dark brown hair, and a decent playoff beard. All he needed was an ax and a U-boat, and he would be a Viking.

Robby had deep blue eyes, blond hair, and fair skin. He was wrapped in the most adorable pajamas and lay right on Nate's naked chest as they walked around the apartment together.

Robby was so tiny and light that Mike was afraid he would forget he was carrying something and drop him. However, Mike managed to walk around the stunning apartment for the next 20 minutes without dropping him.

He showed Robby all the buildings and simulated people about 20 or 30 stories down below in midtown Manhattan.

Mike decided to use this time as a practice run for being responsible for a little human being. So, he offered to change Robby's diaper, which, judging by the smell, housed a natural disaster.

As it turned out, it was far worse than that. It looked like some mixture of spinach, hamburger, and chocolate mousse had combined to plant a bomb in the middle of Robby's diaper, which then proceeded to set off another bomb in the lower half of Robby's back. And the smell—god, the *smell*. Mike wondered why they couldn't give him a simulated character with a broken nose. At least he wouldn't be able to smell this.

Mike began cleaning the remnants of the explosion from Robby's belly, legs, back, and somehow, fingers. He didn't want to know how it got there. In 2032, from what he understood, robotic nannies usually handled this "dirty" work, but given they needed to recharge occasionally, there were times that parents had to step in to change a diaper or two. It was awful. *This* was awful.

After 15 minutes of cleanup and diaper replacement, he brought Robby back to the kitchen, where Eileen was waiting for them both with a big smile.

"Alright, hun, he's all cleaned up—that was fucking nasty." He laughed as he kissed Eileen and handed Robby to her. "I'll get showered and cleaned up and be out for breakfast in 20. I want to get in early for treatment and sit in the hot tub—every little bit helps, you know?"

"I know, honey. You'll be great tonight, and we're here to support you, win or lose. But I *know* it will be a win. I feel it in my heart, okay?

Go do what you need to. I took care of business in the bedroom. You take care of business at the rink. I'll have breakfast waiting for you."

"*Goddamn, this could be the most perfect woman that's ever existed, even if she doesn't actually exist,*" Mike thought. He smiled, kissed Eileen on the forehead, and headed to the shower to wake him up a bit.

His shower was beautiful, with some sort of waterfall setup, a sit-down bench, and an indoor sauna next to the shower. "*They say money can't buy happiness, but it sure can relax the shit out of you,*" Mike thought.

After showering, brushing his teeth, and dressing, he grabbed his bag for the arena. It included deodorant, headphones, some creams for treatment, his favorite gum, and some underwear that he knew was Nate's lucky pair since high school. Mike could only pray that it had been washed at some point, and from the smell of it, it had. So he was fine bringing it with him. Still, kinda gross.

He went to the kitchen and to the smell of eggs, turkey bacon, and toast. Eileen was preparing a plate while Robby, in his highchair, played with his food, his face clearly saying: *Fuck you and fuck your vegetables! I want applesauce!*

This could be the start of the most perfect day in history. Mike sat down at the kitchen counter to have his breakfast.

"I don't blame you, mate. That looks nasty, but you gotta eat it," Mike said as Nate took the spoon from Robby's hand and put it in his mouth. "Open up, buddy…"

"Nate, honey, I'll deal with that—you eat your food so you can get going. The more treatment time you have, the better." Eileen took the spoon from him.

"You're too good to me," Mike said as Nate kissed her again.

"Bring home a Stanley Cup, and we'll call it even," she responded, winking and getting Robby some milk from the refrigerator.

"I'll see what I can do. Whatever happens, I still have you two to come home to, and that's better than a Stanley Cup." Mike took a bite as Eileen laughed.

"You fucking cheeseball. Even I can admit that winning the Stanley Cup is probably the best thing that will ever happen to you. Other than marrying me, of course," she said with a smile.

"Well, I'm not getting ahead of myself. I'll do what I can to be as ready as possible and focus on playing a smart game and not make any bonehead plays that cost us the win. I just want to go out there and give everything I have to say I left it all on the table.

But goddamn, I'm hurting today. How I fell into the boards last game really did a number on my shoulders and lower back. The machine they gave me helped some, but I need to loosen it up before the game. Hopefully, it doesn't cramp up, but I'll see how I feel in warmups." Mike finished his toast. Damn, that was a good egg-white omelet.

Mike's exes never had cooking skills other than the occasional casserole or Thanksgiving turkey. Although, given the advances in food technology in 2032, not many people took the time to cook as good food was readily available to warm up in minutes.

Nothing beats a good omelet, though, and Mike was ready to head out to the arena for his treatment. Nate said goodbye to Eileen and Robby, telling them he'd see them in a few hours.

As their apartment elevator opened—yep, Nate had an elevator in his damn apartment—he and Eileen stood in the doorway. They kissed, a tradition from Nate's college days at the University of Michigan, where he played collegiate hockey for two years before turning pro in his junior year.

"*How cheesy,*" Mike thought, but he played along if it gave him another chance to kiss Eileen.

As he entered the elevator, he felt this would be a good day—even if the Rangers lost—and that being able to get back out on the ice and play professional hockey would be enough for him to enjoy the experience.

▼▼▼

10:15 A.M.

Two minutes later, Mike was in the lobby of his New York City apartment building, Sky Tower, as confirmed by the big sign in the lobby. He stepped outside, finding himself at the corner of 42nd Street and 10th Ave—better known as Hell's Kitchen.

He stopped for a moment to feel the breeze on his face and take in the sights and sounds of New York City. It was a beautiful day for some hockey.

Mike couldn't believe the level of detail around him. Taxis, trucks, cars, and bikes bustled by. Trees, birds, flowers, and plants were scattered on the street in front of him. All sorts of people hurried past him, as if he were actually in New York City.

There were buildings in the distance, as clear as day. He looked down on the pavement and saw cockroaches on the friggin' sidewalk. This was an amazing replication of the city.

"My god, just unbelievable," Mike said quietly, taking a deep breath and smelling everything he would expect to smell in New York City. The good, the bad, and the truck exhaust.

One guy passing by stopped to say, "Good luck, Nate," and asked to shake his hand, which Mike was happy to do. He was going to soak this up because, in 24 hours, he could walk through the middle of the real Times Square and not a soul would recognize him.

Mike had been to New York City a few times, mostly with his family, and was always amazed at the hustle and bustle and the organized chaos that seemed to envelop the city. This was pretty close to what he remembered in real life.

He noticed a man in a dark coat and hat at the side of the street, standing next to a black SUV and waving at him as if to say: *You ready?*

Mike waved back and headed towards the car. "Good morning, Mr. Thompson," the driver said, opening his door.

"Good morning, Felix," Mike responded as Nate, again somehow knowing this guy's name.

Nate Thompson, huh? It was as good of a hockey name as he would have come up with.

Mike sat in the back seat as his bag was loaded into the trunk. Within 30 seconds, they were en route to Madison Square Garden, which, according to the car's GPS, would take approximately 13 minutes—not a bad commute. Mike assumed that this commute would be far different during a weekday rush hour, but on a Saturday morning, not too many people were out yet.

▼ ▼ ▼

As they drove south down 11th Ave, Mike thought about his best memory of New York: when his family visited for Christmas when he was ten, a couple of years before his parents divorced.

They had visited all the usual touristy spots—Times Square, Broadway, and Central Park—but the thing that Mike remembered most was when his dad brought him, his brothers and his sister to Bryant Park to ice skate outside.

The weather was chilly, but not terrible and the rink was relatively empty. As his brothers and sister were either too young or too tired to skate, Mike skated around the rink for probably close to 30 minutes alone with his dad—just the two of them. They had a view of the Chrysler Building on one end of the rink and the Empire State Building on the other. It was an amazing experience for him at the time.

He and his dad skated around the rink just talking, mostly about what he wanted to be when he grew up (a hockey player, of course), if he liked any girls at school (he didn't), and how he needed to be a good brother growing up and take care of his little brothers and sister.

It was a great time spent with his dad and was one of the last good memories he had of his family, as his parents' relationship went sour shortly after that. Two years later, when Mike was 12, they divorced.

Mike took the divorce hard, retreating into his hockey life and going to as many practices and games as possible to take his mind off it. His dad supported him, which he appreciated because it helped them stay close those years after the divorce.

As tough as he was, his dad always encouraged Mike's dream of playing professional hockey and wanted him to be happy.

Even though they grew apart after Mike moved to New York and dealt with his own demons, Mike knew his dad loved him and wanted him to live a good life. But most importantly, his dad wanted him to be happy. Getting sober helped him to realize that.

Mike really missed his father, even four years after his death from pancreatic cancer.

▼ ▼ ▼

Back in the present, Mike was snapped out of his trip down memory lane by Felix's voice. "You ready for tonight, Mr. Thompson?"

"I don't know, Felix. Can you ever really be ready? It's like me asking if you're ready to sit through an hour's worth of traffic tonight. Are you ever really ready? No, but you do your best to prepare emotionally and physically and hope you're still good on the other end. You know?" Mike asked.

"That's a great way to put it, sir," Felix said, nodding in agreement.

"Don't call me sir. Call me Nate. But whatever you do, don't call me Mike." Mike chuckled to himself on that one.

"Okay... you got it, Nate," Felix replied slowly, a bit confused. "Either way, I'll be rooting for you tonight."

"Thank you, Felix. I wanna hear you scream from wherever you're watching or listening tonight. Deal?"

"Deal, Nate. You'll hear me for sure. I'll be at my mom's in Brooklyn, but I'll be watching, don't you worry." Felix chuckled before cursing out a taxi driver for almost hitting their SUV.

"*Gotta love New York,*" Mike thought as he laughed.

▼▼▼

10:36 A.M.

A few minutes later, they arrived at the players' entrance to Madison Square Garden, where Dave, his personal trainer, was scheduled to meet him.

After the last game, when Nate got crushed into the boards late in the game, Dave suggested a two day whole-body cryotherapy session to aid the healing process. Since Nate seemed to be a general mess with lower back pain, cuts on his face, and a bruised rib, Mike was more than happy to come in early to do this.

The thing about Game 7 of the Stanley Cup Finals was that, unless you were physically unable to move your limbs, you were playing. Nothing would stop most players from suiting up unless they determined that playing would be detrimental to the team. At this point, it was about being as healthy as you could right before the puck dropped.

Mike recalled that Dave's plan for today was going to be pretty intense: first there would be treatment, which consisted of a three-minute cryotherapy session followed by a 15-minute sauna session, another three-minute cryotherapy session, and then a final ten-minute sauna session.

Then, he would move on to a 30-minute massage and full-body stretching, followed by a hot shower. All of this had to be done before a 12:30 p.m. meeting with coaches and players to go over video and talk about the strategy for tonight's game before the players went home for a few hours to rest and eat.

As Mike stood outside Madison Square Garden, he could only imagine what it must be like to do this for a career. For professional hockey players, the arena was where they sacrificed their bodies for the sake of their team and a win, all for the ultimate dream of lifting a 37-pound cup of silver and nickel alloy overhead and kissing it with tears streaming down their face.

Mike entered the underbelly of the building, feeling nerves, excitement, pain, anticipation, and probably a handful more emotions he couldn't identify. He was ready to get in and start his morning.

By this point, he wasn't surprised that he knew exactly where to go, although he was still getting used to having two brains and memories inside of him. It was pretty surreal to be walking through Madison Square Garden.

When he reached the locker room, it was more beautiful than he had imagined. The large logo on the floor, the wood-paneled lockers with player jerseys hung up in each, the equipment laid out above the jerseys, and the massive hockey board at the front of the room—it was jaw-dropping.

Pictures of some NY Rangers greats, like Mark Messier, Bryan Leetch, Adam Graves, and Wayne Gretzky, were hung on the walls.

Mike could only imagine walking into this room and knowing it was his home, his sanctuary, where he was most at peace. For him, the locker room was always a place to find his "zen" moment before the game. It was also a place where victories were celebrated, and losses contemplated.

For Mike, seeing a sanctuary like this was humbling. The one thing he missed the most was the feeling of walking into the locker room, seeing his teammates, and knowing they all had a common goal: winning.

That feeling of belonging to something bigger than himself and togetherness only came from playing on a team. Maybe having a child would change that; he hoped it would.

The training room was adjacent to the locker room, where the players could utilize the hot tub, cryo-chamber, and other tables and equipment.

Mike undressed and prepared to enter the cryo-chamber tank for his three-minute session. He had taken ice baths in high school but assumed this would be different. In fact, he knew it would be different because he had distinct memories of Nate doing it. He knew how cold it was going to be.

"*Holy shit, this is going to be cold,*" Mike thought. Or maybe it was Nate. He couldn't tell at this point. He took a deep breath and entered the tank.

"*Holy fucking shit, this is cold!*" Everything in Mike and Nate's body went cold instantly. "Oh my god—this is insane," Nate said out loud.

It was easily the most intense feeling Mike had ever had, and he tore two ACLs. This cold was instant, throughout his body, and directly into whatever soul was in him at the moment.

Mike concentrated on his thoughts: "*Okay, you're good here. Just take deep breaths and think about holding that Stanley Cup in your hands, kissing it, and then handing it to your teammates, all in the heart of Madison Square Garden. Holy fuck, holy fuck...*"

Breathing helped, but only a little. *Ninety seconds to go.* He closed his eyes and thought about Eileen waiting for him at their apartment in Hell's Kitchen. He remembered her smell this morning, how she felt when he was inside her, and how she kissed him. Goddamn, Nate was a lucky dude.

"Time!" Dave interrupted those lovely thoughts of Eileen and helped Mike out of the tank with a towel. Before he could catch his breath, Dave was escorting him to the infrared sauna down the hallway.

"Okay, Nate, 15 minutes in here, please. Here are your headphones. I put them on your favorite station, so enjoy it there. I'll be here when you finish."

Mike and Nate were too cold to respond. Mike took the headphones and put them on.

Apparently, Nate loved hip hop—not Mike's favorite—but at this point, listening to anything in the warm sauna was better than the cold he just experienced.

As he sat in the sauna, Mike thought about how lucky he was to be able to do this. At what other time in humanity could he pretend to be a stud NHL player with a hot wife and a newborn, playing Game 7 of the Stanley Cup Finals at Madison Square Garden?

▼▼▼

Lost in his own head in the sauna, Mike still couldn't believe he was about to be a dad. After years of suffering through depression and alcoholism, he considered himself lucky to be alive. It took him many years to find meaning in a life that was he was hoping would be filled with athletic achievements.

While he tried to find that meaning in his relationships, job, and family, nothing did the trick. Up until about two years ago, the only thing that made him happy was alcohol. And lots of it. Now that he reflected on it, alcohol never really made him happy; it only numbed the pain and the feeling of emptiness he always carried with him.

However, the day Mike learned he would be a dad, something changed in him. It was as if all his suffering had brought him to this point and he was okay with that.

At first, he didn't know what to think. Of course, with him and his ex being separated, it wasn't ideal, but he had faith they would make it work as friends or otherwise and make this kid's life phenomenal.

So, he prepared to be a dad. Mike read all kinds of stupid books and watched videos on how to be a dad, from burping a baby to giving them a bath and how to properly install their car seat. He hadn't yet gotten to the diaper-changing videos, but after this morning, he was fine skipping them.

He had no idea what kind of dad he would be, but he was certainly going to try to do everything for his daughter to ensure she had the best life possible and live up to the type of dad his father was.

▼▼▼

The 15 minutes in the sauna went by quickly, but he felt revitalized as he walked back to the cryotherapy tank for another three minutes of icy hell, followed by another ten minutes in the sauna.

By the time Mike got to the massage table, Nate's body craved stable temperatures and a good massage. Mike had started getting massages regularly about a year ago and regretted not starting sooner—they were amazing.

He lay on the table, stomach down, as Dave prepared warm oil for the massage. As Dave worked on his upper left thigh, Mike couldn't believe how good this felt. It was as if this guy knew exactly where to press, how much pressure to apply, and how long to rub.

Dave moved to the right thigh, then to the lower buttocks, at which point Mike was pretty sure he was getting a small erection, but he couldn't care less.

Dave reapplied some oil and focused on the lower back, where Nate had been injured in the last game.

"*Goddamn.*" That was all Mike could think.

"How does that feel?" Dave finally asked after digging into his back for five minutes.

"Put it this way: I've felt better," Mike responded as Nate. "Just get me good enough to get through 60 minutes tonight, and I'll buy you a steak dinner at Peter Luger's next weekend, win or lose."

Dave laughed. "It's a deal, but I feel good about tonight. You were awesome in the last game, even though the result wasn't what you all wanted. You'll bring the cup home to New York tonight, Nate. But first, let's get this knot out of your upper back. Hold on."

He walked away to get a massage gun and after a minute, he returned and applied it to Nate's upper back for the next five minutes, then to his lower back for another five. Finally, he focused on both upper thighs, which hurt like a motherfucker.

Mike had enough. "Okay, I love you, man, but if you don't stop soon, I'm going to knee you in the balls." He laughed as he got off the table and prepared for his stretching session with Dave.

▼▼▼

12:15 P.M.

Twenty minutes later, after a good session with Dave, Mike was in the shower cleaning up and getting ready for the 12:30 p.m. video meeting with the coaches.

Most players were already there; some had also received treatment, while others came in right for the video session. His locker neighbor, Johan Hedelberg, had just arrived and greeted him as Mike got out of the shower.

"Hey, Nate, how's your back feeling? You looked like shit yesterday."

"Yeah, man, it was hurting pretty bad—fucking Pullock. He was still mad that I popped him good in that fight earlier this season. Fucker should have gotten a game misconduct for that. At least we scored on the powerplay. Hopefully, Dave got me back on track with all the shit we did this morning.

I'll be fine; nothing's stopping me from playing tonight. I'll tell you that much."

Mike looked at Johan, a 6'2" defenseman with a rock-solid body of pure muscle. He was what those in the business called a "stay-at-home defenseman." The guy probably had ten goals in his ten-year career. Still, he was always in position, and very few players could knock him down. You knew you were in good hands with him on the ice.

"You nervous for tonight?" Mike asked, hoping for some deep knowledge from the wily veteran.

"Nah, it's just another game," Johan replied with a smile, revealing at least four missing teeth and a cut above his upper lip. This guy was a dentist's wet dream.

"Yeah, just another game, right," Mike said, grinning. At least he had all his teeth—or so he thought he did. Maybe not. He'd have to check later.

"Your family here tonight?" Johan asked while Mike started to dress.

"Eileen will come with my parents but we're leaving Robby at home with the babysitter. You?" Mike asked back.

"Yeah—my entire family flew in for tonight's game—my mom hates flying but she took the trip all the way from Sweden to be here. It's nuts." Johan said with a huge smile.

"This is the game of our lives my friend. Let's get ready." Mike said as he put his shirt on.

Mike had just finished dressing when captain Zach Stevens called the team into the adjacent video room, where the coaches were waiting.

Through Nate's memories, the prior game against the Oilers wasn't close. The Oilers were up 2-0 after the first period and 3-1 after the second. The Oilers won 5-2 after scoring an empty-net goal in the final minute.

The players weren't expecting a beatdown from their coach, Gary Donaldson, but they knew they had to be better, especially in the defensive zone. If a team gets up on you by multiple goals after the first period, they'll be hard to beat, especially in the Stanley Cup Finals.

Mike settled into Nate's seat next to his linemates: center Dylan Gustaffson, the Swedish star who joined the league four years ago and exploded onto the scene, and Jeremy DeBois, a fifth-year right winger who was the fastest guy on the team and was a natural goal scorer. They usually played on the second line and received some power play time on the second unit.

In front of Mike, Zach Stevens, the Captain and left winger, sat with center Nico Woods, a third-year center who had blossomed this year and was in the Conn Smythe Trophy hunt for the Most Valuable Player for the playoffs, and right winger Olaf Cheradofsky, a lanky Russian-born player who could do it all—score, assist, fight. He was the ultimate hockey player.

To the right of Nate's line sat the third line, led by right-wing Dougie Green, a veteran winger who was injured for most of the year but turned it on during the playoffs, scoring five goals in this series alone. They were relying on him for his leadership. Dougie was joined by left-wing Nick Stolsky, another veteran who was a net-front presence, especially on the power play, and center Adam Right, a fourth-year player who could do it all and was a candidate for the best all-around center in the league this year.

Behind Mike sat the fourth line: center Mike Stillman, a rugged veteran, right-wing Tyler Gruen, a solid overall player who chipped in quality minutes, and left-wing Martin Brady, a rookie.

To the right of them sat the defensemen: Johan with his partner Collin Macfarlane, both bringing a veteran presence to the blue line. Bruce McPherson and his defensive partner, Kenny Matthews, joined them along with smooth-skating rookie Nick Plechton and hard-hitting defenseman Adam Wolf.

Goalie Vladimir Pantelov, known as "Vlad the Destroyer," was in his usual spot in the front row. Vlad had been the team's rock in net this year. He had an off night last game, so they all knew he had to be better this game to have a chance.

Other reserve and injured teammates and coaches trickled in and took their seats as the team's general manager, Tom Forster, and head coach, Gary Donaldson, walked into the room.

"Alright, guys, please settle down and take your seats," Coach Donaldson began, waiting for the rest of the players to quiet down. "Everyone good? Great. Before we start with a quick review of the last game, Tom has a few words about tonight's game. Tom?"

Coach stepped aside, and Mr. Forster moved to the center of the room to address the players.

"Alright, guys, good morning. How did everyone sleep? Like shit? Me too." The room filled with chuckles.

"I know we're all nervous about tonight. The coaches, trainers, and certainly my staff and I. I'm sure you and your family and friends are nervous for you guys as well.

For those of you who have gotten married or have had kids, tonight will certainly rival those experiences for the most emotional night of your lives. If we win, it could be the best night of your lives—just don't tell your wives or kids that." He paused, letting a few more chuckles die down.

"But seriously, this is the moment you've all been dreaming about since you put your first skates on when you were five or six years old. You've likely dreamed of this all through high school, college, major juniors, and all the way through your time in the NHL. Like me, I know you all have thought about hoisting that beautiful cup, raising it above your head, kissing it, and skating around with it in front of your friends, family, and thousands of fans who will be here later today.

I say this with all my heart: No matter what happens tonight, it's been an honor to watch you all grow, develop, and come together as a team this year. No one thought we'd make the playoffs this year, let alone reach the Stanley Cup finals. The fact that you have taken the Oilers to Game 7 is a feat that should be celebrated and remembered. We're fucking proud of everyone in this locker room: the coaches, training staff, and everyone else in the organization who got us here."

Mr. Foster had to pause as he was getting emotional.

"As you can probably tell, I'm a bit emotional. Having played in a Game 7 myself, I know the emotions that take over before, during, and after the game. All I ask is that you take care of yourself today—eat right, nap, get here early, and get mentally prepared for the game of your lives, as you might never play in another Game 7.

With that said, I have full faith in everyone on this team that we can win this game tonight. If we stick to the system, play within our abilities, trust each other, and give everything we have tonight, we can win. Let's play smart, disciplined, and tough. If we do that, win or lose, you'll be able to look in the mirror and you'll be able to look at your teammate and say you did everything in your power to win the Stanley Cup. Alright, gentleman?

I'll return you to your coach now. See you later during pre-game warmups. Gary?"

Tom sat down, and Mike thought it was a pretty good speech—short, to the point, and pretty motivational.

Coach Donaldson resumed. "Alright, boys, Tom summed up a lot of what I wanted to say. I have played in a Game 7 myself and I know what you all are going through. Let's minimize outside distractions so we can focus on the task at hand tonight, control what we can control and get your mind and your bodies as ready as possible for tonight.

We all know the last game got away from us early. We took a couple of undisciplined penalties in the first period, and they capitalized on both. Once they were up 2-0, they locked down, clogged the neutral zone, and shut down our speed. They outshot us almost 2-1, and we just seemed to give up after the end of the second period. That's unacceptable, and I expect to fix it tonight.

Defense: We have to do a better job clearing the zone on 5 and 5. We got trapped too often in the second period on long shifts because we couldn't clear the zone. I don't care what you have to do tonight—get the puck out of the zone to give us a chance at a line change. If you have to take an icing, do it.

Offense: We need to be more flexible with our rushes. If you see them setting up a wall at the blue line, dump and chase. Too often, we tried to get cute with our passes, and they intercepted them and went the other way. Use our speed, but use it wisely. Make sure our passes are tape-to-tape out of the D zone, and if we have to dump in, do it. I'd rather do that than be cute and risk a stupid pass."

Somehow Mike knew that was a reference to a dumb pass Nate made last game. He would need to be more careful with that tonight.

Coach continued, "We need to be smart, gentlemen. Let's not take stupid penalties again, especially in our zone; there is zero need for it. Keep your sticks down, hold up if a player is against the boards, and, for the love of God, watch the hooking calls.

Vlad, the last game was a fluke. Let's get back in the zone and ensure you're seeing and anticipating well, as you did in Game 5.

Power play: Not too many opportunities last game, but your movement was great in Game 5 with Nick on point—so we'll keep that the same. Nate, I'll use you on the first power play to get another left-handed shot. Be ready to contribute."

"*Cool*," Mike thought. A chance on the first power play—he'd take it.

"Penalty kill: You did a decent job last game, but we need to attack the pointmen better. We gave them too much leeway to get set up and dictate their passes. Be aggressive and trust your D and goalie to come up big when needed. I don't want them getting set up and controlling the zone as much as they did last game. It didn't serve us well.

Let's communicate out there. It was way too quiet last game, especially after we went down. Forwards, talk to our D; D, talk to our forwards; and Vlad, I want you talking to everyone. If you see something we're missing, let us know, and we'll get the message across.

Remember, they had the home advantage last game with that thinner air in Edmonton. They don't have that here, so they'll get winded more easily. Let's exploit that and take it to them in the first period. We are 3-0 when we score first in this series; let's get that first goal and play our game, not theirs. Coach Bryce will take you through video from the last game. We'll regroup here at 5 p.m. for our meal and pregame warmups. Any questions?"

Coach Donaldson looked around the room, and Johan raised his hand.

"Coach, given you've played in Game 7, any superstitions you can suggest we follow?" Johan asked, laughing along with most of the room.

"Well, son, if you want me to say 'Don't shower' or 'Wear your dirtiest jockstrap', I won't. But let's just say I smelled *pretty* bad after our Game 7 victory. Needless to say, no one cared that much." Coach laughed briefly before continuing, "Okay, guys, please be here by 4:30 p.m. for the meal, with warmups at 7. See you then."

The head coach exited the room, leaving the other coaches to take over for the next 30 minutes, which were spent watching and re-watching more segments from the last game.

Mike was amazed that this could all be part of the simulation, but, at this point, he was done being amazed and just accepted that this was the level of detail he would be getting.

After the tape session, the players gathered for a players-only meeting. Zach Stevens spoke about how everyone needed to give 120 percent tonight, and anyone injured needed to do whatever it took to get ready to be at the top of their game tonight. Mike felt like that message was aimed directly at him.

Some veterans spoke about how they needed to keep things simple, play within the system, and let the other team make the mistakes.

The message seemed simple, but Mike knew things were always easier said than done. Either way, it was a good time to see his teammates and calm his nerves before heading home.

▼▼▼

1:30 P.M.

Mike stepped into the warm, spring-like day and decided to walk home. It was a 30-minute walk, but he wanted to feel the sun on his simulated face and see the sights and sounds of New York. Along the way, a few people recognized him again, and he shook hands and signed some autographs. So much for avoiding distractions.

He walked up 8th Ave to 42nd Street by Port Authority Bus Terminal and turned left towards 10th Ave. Everything felt real, like he was truly in New York City. He even saw a few rats scurrying across the street to their next meal. It was a beautiful day, and people were everywhere.

During the walk, his phone wouldn't stop ringing. Apparently, everyone knew Nate was usually free in the afternoons, so they called and texted. It was genuinely weird using a phone again as he hadn't needed to do that in the past couple of years, with everything going through virtual glasses or contact lenses.

His simulated parents called and he had a brief conversation with them. Hearing his "dad's" voice was weird, so he ended the call after a few minutes. He just didn't want to call someone else mom or dad that really wasn't. It just felt...wrong.

There were other calls with brothers, a cousin, two friends, and his roommate from college. Mike was generally not interested in speaking with any of them as they held no meaning to him but he played along and placated them with small talk. He told everyone that was physically in New York City that he would see them after the game and everyone that was far away that he would call them after the game and left it at that.

He wanted to get home.

▼▼▼

2:15 P.M.

By the time he got to his apartment, Eileen had lunch ready. Grilled chicken, roasted potatoes, vegetables, and a slice of chocolate cake, which she said would be good luck. God, this woman was perfect. Could he take her back to real life?

After lunch, he played with Robby, swinging him around and tickling his armpits and little belly. Playing with Robby helped calm Mike down. It was amazing how a child's laughter could make you forget everything else going on in your life for that one little moment. It was as if nothing else mattered in the world when a baby laughed.

Mike thought that if everyone heard a baby's laughter twice a day, the world would be a much better place.

After playtime, it was time for both father and son to take their afternoon nap. Nate's body was reminding Mike that he needed all the rest he could get, so Eileen took Robby so Nate could nap.

After climbing into his big, beautiful bed with the most amazing sheets ever, Mike reminded himself to take more naps going forward. They really were amazing. He then asked to skip ahead an hour.

▼▼▼

3:45 P.M.

An hour later, the anxiety levels in the Thompson household had reached an all-time high. Mike had been fine until he skipped ahead.

Mike couldn't tell who was nervous—Mike or Nate. It didn't matter. He was feeling nervous and anxious in a way he had never felt before in his real life.

Sure, Mike had been nervous before—usually before a high school hockey game or during job interviews. He was also pretty damn nervous when he asked his first girlfriend, Marissa, out for junior prom—she was way out of his league, but she said yes.

All Mike could think was that he wanted a shot of something to calm his nerves. Man, what he would give for a Johnnie Walker or a Wild Turkey, and that warm feeling of the alcohol sliding down his throat and into his chest, knowing it was about to do its work.

It had been a while since he had this craving, but he knew he couldn't give in, as tempting as it was. Staying sober would be a challenge, especially if they won, but something Mike knew he needed to do. If having alcohol would be as real as everything else here, he could not give in to the drink. At all.

Mike realized he should have requested that Nate be sober as well. "*Nothing you can do about it now dumbass.*", Mike thought to himself as he showered.

After showering, dressing, and making his final packing arrangements, Mike walked to the elevator doorway, where Eileen and Robby were waiting for him.

"Honey," Eileen said, smiling. "Whatever happens tonight, remember that we love you and will support you, both in hockey and beyond. This game doesn't define you as a player or as a man. We know you'll do your best and sacrifice whatever other parts of your body to help this team win. But I just want to say one last thing: Bring us home the Stanley fucking Cup!" She grinned.

"God, I love you," Mike replied with a wide smile on Nate's perfect face. "Usually, you're the anxious one, and I'm trying to calm you down. Thank you for knowing when I needed the same. You always know what I need."

"Do you need this?" Eileen asked, then gave Mike hoped would not be the last kiss of the simulation.

Either way, Mike would try to get laid once more before 9 a.m. tomorrow. If they won, he'd get celebration sex. If they lost, he'd get sympathy sex. Either way, he was going to go out with a bang.

"Well, no one ever said I was deep." Mike said to himself alone in the elevator. Three minutes later, he was in the car and on the way to the arena.

▼ ▼ ▼

4:30 P.M.

The locker room was tense when Mike arrived in time for the team meal. The team brought in some mostly lean options, such as beef casserole, wood-fired pizza, beautiful brisket, corned beef, and pastrami, roasted potatoes, and lots of vegetables.

Each player would try to consume somewhere between enough food to last them for the next eight hours and too much food that they would cause them to have a stomachache or nausea before game time. It was a delicate balance because the food they brought in was delicious.

Maybe Nate was used to this quality of food, but Mike sure as shit wasn't. The meal was phenomenal. He knew New York had some of the world's best chefs, but the few times he had been there, he was certainly not eating at anywhere that had this type of food. Mike was usually fine with a dollar pizza and some good tacos.

Despite having had a late lunch, he was enjoying the food while chatting with some teammates.

For the most part, there wasn't much laughter or smiling amongst the players; everyone was focused on preparing for the task ahead of them. For the older players, this would potentially be their last shot at a Stanley Cup. For the younger players, it was the game of their lives.

Mike was in the middle of a conversation with his linemates, Dylan and Jeremy, about how they were approaching the game tonight.

"Man, I hope my back doesn't fucking tighten up during the game. I might need you to give me a rubdown during a commercial break."

Jeremy responded with his typical humor, "I guess tighter isn't better in this case, huh?"

"No, definitely not," Mike said, twisting his back a bit. "That asshole Pullock got me good. Normally, I'd take a run at him, but not tonight. Tonight I'll let my play tell the story. Fuck him. The guy's uglier than Coach. Speaking of Coach, I do need to speak with him—any idea where he is?"

Dylan laughed. "I think your ugly coach is with Tom somewhere. Let me know what he says after you speak with him. They'll watch your ass closely tonight, so don't hide anything. But dude, I need to know if you can keep up with Jeremy and me. One of us will be the Game 7 hero. Mark my Canadian words."

Dylan laughed and got up from the table noting that he was going to kick a soccer ball around to warmup. Jeremy and others joined him, as many players loved kicking a soccer ball before the game to get their feet and legs going.

For whatever reason, Mike knew that Nate liked to go for a ten-minute run before the game. It was his way of getting loose and getting the blood flowing. So he went to the training room for a quick run on the treadmill. The workout room was usually empty before games, and today was no different.

He popped in his headphones, pulled out his smartphone, which he had barely looked at, and tuned into his favorite satellite radio station. Mike laughed at how far technology had come in over a decade. Smartphones had become almost obsolete as neurotechnology took over, allowing you to browse entertainment, music and videos without a phone, but he still remembered how to use one well enough.

Whatever Nate liked to listen to was irrelevant now. Mike put on some Tool and started his ten-minute run, which was usually equivalent to one Tool song. He wanted to be careful with Nate's back, so he went for a nine-minute mile, which was unheard of for Mike, but he knew it was slower than normal for Nate.

Mike was amazed at how effortless it felt to run in this body. He wasn't out of breath, and even though he was a little sore, he could move with relative ease for the entire nine minutes. He could only imagine what skating would be like.

He knew one thing for sure: he was ready to get on the ice.

▼ ▼ ▼

6:00 P.M.

Mike put his equipment on as he always did: hockey pants first, chest protector second, skates third, elbow pads fourth, shin and knee covers last.

This equipment was pristine and fit Nate perfectly, a far cry from the beat-up equipment he used back in high school.

His skates were professional ones that fit his feet perfectly, as if they were made just for him. Come to think of it, they probably were made for him.

By 6:15 p.m., he was dressed and ready to go. The only thing left was his helmet and a quick word with Coach.

Five minutes later, Coach appeared. Mike, as Nate, called him to get his attention: "Coach, do you have a minute?" Coach turned to him and walked over.

"Sure, Nate. How are you feeling? Dave said you had a good session earlier and seemed to be feeling better." Coach paused with a face that said: *Please tell me you're good to go.*

So, Mike appeased him: "I'm good to go, Coach. Dave mentioned I might tighten up during the game, so I might need quick heat treatment if that happens to get everything loosened up again. I told Dylan and Jeremy I might disappear for a shift or two if it tightens up, but I also wanted to let you know."

"Okay, thanks for the heads-up. Just see how you feel after warmups, and let's take it a shift at a time. If you need treatment, just communicate with Coach Ross, and we'll manage it for whatever time you need. You excited?" Coach asked as if this wasn't the biggest and scariest night in their lifetimes.

"Excited is one word I'd use," Mike said sarcastically. "I'm excited, nervous, nauseous, petrified, and just trying to take it all in."

"Good, you're all the right things. I'll see you out there." Coach tapped his shoulder before moving on to wherever he was going next.

Mike stood there for a few moments reflecting on what he just said. He really was excited, nervous, nauseous, and petrified. But he had forgotten one thing: he was happy. Genuinely happy for the first time in a long time. And it felt good.

He wondered how the others from their group dinner the night before were doing in their simulations. Were they feeling the same mix of emotions?

His thoughts were interrupted by Zach Stevens shouting, "Alright, guys, let's head out!" as he led the team onto the ice for pre-game warmups.

Mike was heading out with the group in the middle of the pack. The walk from the locker room was short; they made a couple of quick turns, passing some fans waiting on either side of a short glass-lined hallway, and soon they were at the ice-level entrance. The team waited about 30 seconds for the arena announcer to say the famous phrase: "Ladies and gentlemen—welcome to the World's Most Famous Arena. Please welcome to the ice, *your New York Rangers!*"

Mike heard the cheers and music above as he waited to head onto the ice. Zach went on first, followed by his linemates and the rest of the team. Mike followed Dylan and Jeremy, and the Madison Square Garden lights came into view as he got closer.

He paused, taking a deep breath. This was the moment he had been looking forward to for his entire life: a chance at taking the ice in an NHL arena. Mike took another deep breath and then stepped onto the ice. After taking a few long strides, he looked around and just took it all in: the bright lights above him, the screaming fans all around him, the banners hanging in the rafters, the excitement and optimism in the air.

He missed the energy that filled an arena on game day. Even though he only experienced high school hockey with a few hundred fans in the stands, that energy always gave the players a boost before the game.

It didn't matter if everything he saw now was simulated; it felt real to him. He absorbed it all like a kid seeing Disney World for the first time. Nothing in his life could compare to this feeling, which he imagined had to be a similar feeling for any professional athlete that played in this atmosphere.

He took a few laps around the goalie's net, skated back towards center ice, and gathered for the team drills at center ice. It had been years since Mike skated this effortlessly, and it felt good to be flying around the ice, his jersey rustling in the breeze generated by the skating, the wind hitting his hair. Everything felt seamless.

On top of that, everything sounded so real. The players' skates hitting the ice, the pucks banging against the boards and the goalies equipment, the fans cheering for their favorite player. Rock music blared from the huge scoreboard above them, sending a rush of adrenalin—or whatever that was in this simulated body—coursing through him.

Mike appreciated how good Nate's hand coordination, skating, shooting, and accuracy were. Nate's strength and stamina would soon be tested, but Mike wasn't worried. Front-to-back skating was easy, and he was able to cut with ease. Mike felt invincible on the ice. Time would tell how long that would last.

Sitting on one knee towards the end of the warmups, he saw Eileen behind the glass with Nate's parents. Robby was too young for the game, so they got a babysitter. Seeing his simulated parents wave, their faces beaming with excitement, was strange. His dad, a handsome guy in his late 50s, and his mom, an attractive woman as well in her mid-to-late 50s, looked happy. He saw where he got his looks from.

Seeing his simulated parents made Mike miss his real parents; they had always supported him, even after his various injuries, subsequent depression, and, of course, alcohol addiction. He wished he could have told them he was about to be a dad; they would have been so happy.

Mike's mom died in a car crash a little over two years ago, caused by a drunk driver. It was one of the reasons he decided to sober up; he didn't want to have a similar fate happen to someone else because of his stupidity.

For now, he would have to make do with his simulated parents, Arnold and Maureen—good, solid parental names. He waved and gave them a thumbs up; that was all the emotion he could muster.

As the warmup clock counted down, the players returned to the locker room to prepare for the game's start.

Mike felt good. He was ready to play

▼ ▼ ▼

7:30 P.M.

Thirty minutes later, everyone was refreshed, with jerseys changed and gear on, ready for the game.

There was an intensity in the air. Many of the guys were quiet, listening to music and focusing on what they needed to do tonight. Mike missed these moments, when everyone was on the same page and focused on what to do.

After a few minutes of quiet preparation, Coach Donaldson entered for his pregame speech. Mike had heard many coach speeches, but a Game 7 speech for the Stanley Cup Finals was bound to be special. He was glad he didn't have to deliver it.

Coach stood in the center of the room and unfolded a piece of paper from his suit jacket. It looked like a letter, written in large handwriting with pink ink with some sort of picture on it.

"Guys, I want to read you a letter I received yesterday from a little girl named Katherine. She's eight and in the cancer ward at New York Presbyterian Hospital. She has leukemia.

'Dear New York Rangers:

I am eight years old and have leukemia. I watch every Rangers game on television in my hospital room and am so happy when the

Rangers score and win. Please win this last game so I can jump and make all of the nurses happy. Let's go Rangers!

Love, Katherine French."

Coach paused to compose himself.

"Gentleman, I didn't read this letter to make you sad or depressed; quite the opposite. I read you this letter because I wanted to remind you of the important things in life. We get paid a shit-ton of money to play and coach a game that boils down to putting a piece of rubber in a net made of twine.

We *all* know it's not that simple, and we *all* know the significant sacrifices you and your family have made to become the players you are today. However, I want you to remember that hockey is still a game where the outcome is based on one number being larger than another. And that outcome isn't always a fair representation of who the better team was.

I want you to remember that the important things in life will be there tomorrow, whether we win or lose: our parents, our children, our friends, our teammates and all the people that make up this amazing organization.

The one thing I ask of each of you is to take all the emotions you have right now—excitement, nervousness, anxiety, fear, and happiness—and bottle them up for another day. There is only thing you need to be focused on right now: your next shift.

Everyone in this room is feeling the same thing, but we must come together as a team and focus on the task at hand tonight.

Look around. Everyone you see in this room is your teammate and your brother. We win as a team; we lose as a team. Everyone here knows the passion and work it took to be here. Not one person in this room should question that or let that get in the way of the raw emotions of the game.

Tomorrow, I want you to be able to look at your teammate next to you and say, 'I gave it my all yesterday and left nothing on the ice.' When you're out of breath and don't think you have anything left in the tank, you need to find something extra tonight. When you need to make a quick decision with the puck, make the safe and conservative play. When you have the opportunity to punish somebody legally, you take that opportunity.

If we can each say that we gave it our all, we are all winners, gentlemen, regardless of which team puts more pieces of rubber into the other team's net. We all want to win, and our fans want us to win. But sometimes, the better team doesn't win. Let's at least be the better team, the more cohesive team, the smarter team, so tomorrow we can all hold our heads high regardless of the outcome. Okay, gentlemen?

Hundreds of other players and coaches around the league would die to be here right now. Thousands of players worldwide are watching this game, dreaming of being here one day.

Your families and friends will be there tomorrow, so let's give them something to be proud of.

Let's give little Katherine something to be proud of as she fights for her life. Rangers, on three. One… Two… Three… *Rangers!*" He screamed, and the locker room joined in.

"*Wow,*" Mike thought. "*That was a damn good speech.*" He wasn't necessarily jumping to the ceiling, but his nerves were calm.

Zach, the captain, stood up. "Alright, boys, this is the night we've been waiting for our entire lives. Let's play like the team we know we can be and give them hell. Let's go!"

The entire team rose in unison, shouting and screaming while heading toward the arena entryway for the team introductions. The players would be announced by jersey number from lowest to highest, so with Nate at #69, he was towards the back of the lineup, followed by only three players wearing #71, #86, and #88. So, Mike waited as the other players exited first.

As the players started walking out, Coach approached Nate. "Nate, let me know if you need anything with your back. Wanna make sure you're as close to 100% as possible. It's a team game, and we need everyone running at close to full steam. This is no time to be a hero. Okay, son?"

"No problem, Coach. I feel good, but I'll let you know if I tweak anything," Mike noted as Nate.

He could hear the announcer calling his teammates' names, positions, and numbers. Everyone got the same amount of applause as they skated onto the ice, except for #45, Nick Plechton, and #51, Tyler Gruen, the rookies, who got an extra level of cheering when their names were called. Good for them; they both deserved it.

Finally, it was Nate's turn. He gave a thumbs-up to the assistant guiding the players as if to say: *Yes, I am ready to skate onto the ice.*

This was it. He had made it. Not exactly as he drew it up, but fuck it. He was here, about to play one of the most stressful games in all professional sports—Game 7 of the Stanley Cup finals. Where one mistake could mean the difference between winning and losing. Anything could and would happen in this game.

He was ready to go as the arena PA announcer said, "At left wing, number 69, Nate Thompson!" That was his cue. He pushed off to cheers and fireworks and skated next to his teammates at the redline. Not a bad way to enter the rink.

Mike looked around the packed arena, closed his eyes, and took it all in. Amazing.

The final three teammates were announced, joining him to his left to complete the roster. The coaches then joined the skaters at the red line when announced.

The Rangers were holding a pre-game ceremony to honor a former captain, Adam Lemieux, who passed away earlier in the week at 72. His family was on hand for the emotional ceremony. Mike still couldn't believe the number of details that went into this.

Finally, after a TV timeout, it was time for the National Anthem. The players lined up on the benches, focusing on the puck drop in about five minutes. The crowd went silent as an opera singer began: "*O' say can you see, by the dawn's early light...*"

Mike got chills. The last time he heard this song on a bench was the last game of his high school career when he was 18, almost 25 years ago, where he tore his second ACL.

He suddenly felt very emotional and began to weep, albeit with no tears coming out of his tear ducts.

Behind him, Dylan muttered, "You okay, man?"

Mike just nodded and recomposed himself. Nothing like embarrassing yourself in front of your teammates before the biggest game of your lives, simulated or not.

Finally, the opera singer sang, "*O'er the land of the free and the home of the brave?*" and the crowd began to cheer. The players tapped their sticks on the benches and then sat down. It was game time.

The arena was electric, with music blaring and the players pumped but focused. "Let's go Rangers!" was echoing across the entire arena that was literally rocking.

On the bench, there were many "Let's go, boys" and "keep it simple boys."

Mike had to remind himself that these players were actually boys still learning about life and not 43 like he was in reality.

Mike's heart, or whatever it was, was racing, but he wasn't nervous. He felt focused, excited, and ready to get this thing going.

The refs were in place, the goalies ready, and the Ranger's first line was out against the Oilers' first line.

Game 7 was ready to start.

▼ ▼ ▼

FIRST PERIOD

The game's first shift was relatively uneventful, as both teams were feeling each other out after the last game. There were a few puck dump-ins and changes in puck possession, but not much more.

Eventually, the puck went out of play, allowing Mike, Dylan, and Jeremy to take the ice with Nick and Adam. The Oilers had their second line on the ice, which would be the first line on half the teams in the league given how fast and quick their players were. Mike knew he would need to get creative to generate scoring chances.

The draw was in the Ranger's defensive zone. Mike took position and got ready for the puck drop. He wasn't nervous anymore; he was laser-focused on the puck and what he would do if he got it, besides throwing up. This was it.

The puck dropped, and the Rangers won possession. Nick passed it up the other side of the boards to Jeremy, who chipped it out of the defensive zone and into center ice, where Dylan was waiting to take possession of the puck. He turned and shot the puck into the offensive zone, where Mike raced after it in the left-hand corner.

Mike knew he wouldn't get to the puck first but saw an opportunity to lay a check on the Oilers' top defenseman, a 6'3" bull named Kelly Wilson, to set the game's tone immediately. And he did exactly that. He delivered a nice, clean shoulder check, knocking Kenny onto the ice.

The crowd went wild, and a rush of what Mike assumed was simulated adrenaline swept over him like a warm blanket.

"*Man, that felt good!*" he thought as he chased the puck back through center ice.

The Oilers took a shot on goal, which Vlad saved easily. The referee blew the whistle, and both teams changed lines. Mike and his linemates returned to the bench.

"How did that feel?" Jeremy asked Mike.

"That asshole knocked me on my ass a few times last game, so I owed him one," Mike said with a laugh.

"Good. Keep it up, boys. Let's set the tone here," Dylan said, taking a sip of water.

The next few minutes were uneventful; all four lines had been on the ice now, and there were only two shots on goal. Everyone was playing cautiously, but Mike knew that would change and the game would likely open up soon.

After a TV timeout, Mike's line was ready to go back out. This time, the faceoff was in the Oilers' offensive zone.

The Rangers won the draw again. Johan, now on the ice with Collin, controlled the puck and dumped it deep into the Oilers' zone, where Dylan took control behind the net.

Mike took the chance to move toward the front of the net, signaling Dylan with a chirp. Dylan made a blind pass toward Mike, but unfortunately, it was slightly behind him to control. However, it went right to Johan, who took a slapshot that the goalie gloved.

Mike was right in front of the net, and it felt good to be involved in an offensive play. He hadn't controlled the puck yet, but contributing to a good shift that got the crowd going felt great. Looking up at the cheering fans as he returned to the bench, he felt good to get a solid shift in.

So far, the biggest difference in this simulation from how Mike played in high school was that Nate was bigger and better able to withstand a punishment at the front of the net than Mike ever was. When Mike stopped playing, he was probably 160 pounds soaking wet.

These guys were faster and bigger, but so was Nate, so everyone was on a level playing field here.

Back on the bench, the team's attitude was solid. The last couple of shifts had ignited their energy.

The third and fourth lines did their jobs by controlling play and tilting the ice toward the Oilers' zone. While those lines didn't produce a goal, they maintained the momentum of the prior few shifts, especially Tyler Gruen, who continued his amazing play of late.

On the bench, Mike was feeling good, amazed at how easy it was to skate with such power and ease again. He wished he could take this skating ability back to real life. By the time his next shift came, with about ten minutes left in the period, the teams changed on the fly. Mike jumped off the bench and onto the ice, where the defensemen quickly passed the puck to him as he moved toward the offensive zone. It felt great to finally have the puck on his stick.

Mike stick-handled through the neutral zone into the offensive zone, where he put the brakes on and waited for his teammates to join him. Seeing Jeremy racing into the zone, Mike fired the puck around the back of the net where Jeremy could get it.

After some nice moves from Jeremy, he passed it back to the point where Adam was. Adam controlled it briefly before passing it towards his left to Nick, who took a slapshot from the point the goalie saved but left a nice, juicy rebound that found its way to Mike near the goalie's left.

Mike controlled the puck on his stick and immediately took a wrist shot towards the upper part of the net that the Oilers' goalie had to dive across the goal crease to save.

"Motherfucker!" Mike exclaimed, looking up as the crowd groaned in disbelief. He took a deep breath and talked to himself as he skated back to the bench. "Okay, that was your first shot, and it felt good. Nice save by that goalie; they must have given him a 99 rating in this simulation."

Mike laughed as he glanced at the scoreboard, seeing roughly nine minutes left in the first period.

Back on the bench during a television timeout, the positive talk continued. "Keep it up, boys," "Keep bringing it to them," and "Way to go, Nate" filled the air.

The next few shifts were feisty, with the Oilers pinning the Rangers in their defensive zone. Unfortunately, Ilya took a bad roughing penalty after being on the ice for over a minute. With the penalty kill coming up, Nate knew he wouldn't see the ice for a few minutes.

▼▼▼

He took this time to look around at the 18,000+ fans filling the arena, each one looking as real as anyone he'd ever seen in real life. They were partying and dancing to the music during the TV timeout. It felt exactly like being in Madison Square Garden.

He still couldn't believe how amazing and real it all felt. The atmosphere reminded Mike of the time he and his dad went to Game 4 of the 1999 Western Conference finals in Denver against the Stars.

While Mike wasn't a huge Avalanche fan, his dad was, so when his dad asked if Mike would join him for the game, he jumped at the opportunity.

The atmosphere throughout the game was simply electric and when the Avalanche beat the Stars 3-2, thirty seconds into overtime, sending the crowd into an absolute frenzy, Mike couldn't believe how happy his dad was. It was as-if nothing else in the world mattered but being there with his dad and it was on the of the happiest memories Mike had as a child.

Mike hoped to recreate that type of moment tonight in this version of New York City.

▼▼▼

As the penalty kill began and the Oilers controlled the play, the fans started chanting: "*Kill, kill,*" urging the Rangers to prevent the Oilers from scoring on the power play.

Unfortunately, their chants didn't have the desired effect. Fifteen seconds in, a shot from the point was deflected into the net by an Oilers forward standing right in front of Vlad. 1-0 Oilers. A hush fell over the crowd as the scoreboard at the center of the ice started playing "Let's Go Rangers."

The sentiment on the bench was quiet as Mike's line jumped back on the ice. Mike took a deep breath and told Jeremy and Dylan, "Let's go get it back right now."

As the puck dropped, the Rangers controlled it and immediately brought it up ice. Dylan crossed the blue line and dropped a pass to Mike, who was skating behind him.

Mike saw Jeremy heading towards his right and slipped a beautiful pass to his stick. Jeremy made a power move toward the goal but was tripped up by an Oilers' defenseman before he could get a shot off.

Oilers' penalty. The Rangers were going on the power play.

"Nice play, baby! Way to go!" Dylan shouted as Mike returned to the bench.

Coach decided to leave Nate on the power play with Dylan, Jeremy, Nick, and Will. Mike was excited to get a chance to play on the power play, something he had excelled at in high school.

The keys to the powerplay were patience, control, movement, and knowing when to take a shot. As a defenseman, you had to get the puck to your playmakers in the right areas while being ready to shoot if a lane opened. For the forwards, it was about moving the puck quickly and carefully to keep the other team on their toes.

You couldn't hold onto the puck for too long and waste time; quick, decisive movements of the puck were important, while always maintaining a shooter's mentality.

With the draw in the Rangers' offensive zone, Mike was ready to shoot. The Rangers controlled the puck off the draw and set up on the power play. Mike maneuvered to the left of the goalie, received the puck from Nick, controlled it for a moment, and passed it back to Nick, who sent it over to Will and then back to Nick.

Nick faked a shot and got the puck to Mike, who had some room to move toward the goalie. As Mike prepared to shoot, from the corner of his eye, he noticed Jeremy skating towards the net to his right. Mike make a quick decision to make a hard pass through a pair of legs right to Jeremy's stick, who one-timed it into the empty net above the goalies' shoulder. *Goal!*

The crowd erupted as Mike skated over to jump on Jeremy, and the rest of the power play unit joined them as they went up against the glass dividers. "Fuck yes!" Jeremy exclaimed. "What a fucking pass!"

A collective "Yeah!!" came from Dylan, Nick and Will as the group headed to the bench.

The Rangers' players stood on the bench, ready to fist-bump the unit as they made their way toward the bench. The arena music was blaring; the crowd was going wild, as was the bench.

Mike was in heaven. While he didn't score, his pass was perfect, right to Jeremy's stick with an open net in front of him. His ex-girlfriend could have scored on that much net.

Mike was skating well, playing a physical game against the boards, and even delivering a few hard checks along the way. He was playing hockey again, and it felt incredible.

As he sat on the bench, all Mike could think was that while he knew this wasn't real, the joy, the euphoria, and the excitement felt as real as anything else he had experienced in his life.

The next couple of shifts were uneventful, and the buzzer sounded, with the score tied at 1-1 after one period.

As they left the bench, the Rangers' assistant informed Mike that the TV broadcast wanted a quick interview with him before they went to the locker room.

"*Cool*," Mike thought. A chance to get on simulated television.

"Let's do it," he told the assistant, who guided him back to the bench and handed him a headset and microphone.

"Steve and Ray are the announcers; they'll ask you a few questions. It should only take a minute."

Mike put the headphones on and heard Steve say, "Congratulations on a great first period, Nate. We know you were a little beat up after the last game—how is the back feeling?"

"It feels good," Mike responded as Nate. "I received some treatment this morning to loosen it up and help the healing. I'll just keep pushing forward. No way I was going to miss this game tonight."

Ray said, "You had a great opportunity earlier in the period, and that pass on the power play goal was just insane. Take us through that pass—I'm sure it felt great to respond after that first goal by them."

"Yeah, we knew they would come out hard, and we wanted to match their intensity. Obviously, that first goal hurt, but it was good to get one right back. On the power play, I had a shooting lane but saw J-Dog out of the corner of my eye. Luckily, that pass made its way to him through a few legs, and he had an open net. Glad we were able to get one back like that towards the end of the period."

Steve continued, "This is your first Game 7 experience. What's it like on the bench tonight?"

"Yeah, it's really intense right now. Every shift, pass, and decision is important, you know. We need to stick to our game, be patient, and wait for the right opportunities to hopefully get a few more in the net the rest of the game."

"Okay, Nate, we appreciate your time. We'll let you get back and rest for a bit. Good luck the rest of the way," Ray concluded and signed off.

Mike took off the headset and headed to the locker room.

▼▼▼

FIRST INTERMISSION

The locker room was in good spirits when Mike arrived. He took most of his equipment off and asked Dave for some quick treatment on his back. Though he didn't feel his back stiffening, he wanted to keep it as loose as possible.

Dave applied heat and massaged his back for about five minutes. It felt amazing. Mike wondered if he was moaning in his chair back in the room with Charles; he hoped he was.

Mike wasn't sweating in the simulation, but he was still thirsty, which was weird. He spent the intermission sitting by his locker, gathering his thoughts on the first period and this experience overall. He kept thinking about how incredibly real it felt, and he didn't want it to end.

After ten minutes, Coach came in for his between-period speech.

"Alright, boys, nice first period there. I'm glad we got one back there. Nate, that was an amazing pass. Jeremy, great finish. Let's build on that here in the second period. Dylan, Tyler, and Nick, great play out there. Let's keep it up.

They're playing smart and patient tonight and taking short shifts. Offense: Let's try to keep them pinned in our offensive zone and get our cycle game going. I want to wear their defense down so our speed becomes more of a factor.

Defense: You're doing a nice job limiting them to six shots. Let's keep making smart clears so they can't get going offensively. I don't care if we play a boring game the rest of the way, as long as we play smart and together. Okay?

Nate, your line is going to start the second period. Let's get another one and build from there. Keep it going, boys."

Coach left the room. Mike grabbed a quick energy bar and a banana from his locker to re-energize.

He hoped they could maintain the momentum into the second period. After a few sips of water, he began putting his fresh equipment back on. It was nice to wear clean pads and jerseys between periods; in high school, everything was soaked in sweat by the end of the game.

After a few more minutes of recuperating, it was time to head back onto the ice.

Zach Stevens took his position at the front of the locker room. "Alright, boys, let's keep this energy going into this period and take it to them. We're the better team, so keep the physicality going and the skates moving. Rangers, on three." The players brought their hands together and shouted, "Rangers!" after Zach's count.

Mike had always thought things like that were cheesy, but now he was pumped and ready to get back on the ice.

▼ ▼ ▼

SECOND PERIOD

Back on the ice, Mike didn't feel any butterflies. He was ready as the puck dropped, and the Rangers controlled it with a dump-in to the Oilers' offensive zone by Dylan.

Mike rushed in, cycling the puck with Jeremy and Dylan as Coach had instructed. For a solid 20 seconds, they passed the puck along the boards behind the Oilers' net. Finally, Mike passed to Dylan at the top of the zone. Dylan fired a shot, but the goalie saved it.

The crowd clapped as they changed lines, and Zach's first line came on the ice.

Back on the bench, Dylan, Jeremy, and Mike congratulated each other on a good shift, vowing to keep it up for the rest of the game.

Zach's line had a couple of good shots, but the Oilers's goalie was on his game tonight and made some solid saves.

The third and fourth lines had strong shifts. Dougie, Nick, and Adam controlled the play, while Mike, Tyler, and Martin delivered big hits, preventing the Oilers from generating any opportunities until a TV timeout paused action with around 15 minutes left in the period.

Mike's line was back on the ice after the TV timeout against the Oilers' top line. The puck dropped, and the Oilers controlled the play in the Rangers' zone with some nice passing and control.

Finally, the Oilers worked the puck to the defensemen at the left point near Mike, who passed it over to the defensemen at the right point. He fired a shot that somehow made its way through about five players and passed Vlad for a goal.

"Damn, 2-1 bad guys," Mike thought. The crowd groaned again and went silent. While there was nothing Nate or Mike could have done about it, Mike still felt down about being on the ice for a goal, especially in a game like this.

Back on the bench, the players noted how the Oilers were mimicking the Rangers' style, trying to cycle the puck and pin the Rangers in their zone, with the defense pinching slightly more than in the first period.

The assistant coaches advised the defensemen that if the Oilers continued to use this style, the defensemen should try to flip the puck high and far and see if one of the forwards could get a breakaway attempt out of it, especially if speedier forwards were on the ice.

The next few shifts were a lot of back-and-forth. The Oilers had some momentum and were picking up their attacking and aggressive style.

Mike's next shift was with about ten and a half minutes left in the period and it was fairly uneventful. That is until the end of the shift where Mike was trying to get off the ice as the puck came bouncing to him. He controlled it for a second before dumping it into the Oilers' zone. As soon as he did that, Kenny Wilson, perhaps remembering Mike's check on the first shift of the game, came barreling towards him and knocked Mike right into the Ranger's bench. The resulting motion extended Mike's back in a weird position and he felt it pop immediately.

Something tweaked in his lower back. "*Ouch,*" Mike thought as he slowly climbed over the bench. The Rangers' training staff immediately approached him and asked if he was okay.

"That one definitely got me a little," he responded, hunched over on the bench. It felt like someone shot a hot needle into his back. He needed to sit for a few seconds to see how bad it was.

After a minute, the training staff told Mike to head back to the locker room to see if they could give him some quick treatment.

"*Dammit,*" Mike thought as he walked gingerly towards the locker room. "*Why couldn't they give me a fully healthy body for the simulation?*" He was fuming.

Obviously, there is injury risk in any professional sports game, and by Game 7 of the last round of a long playoff season, everyone is hurting somehow. But it would have been nice to have at least *started* with someone who was closer to 100% healthy.

"Why would they not give me a healthier body? Goddamn it!" Mike murmured out loud as he returned to the locker room with the training staff. This generated some puzzled stares from Dave and Jon, the head trainer. Mike ignored them.

"Alright, Nate, take your jersey off. Let's apply some more heat to the muscle and see if we can continue loosening it up," Jon said.

Mike removed his jersey and some padding and sat shirtless on the table as the trainers rubbed some atomic balm on the left side of his back, glutes, and hips.

"How are you feeling?" Jon asked. "Is it tightening up a lot?"

"It seems okay for now. I can sit up. If it gets much tighter, though, skating will be tough," Mike replied.

Jon continued, "Okay, let's give the cream a minute to heat you. We'll continue rubbing you down, and hopefully that will loosen you up until the period break. Then we can continue some other treatment, okay? I know you wanna get back out there."

Mike lay down, letting them massage his back for another few minutes. He could hear the broadcast in the locker room 20 feet away, and it sounded like they were at another commercial break. He hoped to get back on the ice for the final few minutes of this period to test his back.

After what felt like an eternity, he finally returned to the bench with two minutes left. He told Coach he was okay and wanted to get back on the ice. Coach agreed, putting him on the ice with Nick Stolsky and Adam Right. The defensemen were Bruce and Kenny.

The puck drop was in the Ranger's defensive zone, which the Oilers won and controlled possession of. Again, they started cycling the puck with passes up to the defensemen, back down to the forward, and back to the defensemen.

After about ten seconds, the defensemen near Mike pinched in to keep the puck in the zone, which he did, but it went right to Kenny, who controlled it. Seeing both Oiler's defensemen stuck in their offensive zone, Mike seized the opportunity to move up ice as Kenny flipped the puck up in the air toward center ice. Mike raced as fast as he could towards the puck as it landed about five feet in front of him.

With nothing but open ice between him and the Oilers goalie, Mike had flashbacks to high school, where he had several breakaways. He remembered his favorite move: pretending to shoot forehand, faking the shot, and bringing the puck to his backhand to roof it over the goalie's left shoulder.

It was his signature move, and he was most confident in it.

As he raced in, he saw the goalie begin to come out towards the edge of his crease to meet him. "*Perfect,*" he thought, hearing the crowd growing louder.

He could see the goalie's eyes, wide as ever, watching his every move like a hawk.

Ten feet, eight feet, six feet. With about five feet left, he made the motion as if he were going to shoot until he was about three feet away from the goalie, and then quickly moved the puck to his backhand. He edged as far to the right of the net as he could before shooting toward the upper right part of the net.

As he skated away from the net, he glanced back to see that it went *in!* "Holy fuck!" Mike shouted as Nate as he crashed along the boards. He couldn't believe it!! It went in!!!

Mike instantly flashed back to when he used to shoot pucks in his driveway dreaming of how he would celebrate if he ever scored a goal in the NHL. Usually it involved riding with one knee on the ice and doing some sort of shooting gesture with this stick.

Here he didn't have time to do that. He backed up against the boards and waited for his teammates to come meet him. And meet him they did.

"What a fucking move, Nate!" Nick yelled.

"Holy shit, what a move!" Adam shouted, jumping on them.

"That's how we do it—right back in it!" Bruce cheered.

"*Yeah!*" Kenny added, as he was the last member of the unit to get to the mini pileup of players along the glass.

Once again, Mike was in heaven as he skated towards the Rangers' bench, glancing up at the game clock: 1:25 left. There was no comparison to this feeling. Maybe the birth of his baby would come close, but he wasn't sure it would exactly match this. This was insane.

He had never felt anything like this in his life. It was a mixture of pure adrenaline, excitement, happiness, and a sense of achievement.

As the final 90 seconds ticked away without any further excitement, he closed his eyes, repeatedly whispering "thank you." He wasn't sure who he was thanking, but he felt grateful, so he figured saying it aloud was enough.

"Hey Nate." He turned to see Kenny leaning over him from the other end of the bench. "Great fucking move. Let's do that again in the third."

"Fuck yes, I can beat that guy again," Mike said, firmly believing that now, as the horn blew, marking the end of the second period.

▼▼▼

SECOND INTERMISSION

Back in the locker room, between periods, Mike continued to receive treatment. It seemed to help. He knew that if this were real life, tomorrow would be absolute hell recovering from this, but since he would be back in his own body tomorrow dealing with his other real-life ailments, he didn't care.

Surviving the next 20 simulated minutes was all that mattered.

Coach came in to give his between-period speech:

"Alright, gentlemen, we're right where we want to be here. It's a tied game, so nothing has changed. Nate, what a fucking move, man!

Let's remember what we are playing for here. You have spent most of your life working toward this final period. Regardless of what happens, I don't want *anyone* to look in the mirror tomorrow morning and say they didn't give their all in these final 20 minutes.

Stick to our structure and make smart plays. If you see an opportunity, take it, but make sure there's back-end coverage.

We want to keep our shifts short, so let's aim for 40-50 seconds before changing.

Nate, I know you're hurting despite playing a great game. If you can't give it your all, please tell one of the coaches. We can't afford to have someone out there who's struggling to skate at close to 100%. There is no shame in it, son; you've been a warrior out there."

Coach looked at Nate as if expecting an affirmative response.

"Understood, Coach," Mike responded, not quite sure what to say.

"Alright, boys, coaching you this season has been an absolute pleasure. Win or lose, you're champions in my book. Let's give them hell this period.

One...Two...Three... Rangers!"

▼▼▼

THIRD PERIOD

As the third period began, the anxiety on the bench was palpable. Everyone was focusing even harder on their next shift. After six and two-thirds games, both teams knew each other well, so there weren't many surprises left to unveil.

Each team would be careful with their passes, making it more critical to choose moments to be aggressive wisely.

Nate's line didn't get on the ice until three minutes into the period, and two quick whistles—one for offsides and one for icing on the Rangers—moved the puck back into the Rangers' defensive zone.

Mike could tell Nate's back was holding up, but he was nervous it could seize at any moment. He continued to move it and try to keep it as loose as possible.

After the puck dropped, the Oilers started cycling again with their top line on the ice. As Nate's line had been on the ice for about 45 seconds, they were becoming a bit winded, and the Oilers took advantage with several shots on goal.

Johan gained control of the puck but made a mistake, sending it out of the zone and into the crowd without touching the glass, resulting in a delay of game penalty on the Rangers.

Mike returned to the bench, hoping the penalty kill could do its job, which it did over the next two stressful minutes where Mike was sure he needed to shit his pants as the Oilers controlled the puck for most of the time in the Rangers' zone.

Fortunately, Vlad the Destroyer made a few huge saves, keeping the game tied at 2-2.

As the penalty kill ended, Coach decided he wanted the third and fourth lines to tilt the ice back in the Rangers' favor and try to build some momentum back, which they did by controlling the puck and spending more time in the Oilers' zone.

Next up was Zach's line, which continued the play in the Oilers' zone, resulting in some excellent opportunities but, unfortunately, no goals.

Finally, after a quick TV timeout, the arena buzzed with a nervous energy. Mike's line was back on the ice with ten and a half minutes left in the third period.

After the puck dropped in the Oilers' offensive zone, Mike was able to control it and begin the cycling process with Dylan and Jeremy.

Jeremy controlled it for a bit and passed it up to the point for a shot on goal, which went wide but right to Dylan, who controlled it behind the net and went for a wrap-around attempt on the goalie, which the goalie stuffed.

Mike moved to the front of the net, and he and Dylan both whacked at the puck to try to knock it into the net as a scrum broke out with the Oilers' defensemen, who apparently were not happy with the whacking taking place.

The scrum was pretty intense as Mike wrestled with one of the smaller Oilers' defensemen, and they eventually wrestled each other to the ice, screaming and cursing at each other. The crowd roared as a few other players jumped in to help their respective teammates.

"Fuck you, you asshole. Didn't you hear the fucking whistle?" one of the Oilers' defensemen was yelling to Mike.

"No I didn't hear the fucking whistle. The ref was on the farside of the net, you prick." Mike quipped right back.

"Take some money and go get your ears checked this offseason after we send your asses home." Boy this guy was a real comedian.

"Gotta stop me first, asshole." Mike stated right back as the linesman dragged both of them to their respective penalty boxes.

They were offsetting penalties, meaning there was no power play due to the little skirmish. Mike was relieved, as he didn't want to put his team in a bad position on the penalty kill.

As his simulated adrenaline wore off, he realized his back had seized up on him a bit. In hindsight, trying to wrestle someone thirty minutes after getting treatment on his back was probably not the best idea.

Hunched over in the box, he tried to control his breathing as much as possible.

The last thing Mike wanted was for the coaching or training staff to notice his pain and force him to sit for the final minutes of the period. He estimated there would be roughly seven and a half minutes left by the time he got out of the penalty box, and he would have a few more shifts. He was going to suck it up and play through this pain.

The next two minutes went by *really... fucking... slowly,* but they gave him a chance to continue loosening his back. By the time the penalty expired, he felt better.

Unfortunately, the play continued for another two minutes before there was a whistle for an offsides play.

When he got back to the bench, only five minutes remained in the third period, with the score still tied 2-2.

Mike had skated well enough from the penalty box, so he didn't think his back would prevent him from skating normally. He was controlling his breathing and could sit on the bench in a position that didn't hurt too much, so he thought he'd be fine to take another shift or two. If the period ended tied, he'd go back into the locker room and get some more treatment.

The atmosphere in the arena was tense. Everyone—the fans, players, coaches, training staff, and even the TV announcers—was sitting at the edge of their proverbial seats.

During the TV timeout, Coach said that he was going to put Zach's line back on the ice when the timeout ended, followed by the third and fourth lines to control the play. Mike's line would go on with around 90 seconds left in the period.

The next several minutes were a lot of back-and-forth, with only a couple of shots on goal that were easy saves for the goalies. The players were gripping their sticks harder to make sure they were not the ones who made a mistake that would cost their team the victory.

Finally, with a minute and fifteen seconds left in the period, Nate's line got back on the ice. The theme was to be careful and not make mistakes, but if an opportunity presented itself, to go for it.

The puck drop right outside the Rangers' defensive zone was won by the Oilers, who dumped it into the Rangers zone. Nick controlled the puck and passed it over to Adam on Vlad's left. Adam controlled it for a second before passing it up to Jeremy towards center ice. Jeremy, tangled with one of the Oilers' defensemen, but managed to perfectly tip the puck to Dylan, who was racing through center ice. Dylan picked up the puck as Mike raced with him, developing a two-on-one in the Oilers' defensive zone.

As Dylan slowly headed towards the goalie, with Mike to his right, Mike knew he needed to be ready for a shot. Dylan was a skilled passer and had a pass-first mentality, which Mike needed to be ready for.

Coming down the right side of the ice was not natural for a lefty, so Mike had to twist his body to get in position for a potential pass. As soon as he twisted his body, the pass was on it's way. He tried to breathe to calm himself, as he knew if he got a good shot, it might go in the net. As he breathed deep, the right side of his back seized up just as the puck hit his stick.

Mike tried to muster some power in his back to generate a quality shot, but the pain was too intense. He took a weak shot that missed to the right of the goalie as he crumpled to the ice in pain, sliding into the boards.

The puck took a strange bounce off the boards, landing on an Oilers' forward's stick, who was backchecking on the play. Immediately, the Oilers turned up the ice, realizing that Mike was down on the ice and that they would have a man advantage going the other way.

Within a few seconds, they had made their way into the Ranger's zone. One pass to the forward, another to the trailing defenseman on the play, and within ten seconds of Mike's back going out, the Oilers had put the puck in the back of the net.

3-2 Oilers, with 30 seconds left in the third period.

Mike was unable to move. It was as if his back was completely solid like cement, and all he could do was lay there and ponder what the fuck had just happened.

The arena had gone completely silent, aside from the Oilers' bench going wild and a few cheers from their fans in the crowd.

He could also hear his coaches and some players yelling at the referee for letting the play continue while Mike was down on the ice. The referees didn't seem to respond.

Soon, the team trainers rushed out to check on Mike. He barely registered them being there, still in shock.

Lying on the ice, seeing his simulated teammates' faces, Mike could not help but realize that this was one of the most painful and upsetting experiences of his life.

This came from a guy who had torn two ACLs, battled alcoholism and depression, lost his parents as well as two dogs, and gone through countless breakups with women. The feelings he had right now could only be described as utter sorrow and dejection.

He had gone from such a high at the end of the second period to such a low right now that it was almost unbearable.

The trainers helped him to the bench, where he still heard the coaches arguing with the referees that the play should have been blown dead. The referees argued back that they had the discretion to blow the whistle while the other team had possession of the puck, and because the play happened so fast, they did not feel the injury was serious enough to warrant a whistle.

The crowd booed mercilessly, throwing cups, hats, and other objects onto the ice.

Mike sat in silence, staring at his pants. He was in pain, but he hardly felt it anymore as he was in shock. He had made a selfish decision to do what was best for him instead of his teammates, and it likely cost them the Stanley Cup.

It was a pattern in his life that just kept repeating. It was why he could never last in relationships and why he didn't have a great relationship with his remaining family. He was selfish, and this was one more example of how his selfish decisions caused harm and pain to others around him.

He had hoped to experience the joy and excitement of winning a Stanley Cup, but his selfishness cost him that opportunity. He was devastated. The looks on his teammates' faces said it all. Utter devastation.

As the final 30 seconds ticked off the clock and the horn sounded, Mike sat staring at his skates, wondering how such an incredible and life-changing experience could turn bad so quickly. He had gone from such a high of making an amazing pass on the first goal, scoring the tying goal, and playing a great game of hockey to... one of the lowest points of his life.

Mike couldn't bear to look at his teammates at the moment, though they all came to offer their support as they headed out on the ice for the final handshake line. He couldn't watch the Oilers celebrating with their goalie on the far side of the rink. He couldn't look at the crowd and see Eileen and his simulated parents.

No, he could only sit there, staring at his skates. After a few moments, Coach came over and said, "Come on, son, we have to shake their hands. I know it hurts."

Mike finally looked up and saw the Oilers gathered around their goalie, hugging and high-fiving each other, making their way toward the middle of the ice for the traditional handshake line, where both teams shook each other's hands after a hard-fought series.

Slowly, Mike worked his way off the bench and onto the ice. The handshakes and congratulations came, along with the "good game" and "you played your heart out," but it didn't matter.

All Mike could think about was the visual of lying on the ice, watching the Oilers score that last goal just after he was so close to winning it. He knew if Nate's back hadn't gone out at that exact moment, he would have scored and been on the other side of the line right now with the opposite emotions.

He felt sick. That was the only way to describe it. He wanted out. He didn't want to return to that locker room and see his coaches and teammates looking discouraged and disappointed when he knew it was his fault.

Nothing would help him overcome this. Not Eileen, not Robby, certainly not anyone from that locker room.

He just needed this to end.

As he stood on the ice, watching his teammates head off to the locker room, Mike knew this was the end of his journey. He couldn't remember what he had to say to be extracted from the simulation, but he thought it was something like, "Stuart, please get me out of here. Extract me—it's an emergency."

▼ ▼ ▼

MARCH 8. 2032
5:15 P.M.

A few moments later, he slowly opened his eyes and saw Stuart staring at him with his giant, non-human eyes.

"Are you okay, sir?" Stuart asked.

"Huh? I'm okay, I think," Mike responded, slowly adjusting to the light and his surroundings. "Can you raise me a bit, please?"

"Certainly, sir," Stuart said quickly as he raised the chair to allow Mike to sit upright. "Charles will be in momentarily; I have alerted him about your request to be extracted. Please sit here for a moment. Here is some water." Stuart handed Mike a cold glass of water, which he drank quickly.

A moment later, Charles entered the room with a doctor beside him.

"Hi, Mike. How are you doing? Do you know where you are?" Charles asked.

"Yeah, give me a minute, please," Mike said slowly, taking a few minutes to get his bearings. "I'm in the facility—the simulation facility, right? You're Charles? Just give me a few minutes."

"Okay, sir," Charles responded. "We'll continue whenever you're ready."

After three or four minutes, Mike nodded, signaling he was ready. Charles continued, "I hear you requested an extract from the simulation a little early. This is Dr. Browning. He is here to ensure your vitals are okay and you don't have any conditions that would necessitate further action."

Dr. Browning took it from there. "Hi, Mike. Can you tell us why you asked to be extracted a little early from the simulation? It looks like the game had just ended, which did allow you to leave the simulation, but you indicated it was an emergency. Can you please elaborate on what happened?"

"Yeah, I didn't feel like being in there anymore. Am I able to get out of here?" Mike asked slowly, still adjusting to being back in reality.

"Not quite yet, sir; we must ensure you leave here physically and mentally okay. We have access to your simulation so that I can look back. Why don't you just tell me what happened, please?"

"Goddamnit, Doc, you're not going to make this easy on me, are you? Fine, I shit the bed, okay! I had an opportunity to score a game-winning goal in Game 7 of the Stanley Cup Finals, and I blew it because you fucking people gave me a broken body that went down at the worst possible time. I should sue your fucking asses for giving me a body that didn't work."

Mike was sitting up in his chair, his face contorted with anger.

"Okay, sir," Dr. Browning replied, stepping back from the chair. "You need to calm down first before we can continue."

"Fuck that," Mike said, glaring. "You people set me up for failure." He jabbed his finger towards the doctor. "Who the fuck thinks of that? Yeah, let's give a guy, who had multiple injuries that derailed his real-life career, injuries in the fucking simulation! Really fucking fair! Was this some sort of sick, demented game you were playing with me? Sick fucks you all are!"

At this point, two large gentlemen entered the room and held Mike down in the chair as a nurse stuck a needle in his arm.

The last thing Mike remembered before falling back asleep was pure rage.

▼▼▼

MARCH 22, 2032

Mike had done this before. He had been sequestered in a windowless and television-less hospital room before. From his multiple stops in rehab, he knew how to pass the days and find comfort in complete boredom.

His friends and family weren't allowed to visit him for a few days after his admission to the short-term recovery facility. His emergency contact was Stacy, so she came as soon as possible to make sure he was okay. That helped a little, but he was more concerned about her being okay.

During the rest of his time in the facility, he focused on being polite and calm with the nurses, avoiding anything that would make his time here longer than it needed to be.

He tried to focus on the positives: He had scored a goal and had a beautiful assist. He also tried telling himself that he couldn't control what the simulation gave him. It was what it was.

Still, rage and devastation were eating him up inside. He felt the simulators, who knew his background and injury history, had set him up. It felt like it was done intentionally, and he wasn't happy. Would he ever be able to prove that? Probably not, but he was furious at how the simulation went.

However, the realization that his selfishness might have cost him the experience of hoisting the Stanley Cup was something he could not let go of, even if it wasn't real.

Mike should have known it was no place for him to be brave. If he was hurting, he should have told his Coach. Any professional hockey player would have reported their injury in real life and prioritized their team. Not doing so in the simulation was stupid and selfish.

He could have let his teammates handle the rest and still had the chance to hoist the Stanley Cup, which was his goal of the experience.

So, he spent the next two weeks assuring doctors and visitors that he was fine. He knew the drill; they wanted to make sure he wasn't a harm to himself or others.

Finally, after being held for two weeks, Dr. Browning was ready to send Mike home. On the evening of Mike's release, Dr. Browning walked into Mike's room to relay the requirements of monthly physical and mental wellness checks that Mike had to comply with to be eligible for next year's Anticipation Day experience. Mike gave his approval through a simple phrase: "I understand."

"Okay, Mike. Please hold on for a few moments while we get your paperwork ready," Dr. Browning said as his final parting words to Mike.

Thirty minutes later, Mike left the facility and got in a car, hoping his negative feelings would soon be replaced by positive thoughts of his daughter's birth in a matter of months.

He clung to those thoughts as he drove off into the Denver night.

▼▼▼

JULY 14, 2032
2 P.M.

Mike walked out of Intermountain Health Hospital and headed towards the parking garage. His emotions were all over the place.

He was, tired, nervous, scared, but mostly confused. Confused as to why he didn't feel even a *tinge* of happiness on what should have been one of the happiest days of his life.

Sure, seeing the birthing process is traumatic for most people. However, at the end of that process, when a parent holds their newborn for the first time, happiness should be one of the foremost emotions.

When Mike first took little Isla into his arms, gazing into her blue eyes and holding her tiny fingers, the strangest thing happened. Mike didn't feel happiness. He felt pride in fathering this beautiful human being, nervous that he was not responsible enough to take care of her, exhausted from nearly 30 hours of no sleep, and certainly hungry, as his growling stomach reminded him.

Yet happiness was not an emotion he felt, and he kept asking himself why.

Deep down, he knew why. He knew the reason he didn't feel happiness right now was the same reason he battled alcohol and drugs for most of his life.

That feeling that he hoped would never return had returned.

As he got into his car and pulled out of the parking lot onto 18th Ave, he had two options.

To the left was home, food, rest and a return to the hospital tomorrow to check on mommy and daughter.

To the right was his old liquor store on 17th Ave, where he used to stop by every Friday night on his way home from work to buy a six-pack of beer or a bottle of bourbon before heading to the City Park Pavilion, where his contact supplied him with methamphetamines and the occasional vial of crack.

Both directions led to two very different results. So, when the light turned green, Mike sat there for a few seconds and eventually turned his signal on and made the turn he knew he had to make.

CHAPTER 3

− MARYANNE − ONE DAY WITH HER DAD

MARCH 8, 2032
7:15 A.M.

"*Wow, what a difference two years makes,*" MaryAnne thought as her self-driving car drove through the streets of Denver on the way to the simulation facility early on Sunday morning. She was tired, but excited to be embarking on this journey.

Working for the NSA certainly had its perks: seeing some kick-ass technology, working on exciting projects with committed people, and getting an early retirement.

However, she could have never imagined that when she joined the NSA 13 years ago, getting to do a trial simulation experience that was supposed to make you forget all about your everyday life would be one of those benefits.

Her mind drifted to her first experience as she made her way towards her next one.

▼ ▼ ▼

Two years ago, MaryAnne was part of the first group in the country to apply to experience these simulations. The application process was optional for government employees, and many opted out, preferring to let others be the guinea pigs.

She never admitted it to anyone, but she did have concerns about the neural linking's possible short-term and long-term effects. From what she was briefed on about the technology, it seemed safe and unlikely to cause any long-term issues. Still, as they said, "Failure is the opportunity to begin again more intelligently." She hoped she wouldn't be one of the "failures."

The program's timing was perfect for MaryAnne, given her recent divorce from Kevin, her ex-husband who she happened to meet on the first day of NSA training a decade earlier.

When they first met, she couldn't take her eyes off him—tall, dark, and handsome—the usual type of guy she was attracted to.

Soon after, she approached him at an after-work event and they ended up talking for most of the evening, which led to dinner, an overnight sleepover, breakfast the next day, and eventually dating for a couple of months. While there was no official policy against dating a fellow employee, they decided to keep it quiet until they were sure their relationship was serious enough to warrant revealing it to their superiors.

Once they were sure, they decided to come out in the open with it. Because they were in different divisions of the NSA (Kevin was in the SIGINT division and MaryAnne was in the Information Assurance division), their superiors saw no immediate risks and allowed them to continue their relationship, with the caveat that any changes must be reported to their individual superiors to ensure no breaches of confidentiality.

They became more serious after that, leading to Kevin popping the question three years later. While she loved him and wanted to spend the rest of her life with him, she wasn't sure if he was ready for marriage. His parents had been pressuring him to tie the knot for a while, and she felt he was doing it to appease them more than because he really wanted to marry her.

MaryAnne put those doubts aside and said yes, hoping their love would be enough to make their marriage work. And it was. They were happy together.

Kevin's work required significant travel, and he would be away for weeks at a time. MaryAnne told herself that this was part of what she signed up for, and she had to accept it for the short term. Eventually, he would ascend through the ranks of the NSA and get promoted to a head management position, which would result in less travel and a greater pension upon retirement.

Unfortunately, as she discovered later on, his time away wasn't all business. There was also a significant amount of pleasure for him involving a few women scattered around the country he visited routinely.

Even after relocating back to Denver for MaryAnne's work at the NSA office in Denver, Kevin's travel around the country continued.

The night he accidentally left his phone by the bedside and she saw a text pop up from "Sarah—Cloverfield", was one of the worst nights of her life. She had suspected something was going on, but finding multiple text chains with multiple women absolutely devastated her. For someone in the NSA, he really was a fucking moron when it came to having these messages out in the open.

It was as if her entire life up to that point had been a nightmare that she couldn't wake up from. Her sense of worth was shattered.

Divorce proceedings followed, along with a severe bout of depression. She informed her superiors, who recommended a leave of absence to get her head straight, which she took.

As she was still employed by the NSA, she was eligible for the simulation experience. The timing of the simulation was perfect as she really needed to "let loose," and let loose she did. In the mindset of purely wanting to feel good again, she had simulated sex with over 50 guys on her journey across Europe.

Some were absolute studs; others were not, but what did she care? There was no risk of diseases, pregnancy, or hurt feelings. She was able to feel the sensation of an orgasm, so why wouldn't she fuck her way through Europe?

After what Kevin had put her through, she needed a release, and boy did she get one. She didn't care that it wasn't "real." It felt real to her, and that was all that mattered. It was a beautiful, incredible, refreshing, surreal, and otherwise fantastic trip.

She came out of the simulation feeling rejuvenated and ready to move on with her life. Fuck Kevin and the multiple women (that she knew of) he cheated on her with. She realized it was a blessing in disguise to be able to move on from him and focus on her physical and mental health, which she was trying her best to do.

Therapy helped her work through these issues so she wouldn't hold onto everything on the inside. No matter how tough of a woman she projected to the world, she had been hurting for a long time. After her simulation experience, she was a new woman ready for the next chapter of her life to begin.

The one clean aspect of their relationship was that there were no children. Although MaryAnne still harbored the idea of becoming a mom one day, she realized it might not be in the cards for her, and she was fine with that. It allowed her to focus on herself and have a clean break from that asshole.

Over the past year, she had started dating again, including a fling with Patrick. Some men were more serious than others, but she never developed a deep enough connection with any of the men. And she was fine with that.

At 40, MaryAnne was now focusing on work, yoga, eating better, and getting her mind right. With everything going on with her dad's health, she was spending most of her time with her parents, knowing his time was likely limited at this point.

With the government stipend for Anticipation Day, she was a little more financially secure and could afford to put her career on the back burner for a short period of time to spend as much time with her dad as possible.

Similar to last year, the timing of this year's simulation couldn't have been better, and the theme wasn't hard to pick. Spending a day reliving a day with her family was an easy choice, as this day was close to her heart for many reasons.

The day, July 11, 2026, was the last night of her parents' 50th-anniversary cruise to Bermuda, which MaryAnne and her brothers, James and Robby, paid for in honor of their parents' special occasion.

The attendees were MaryAnne and Kevin; her 34-year-old brother James and his family; her 31-year-old brother Robby and his family; her dad's sister Lori and her husband Bill; and, of course, her mom and dad.

MaryAnne always got along with her family, seeing them as much as possible. Even after her brothers moved away from the Denver area, she still tried to see them a few times a year, mainly for holidays and birthdays.

Her nieces and nephews loved when "Auntie MaryAnne" came to visit, as she always came bearing lots of presents for all of them. She treated them as her own kids, dishing out advice when needed, taking them out when she was in town and buying them a present or four.

"That's what aunts are for," she would always tell her brothers. "Especially aunts without kids of their own."

Unfortunately, her relationship with her parents, especially her mother, became strained after the divorce. Her mother seemed more disappointed that MaryAnne still had no children than about what Kevin had done to her. However, with her dad's health ailing, MaryAnne decided to set aside her negative feelings towards her mother and be there for her parents as much as possible.

Her parents had appreciated MaryAnne and her brothers organizing the cruise and had looked forward to the trip for a long time. The cruise departed from New York City, which was perfect since everyone had wanted to revisit New York. After a few days wandering the streets of New York, they spent two days at sea, two days in Bermuda, and two days back at sea before returning to New York a week later.

Between the beautiful and fun cruise ship, the pink sands of Horseshoe Bay, where Kevin, James, and Robby jumped off four-story-high cliffs, and driving around the island to visit the local beaches and restaurants, it was an amazing trip.

On the first night in Bermuda, the entire family joined for an anniversary dinner in Hamilton, the capital. They enjoyed a delicious meal with a beautiful sunset view and everyone was in a great mood and happy.

They spent the other day on the island exploring on their own and shopping. Bermuda was a beautiful place and MaryAnne wanted to go back one day.

On the ship, her nephews and nieces had fun, mostly playing in a water playground, basketball, or any of the hundreds of other activities the ship had to entertain them. Truthfully, MaryAnne didn't see too much of the family during the day; everyone got together at the family meals to discuss their day.

By the last day, everyone was tired but relaxed, ready to return to New York. All the effort put into planning the cruise and getting dates picked out came together with the family for one final day together at sea.

This was the day that would help her remember her dad as she wanted to: a loving and fun man, passionate at times, and able to take in moments for what they were.

He always supported her career, and she knew he was proud of her. She hoped this simulation would provide the warmth she needed to face her dad in his current state. She would find out soon enough.

▼▼▼

8:15 A.M.

MaryAnne and her nurse, Emily, arrived at room 305, where Emily instructed MaryAnne to put her effects in the locker so they could confirm the simulation. As MaryAnne was doing this, a robotic assistant approached them, announcing itself as "Maria."

"Maria will assist with monitoring your vitals during the simulation and alerting us if anything seems off," Emily explained. "Just to confirm, your simulation will recreate a day from your actual life. July 11, 2026. Is that correct?" She glanced at her tablet.

"Yes, that sounds right. That should have been six days after it left, which was the day after the July 4th holiday, so that sounds right," MaryAnne replied. "By the way, Maria is my mom's name too! Isn't that weird?" She chuckled.

"That is weird! Do you want me to request a different assistant?" Emily asked.

"No, it's fine. It's a great name," MaryAnne said.

"Perfect," Emily said. "It sounds like a fun trip. I can imagine why you'd want to recreate that."

"It was, for the most part," MaryAnne responded. "My ex-husband and I needed the trip after our house was partially hit by a tornado a few months earlier. Plus, it was my parents' 50th anniversary, so it was good timing."

"Oh my god, that sounds terrible. I hope everyone was okay from the tornado?" Emily asked, genuinely interested.

"Yeah, everyone was okay, luckily. It hit when we were at work, so no one was home. Our roof was totaled, though. I guess it comes with the territory when you live in eastern Colorado. But thank you," MaryAnne said with a smile.

"Please don't repeat this, as I could get into trouble, but ironically, I was just with a man going tornado-chasing in his simulation. Sounded scary." Emily winced as if to say: *Who would do that?*

MaryAnne wondered if that was Patrick. How many people could be here for a tornado-chasing simulation today? It's a small world, but not that small.

"A few more questions, and we can get you going," Emily continued. "Have you had any changes in medicines, health conditions, both physically and mentally, or significant trauma in your life since you last saw us two months ago?"

"No, nothing," MaryAnne replied.

"Perfect, thank you," Emily said, tapping on her tablet. "Now that that is confirmed, let's review what will happen next. I know you did this two years ago during the trial run. The process will be similar but with some differences since you're reliving a day from your history.

As you know, we'll sedate you before placing the ring on your head. The sedative dosage was calculated based on the 6.5-hour run-time and your height, weight, and body mass index. Maria will monitor your vitals, and a team of medical professionals will come by every 30 minutes to review your vitals while in the simulation. As you know, once you wake up in the simulation, you may feel confused for a few minutes as the ring adapts to the environment and learns your neural pathways. This should pass quickly as you acclimate to the simulation, just like last time."

"Sounds good," MaryAnne responded.

"Now, let's go over what the differences will be. Sorry for the list, but it's important for you to understand how this simulation differs from what you did last time.

One: The simulation will recreate your chosen day as accurately as our technology allows, based on the memories we were able to retrieve from the downloading process. It's important to remember that what you see may not exactly be what happened that day but rather how you remember it. For instance, you may have remembered a relative wearing glasses when they actually wore contacts. So, if they mention needing to take out their contacts, there may be discrepancies. Does that make sense?" Emily paused, noticing MaryAnne's confusion.

"I think so… You're saying I might have remembered things from that trip differently than how they actually happened, and I need to keep an open mind, right?" MaryAnne asked.

"That's right. The overall day should be accurate, but some details may not make complete sense as you rewatch your day. And that's okay. It was likely just some inconsistencies from how your brain acquired the memory to how it stored and retained it. Our technology can only pull what was retained, so don't freak out if things don't perfectly align. Okay?"

"Got it. Thanks for the warning." MaryAnne laughed.

Emily continued, "Great.

Two: There may be gaps in the day where memories couldn't be retrieved. No one remembers everything about each day. It's impossible. But that's okay. Think of it like the night sky." She pointed upward with her tablet pen. "Bright stars are the easiest memories to recall and should have lots of details to recreate. Dimmer stars are recallable memories that can be retrieved, but they may not be perfect. Barely visible stars are those we used a 'technological telescope' to zoom in on to get enough memories to recreate them in the simulation. Again, they won't be perfect, but they will get you close enough to what happened. Finally, some areas have no stars, meaning we had to skip ahead as no memories could be recalled. Hopefully, those are minimal. Okay?"

MaryAnne could only muster a simple "Okay."

"It's a lot, but this is all to prevent you from freaking out and ending the simulation for no good reason.

Three: You won't have real-time access to your thoughts from *that* day. It'll be like watching a movie from a first-person perspective without any insight into what you were thinking at that moment. You might recall some thoughts from that day as you rewatch, but unfortunately, we can't recreate them. You can think fully in real-time, but if you go into 'la-la land,' you might miss parts of the simulation as it will continue to play out.

However, you will be able to feel emotions through your memories. If you remember being angry, you will be able to feel that. Same with happy, sad, relaxed, tense, etc. Don't ask me how they can do that; they are able to.

Four: You'll be able to hear, see, smell, and touch everything you come into contact with as if you were actually there. This remains the same as before.

Five: We've recreated the timeline as accurately as possible based on the details of the memories the technology could pull and additional details like daylight or indicators of time that we could pull, like a clock. However, there may be some memories that could not be perfectly put in order. Again, this should be minimal, but I'm letting you know in case it freaks you out.

Six: Like last time, you can skip ahead in the simulation. However, this time, when you skip, it will be to your next memory. You only need to say 'Skip to the next memory.' As a government employee, you are allowed unlimited skips, though you hopefully won't need them as there are only a certain number of memories included within the simulation.

Seven: If you feel uncomfortable or have a question, just say 'Maria' followed by your question. Maria will be able to communicate with you as needed.

Eight: To be extracted from the simulation, say 'Emergency, please extract.' We'll stop the sedation, remove the ring, and work to understand what the issue is on your end. We have 15 minutes to continue the simulation before we must permanently end it, so we will talk with you to determine what the issue is. If you want to continue, we'll need your verbal consent; otherwise, we'll ask to confirm that you want to cancel the simulation.

Nine: If you recall, you could end the simulation early last time. In this case, we can end the simulation once it's past 10 p.m. on the simulated day. Just ask Maria to end it, and we'll proceed.

Any questions?" Emily finally asked.

"No, that all sounds straightforward." MaryAnne laughed. "I feel I am just going to have to get in there and figure it out from there."

"You'll be fine. Just remember, you'll feel like you're actually there, but you can't control anything. Go along for the ride, enjoy it, and hopefully, your memories are accurate!" Emily laughed.

"Me too. It was a funny day," MaryAnne said with a warm smile.

"Alright, let's get you started then. We'll start the process, put the ring on, and the next thing you'll see is your first memory from that day, which begins right when you wake up. Have a pleasant journey, and we'll see you on the other side."

The last thing MaryAnne remembered before blacking out was Emily's smile and thinking about how white and perfect her teeth were.

▼▼▼

JULY 11, 2026
10:15 A.M.

The first thing MaryAnne felt was something rubbing against her butt. Was Emily trying to shove a tube up her ass, or was this from her memory? She heard rustling behind her, but again, she was unsure what it was. She could feel something beneath her, like a sheet or a blanket, which covered her waist, warming her.

A distant sound, maybe a television, reached her ears, but all she saw was blackness. What was going on? Had they screwed up the simulation?

Should she call for Maria?

After 30 seconds, something that felt like a finger reached into her inner thigh. Did she and Kevin have sex on the morning of this day?

She couldn't remember but figured she was about to find out.

Her head throbbed, and her mouth was dry. Was she hungover or did Emily mess something up?

Present Day MaryAnne vaguely remembered going out with Kevin to one of the clubs on the top deck but didn't recall getting drunk, although given how she was back then, it wouldn't be surprising if she did, in fact, have a hangover.

It was still mostly dark, but MaryAnne could see a little better. Was she opening her eyes slightly? She could vaguely make out the room's sliding glass door.

The hands, now fully engulfed around her groin, had to be Kevin's. He was always horny in the morning after drinking too much the previous night and passing out with a hard-on, or at least a semi-hard-on.

He was kissing her neck now. Okay, this did feel good and certainly helped her forget her raging headache. He slowly pulled the blanket down, kissing her shoulders and going down to her back. His fingers, now inside of her, combined with his kisses, were getting her worked up. She could feel his penis growing.

She hated that this was the way this day started. Should she skip ahead to the next memory?

As she pondered this, he flipped her onto her back, his face now between her legs.

"*Well, what's the harm at this point?*" Present Day MaryAnne thought. "*You can still hate him and remember what it was like to have sex with him.*"

The memories of this simulated morning were slowly returning to her.

His tongue felt amazing, and it didn't take long for her to orgasm. If she'd known then what she knew now, she would have wrapped her legs around his stupid face and choked him out. But goddamn, the man knew how to please her.

"I want you inside of me," MaryAnne told Kevin. It wasn't Present Day MaryAnne speaking, but she heard it, and her mouth definitely moved, so she must have said it on the cruise. It was bizarre hearing her voice inside her simulated head and her mouth moving without her control. She sounded a little tinnier, but maybe that was just her "hungover voice."

"Your wish is my command," Kevin said, slowly climbing on top of her and inserting his hard penis into her. The sensation was amazing and overwhelming for Present Day MaryAnne—even though he was an asshole, his penis was the perfect combination of size and girth.

She hated that she loved the sex so much, but she should have assumed that Kevin and she were intimate on the cruise and expected some of these memories to appear.

Even in the simulation, Present Day MaryAnne could feel every thrust as if it were real. She had had sex with men in the simulation last time, but this was different. This was a reenactment of real life, and even though she hated Kevin now, she felt the same passion she had six years ago when she was in love with him and enjoyed fucking him. And this was *way* more intense.

After two mind-blowing orgasms in missionary, Kevin rolled over, and MaryAnne climbed on top, her body shaking. She could fully see now, and as she looked down at him, Present Day MaryAnne remembered what a gorgeous man he was. Short brown hair, hazel blue eyes, a wisp of facial hair, and a perfectly structured face. His body was still in good shape, and he still had the nicest ass of anyone she had ever been with, which was a respectable number by now.

It didn't matter what hour of the day it was; he always turned her on, and this morning was no different. She grinded herself to a third orgasm, then bent down to kiss him and whispered in his ear, "I want you to come."

She remembered how incredible it felt to feel him come inside of her. During the cruise in 2026, she had just gotten off birth control with the hopes of becoming pregnant. They had been trying to conceive for about six months but hadn't succeeded. But it certainly wasn't for a lack of trying.

As she thought about this, Kevin flipped her onto her stomach, flat against the bed, with her face buried in the pillow. He entered her again, and holy shit did he hit her spot. She exploded in a mixture of pleasure and more pleasure. She moaned deeply into the pillow, and he hit her spot again and again. She knew he loved taking her from behind, and it would only be a matter of moments before he came, just as she was moments away from her fourth.

She came in euphoric pleasure as Present Day MaryAnne felt the warmth build inside of her. He moaned deeply and collapsed on her back, his throbbing dick staying in her for another 30 seconds or so.

What woman wouldn't want to start a day with four orgasms on a cruise with their hot husband lying on top of them? Present Day MaryAnne wanted to raise her hand, but she couldn't.

As he got off her, Present Day MaryAnne swore she heard Kevin fart, but she didn't laugh. She *always* laughed when he farted, much like a 5-year-old would. Kevin's farting, especially after sex, would normally make her burst out laughing. But not this time.

Maybe this is one of those situations Emily mentioned, where MaryAnne remembered something differently than how it actually happened. She always associated farting with Kevin, so it's plausible she naturally worked a fart into her memory that didn't actually happen.

Either way, MaryAnne got up from the bed, put on her cruise robe, and walked into the bathroom to pee. Looking in the mirror, Present Day MaryAnne saw a much younger version of herself. It was only six years earlier, but her face seemed 15 years younger than it looked today.

Her blonde hair was ruffled from the roll in the hay but still healthy-looking. Her hazel eyes oozed youth and excitement, and her face was generally wrinkle-free. "*Man, what a difference six years makes,*" Present Day MaryAnne thought as she sat down to pee.

She wanted to scream to her prior self: "*Get out, run away, and don't look back! Save yourself the trouble, trauma, and pain of what is going to happen and leave his sorry ass!*" But she couldn't. All she could do was stare at the inside of the small bathroom on the cruise ship as she peed.

Walking out of the bathroom and onto the deck, it looked like midmorning. Apparently, it wasn't too early for a blunt, as MaryAnne was taking one out, lighting it, and putting it in her mouth.

Present Day MaryAnne forgot that weed wasn't legal to take on a cruise back then, so she had to sneak it on board through her luggage. Well-hidden, of course, as she had to be careful, given her job with the government.

By the last day of the cruise, she must have gone through about 90% of her stash.

MaryAnne stood on the balcony, looking over the sea on a beautiful, cloudless morning. Present Day MaryAnne distinctly remembered thinking in this moment about how good life was: she was smoking a blunt on a beautiful day after a wonderful vacation with her family, and she had just had four orgasms. Life *was* good then.

She felt relaxed. Emily was right; Present Day MaryAnne *was* feeling what she felt that day, and right now, that feeling was full relaxation. *Pretty. Fucking. Cool.*

She stayed on the balcony for another ten minutes, smoking, until Kevin came out.

He stared at the ocean for a minute before turning to her. "You hungry? I could eat—that pizza last night at 2 a.m. messed me up something good. You do not want to be around this room in about an hour."

"Lovely. Well, this thing will make me crave pancakes and syrup. Let's go down and see if anyone's eating. I'll shoot everyone a note to let them know we are heading down. My parents were up three hours ago and are probably ready for lunch."

Present Day MaryAnne laughed on the inside, remembering how she always loved pancakes with syrup when she got high. She always craved something sugary, but syrup always hit her spot, much like Kevin did a few moments earlier.

She started getting dressed as Kevin did as well.

"What do you want to do today? Gamble or spend time by the pool?" Kevin asked.

"Babe, remember you booked me a massage at the spa at 12:30? I'll do that and then spend the rest of the day by the pool. Take advantage of the sun, you know? I haven't seen James and Robby much, so it'd be nice to spend time with them and the kids," MaryAnne said while searching for her room keycard.

"Sounds good to me. I'm not sure I can drink until dinner; those margaritas from last night are sitting with the pizza and need to be evacuated soon." Kevin said pointing to his asshole.

"Lovely. I'm a lucky woman," she said, rolling her eyes.

"Pretty sure you thought so 20 minutes ago," Kevin said as he kissed her neck again.

"*Gross!*" Present Day MaryAnne thought.

"Okay, if you keep doing that, we're never going to eat." MaryAnne laughed, breaking away from him and walking to the door. "I'm hungry. Let's go."

▼ ▼ ▼

11:05 A.M.

The next thing Present Day MaryAnne saw was her family seated around a table in the ship's buffet area. Her mom and dad were laughing at something her brother James said.

"*My god, this is amazing,*" Present Day MaryAnne thought. She was still getting used to watching this day play out. She couldn't control anything, but she felt herself move, and when she spoke, her mouth definitely moved, but she couldn't change anything. It really was just like watching a movie play out, but in first person. This was definitely a *trip.*

Seeing her dad smile and laugh warmed her heart, though she couldn't tell whether her feelings were from that moment or her current self. It hardly mattered; she hadn't seen her dad laugh like that in years since his diagnosis. He had the greatest laugh. If you heard it from the next room, you knew it was him.

While Present Day MaryAnne longed to hear that laugh again, she knew it was unrealistic at this point. These memories would have to do, which was okay; this was why she had chosen this day.

Her gaze shifted to her mom. "*Aww, my poor mom,*" Present Day MaryAnne thought, instantly noting how the years of caring for her dad had worn on her. This version of her mom looked so different from the one awaiting her next weekend.

She looked... happy.

Seeing James was good too. He was always so much fun to hang out with, especially on a family vacation, with his big blue eyes shining bright this morning. Her nieces and nephews had grown *so much* since the cruise. Aly was almost in college, Lilly had just gotten her driver's permit, and Joey was ten and playing football.

Here, in this world, Aly was 11, Lilly was nine, and Joey was four. They were eating eggs, pancakes, waffles, chicken fingers, and fruit. Aly, with her curly brown hair and warm brown eyes, had just joined her school's band back in 2026. Lilly had curly blonde hair and was always looking for her next fun adventure at this age. Joey was so tiny and cute here, with his thick brown hair trying to hide his big, brown eyes.

James' wife, Gaby, was not there. MaryAnne Present Day remembered she was getting a massage of her own this morning.

Robby and his family were missing too. MaryAnne figured they were at the pool, on the waterslide, or playing somewhere on the ship. Her aunt and uncle were also not there; she imagined they were reading somewhere on the ship, away from all the craziness.

Her mom turned to MaryAnne and Kevin. "So, what time did you two crazy kids stay out until last night?"

"Oh jeez, what was it, 1:45, 2 a.m.?" Kevin asked MaryAnne while shoveling scrambled eggs into his mouth.

"I don't remember much past midnight, to be honest," MaryAnne said with a laugh, her mouth full of pancakes. After swallowing, she added, "I just can't drink like that anymore. Maybe in college, but definitely not now."

"Cheers to that," Kevin interjected, buttering a bagel.

MaryAnne sighed. "All I know is that on Monday, it will be back to the real world and starting this crazy project that I can't tell anyone about."

"I can't believe they're making you spend so much time in D.C.," her dad said as he took a break from playing with Joey.

"Yeah, I saw this coming. It should only be for a few months, but it's all hands-on deck. Since the President prioritized this for his campaign, we knew this would fall on our shoulders if he got elected.

It's exciting, Dad. I get to deal with some of the biggest national security challenges since 9/11, you know? This time though, we're trying to be more proactive in figuring out what we know and what we don't. Since China backed out of the International AI Agreement in March, they're now investing billions in advancing their capabilities. So, we have to be prepared to identify and respond to the advancements they are making. I'm actually looking forward to it." She paused to finish her pancakes.

Her dad stared at her, then chuckled. "You know, I remember watching *Terminator* when I was younger and thinking how crazy it was to think robots could take over the world. But now, it's only a matter of time before that happens."

"Dad, do you mind? The kids don't need to hear this," James said.

"Sorry..." her dad whispered. "They probably know more about this crap than you and I combined. If not, I'm sure they will soon. They're teaching all about artificial intelligence in high school, so they should be aware of it."

"I know they are aware, but it's our last day. Let's enjoy it without focusing on robots taking over the world, okay?" James said, laughing as he helped Joey finish his waffles.

Her dad glanced at MaryAnne before continuing. "Well, either way, I'll call you daily to see if I need to get into my safe room. If I don't hear from you after a few days, I will have no choice but to assume we're under attack and World War 3 is about to begin. So you better call me back everyday."

"Dad, you're ridiculous," MaryAnne said, cracking up. "If you don't hear from me, it's probably because I blocked you, and I'm just communicating with Mom."

"Well, whatever. I think it's amazing you're working on this, and I'm proud of you for being involved at this level." Her dad tapped her on her shoulder. "I always knew, since you were young, that you'd do something amazing. Just don't fuck it up."

"Allen!" MaryAnne's mom scolded, giving him a gentle smack on the shoulder. "Language!"

"What? Oh, I'm just kidding, kids. You know I'm proud of Aunt MaryAnne's career and what she's accomplished. I just want her to be careful, that's all. The government can't be trusted, no matter your clearance level. All I am asking is that if she hears anything about the end of the world, I'd appreciate a little heads-up. I'd like to spend my last days enjoying myself with your mother." He kissed her mom's hand with a smile.

That was what MaryAnne loved most about her dad. Even if he was rough around the edges, deep down, he was a sweetheart, and it always showed at the perfect time, especially with her mom.

"Get a room, you two," James said, laughing.

"Alright, alright," MaryAnne's mom said, laughing as well. "What's the plan for today? Your dad and I want to check out some art downstairs before the auction closes. Are you all planning to hang by the pool?"

"That's the plan," James replied. "Gaby should be done with her massage soon, and then I'll hit the gym for a bit. The kids want to play in the pool and go on the waterslides with Lia and Danny. I assume Robby and Lauren will be drinking by the time we get out there, so I'll join them when I get back from the gym."

"Cool," Kevin said, finally done with his meal. "I need to head back to the room for a bit, but I'll meet everyone on the deck at some point."

MaryAnne added, "I have a massage at 12:30, so I'll catch up with everyone after that. I'm not sure I'll be drinking until dinner, but don't forget I wanted to go to that couples' game show tonight to get Mom and Dad on. I think it's like the Newlywed Game, where they ask questions about the couples to see who knows each other better. It's at 8 p.m., so Mom and Dad, take a nap if you need to."

MaryAnne looked at her parents, as everyone was starting to get up from the table to get on with their day.

"*If they only knew what was coming tonight...*" Present Day MaryAnne thought, chuckling to herself.

▼ ▼ ▼

12:15 P.M.

The simulation picked up next with MaryAnne walking on the top deck of the ship towards the spa entrance. She passed people coming from the gym, as well as others walking in and out of the spa.

As she approached the entrance, she spotted Gaby walking out. "Hey you," Gaby said as she gave MaryAnne a hug. "How are you feeling this morning?"

"To be honest, I'm hungover, tired, somewhat nauseated, and sore, if you catch my drift," MaryAnne responded, pointing down at her crotch.

Gaby snickered. "Oh, yeah? You two kids have a little fun this morning?"

"It always happens like this," MaryAnne said while throwing her hands up in the air. "Kevin gets wasted and horny, but before we can take advantage of that, he passes out. With a raging hard-on. So, of course, he wakes up all ready to go. I didn't have much choice in the matter this morning, but I still feel like shit. I'm hoping this massage helps. How was yours?"

"Oh man, it was so peaceful and relaxing—no kids, no James, no brothers or aunts or parents or parents-in-law. Just a pair of oily hands rubbing me down. Exactly what I needed. Which one are you getting?"

"Kevin booked me the hot stone massage, I think? I'm not sure. I've never tried it, but I've heard good things about it. My friend

Alexandra just had it done; she said it was amazing. So, we'll see!" MaryAnne shrugged.

"Sounds great. I hope you enjoy it. I'm gonna get back to the kids, but we'll see you for a late lunch or photos or something. Just find me later—I'll be the one screaming," Gaby said while laughing.

"Will do, honey. Glad it was peaceful for you. I'll see you later," MaryAnne replied, hugging Gaby again.

After parting ways, MaryAnne continued towards the spa entrance. It was good to see Gaby happy; her laughter could light up a room. MaryAnne was happy knowing she and James were thriving back in 2032. They deserved it.

Present Day MaryAnne could feel a combination of nervousness and excitement for the massage. While weekly massages were now part of her life, she hadn't been into them back in 2026. The thought of other people touching her? *Yuck.* That probably explained the nervousness.

The excitement? That was probably because she *really* needed to relax.

The trip had been fun to this point, but the weeks and months leading up to it had been stressful, with the tornado damaging their house, work being insanely demanding, and Kevin being, well, *Kevin.* That stress was really getting to her, so when Kevin told her he'd arranged this as a gift, she thought it might help relieve some of it.

MaryAnne approached the spa's front desk to check in.

"Hi, I'm MaryAnne Jackson. I have a reservation for a 12:30 massage."

"Oh yes, Mrs. Jackson, here you are. You're booked for a Hot Stone Massage. We'll be right with you. Here's a robe and some slippers; please change in the women's restroom and come back here. We'll call you when we're ready. Here's a bag for your clothes."

"I've never had one before. Are they better than a regular massage?" MaryAnne asked the young lady behind the counter.

"Well, ma'am, hot stone massages are designed to improve blood flow to your muscles through a combination of heat and massage therapy. We recommend them for people with a lot of pain and tension in their upper back, including their scapula and rhomboids. It's worth a try! If you don't like it, the therapist can switch to a regular massage."

"Okay, that sounds fine to me. Where's the locker room?" MaryAnne asked, looking around.

"It's back down that hallway, ma'am, on the right."

MaryAnne walked towards the women's locker room and entered to see a rather attractive blonde woman undressing. MaryAnne had experimented with women in college and was fine acknowledging when women were attractive. This woman was a *bombshell*—blue eyes, a tanned, perfect body, natural breasts, and an impressively flat stomach.

"*Damn, she is good-looking. Was she really that attractive, or is this just how I remembered her?*" President Day MaryAnne thought. She wasn't sure.

"Oh, they are wonderful, the heat is amazing, and you feel totally refreshed afterward." the woman was saying as they must have been talking about hot stone massages while Present Day MaryAnne was lost in thought. "Just make sure they're careful around the ribs, spine, and other bones in your back. You don't want those stones hitting too hard against the bone—it can hurt. These people are professionals, though, so you should be fine. I'm Hillary. What's your name?" Hillary extended her hand.

"Hi, nice to meet you. I'm MaryAnne. Where are you from?"

"We're from Dallas. I'm on my honeymoon with my husband, Austin." Hillary smiled. "Yes, his name is Austin, and he's from Dallas. His parents were a little twisted like that, but he's gotten used to the question." She laughed.

"*Oh my god, I completely forgot about this interaction. That's so funny,*" Present Day MaryAnne thought. Before the simulation, MaryAnne had wondered whether they would be able to pull memories that she had forgotten about from that day. This was one of those things she had totally forgotten about. "*Pretty cool,*" she thought as the scene played out in front of her. She refocused her attention to the simulation.

MaryAnne was talking. "I'm here with my husband and family for my parents' 50th wedding anniversary. We had never been to Bermuda, but we absolutely loved it. Somehow, I've survived the trip so far. Congratulations on your wedding. I'm so happy for you." MaryAnne took her bra off and slipped it into the bag.

"Aww, thank you!" Hillary replied cheerfully. "That is so sweet of you. Wow, 50 years, huh? I can't even imagine that. Congratulations to them—that's an amazing milestone. Where are y'all from?" Hillary asked with that Texas drawl.

"We're from Denver. We lived in New York for a bit and then in D.C., but finally made our way back to Denver to be closer to family. I've visited Dallas a few times. It's beautiful there. Hot, but beautiful." MaryAnne took her shorts off, leaving her panties, then slipped into the robe and took her panties off under it.

"Well, I hope you have an amazing time here and that you enjoy that massage. Maybe I'll see you around the ship, but I have to shower to meet my hubby for lunch. Pleasure talking, MaryAnne. Bye now!" Hillary smiled as she walked off towards the showers, leaving MaryAnne alone.

She threw her bag into a locker, took one brief look in the mirror, and headed back toward the waiting room. *"My God, I was a fucking hot mess,"* Present Day MaryAnne thought, laughing.

▼▼▼

12:35 P.M.

The next thing Present Day MaryAnne saw was her other self laying on the table, with her massage therapist standing over her. The therapist had a nametag on that said "Lulu". MaryAnne had a towel wrapped around her waist, apparently already having taken her robe off. Lulu asked a few questions about her history with massages and whether she had any preferences.

"This is my first hot stone massage. I'm excited to try it out," MaryAnne replied.

Present Day MaryAnne remembered how good this massage felt and was excited to feel the relaxation again. *"A simulation and a massage—what a combination!"* she thought, as Lulu began rubbing oil on her back, while explaining that hot stone massages required more oil than a normal massage for the stones to glide smoothly against the back.

"Oh, this is going to feel good," Present Day MaryAnne thought as she got lost in her thoughts.

▼ ▼ ▼

On the cruise, MaryAnne had been generally happy, but at that time, she believed something was off with Kevin. After the divorce, she spent a lot of time in therapy looking back on their relationship and realized she had ignored the signs of his unhappiness and potential unfaithfulness: the constant bickering, comments about her weight (which she took very personally), and his constant traveling to the same places for "work."

MaryAnne had wanted a family with Kevin. Deep down, she believed that if they had a child, he would find true happiness with her, and they would work through their differences.

Little did she know that soon after their divorce, Kevin would have a child with one of his mistresses—a client from Nashville who was ten years younger than him. MaryAnne didn't envy him; from what she heard, this woman was psychotic and was taking him to court for a shit-ton of money. Good. He deserved it.

While MaryAnne was undoubtedly happier now than during the divorce two years ago, she still had a long way to go. Her career and mental health were her focus now, but she knew that eventually she would want to find another partner who treated her with the respect and admiration she deserved.

However, MaryAnne needed to be happy with herself before she could give her heart to someone else, which would take time and patience. She hoped this simulation would be the first step in finding her true happiness again.

▼▼▼

"Wow, that's hot!" MaryAnne exclaimed in the simulation, interrupting Present Day MaryAnne's thoughts. Apparently, the massage had begun, and yes, it was hot.

"Wow, I forgot how fucking hot these stones were at first. Shittt," Present Day MaryAnne thought, feeling the heat as if the stones were on her. *"How the fuck do they do this? Oh well, if I was able to feel an orgasm, I should be able to feel this!"*

Lulu said something about "getting used to it," but MaryAnne was lost in how good the stones now felt on her back. Lulu rubbed the stones from her upper back down to her lower back, delivering intense heat.

Goddamn, this felt good. It was hot, but the relief was almost instant, lifting the pressure off their collective shoulders.

As Lulu finished with the first set of stones, she tucked them under MaryAnne's body and began with the second set, kneading the side of MaryAnne's body, working around her hips and up towards the shoulders.

Both of their bodies went limp. Present Day MaryAnne thought she heard her 2026 counterpart say something but couldn't tell.

Now, Lulu was doing circles around MaryAnne's scapula while she continued kneading her back. Present Day MaryAnne was sure she was drooling, both in the simulation and probably back in her chair in Denver. *"Mental note to book one of these the next weekend,"* she thought.

After about 20 minutes, Lulu said, "I'm now going to do something called the piezoelectric effect, where I tap and move the stone along parts of your back, including your rhomboid muscle. This will send a shockwave into your muscle fibers to disperse stagnation. It may be noisy, but it's good for muscle tension."

"Okay," MaryAnne said quietly, her voice muffled by the towel.

Lulu started tapping the stones together, and Present Day MaryAnne felt the shockwaves in her back. It was a mix of pleasure and pain. This continued for another 15 minutes before Lulu switched to a knuckle massage up and down her back for the final 15 minutes.

Present Day MaryAnne was hoping this massage would cure her back pains in real life. She would have to see how she felt tomorrow.

"Wow, that was amazing," MaryAnne was saying as Lulu took a step back and let MaryAnne know her time was up. MaryAnne slowly sat up and sat on the massage table for a minute or so before getting up and putting her robe back on. "Will you come home with me?" She laughed as she thanked Lulu and began the walk back to the locker room.

MaryAnne felt so relaxed. She remembered thinking in this moment six years ago that between the morning sex and this hot stone massage, this was turning into a pretty good day.

Present Day MaryAnne laughed as her 2026 counterpart went on to shower, dress and leave the spa without a care in the world.

▼ ▼ ▼

1:55 P.M.

The next thing MaryAnne saw involved her walking near one of the pools on the sundeck. The sun shone brightly, reggae music blasted from the center of the pool, and most people wandered with either a drink in their hand or a plate of food from the buffet.

These were the days that Maryanne missed having kids of her own the most. She imagined the joy of bringing her children on a cruise like this and how much fun they would have. It was the one part of her life that felt empty, and while she hadn't yet given up on having kids, time was certainly running out, which made her genuinely sad.

Back on·the ship, she finally saw her brother Robby with his kids, nine-year-old Lia and five-year-old Danny, hanging out by the big water playground. Lia was a rambunctious little girl back then, always trying to get into trouble, especially around her older cousin Ali. She was a cutie and looked just like Robby. Danny was a handful as well—a little bundle of energy, as most five-year-olds were.

"*Oh my god, Robby,*" Present Day MaryAnne thought, as the Robby before her was so different from the Robby back in 2032, after the bike accident three years ago that shredded his right leg and prevented him from walking for almost a year. Since the accident, he had stopped working out and gained some weight as well.

MaryAnne hoped he would get back into shape now that most of the physical rehab was complete. Still, she knew that he was likely depressed, as soon after his accident, advancements in artificial intelligence had threatened his job as a tax preparer. After the conversation with Eric the night before, she realized she should introduce the two—maybe Eric could help him find something on the side. She made a mental note to introduce them after the simulation was done.

But at the time of the cruise, he was still muscular with a lean build, blond hair, blue eyes, and a great jawline.

She walked up to Robby, hugged and kissed him, and asked, "Have they been in this playground thing all day?"

"Pretty much," Robby responded. "They took a break for some ice cream, but they haven't stopped since probably 10 a.m. when we got out here. I hope they have enough energy for that show tonight you wanted to go to."

"Wow, that's amazing." MaryAnne laughed. "They are so cute together! I love seeing them have so much fun. And yeah, for that show, it's at 8 p.m. in the Mermaid Amphitheater, which is down on four or something. It should be fun; based on the description, I think it's like The Newlywed Game, where they just ask questions and the other person has to guess. If we say we're here for their 50th anniversary, I'm hoping they can get on. It would be a funny way to end the trip. If the kids can make it, great; if not, I understand."

"Yeah, it sounds funny. I'm sure Lia will be fine," Robby noted. "We'll have to see how Danny is behaving. This sun might wipe him out, but some combination of us will surely be there."

"Perfect. I can't believe this is the last day," MaryAnne said sadly. "I think we all had a fun time, right? I'm glad Ali is feeling better; it sucked for James not being able to do much at night. Speaking of not feeling well, how's Lauren?"

"I think whatever Ali had, she caught," Robby said, rolling his eyes. "She's resting in the room, but texted me that she was going to come up to hang with us, so hopefully that's a good sign. What would be a cruise without someone getting sick?" He smiled and took a sip of his pink drink with a little umbrella.

"Yeah, no shit," MaryAnne said, then pointed at Robby's drink. "I don't know how you're able to do that. I don't think I can drink anything today after this morning's hangover. That massage I just got was amazing, though—just what I needed. Hot stones are awesome. That's going to be my new 'go-to' when Kevin pisses me off. Absolutely amazing and relaxing."

"Really? I'm glad you enjoyed yourself. I assume Kevin is pissing you off again?" Robby chuckled to himself.

"No, we've been good this trip. I haven't wanted to throw him overboard—much. But we still have a night to go. He certainly behaved this morning, if you know what I mean." MaryAnne playfully nudged her brother on his ribcage.

Robby pretended to gag. "Jesus, MaryAnne, I didn't need to know that. I'm drinking, not drunk. Don't make me vomit."

MaryAnne laughed. "Sorry. Did you have fun last night? It was nice seeing you and Lauren out for a while. I'm glad Mom and Dad took the kids for a night. That was nice of them."

"Yeah, we needed it." Robby sighed. "We haven't been out that late in years. I forgot how much weed helps me take the edge off and not give a shit about anything. I'm glad we found that karaoke—you were hilarious. Screaming your ass off to the best of the 2000s. There were some classics from our childhood. I'm sure Taylor Swift would have been proud."

"Ugh, so embarrassing. I'm glad you both were there to witness my karaoke powers. Speaking of the other one, where's James?" MaryAnne asked, looking around.

"He was at the gym and just got back. The kids wanted some ice cream I think, so they'll be back soon, I imagine," Robby replied just as Lia approached, splashing through the playground. "Hi, Aunt MaryAnne!" She yelled, running over.

MaryAnne kissed her forehead. "Hi kiddo! Are you having fun? This looks awesome."

"It's so cool. I've been going up and down the slides for like an hour!" Lia said, just exuding happiness.

"It's actually been 2.5 hours, kiddo." Robby corrected.

"Okay, well, I'm going back to play, Daddy. Can we go on the slides?" Lia asked, seemingly ignoring the correction that had just been made.

"In a few minutes, baby. I'm just finishing talking to Aunt MaryAnne, okay?" Robby said as he patted Lia on the back.

"Okay, Daddy. I'll be back," Lia responded, already running back into the mist of the water playground.

Just then, MaryAnne saw her mom and dad come outside from the inside area and walk over to them with smiles.

"Hi, guys! How is everyone?" Her mom asked as she approached MaryAnne and Robby.

MaryAnne hugged her mom, saying, "Good, good. I was just telling Robby about my massage and how amazing it was. It was so relaxing and helped me forget everything else going on with me."

"That's great, honey. Robby, honey, where are James and the kids?" Her mom asked, seemingly ignoring MaryAnne's statement. "*Ah, there it is…*" Present Day MaryAnne thought, quickly remembering how her mother made her feel sometimes.

She and her mother had always had some issues, but back in 2026, her mom had become more focused on Robby and James and their kids than what was going on in MaryAnne's life. It was fine. MaryAnne had accepted it a while ago, after many trips to her therapist. It still stung when it happened, even in her memories.

"They went to get some ice cream. They'll be back soon," Robby said in the simulation, breaking Present Day MaryAnne's train of thought.

"Oh great. I want to get a family picture now that everyone's finally here and hopefully in the same place. I also asked Lori and Bill to come up. I think they were reading downstairs," her mom said, looking around in case they were around.

Her dad kissed MaryAnne's forehead and said, "Hey honey, I'm glad your massage went well. I'm sure you needed it." Her dad always knew what she needed to hear.

"Thank you, Daddy. It was, honestly, amazing. I needed it. How was your morning? You saw some art?" MaryAnne asked, hugging him.

"Yeah, I saw a cool painting yesterday that was very interesting, so I wanted to see the pricing," her dad responded with a big smile. "They said it was an auction process until 4 p.m., but to stop by at dinner to see if anyone put a bid in. No bids yet, so I'll stop by after we eat and see if I can make a deal. I'm good at negotiating, so I think I'll be okay if it's still available. Your mother isn't happy about the painting, but she bought some jewelry, so she doesn't really have a leg to stand on."

Her mom was talking to Robby, but she interjected, "I'm right here, Allen, and I can hear you."

Her dad laughed. "What? It's the truth. I like the painting and think it would go great in the hallway. What's the problem?"

Her mom rolled her eyes and sighed.

"Oh, stop, Maria—you're worse than my mother was. After 40 years of hard work, I'm entitled to get a painting I enjoy." Her dad was getting frustrated.

"Do we have to do this now? All I wanted was to talk about it before deciding that. You went ahead and started deciding like I wasn't even there," her mom said defiantly.

"I didn't make any damn decision. I just asked the guy what the price was currently, and he told me to stop by later, after dinner. How is that deciding?" Her dad asked, visibly angry at this point.

"Okay, forget it. I guess I'm wrong; you're right." Her mom sighed. "Let's just take this picture, and we can stop by later to check what the pricing is. Okay?"

"Sir, yes, sir." Her dad put his hand to his forehead and saluted.

Present Day MaryAnne remembered how much her parents used to bicker and how tough it was to hear sometimes. When her dad's dementia started to kick in, the bickering worsened initially, as he could still hold conversations. However, as the disease eventually progressed into an Alzheimer's diagnosis, the one blessing was that the back-and-forth stopped.

In a weird way, it was nice to hear them like this again, as it reminded MaryAnne of how sharp and funny her father used to be.

"Hey, everyone!" MaryAnne turned around and saw James walking toward them with Joey in his arms and Gaby, Ali, and Lilly following.

"Hey guys, how was ice cream?" Her mom asked as they approached.

"It was good, grandma—the same flavors they always have," Ali replied quickly.

"Good, honey, I'm glad you got to have some yummy ice cream! How are you feeling?"

"I'm good. I'm going to go on the waterslide with Dad and Lilly. I think Mom is going to stay with Joey." Ali started talking to MaryAnne's parents about something she wanted to do on the waterslide, which distracted them.

James turned to MaryAnne and Robby. "Yeah, I got roped into the waterslides by an 11-year-old. Good thing I haven't started drinking yet; I'd be chasing my vomit down the slide. What are you up to?"

MaryAnne laughed. "Oh, I just had my massage; it was absolutely amazing. I think I'll lie down and read a book for a bit and get some last rays before we go back to reality."

"I hear you—today is gorgeous. Where's Kevin?" James asked, looking around.

Not sure, I think he was taking a shit. I just came from the room, and he was still recovering from last night. I told him to come up to the pool when he's done, so imagine he'll be here soon," MaryAnne noted matter-of-factly.

"Okay, I'll see you around, I guess." James responded. "Let me know if you want a drink before dinner, assuming you're not still hungover from last night! That was a great time. I haven't done that with you two in probably ten years. I think old age is catching up to you, sis. You used to be able to hang with us!" he exclaimed, punching her in the shoulder.

As he said that, Gaby came over, put the kids down, and kissed MaryAnne.

MaryAnne signed. "Ha, I know. Well, I *am* getting older."

Gaby chuckled and added, "Hell, I'm a two-beer queer at this point. James probably wishes I was this cheap of a date when we met in college. I could drink a shit-ton more back then."

"Yeah, that would have helped my wallet for sure. You certainly played the game well with me, darling." James laughed as he gave her a kiss on the forehead.

"Thanks, darling," Gaby said dryly. "Oh, hey, speaking of games, did you still want to check out that game show tonight for your parents? We'll try to keep the kids up for it. I'm not sure how Joey will feel, but Ali and Lilly should be okay with it. Any idea what it is?"

Present Day MaryAnne laughed as she heard that question.

Her 2026 counterpart raised her hands in a shrug: *I have no idea.* "The app didn't give much information, but it sounds like the Newlywed Game. They ask a bunch of questions, and the other person has to answer. It's at 8 p.m., so hopefully everyone can join."

"Well, Mom and Dad sounded up for it, so we'll check it out. Alright, honey, alright, we'll go," James said as Ali tugged at his arm.

MaryAnne watched Ali pull James away to get to the waterslides. Present Day MaryAnne adored Ali and couldn't believe how cute she was. Ali had been sick for most of the trip, so this was her time to be an 11-year-old and have fun on this cruise.

Her counterpart in 2026 yelled after them, "Go! I'm going to read a book. We'll catch up later, okay? Have fun, Ali!"

James and Ali disappeared on their way to the waterslides. Gaby said goodbye and went to watch the remaining kids. MaryAnne said goodbye to her parents and made her way up to the sundeck to find a quiet spot away from the noise of the pool area, hoping to lie down and nap.

▼▼▼

3:35 P.M.

"Hey, you okay?"

That was the next thing Present Day MaryAnne heard, but she couldn't see anything but darkness. What the fuck? Was the simulation broken? She was about to call out for Maria when it looked like her eyes opened. Kevin was sitting on the chair beside her with a book in hand.

"Oh, right, I took a nap on the deck. Duh," Present Day MaryAnne thought.

Her past self responded, "Oh man, I must have fallen asleep. Sorry. What time is it?"

"3:35 p.m., honey," Kevin replied. "You had to be out for an hour. Good thing I put sunscreen on your back before I left—you would've been burned to a crisp."

MaryAnne sat up in the chair to face Kevin eye-to-eye. "That massage you got me really relaxed me. That was so sweet of you. Thank you. Plus, the way you woke me up. I just needed to take a nap, I guess."

317

They kissed briefly before pulling away and lying down on their respective chairs. Present Day MaryAnne felt gross kissing him.

"Do you want to move to get more sun?" Kevin asked.

"No, I'm good," MaryAnne said. "We were in the sun for a few days in Bermuda, so I need to be careful. Where did you go again? I was so tired before you left, I forgot."

"You must have been exhausted." Kevin laughed. "I went to the gym. Thought I might as well get a workout since it may be a few days before I can go again. How was the massage?"

"Do you want a drink?" MaryAnne asked as a server passed by to take orders.

"Sure, if you're having one. Figured you were taking it slow after last night, but if you want one, I'll join you," Kevin said, lying down in the chair.

MaryAnne signaled to a waiter. "Hi sir, could we get two rum and cokes? Room 5492. Here's my card. Thank you. No cherries, please."

She lay back down and turned to Kevin. "Okay, sorry, you were asking about the massage, right? It was amazing. They start with lots of oil, massaging it in with their hands. Then they take these hot stones and rub them in circles. I guess they have to be careful with the spine and clavicle because the stones can burn, but it's totally relaxing. She finished with a nice deep knuckle massage. It was relaxing so thank you again. I definitely needed it."

"Good, I'm glad you could relax," Kevin said, smiling. "I know it's been stressful thinking about this new project of yours and being away for weeks at a time. But it will definitely benefit your career and could get you catapulted within your department. Plus, it's only for six months, and I'll visit as much as possible. Okay? We'll be fine."

"*Oh, fuck you, you asshole. We'll be fine? Fucking liar.*" Present Day MaryAnne felt her anger boiling. She wondered if the chair she was lying on in the facility in Denver was starting to steam. "*You were fine fucking that whore from Nashville behind my back. Oh, and that bitch from down the street, who was always so nice to me. Now I know why she was so happy—she was fucking you too. Don't worry, if she ever says shit to me, I have dirt on her that her husband might not like.*

I should take this glass from this rum and coke and smash it over your thick fucking skull. Then take the shards and cut off your disgusting dick."

Goddamn, if only she could go back and end their relationship one of the 200 times she suspected he was cheating. If only she had been strong enough to trust her instincts and walk away, her life would be heading in a different direction now. But she chose to trust him, hoping a baby would keep him tied to her. That never happened, and the rest is history.

Present Day MaryAnne felt a little better as her counterpart said, "I know, babe. It's just been weighing on me lately. I shouldn't be sacrificing so much time with you for my career when we're trying to get pregnant. I feel like you're upset at me. I don't know."

"MaryAnne, seriously?" Kevin looked at her, confused. "I'm not upset at all. I've always supported your career. I get why you're doing it, but I need you to understand that I have a career too and need to do what I need to do."

Present Day MaryAnne felt her anger rising again. *"I'm sure you did, you fucking asshole. You did what you needed to do and who you needed to do."*

"I wish it was different and they could let you work remotely, but I get it. This is only for the short term. By next spring, we'll be back together all the time, okay?" Kevin said assuredly.

"Thanks. I needed to hear that. I love you for understanding and supporting my career. Always have. Just don't forget me, okay?" MaryAnne asked, chuckling.

"After this morning, I don't think I could forget you. You were pretty ready to go. You used to get like that every morning after drinking. I didn't have to do much, and you were wetter than the Indian Ocean." Kevin laughed.

"Oh my god, Kevin!" She was cracking up now.

▼▼▼

It was nice to hear herself laugh. It had been a while since she had laughed like that. Years earlier, before shit hit the fan, she used to laugh like that all the time.

After everything was said and done with her project, she was away from Kevin for over a year. At first, they saw each other every weekend, usually with Kevin flying to her, but after a few months, the visits reduced until it was once a month for a few days at a time. Kevin blamed his busy schedule, but he was more distant and less affectionate when she did finally return home after a year of working remotely.

By that point, they were having sex maybe once a week, but it was routine, like a chore he had to complete to get on with his day and stop MaryAnne from bringing it up since she still wanted to get pregnant.

Kevin blamed it on being tired and hurting his back from lifting at the gym. But she never bought that.

Seeing Kevin again in her memories was fine initially, especially with the ability to feel an orgasm earlier in the day. But now that she heard him say all this shit, it just reminded her of how much she hated his guts. Despite all the therapy she had taken for years since their separation, nothing compared to being right next to him and yelling in his face, even if he couldn't hear her.

As they both sat on their chairs back on the ship, drinking rum and coke, all Present Day MaryAnne could think about was how rageful she was. *"Why couldn't you just be a man and say how unhappy you were instead of living a lie? I wasted over ten years of my life with you!"*

There was something more primal and more freeing about voicing her anger and hatred of him directly at him, especially knowing he couldn't yell back at her. She felt herself calming down a little bit and was able to focus back on her memories.

Amidst her rage, she had missed some of the conversation, and now they were walking back to the room.

"*Oh no!*" Present Day MaryAnne thought. She remembered they went back to their room and had sex again. "*Fuck this!*" As much as she would love to orgasm again, she was not watching herself in bed with his maniacal asshole. "*Should I skip ahead?*" She asked herself before realizing it was an easy decision to make.

"Maria, can you skip to the next memory, please?"

Maria: "Confirmed. We are skipping ahead to the next memory."

▼▼▼

5:50 P.M.

"*Wow, what a beautiful dress that was,*" Present Day MaryAnne thought, looking at her past self in the mirror. She was wearing a stunning green dress that highlighted her cleavage as well as her dark and toned legs, paired with black high heels and the elegant earrings Kevin had given her the year before for their anniversary.

The dress was a treat from their time in New York City before the cruise. They had shopped along Fifth Avenue, and although MaryAnne had promised herself she wouldn't go crazy, she couldn't resist when she saw the dress in a window of one of the upscale shops near Central Park. She hadn't told Kevin the price, but she knew he would like it.

Her makeup—mascara, rouge, and eyeliner—rounded out her outfit. She looked *hot*.

Kevin was heading towards her, dressed in a sharp blue three-piece suit with a matching blue and green tie.

It was formal night on the last night of the cruise, and it ended up being the first dinner the entire family would attend together.

"You look great," Kevin said, kissing her cheek.

"You look pretty good too." MaryAnne kissed him on the lips. "*Yuck! Please stop!*" Present Day MaryAnne thought.

"You ready to go?" He asked. Present Day MaryAnne felt hungry, likely due to her 2026 counterpart not eating much all day combined with multiple romps in the hay and the sun all afternoon. So they left for the dining room on the third deck with MaryAnne looking forward to this dinner.

As they walked down, Present Day MaryAnne admired the beautiful outfits around her and thought about how formal night always reminded her of the *Titanic* with everyone in their best outfits.

When they arrived at the dining room, the entire family was already seated so MaryAnne and Kevin took their spots at the end of the long table.

"Hi, everyone. You all look absolutely fabulous tonight! I'm sorry we're late," MaryAnne said as they sat down. "I fell asleep after that massage, and it messed us up."

"Sleeping, huh? Must've been a good nap!" Robby said, winking at her.

MaryAnne glared at Robby as if to say: *Please shut up!*

The kids were at the other side of the long table, coloring and discussing their day. MaryAnne raised her voice. "Hey kids, how were the water slides?"

Ali spoke first. "They were so cool! I think I went on all of them like 200 times."

Lilly followed, "One was super-fast, the other was okay. The one with the tubes was the best; we kept going backward."

Lia was too busy coloring to answer, but MaryAnne was sure she felt the same.

"That sounds like so much fun! I'm glad you guys enjoyed it," MaryAnne exclaimed. She turned to her Aunt Lori and Uncle Bill. "So, what did you guys do today? Just hang out?"

Aunt Lori answered, "Yeah, we read some books, saw everyone at the pool for a bit, and just relaxed. It was so nice out on that pool deck, so we took advantage of it. We saw the kids running around briefly, but then they disappeared. Poor James and Robby were chasing them all over the place. I felt so bad for them!"

Uncle Bill added, "What about you guys? Get some sun?"

"Yeah, I had a massage earlier today, then sat by the pool to read. Apparently, I fell asleep. We had a few drinks before returning to the room. It was a nice, relaxing day, for sure. So, what's everyone having for dinner? Dad, did you see they have ribeye? Mom, they have salmon tonight."

Her mom replied, "Yeah, I saw that. Allen, are you getting the ribeye? Maybe we can share?"

Her dad said, "Sharing? Honey, you can order as much as you want. Get both the salmon and the ribeye, and we can split them. I'll get my own ribeye, though; the portions aren't huge here."

MaryAnne turned her attention to Kevin. "What are you going to get? I think I'll go with the pasta. I need some carbs."

"I was going to get the same. Why don't I get the salmon too, and we can share it?" Kevin suggested.

The waiter came by their table and they all placed their orders. MaryAnne was busy savoring some delicious rolls with butter when her brother James clinked his glass with his knife and stood up.

"Well, I figured I'd start this. I just wanted to thank everyone for coming on this trip." He looked at their parents. "We wanted this to be a fun way to celebrate your 50th anniversary, Mom and Dad. I hope it was a great experience for you both. That dinner in Bermuda was awesome, even if it took three hours! I'm also sorry a few of us got sick; I blame Gaby for that!" He glanced at Gaby, who playfully hit him on the arm.

"But seriously, I'm glad everyone is here tonight, healthy and ready to have a good last night. So, here's to you, Mom and Dad, and your anniversary. May you have 50 more years together! Let's enjoy tonight before we return to reality in a couple of days!"

Everyone raised their glasses and said, "Cheers." Her dad looked at her mom and said, "50 more years, huh? I can make it, can you?"

Her mom smiled back. "We'll see."

James sat down, and Robby got up. "Alright, alright. Let the funny guy go next. Well, I guess not to repeat what James said, but thank you everyone for joining. It was a helluva time organizing this trip and finding the right date and location, but I think we made a good decision, right? That cliff jumping in Bermuda was amazing, and the kids had a blast at that blow-up water park next to the ship that we paid way too much friggin' money for.

You know, I remember the first cruise I went on with Dad's and Lori's parents up to Alaska. It was so much fun. Remember that one? Where my jeans were stolen and I had to go with Lori to a friggin K-Mart in Juneau? That was an experience. I remember grandma stealing rolls from the dinner table, and Grandpa complained about everything to try to get a discount, even though we kept explaining to him that all the food was included. It was a great time just being able to spend time together. With our hectic lives these days, it's tough to find time to spend together, so I just wanted to say how much I enjoyed seeing everyone happy... when we weren't throwing up or dealing with fevers.

To Mom and Dad, Happy Anniversary. I hope you had a great time and, most importantly, no one threw anyone off the boat. I'd call that a victory! Cheers, guys."

Everyone cheered once more.

"*I should have thrown someone off the boat!*" Present Day MaryAnne thought. "*Oh, it's my turn to speak, isn't it?*"

It sure was. As the appetizers and salads arrived, MaryAnne stood up. "I'll make this quick because I'm starving, but I just wanted to say: Mom, Dad, this trip was for you. We wanted to repay you for always being there for us growing up and helping us succeed in our careers and lives. Hopefully, having everyone together, including the grandkids, was a blast for you, and you'll remember it forever. That's the most important thing. If it was a blast, then we did our jobs, and we couldn't be happier. Also, Dad, get that painting, will you? You'll regret it if you don't. Cheers!"

MaryAnne smiled and sat down. Her dad looked at her, tearing up a bit. "Thank you," he said.

▼▼▼

Fifteen minutes later, after everyone finished their appetizers, her dad stood and raised his glass.

"Alright, everyone, you knew this was coming. I'm not very good with words, but I wanted to say how thankful your mom and I are that you could all be here with us to celebrate our 50 years together. Fifty years, huh, Maria? I remember meeting your mom during our sophomore year of college; she was a beautiful, vibrant young woman studying French to be a teacher. When I first met her, I tried to woo her with my basic French from two years of high school, but I certainly couldn't compete with her. The first time I said 'Je T'aime,' I meant it, and I still do all these years later. I couldn't have asked for a better life partner, even though we occasionally argue and disagree." He smiled and nudged her mom with his elbow. "Am I right, Maria?"

"Occasionally, sure..." Her mom smiled and sipped wine.

Her dad continued, "Well, anyway, the point is, your mom and I wanted to thank you all for joining us on this trip and celebrating 50 amazing and fruitful years together. It has been the joy of our lives to watch you kids all become the mature, caring, beautiful, and successful human beings you are today. Nothing makes us happier than having you kids together, along with my beautiful sister Lori and Bill. Here's to doing this again for our 100th anniversary, although you might have to help me up the stairs by then. I love you all. Thank you from the bottom of our hearts."

Her dad patted his chest a couple of times before sitting down, with tears rolling down his cheeks. MaryAnne's mom took his hand and kissed him on the cheek. It was nice to see them like that—it was rare.

MaryAnne felt herself tearing up, but she wasn't sure if that was in the simulation or real life. It didn't matter. She remembered how much her dad's speech meant to her and her brothers, knowing it took a lot of work and effort to organize this trip.

Everyone said, "Cheers," while clinking their glasses together, even the kids.

"I have to echo what your dad said, guys—job well done on the trip," MaryAnne's mom added, tears welling up in her eyes. "Your dad and I couldn't have asked for a better way to spend our 50th. Thank you all again for organizing and planning this with everything else going on in your lives."

The rest of the meal was fairly mundane. MaryAnne had her salmon and pasta with Kevin, and enjoyed some delicious chocolate lava cake with ice cream for dessert.

Overall, it was a nice meal to end the trip.

They finished dinner around 7 p.m. and planned to meet at the show around 7:50 p.m. The kids headed to the arcade while some of the adults grabbed a quick drink before the show.

▼ ▼ ▼

7:25 P.M.

"*Sing us a song of a Pianoman, sing us a song tonight,*" MaryAnne heard as the next memory began. A man in a tuxedo was singing the famous Billy Joel song at the piano, while some of her family sat around, listening and singing along.

Her dad laughed to her right. "This guy's a riot," he said. Her mom was on his right, with Aunt Lori and Uncle Bill across from her at a small table.

Kevin was to MaryAnne's left, sipping on what looked like whiskey on the rocks. She looked down at a glass of wine sitting on her right leg and brought it to her lips, taking a sip.

James, Robby, and their families were absent. She recalled meeting them at the show later. They were at the arcade or running around somewhere.

As the piano player wrapped up "Piano Man," her dad called out, "MaryAnne, thanks again for organizing this. I know it was a lot of work, and you handled a lot of different personalities and requirements, but this has been a great trip. It means a lot to your mom and me that we're together as a family. Who knows how many more of these trips we can take?"

"Oh, stop, Dad," she replied. "I'm sure we'll all get together for something next year. But you're welcome. I am glad it all worked out... for the most part."

Of course, that trip was the last big one the family made. Between Robby's accident and her dad's diagnosis, it became hard to get everyone together again. Present Day MaryAnne felt a pang of sadness, knowing the next time they'd likely all be together would be at her dad's funeral.

"I know, honey, sickness is hard to control, especially with kids," her dad responded. "You'll see one day. It's just nice to see you kids happy and all in one place. With your work schedule, I know it'll be hard to get together next year, so celebrating like this was special to us."

He sipped his drink. "Anyway, I hope this show is as good as it sounds."

He glanced at MaryAnne's mom. "Hey, if we get picked, should we talk about what questions they might ask?"

"Who knows if we will, but I bet the questions will be something stupid like what type of underwear you own or how many times you fart a day," her mom said, smiling.

MaryAnne was relieved to see her mom smile; she was always more relaxed with a glass of wine in her hand.

Lori turned to Maria and asked "Well, you've lived with my brother for 50 years; how many times *does* he fart a day? I gotta know. When we were growing up, it was probably 15-20 times a day, and good lord, they were nasty."

"Oh geez, I lose track sometimes, but it's at least 10-15 per day." Her mom laughed. "Depends on what he's eaten."

"Well, darling, it must be your cooking," her dad replied, chuckling.

MaryAnne turned to Lori. "How are you feeling, Aunt Lori? I know this cruise has been a struggle, but I'm glad you could make it tonight."

"I'm okay," she replied. "Feeling better than I was a couple of days ago. Bill will probably need to see the doctor when we return home in a few days, but he seems okay. I'm so glad we could come; it was great seeing you, James, Robby, and all the kids. Catching up in person is always fun."

MaryAnne got lost in her thoughts as Lori continued the conversation from her memories. MaryAnne was thinking about the special place in her heart for her aunt, who was always honest with her and offered great life advice. Plus, she was a blast to hang out with. MaryAnne related to her the most out of anyone in her family.

Lori and her uncle had been married for some time, and MaryAnne saw them once every other year due to the distance. She absorbed as much of Lori's time as she could on this trip since she didn't know when they would see each other again.

Present Day MaryAnne tuned back into the conversation. Her 2026 self was saying, "I always loved watching Grandma gamble at the slot machines. I'd sit with her for *hours*, watching her play and putting coins in the slot machine. When I won, I remember how awesome it felt. I miss them so much."

"I know, I miss them too," Lori said. "Remember how your brother mentioned her stealing the rolls from the dining hall? She'd take ten rolls, some butter, wrap them up, and toss them in her purse. No shame at all. She just did it. I have no idea what she did with them." She laughed. "I assume she ate them at some point. Allen, do you know?"

"What's that?" MaryAnne's dad turned to them.

"Did Mom ever eat those rolls she took from restaurants?" Lori asked.

He thought for a moment before answering. "Oh yeah, she'd bring them home, freeze them, and use them as needed. Every restaurant we went to, rolls would be in her purse before the waiter even set the basket down. It was unbelievable."

"I think she fed them to the birds from her balcony. Remember?" Bill chimed in. "On that one cruise, we had the room next to your parents, and we'd hear the seagulls at 6 a.m. because she was feeding them bread from her balcony. We got so pissed—we had to tell her to stop!" Bill laughed.

"Oh my god, you're right. That's so funny. She was nuts. But I miss her," Lori said, staring at her drink for a few seconds.

Her dad broke the silence: "Yeah, she loved these cruises. Especially with you guys."

The group spent the next fifteen minutes chatting, listening to music, and drinking. It was a fun time for MaryAnne to relax and be with her family.

Present Day MaryAnne couldn't help but laugh, thinking about what would happen in a matter of minutes.

▼ ▼ ▼

8:05 P.M.

The simulation jumped to the entire family seated on red leather chairs in the large amphitheater, waiting for the gameshow to begin. The crowd of a hundred or so people seemed to be in a good mood, buzzing with excitement.

The elevated stage was in the center of the room with the crowd sitting all around it like a horseshoe.

MaryAnne and her family were towards the back left of the crowd in the elevated part of the theater, looking down towards the stage below.

Her mom and dad were sitting in front of the rest of the family on two swivel chairs. MaryAnne, Kevin, James, Robby, and Gaby were behind them. The kids were to their right playing cards with Lori and Bill to stay entertained until the show started.

Lauren and Danny were not there. MaryAnne remembered Lauren wasn't feeling well and had offered to take Danny back to the room to put him to bed.

MaryAnne turned to Robby, James, and Gaby. "So, we'll just scream '50th anniversary' when the show starts?"

"Yeah, I guess." Robby replied. "I assume they'll pick a few couples from different age groups. That's what I've usually seen. I guess Mom and Dad will be in the 'experienced' category. Can't wait to see what questions they ask."

"Oh man, this is going to be interesting," James added. "I mean, they know each other pretty well, right? It's been over 50 years. I hope they can answer at least a few questions correctly."

"They'll probably do better than we would," Gaby quipped.

"Yeah, you think? I think we'd do alright. As long as they don't ask about our sexual pasts, we'd be fine," James said.

"Oh, stop. You know everything about mine. And I'm pretty sure I know all about yours, but who knows? There might be things you haven't told me," Gaby said, giving James a death stare.

"Oh, really?" James retorted. "We just figured out that you thought we met when you were 19, but you were actually 20. There's a whole year I know nothing about. I am sure you weren't sitting around reading books that year. So, yeah, I'm pretty sure we would not do too well if some question came up about your sexual history."

"Oh my god! Can you not in front of your brother and sister, please? I'm embarrassed enough that I missed an entire year," Gaby said, laughing as she covered her eyes.

Present Day MaryAnne laughed, thinking how perfect they were for each other.

"What do you think, honey? How would we do?" Kevin asked MaryAnne in 2026. "I think we know each other pretty well." He put his arm around her.

"Get your fucking arm off of me", Present Day MaryAnne thought, wondering if she could reach through the simulation and chop his arm

off. Given what was about to happen, there was no point in getting angry again, but it still disgusted her.

"I think we do, but I'm sure as hell not getting up there to find out." MaryAnne laughed.

The lights dimmed, and the show's host appeared: a petite Spanish woman with beautiful light brown hair and a sleek dress showing off her ample cleavage. She was definitely Kevin's type, given the way he was gawking.

"*What an asshole,*" Present Day MaryAnne thought.

"How is everyone doing tonight?" The host asked. The crowd clapped rather unenthusiastically.

"Folks, come on," she urged. "I know you're not going to do me like that. It's the last night of your vacation; we're on a beautiful ship; and you've eaten, drank, and partied like kings and queens all week. So, I'll ask again: *How are we doing tonight?*"

This time, the crowd roared with applause, hoots, and hollers.

"Okay, okay. That's more like it. Thank you." The host laughed, waiting for effect. "I want to be the first to welcome you all to the 'Perfect Couple' gameshow. My name is Fantasia—yes, like the singer, only *way* more fabulous." The crowd laughed. "So, tonight, we are going to select three fabulous couples from the crowd to play a little game that will help us figure out which one of the couples are most in sync. You all ready to play??"

Fantasia held the microphone out to the crowd as there were more cheers, hoots and hollers scattered throughout the room.

"We'll have three categories for the couples tonight:

The first will be a newlywed couple, one that has been together for less than a year. You know who you are—the ones who still think you'll be married forever. The couples the rest of us want to strangle because they're still so damn happy! Am I right?"

The crowd laughed and clapped. MaryAnne and Kevin had been married for five years, so they didn't fit into that category.

"For the second couple, we need a slightly more experienced couple that has been together for over a year but less than 40 years.

That's a wide range, but you are the folks that should be in total sync with each other by now and should do pretty well in this game. You're somewhere between hating, liking, and loving each other. Who are my couples out there that fit into this category?"

Fantasia held the microphone out to the crowd again and a good portion of the room clapped, including all of the siblings and their spouses.

Fantasia continued; "Finally, we want a couple that has been together for a *long* time. We're talking 40 years or more. I can't imagine being with someone that long, can you? These folks should know each other inside and out, even if they struggle to get out of bed in the morning."

The crowd laughed again. "You couples know what I'm talking about—it hurts to get up, and that's okay! We love you and want to learn from your wisdom and experience. And maybe find out how much medication it takes to get through the day."

Fantasia laughed, then continued. "Alright, so let's get the search going for our first couple. Do we have any newlyweds or couples who have been together for less than a year?"

A dozen couples eagerly raised their hands. After some back-and-forth, Fantasia chose a cute young couple from New Jersey, Rob and Nicole, who were on their honeymoon.

"Now, for our second couple. Do we have any more experienced pairs, those who have been together for more than a year but less than 40 years? That will probably be a lot of you, but who's out here tonight?"

After some back-and-forth with the crowd, Fantasia selected a couple from Virginia, Jeff and Mandee, who had been together for around ten years to join them on stage.

"Now for our final couple, we're looking for the most experienced couple in the room." Fantasia scanned the crowd, looking for the perfect couple. "This couple would normally be asleep now but are here with us for this game show. Anyone celebrating something special for this cruise?"

MaryAnne, James, Robby, and Lori screamed in unison, "50th anniversary!" and pointed to MaryAnne's parents sitting in front of them.

Fantasia turned to them. "50 years? Wow, that's a *long* time! What are your names?"

"Maria and Allen!" Her dad shouted.

"Maria and Allen, welcome. So, it's been 50 years of marriage, huh?" Fantasia asked.

Her mom responded, "We've known each other for 53 years but have been married for 50. We met in college and are celebrating our 50th anniversary with our family this week."

Present Day MaryAnne remembered thinking how excited they seemed to participate in the show, at least in that moment.

"Okay, wow! That is amazing. Let's see if anyone can beat 50 years. Anyone else?" Fantasia asked.

Someone in the crowd shouted, "56 years!"

"56 years? Woah! Really? Where are you?" Fantasia searched for the folks who said that.

MaryAnne felt her heart sink, but that must have been in the simulation.

"Oh, they're not here yet?" Fantasia asked. "Do you know when they will be? No? Oh, jeez. If they've been married for 56 years, it may be a while before they get here. No offense." She laughed.

"Alright, folks, I think we've found our experienced couple. Maria and Allen, please come join us on stage."

"I totally forgot they nearly didn't get picked. This whole thing I'm about to relive almost didn't happen. Good thing that other couple was in the bathroom," Present Day MaryAnne thought.

The entire family clapped to encourage her mom and dad, as did the rest of the crowd. Soon, MaryAnne's parents were on stage, joining the newlyweds, Rob and Nicole, and the slightly more experienced couple, Jeff and Mandee.

"Okay, great!" Fantasia exclaimed. "We have our three couples. Now, here's what will happen tonight. Are you ready? We're going to play a series of adult games and activities to see how harmonious you all are with each other. The scoring will be time-based, so the quicker you complete each activity, the better. Make sense?"

Present Day MaryAnne felt her heart race at this moment as her counterpart in 2026 was likely realizing this would definitely *not* be the "Newlywed Game" with some PG-13-rated questions.

MaryAnne glanced at James and Robby, who both wore concerned expressions that said: *What the fuck did we do?*

She turned to Lori and Bill, who looked equally worried.

Kevin eventually turned to MaryAnne and said, "Uh, I don't think this is the Newlywed Game, MaryAnne. What did we just do to them?"

"I don't know, but my dad does *not* look happy," MaryAnne replied. Her dad's scowl was not something she'd seen in a long time. He was nervous, and so was her mom—she could tell.

"Should we get them off the stage? What do we do?" Lori asked, half laughing, half concerned.

"I don't think we can get them off the stage now," Robby replied. "Oh my god, my dad is so pissed." He laughed. "I haven't seen him like that in a long time. Let's see what they have to do."

Fantasia continued, "Okay folks, for the first activity, each lady will take this ball"—she held up what looked like a soft pool ball—"and roll it from the bottom of their gentleman's pant leg, up through the middle of his pants, and down the other pant leg. Ladies, you have to do this four times using only one hand; the other hand must be behind your back. Take your time and make sure you don't lose the ball in your partner's pants."

MaryAnne looked around and saw her siblings' faces turn pale. She was sure she looked the same. This was quickly turning into an extremely uncomfortable experience for them.

On top of that, the grandkids were fully engaged now that Grandma and Grandpa were on stage.

"Oh my god, this is insane. They're going to kill us. I gotta get this on video." Robby stood up and went to the back of the theater to get a better view. Ali joined him.

Fantasia continued, "Okay, we'll start with the newlywed couple first. Rob and Nicole, come over here and let's see what you can do."

MaryAnne remembered hearing the crowd laugh, but all she was doing was staring at her parents and wondering what they were thinking. She heard her family members laugh watching Nicole try to get the ball up and over her husband Rob's pants four times, but all she was focusing on were her parents.

She was feeling a combination of awful, giddy, and nervous for them. If this went well, they would look back and remember it fondly. If not…

After a couple of minutes, Nicole completed the four balls, and the crowd cheered.

"Great job, guys!" Fantasia exclaimed. "Way to get us going! What's that, Rob? You wish your balls were that big? Well, we'll just keep that to ourselves, won't we?" Fantasia and Rob laughed together.

"Okay, Jeff and Mandee, you're up next. Let's see if you can beat their time here of 2 minutes and 25 seconds."

"James, they're going to kill us. I'm not sure I can watch this," MaryAnne said.

"Well, we did this to them, so we have to watch. I can only imagine what they're thinking right now. I might pee myself and vomit at the same time." James laughed and turned back to the show.

MaryAnne looked at the kids, who were all watching, curious about what was happening. The crowd was laughing, and when Jeff and Mandee finished around three minutes later, her jaw clenched, and she felt a wave of nervousness hit her.

Fantasia chimed in, "Great job, Jeff and Mandee! You weren't as fast as Rob and Nicole, though. Sorry, guys. Jeff, I guess Mandee isn't as good with balls as you thought!" The crowd laughed again.

"*This girl was just a hoot, wasn't she?*" Present Day MaryAnne asked, though no one could answer.

"Alright, our experienced couple, Maria and Allen, come on up and let's see how you do!" Fantasia beckoned her parents to the stage.

Her mom and dad slowly walked up. Her mom bent down on one knee in front of her dad with the ball in her left hand. Her dad looked up towards where the family was sitting and just shook his head in anger. MaryAnne felt awful.

Fantasia said, "Go!" and her mom began inching the first ball up the inside of her dad's right pant leg. It fell a couple of times but finally her mom reached his crotch and the crowd went wild.

Her dad looked up surprised and said, "Ooh, careful," which made the crowd laugh harder. Her mom's hand was literally on her dad's crotch. Her mom proceeded to slow roll it down the other side of his pants.

She was doing well!

MaryAnne couldn't look. Her hands covered her face, so the scene went black, but she could hear James, Kevin, and Lori laughing like never before.

Gaby said, "Oh my god, this is hilarious," and she heard the kids asking, "What are Grandma and Grandpa doing?"

After what felt like an eternity, but was actually only a few minutes, her mom completed all four balls.

Fantasia exclaimed, "Alright, Maria! Great job. How are you doing, Allen? Was that fun?"

Her dad slowly turned and replied, "It was great."

The way he said it, MaryAnne could tell he was pissed. Usually, he was as witty and sarcastic as they come. When they returned to their spot next to the other couples, she could see her dad scowling at them. Eventually, he just pointed at them, as if to say: *You're going to get it when this is over.*

MaryAnne saw Robby with Ali at the back of the room, videotaping on his phone. They were both laughing hard. Lori was still cracking up and telling Bill, "Allen is going to strangle us when this is over."

Present Day MaryAnne remembered wondering if she should laugh or run to the back to join Robby. But before she could decide, the host was ready for the next activity.

"Okay, couples, I bet you never had that much fun with balls before, huh?" She laughed, and the crowd joined her. "Now, for our second activity, we are going to have to break the blindfolds out! I know some of you out there enjoy blindfolds, am I right?"

A few drunken members of the crowd cheered wildly and whistled.

Fantasia laughed. "Okay, calm down, folks. Save it for later tonight, haha. For this activity, ladies, you'll be blindfolded on the stage and we are going to give you a long, folded piece of wire, okay?

How this is going to work is that your husband will stand on stage holding an empty toilet paper roll near his midsection. The goal is to get the folded wire into the toilet paper roll as quickly as possible. Husbands, listen up. We are going to spin your partner around four times blindfolded to disorient them. You'll need to guide them with your voice so they can get their stick into your hole. Understand? Again, the couple who does this the quickest wins. Are we ready?"

MaryAnne covered her eyes again. "Oh my god." She peeked at James and Gaby, who looked equally bewildered.

"Holy hell. I don't know if I can watch this," James said, laughing as he hunched over. "Is this really happening?"

Gaby was laughing too. "This is insane. I had no idea this was going to be like this."

"None of us did," Kevin said. "That's why it's so great. I don't want to look, but I know I won't be able to help myself."

MaryAnne couldn't speak; she just watched her parents to see their reaction. They were talking but otherwise emotionless.

"Rob and Nicole, you're up first. Let's see how quickly you can get it in the hole!" Fantasia exclaimed.

MaryAnne looked at her parents, then at James and Gaby, and finally at Robby and Ali at the back of the room to see how they were reacting. She turned to Lori and Bill, sitting to her right with the kids. Everyone seemed nervously excited, mirroring pretty much how she was feeling.

By the time the crowd finished laughing at Rob and Nicole, and then Jeff and Mandee, MaryAnne couldn't bear to watch her parents do this. No child should witness their mother blindfolded, trying to insert a long stick into an empty toilet paper roll held by their dad near his crotch.

Fantasia seemed indifferent to MaryAnne's feelings, though. "Allen and Maria, are you ready? It looked like you were strategizing over there while Jeff and Mandee were up. Let's see how you do! Crowd, let's cheer them on as they try to beat the other couples' times."

Her parents made their way to the center of the stage. Her mom was blindfolded, and her dad stood 8-10 feet away, holding a toilet paper roll near his crotch. After being spun around four times while holding the folded metal wire, her mom was a little wobbly and disoriented, so she took a few seconds to get her bearings. Now, she looked for her dad's voice in the darkness.

MaryAnne heard her dad guide her mom: "Left, Maria, left. Stop. Now go forward about three feet. Okay—keep going. Keep going. Stop! Okay, now a little to the right! Nope. Too far right. Back to the left. Okay stop there. Just stop! Now straight again. You're right in front of me. You'll need to kneel to get the wire in."

"How far down do I need to go?" Her mom asked.

"About six to eight inches," her dad responded. "Okay, keep going. No, you're too low. You gotta come up a few inches."

"How many? I don't want to stab you," her mom said.

"Two inches! Higher, higher. Okay, good. Keep going." He stopped, looking at the crowd. "This reminds me of college."

The crowd roared with laughter, and MaryAnne could finally breathe a little.

He turned back to her mom. "Keep going forward. The tip is almost in. Keep going. No, damnit! You're too high. Lower, lower. Good. Keep going. More, more. Got it!"

Fantasia broke in, saying, "Yes! Good job, Maria!" The crowd laughed and applauded as they finished.

MaryAnne clapped, noticing her entire family clapping too, even the kids. Robby and Ali were dying of laughter; Lori's laugh permeated the room; James and Gaby were clapping while Kevin was just staring at the stage.

"Oh my god, Kevin. I can't breathe. Please tell me this will be over soon," MaryAnne said.

"They're doing great! The crowd loves them. They're fine, MaryAnne," Kevin replied, calming her a little bit.

"I know—I'm just afraid of what the last game will be," MaryAnne said while managing a small chuckle.

Fantasia continued, "Alright! Maria and Allen, great job. Now, Allen, I *gotta* hear how that reminded you of college!"

"My kids are here, I probably shouldn't say. It was a long time ago," her dad said, pointing up at them.

James looked at MaryAnne as if to say: *I have no idea what he's talking about.*

"Fair enough," Fantasia replied. "Alright, everyone, great job so far. Now, we're at our final challenge. Couples, this one involves one of our favorite things from childhood. No, it's not silly putty or Sunny D—it's balloons!"

Fantasia went behind the stage, grabbed a bucket of red balloons, and brought it to the couples. "For your last challenge, you must pop three balloons without using your fingers or any sharp object. You'll have to use your weight to pop them.

There are three ways you'll have to pop the balloons. First, each couple will face each other with the balloon between you and you will have to press your bodies together to pop it. Simple enough, right?

Second, ladies, you will straddle your husband while sitting on this chair, with the balloon between you both. You will have to pop it in that position." Fantasia said while walking over to a chair at the edge of the stage.

Finally, gentleman, you'll kneel on this chair with your butt facing your lady and your face toward the audience. Ladies, you'll put the balloon between your midsection and your husband's rear end and attempt to the pop the balloon. The couple that does this the fastest wins. Any questions?"

MaryAnne exchanged glances with her brothers, Gaby, Lori, and Bill. Once again, they all shared the same look: *Oh no.*

Fantasia called up the first couple: Rob and Nicole. MaryAnne watched them do the three pops: first standing face-to-face, then with Nicole straddling Rob, and finally in a doggy-style position, which nearly had Rob faceplanting into the crowd. It was hilarious to watch and the crowd went wild, laughing and cheering. It took them a few minutes to complete all three positions as the balloons seemed hard to pop.

MaryAnne kept an eye on her parents, who were strategizing again. She knew her dad was up to something.

Jeff and Mandee went next. They did okay but had some trouble with the last position, leading them to take much longer than Rob and Nicole to pop all three balloons.

Finally, it was her parent's turn.

MaryAnne remembered her stomach sinking at this moment. She felt bad for her parents having to go through this but hoped they'd appreciate the humor in it.

Fantasia announced, "Maria and Allen, you're up next. You've seen the first two couples pop these balloons; now it's your turn. Are you ready?"

"Do we have a choice?" Her mom asked wryly.

Fantasia turned to the crowd. "What do you think? Are you ready to see Maria and Allen pop some balloons?"

The audience clapped, hooted, and hollered in encouragement. MaryAnne glanced left, seeing James and Gaby clapping and cheering, then to the right, where Kevin, Aunt Lori, and Uncle Bill were cheering with the kids joining in loudly.

Fantasia said, "Sounds like they all want to see you do it. So, Maria and Allen, here's your first balloon. Get ready, get set... go!"

MaryAnne watched as her parents squeezed the balloon between them, pulsating together to try to pop it. Her dad looked like he was going to break a hip as he thrust his body awkwardly towards her mom. She thought this would be the easiest one to pop after all the food they'd eaten on the cruise.

Her parents continued to pulsate together and finally, after about 20 seconds, the balloon burst against her mom's chest. One down.

They moved to the second balloon. Her dad sat on the chair and her mom slowly straddled him with the balloon in the middle of them. MaryAnne put her hands in front of her eyes briefly before looking at her nieces and nephews, who were staring at their grandparents in amazement.

She saw Robby videotaping and laughing at the back, with Ali standing beside him, cheering on her grandparents.

Her parents were still struggling on the stage when she turned back. Her mom was literally grinding and jumping on her dad's crotch. No child should ever have to witness their parents doing this. It took a good 30 seconds of grinding on her dad before the balloon popped. Whoo! Two down.

For the finale, her dad got on his knees on the chair, with his butt facing the stage and his face toward the crowd. MaryAnne watched him trying to get comfortable, nearly toppling over the chair into the crowd before he got settled.

Her mom got the third balloon and raced toward her dad with the balloon and positioned it in between her crotch and his behind, which was, unfortunately, sticking out a little from his pants. She pounded the balloon against her dad, attempting to pop it and almost knocking him over into the crowd again. At this point, the crowd was going absolutely crazy with laughter.

MaryAnne could barely hear her family's screams as she was laser-focused on watching her parents try to pop this balloon. It just refused to pop, no matter how vigorously her mom pushed against her dad's bum.

Present Day MaryAnne noticed her mom take something out of her pocket and poke the balloon. Was it a key or a pen? She couldn't tell, but she couldn't recall that detail from six years ago. Maybe it did happen; maybe it didn't, but it was still amusing to see how she had remembered the game.

Finally, after what felt like an eternity, the third balloon popped, and the crowd cheered wildly. MaryAnne cheered, as did James, Gaby, Kevin, Lori, Bill, and the kids.

Fantasia gathered the couples at the front of the stage. "Oh my god, Allen, are you okay? I thought we lost you for a second there."

"That took me back to college as well—holy moly," her dad said, slightly out of breath.

Fantasia chuckled. "What college did you attend with all these fun memories?"

"The University of Albany—it's cold up there, not much to do," her dad replied, earning a laugh from the crowd.

"Maria, are you okay? How was it being behind Allen for once?" Fantasia asked.

Her mom winced. "Oh my god, my kids and grandkids are here. I'd rather not answer that."

Fantasia laughed again. Present Day MaryAnne wanted to punch Fantasia for asking such a question, knowing they were here with their family.

"Hah! I completely understand. I'm sure they're proud of you; you two were amazing. Alright, folks, let me tally the scores, and I'll be right back with the winner."

Fantasia finally left the stage, leaving everyone with their thoughts for a minute. Everyone looked at each other like: *Thank God that is over, and we can breathe again.*

Robby and Ali walked back to the rest of the family.

James looked at Robby. "Please tell me you got all of that on video? That was the most amazing thing I've ever seen."

"Oh yeah, the whole thing," Robby answered proudly. "We'll need to edit some parts before uploading it. That was hilarious, yet scarring at the same time. I hope they don't kill us when they get back here."

"They might kill me for suggesting this," MaryAnne said. "But it looked like they had fun, and the crowd loved them."

Aunt Lori walked over to the rest of them, still laughing. "You guys, that was the funniest thing I've seen in a while. Your parents are going to kill us, though. Did you see your dad? I swear I saw steam coming off his head. That was *amazing*."

Fantasia returned to the stage, ready to announce the winners. "Alright, folks. Did you enjoy that show?" The crowd cheered loudly. "Let's give all the couples a big round of applause for their bravery tonight. There may be some long conversations after this show is over, but we have the results. Are you ready? The winners of tonight's Perfect Couple game, showing that experience truly matters, are… *Maria and Allen!* Come on up, you two—you were amazing."

The entire crowd cheered as MaryAnne's parents walked over to the host. Her dad raised his hands in the air and high-fived Fantasia.

Fantasia held up a big basket. "You guys were fantastic. We have a beautiful bottle of wine, a gift basket, and two medals for showing the other couples how it's done. Thank you all for joining us and remember, there's dancing in the Elephant Club until 2 a.m., late night comedy shows and plenty going on the ship all night. See you around! Goodnight!"

MaryAnne watched her parents walk off the stage, her mom smiling and her dad playfully glaring as if to say: *I'm going to strangle you all.*

As Maria approached the group, MaryAnne walked over to her and said, "So you're saying that wasn't like the Newlywed Game? You guys were great." She laughed, hugging her mom and dad.

The rest of the family joined in, hugging and congratulating them. A few random people approached with variations of "good job" or "you guys were awesome."

Present Day MaryAnne remembered feeling a bit relieved that her parents didn't seem too upset.

As they started to leave the theater, MaryAnne asked if anyone wanted to go to the helipad area of the ship to see the stars before calling it a night.

Kevin indicated he wanted to gamble, which was a blessing in disguise, as Present Day MaryAnne didn't want to see him anymore. Gaby took the kids down to bed, and Aunt Lori and Uncle Bill also decided to turn in. They said goodnight, exchanging hugs and kisses with everyone.

James, Robby, and her parents said they were happy to spend a few minutes stargazing.

After everyone else said goodnight, MaryAnne led James, Robby, and her parents to the helipad.

▼ ▼ ▼

9:35 P.M.

Her memories picked up with them walking on the ship toward the helipad. It was a beautiful night out—it was cool but not too chilly, not a cloud in the sky and a gentle breeze on the ship.

They walked along the 4th deck, climbed a small set of stairs, and passed through a tunnel-like walkway where the winds picked up strongly. After about 20 seconds, they made it to the other side of the tunnel to the area of the helipad.

MaryAnne knew this part of the ship was usually the darkest to help the boat crew with navigation, so she loved looking at the night sky here. Tonight was no different, as it was a moonless night, leading to almost complete darkness, except for a few lights from people's rooms at the front of the ship. A handful of people were on the helipad, talking quietly.

As James, Robby, and her parents walked up the few stairs onto the helipad area, they all looked up in awe at the incredible number of stars visible on the moonless night.

Present Day MaryAnne imagined her memories probably didn't do justice to what it was like that night. It was still so beautiful and stunning to see again, even in her memories.

Her mom and dad sat on a bench while Robby and James lay down at the center of the helipad, staring at the sky.

"This is insane," Robby said slowly. "I haven't seen this many stars in forever. You can see the Dippers and Orion's Belt. Pretty sure that's Uranus over there as well."

"Been a while since I've seen Uranus." James snickered.

"I should have seen that coming. You're an imbecile," Robby replied.

"This is beautiful, honey. Thank you for bringing us here," her dad said, gazing at the sky. "This is the perfect way to spend the last night. I was ready to kill you about 20 minutes ago, but you're forgiven. Come here."

MaryAnne walked her way to sit down next to her parents. Her dad kissed her on the forehead.

"Thank you, MaryAnne. I couldn't have asked for a better way to end the cruise with my family," her dad said quietly, rubbing her head as she leaned on his shoulder.

Present Day MaryAnne felt herself getting emotional remembering this moment.

"I'm so glad you enjoyed yourselves. I was worried something would go wrong, and while a few people got sick and you nearly broke a hip trying to pop a balloon, I think we all had fun, right?" MaryAnne looked up at him.

"I think so. No trip is perfect, but we enjoyed ourselves, and the kids had a blast, especially after what just happened." Her dad laughed for a few seconds. "I can't ask for anything more than that."

"Yeah, I can't wait to get back to the real world and see what's waiting for me at work," MaryAnne said slowly, looking back at the sky.

"You'll be fine, MaryAnne. You're so talented, and they obviously asked you to be a part of this program for a reason. Just take it day by day. I'm sure you'll kill it." Her dad always knew what to say to her.

"Thank you, Daddy. That means the world to me." She stared at the sky, amazed at the amount of stars flickering brightly.

James and Robby were still lying on the ground, discussing sports. Her mom was also staring at the sky, taking it all in.

Present Day MaryAnne remembered that she went to meet Kevin at the casino after they were done on the helipad, but she didn't give a shit about that now. From what she remembered, they gambled for a little, got some pizza and then went to bed, but she didn't want to see any of that.

MaryAnne was content to end her simulation with her head on her dad's shoulder, staring up at the sky, surrounded by her family.

She had gotten to relive this perfect day and was now filled with a sense of calm and peace. Seeing her dad again like this—alive, funny, and able to converse with her—made her so happy.

Whether everything was recreated exactly as it happened was irrelevant. This last memory on the front of the boat, all of them together, staring at the night sky in wonder, was how she wanted this simulation to end. Noone cared what the future held, only caring about being together and enjoying each other's company.

This was how she wanted to remember her dad, and she knew this was the perfect time to end the simulation.

MaryAnne had loved every minute of this experience, both on the cruise in 2026 and in this simulation.

Achieving closure with her relationship with Kevin had been hard. While she was still angry at him, she knew she had to let go of her rage to make herself vulnerable to love again. It was the only way she would be able to move forward.

MaryAnne also found some closure with her dad. Remembering him as he was back then was helping her to accept how he was now. He was a loving, fun, and caring father. No matter his condition when she saw him the following weekend, this was the father and man she would always remember.

Now, she could embrace the path to his eventual passing with dignity and grace and support her mom as much as needed.

As she saw from her watch that it was after 10 p.m., she decided to end the simulation early.

Sitting with her head on her dad's shoulder, staring up at the sky, she asked Maria to end her simulation with her last thought being "*I love you Daddy.*" before everything faded to black.

CHAPTER 4

ERIC - LEWIS AND CLARK EXPEDITION

MARCH 8, 2032

7:15 A.M.

Eric was exhausted. Sundays were usually his day to sleep in, but today, he had to be at the facility by 7:45 a.m., which meant waking up at 6:30 a.m. It wasn't ideal, especially after a few strong whiskies the night before. He reminded himself that this experience was only once a year, and hopefully, it would live up to the hype.

He hated the feeling of being hungover the morning after drinking. He had his routine down of drinking lots of water and taking an Advil before bed, but it still didn't cure everything. Every time he had a hangover, he swore he would cut down on drinking. Yet, every time the opportunity to drink came up, he took advantage of it. He really needed to stop the cycle somehow.

Driving through the quiet Denver streets on this early Sunday morning, Eric realized that he really needed this break from his life; more than he wanted to admit. Between work, Alexandra, the kids, and the drinking, he hadn't been feeling well these days—mentally, emotionally, or physically.

▼▼▼

Eric often felt shame when complaining about his life as he knew others had it much worse. He had a great job, at least for the moment, great kids, a supportive wife, and decent health. Now, there was money coming in from the government for participating in a supposedly life-changing simulation.

Yet, something was missing—the excitement of something new. His life had become routine and mundane. He felt lost and yearned for something *more* than just being known as an accountant and a dad.

As a partner at a large accounting firm, Eric had built a successful career. However, with recent advances in artificial intelligence and the state of the world economy, businesses were finding ways to integrate AI into their internal financial systems. This trend was causing a reduction in the need for services provided by most accounting firms across the country, resulting in reduced revenues, headcount, partner compensation, and even the threat of partners being let go.

Firm leadership put him in charge of reviewing the firm's strategy for AI offerings and combating the impact of AI. The truth was that the technology was evolving too rapidly, changing the underlying nature of how businesses operate. Why pay $700 an hour for third-party accounting services when a software tool could do the same job just as accurately for a fraction of the cost? Sure, there would always be a need for human oversight, but not at the same level as there was a decade earlier.

So, needless to say, the past few years had been stressful, as he saw this coming long ago.

The stress from work, coupled with the daily exhaustion of managing the kid's activities, left Eric with little time for himself. This led to more drinking, more arguments with Alexandra, and eventually, thoughts of divorce. It was no wonder Eric was in a place where he needed a vacation from his life.

So, when the government approved Anticipation Day, he was excited to sign up.

Eric knew he wanted an experience set in the past; somewhere few people existed and somewhere outdoors amongst nature. Eric wanted a place before the footprint of humans dominated the landscape with mini-malls, gas stations, and fast-food joints.

After a few weeks of contemplation, he decided to do the Lewis and Clark expedition as his simulation.

This choice was close to his heart, as in eighth grade, Eric was reading a story about the Lewis and Clark expedition in history class when the school nurse came into his classroom to take him to the principal's office, where his mother was waiting.

It was in that office that he got the news that his father had died in a car accident earlier that day. While Eric tried to forget most of that day, the one thing he did remember was wishing he could travel back in time and actually be a part of the Lewis and Clark expedition to escape the pain he was feeling.

This simulation was, in a way, a tribute to his dad, who *loved* the outdoors and used to take him and his brother Richie camping in the Rocky Mountains. Eric felt this was something his father would have considered doing if he were alive today.

He often thought about those camping trips, as those were one of the few times he remembered his dad sober. It made sense—leading a couple of kids deep into Rocky Mountain National Park required a clear head. They usually went to an area known as the Wild Basin, roughly 15-20 miles from the nearest parking lot, which would take them a day and a half to hike to. Once there, they would pitch their campground near Ouzel Creek, and depending on the weather, they would stay for two or three days, before hiking back.

Their father started taking them camping here when Eric was eight and Richie was 13. While it was a relatively tough hike to get to and from the campsite, the time spent there was filled with good food, fun games, and lots of laughter.

His dad was a funny dude when he was sober—full of laughter and life, but when he drank, it was a different story, as the house was full of yelling, cursing, and fights with his mother.

Eventually, his mother couldn't take it anymore and left, taking Eric and Richie to their aunt and uncle's house before finding an apartment a few months later.

Even after the divorce, their father continued the camping tradition until his death a few years later.

Ironically, Eric would think about those trips while drinking alone in his home office or a hotel room on the road.

When he talked through this simulation idea during his intake three months earlier, the personnel noted he had two options: 1) live as one of the actual expedition members, based on reconstructions of available historical documents, or 2) assume a new character created by the simulation with a unique background for the expedition.

Eric thought about it for a week before choosing the second option of a new character. He wanted to see what this simulation could come up with.

Due to the government restrictions, he could only experience up to a year of the roughly 550 day expedition to the Pacific Ocean. Since the latter part of that first year involved winter camp, with the individuals likely freezing their asses off, Eric decided to end his simulation in early November of 1804, around the time the expedition reached their winter camp near North Dakota. He was not interested in spending a few simulated months in a freezing and miserable environment, longing to be in a warm room somewhere, when he actually *could* be in a warm room back in his house in Denver.

As such, the last day of the simulation was slated for November 13th, 1804. November 13th was his birthday, so it was as good a date as any to stop. He would be spending 183 days in a simulated world, while only being in the Denver facility for 6.5 hours. Talk about a mind-fuck.

Even at 183 days, it would be a grueling journey with hot summer days, exhausting days of rowing and pulling their boats up-river and likely awful food to fill their bellies.

Most people would have said he was crazy but Eric was fully looking forward to this experience.

▼ ▼ ▼

Speaking of cold, the facility waiting room was freezing. Holy hell. They had asked them to dress warmly, but Eric hadn't expected this.

After about twenty minutes, a male nurse named Ramiro walked through the door and called his name. Eric followed him through the metal doors into the facility's back area, which was huge. After weaving through hallways, they reached the elevators and went to the fifth and top floor.

They turned right and entered room 595. *"My favorite whiskey brand—of course."* Eric thought, laughing on the inside, thinking about the new brand of whiskey he had recently discovered.

Once Eric put his personal affects in the locker and sat down in the chair, Ramiro went over the details of the simulation and the rules attached to it. Eric couldn't help but laugh when he heard he wouldn't have to shit.

"Yeah, my friend mentioned that last night. So strange. Who would think of that?" He asked Ramiro, who chuckled and replied, "No idea man, but it's a trip. I did the full year simulation. You literally never have the urge to piss or have a bowel movement. To go without that for a year? It's weird, but amazing. You get used to it. And when you finally do need to go after coming back to reality? That's weird too, but also kinda amazing."

Next, Ramiro explained the skipping process. Eric had been given 125 skips, given the long and tenuous nature of this experience. He mentioned a rule about skipping up to 50% of the remaining simulation, but it was too early for Eric to do the math, so he would have to rely on Ramiro if he did decide to start skipping ahead.

After confirming he wasn't planning to deviate from the simulation's parameters, Eric was ready to do this. Although, for a second, he did consider purchasing an add-on—maybe he could run off with a beautiful Native American woman, *Dances with Wolves* style. However, he decided to stick with the plan to recreate the expedition as it happened. Maybe next year, he would have a romantic experience in a simulation where electricity, heat, and hot water already existed.

As Ramiro and his robotic assistant, Brian, were getting him hooked up to the monitoring stations, and his ring was being prepared, Eric realized that he was really nervous, but also really excited.

Eric wondered what Alexandra's experience would be. Knowing her, she would likely pick something near the beach, surrounded by beautiful sand, ocean, and people. All she would probably do is lounge in the sun, enjoy good food, and feel at peace.

He doubted she'd have sex, but he wasn't sure. Lord knows their sex life had been nonexistent, so maybe she would? Given his past indiscretions, he didn't have much of a hill to stand on if she did.

Either way, he hoped she found some happiness and came out of it relaxed and rejuvenated. She needed and deserved it.

"Okay, Eric," Ramiro said, walking over with the ring. "I'm going to place this on your head, hook you up, and then start the drip. You will feel some tingling in your body and a little warmth in your chest—that is totally normal. You'll be out in about 30 seconds. The next thing you will see, hear, and smell will be in 1804." Ramiro paused before continuing. "I wonder what one smelled back then—I can only imagine," he added with a dry laugh.

"Sounds good." Eric laughed. "Hopefully, it's not horse shit or, worse, human shit. Maybe start me off in a strawberry field or something."

"That's not up to me man, but good luck. I will see you in about 6.5 hours. Sweet dreams." Ramiro closed the ring around his head and returned to his computer to do whatever he had to do to shoot Eric back in time.

A minute later, Eric was out.

▼▼▼

MAY 14, 1804

The first thing he felt was wind. It wasn't warm, but it wasn't cool either. It was just pleasant. The breeze on his skin felt refreshing, reminding him of the fan next to his bed at home.

It instantly brought him back to those camping trips with his dad and Richie to Rocky Mountain National Park, where they would spend a few weeks every year, once in the spring, once in the summer, and once in the fall.

Eric remembered waking in the morning before his father and brother were up and sitting outside their campground, taking in the sights and sounds of whatever wooded area or lakeside setting they had decided to stop at. The air was always fresh, the wind usually light and pleasant, and the atmosphere peaceful.

In a way, those trips made him confident he could take on the rigors of this simulation experience. Being out in the elements and battling nature was how he grew up. Sure, this would be with less comfortable clothing and rudimentary equipment and for much longer than his hikes with his dad, but he was confident he could handle this simulation.

"*Wait! Simulation? Lewis and Clark?*" Eric thought. "*Holy shit, am I in it already?*"

Eric could now see a little better, and he saw what looked like a wooden cabin coming into greater detail. He appeared to be lying on a hard (very hard) mattress on the lower bunk of a bunk bed.

As he sat up and swung his legs over the edge, he could not believe what he was seeing.

Everything looked *real*. He wasn't sure what to expect, but he looked at his hands, noticing they appeared younger. A warm grey cloth shirt covered his torso, and he wore an equally warm pair of white pajama pants. He glanced down at his feet—pretty ugly, with long toenails and thick layer of hair. *Gross.*

In front of him was a red square table surrounded by four empty chairs. Two candles flickered on the table, with a few cups, bowls, and various silverware scattered. A small fire crackled in the fireplace to his left, adding warmth to the room.

He felt the cool, bare floor as his feet touched it. It was amazing. "How the fuck did they do this?" He asked out loud to no one, surprised by the younger, healthier sound of his voice.

Standing up, he saw a pair of socks on the chair next to him and slipped them on. The cabin was small, furnished with a triple bunk bed, the small table and chairs in the middle, a smaller table with a chair against one wall, and two barrels along the other.

A handful of pots and pans hung on the far wall, presumably for cooking whatever food these guys had back then. An axe was mounted on the opposite wall beside a red backpack, which was strapped to a small bag and a black canteen, both marked with "US" in white letters.

Under the bed, he found a large black trunk. "Wow, they really thought of everything, didn't they?" He asked out loud, again to no one.

As his ears adjusted, he heard commotion outside through the two small windows beside him. He walked to the door, opened it, and peeked outside. It was a beautiful cool sunny morning, with blue skies and the sun peeking through the trees off to the right. Birds were chirping cheerfully.

To his left, about 20 yards away, two more buildings stood, with 30 to 40 men gathered in front of them, talking about something.

Feeling that this might be important, Eric decided to go inside, get dressed, and join them. He was still adjusting to the simulation and feeling a little nauseous, but he hoped that would subside as he got used to his surroundings.

After putting on his boots and pants, Eric returned to where the men had assembled.

As Eric approached, he saw a variety of outfits: some men wore white garb with guns, belts, and sand-colored shoes, while others had red vests under black jackets and hats. A few wore blue garb with pointed hats on.

A handful appeared to be in plain clothes. Maybe they were local residents or farmers just hanging around. Eric couldn't tell.

He also noticed a dog standing near two men in the center. It was one of the largest dogs he had ever seen, with dark brown, almost black fur draping over its body, long floppy ears, and a big nose. It must've been the Newfoundland dog he'd read about as a child. The dog looked beautiful and appeared to be very well-behaved.

Eric joined the crowd and listened to the gentleman speaking in the center, who was about six feet tall, with a pointed nose, narrow brown eyes, and dressed in full gear, including a black, pointed top hat. Eric caught the conversation mid-sentence:

"You gentlemen understand the responsibility of the task you are about to undertake. For some of you, it will be the most difficult thing you have ever encountered. For others, this will just be another period in your life.

There will be challenges, and there will be moments when you may question whether you can continue. When you find yourself filled with doubt, and you will, I ask that you continue—not for yourself, but for your brothers on this journey with you. For your family, who will benefit from the success of this journey. For your fellow countrymen, who are counting on you to explore, research, and discover new lands. For your President, who has tasked us with exploring the vast territory of the Louisiana Purchase, establishing trade with indigenous people, and claiming new territory for the United States, all with the hopes of reaching the vast ocean to the West.

Gentlemen, if we succeed, people will speak of us for centuries after we have all met our eventual demise.

You men have been handpicked because we believe you are the best and most respected men in your field to undertake this duty. I expect your full dedication to this journey, your respect and curiosity for the people, animals, and lands we will encounter, and your cooperation in obeying orders from Captain Clark, myself, and your squad leaders.

Any actions that violate Army rules and regulations will be dealt with swiftly and harshly. Most of you have served and should understand these rules and regulations. If you're unfamiliar with them, speak to Captain Clark or me, and we can review them."

The man put his head down before continuing.

"I ask God for a safe and successful journey and put faith in Jesus Christ, our Lord and Savior, to watch over and protect us on this trip.

Captain Clark would also like to say a few words before we begin. Remember, we sail at 4 p.m., in approximately six hours, so please make preparations and we will set sail then.

I'll be traveling to St. Louis to gather some last-minute supplies, and aim to meet you around St. Charles in a few days. Captain Clark, please proceed."

The man to the right removed his hat, revealing reddish hair and a fuller face. He addressed the men.

"Gentleman, not to repeat everything Captain Lewis just said, but I am honored to be entrusted by Captain Lewis to be a part of this extraordinary expedition into the great unknown. We bring years of experience as scientists, mapmakers, surveyors, and general adventurers. We both desire to learn about and understand the natural world around us, and share that knowledge with others.

We are humbled and excited that you gentlemen have offered your services on this journey. The risks are severe, and the likelihood of perishing is ever-present. However, if we are to succeed, gentlemen? Well, the world will be ours for the taking. We will have brought an unseen land to the rest of this grand country, with countless tales of new species of plants and animals, interactions with the natives, and lands that have never been documented before.

This is what excites me, and I hope it excites you too. I look forward to working with you, gentlemen, and I pray to God for a safe journey."

Captain Lewis mentioned they would begin making final arrangements and would sound a horn when ready to leave.

Eric walked back to his palatial lodge, where two men greeted him with smiles.

"You ready, George?" asked one of the men, a young but sturdy-looking fellow.

After a few seconds of nobody answering, he added, "Hey Georgy—you sleep yo'self deaf?"

Eric realized the man was staring right at him and his name was, in fact, George. "Oh, right, sorry. Yes, I'm ready. Apologies, Robert. I'm still waking up. Too much brandy last night, I feel."

How did Eric know this guy's name was Robert? There was no way he could have guessed it. This must be part of that known memory thing Ramiro mentioned a little while ago in Denver. It just hit him again—his real body was lying somewhere in a facility in Denver in 2032, while he was seemingly here in 1804, talking to some guy named Robert. What a fucking trip!

"No worries, mate. You certainly kicked back like it was your last night!" The other gentleman chimed in from across the room.

"Yeah, it was a rough night, I suppose," Eric said as George.

Now that they mentioned it, he did feel hungover. He was too freaked out by what he was seeing and hearing to realize he had a headache in addition to his nausea. At first, he assumed the nausea was just him getting used to this world. Damn, even in his simulation, he appeared to be a drunk. "Where is my water?" He asked to no one in particular.

"Here, George, have some of this. My special of the day," the guy across the room said, pouring a dark liquid from a nearby pitcher and handing it to Eric.

Eric sniffed the drink; it smelled sweet. *"Why the hell not?"* he thought. *"What's the worst that could happen? It's a fucking simulation."*

He drank the concoction, which was quite delicious, sweet, and earthy, unlike anything he'd ever tasted before. Instantly, he felt his simulated body slightly rejuvenate.

"Thank you, Hugh." He just knew the man's name was Hugh. Again, weird.

"Yeah, that brandy done made you straight stupid last night," Hugh said while laughing, exposing some damn ugly teeth. "You were singing your arse off. It was God awful to tell you the truth."

Fantastic. George was officially a singing drunk. Eric sat down, rubbed his simulated temple, and vowed not to touch another drink for the rest of the trip.

After spending much of the last six years drinking to cope with life's stresses and unhappiness, Eric decided to use *this* time, in *this* place, to take a break from alcohol.

Maybe it would be easier here than in the real world; maybe it wouldn't. Would he feel like he had gone 183 days without alcohol when he woke up back in Denver or would it not make a difference at all? He wasn't sure, but he was determined to find out.

"Ha, I can imagine. Last time I drink for a while then," Eric, as George, replied to Hugh.

"We'll see about that, mate," Hugh said with a broad grin.

▼▼▼

The next few hours were spent talking with Hugh and Robert about what they were most excited about, ensuring they had all the necessary supplies, what women they might meet along the trip, and other random topics.

Eric then helped lug boxes, crates, and other supplies from the cabins to the central staging area and then onto the boats. He tried to take in the different dialects he heard—an amazing mix of British, Southern, Creole, and a few others he couldn't easily identify.

Finally, by around 4 p.m., the final supplies were loaded onto a boat that looked like something out of an old pirate movie. It had to be

50 to 60 feet long, with a large white sail at the front of the boat and a raised, covered wooden canopy that could easily hold 5-10 men sitting above the rear of the boat.

Eric noticed oars on the floor along each side of the boat and, counting 10 oars per side, quickly calculated that 20 men would be responsible for rowing at a time. He *was* an accountant after all.

Something in him knew he'd be one of the rowers, which he didn't mind. He always enjoyed rowing and occasionally used the rowing machine at the gym.

Eric realized that this boat and the river floating by would be his home for the next several months. Though he would miss his kids, it would only be a day in the real world. His focus now had to be on the river and the journey ahead.

Off to the side of the large boat were two smaller boats, each carrying around half a dozen men and some small boxes of supplies.

On the main boat, men moved about in different directions, making final preparations. Eric helped organize a wide array of supplies, including surveying equipment, clothes, tools, knives, guns, liquor, grain and plenty of cans labeled "portable soup," which he couldn't *wait* to try later.

He was busy moving a box of grain when a whistle blew, signaling the men, including Eric, to gather at the ship's center. He lined up next to his new friends Hugh and Robert. After a few minutes, Captain Clark boarded the boat and approved the launching the boats.

Eric felt a thrill. Though the weather was turning cloudy and it looked like it was going to rain soon, this was what he had been looking forward to: being out in nature, setting sail into the unknown lands of the United States.

It was the same feeling he used to get before those trips with his father into Rocky Mountain National Park. *Anticipation.* What a great feeling it was indeed!

Sitting beside his ore, Eric wondered how physically painful this experience would be. While he had considered the pain and effort that would be involved here, he knew he'd soon find out how tough it really would be.

He had basic gloves on, far from the thick pairs of garden gloves he used for landscaping back home. These would likely result in calluses and blisters on his hands. The constant lifting of supplies and the actual boat itself when it got stuck, would strain his back and legs. Walking would be a painful experience, as his shoes were pretty thin—nothing like the warm and thick boots he had at home.

Then there were the natural threats that could inflict pain: bears, wolves, poisonous berries, snakes, bugs, hail, and lightning.

It would also be chilly, especially at night, and with the current weather, the expedition would likely face rain and other elements of simulated nature that could cause sickness. Eric could only hope that whatever malady befell him would be treatable with the expedition's limited medicine. Otherwise, this could be the quickest simulation death ever.

While Eric could skip ahead, that felt like cheating. He wanted to embrace the pain and suffering of this journey, within reason, of course.

In a twisted way, Eric was hoping whatever pain he experienced here would help him appreciate the life he had back home in Denver. While not perfect, he knew he was blessed with an amazing wife, three beautiful children, and a good job. Most of his pain came from his past, and he needed to move on from that, for his family's sake as well as his own.

▼▼▼

A gunshot rang out from somewhere on land, breaking his train of thought. The expedition cheered and began rowing. Eric joined in, syncing his strokes with the others. It felt silly, knowing it wasn't real, but he couldn't wait to see what this adventure had in store for him: the sites he would see, the animals he would encounter, and how much he would learn about living in this time period.

As the group rowed away from the shore, Eric closed his eyes and just listened. There were no cars, no screaming children, no planes overhead, no co-workers or clients calling, no wife yelling or complaining, and no music or electronic noises. Nothing but the sound of the river flowing past them, birds flying overhead, the wind rustling the sails, and currently, the cheers of locals who had gathered to send them off.

Gradually, those cheers faded, replaced by the grunts of twenty men rowing in unison upriver. If nothing else, Eric would develop some nice muscles in the simulation.

As he rowed back and forth, he realized that, for the first time in a long time, he wasn't worried about a damn thing. Not work. Not the kids. Not Alexandra. Not AI. Not money. Not life. Not death. Nothing.

A part of him wished he had some music he could turn on to help him relax, but the sounds of nature would have to suffice here.

Soon after departing, they reached the confluence of the Missouri and Mississippi Rivers. The men stopped rowing for a minute to turn around and take in the breathtaking sight. Eric was amazed at how easy it was to see the two rivers, as their colors contrasted significantly.

The Missouri's water, on their left, looked browner than the blue-green Mississippi on the right. Eric assumed the browner hue was due to the different sediment in Missouri River, though he wasn't sure.

They veered towards the left to head up the Missouri, rowing hard to combat the strong currents where the rivers met.

For the next few simulated hours, they rowed steadily, pausing briefly to re-energize. A light breeze and some light showers began to fall as they docked at a small island along the river in the early evening.

Eric helped set up a simple camp on the island while the other men prepared food and started a campfire for dinner, with everyone working like a well-oiled machine.

Around the first campfire, Eric got to know some of the other men on the expedition.

The group seemed to be organized into three squads, including the dog. Eric, as George, was part of the second squad, led by Sergeant Charles Floyd, who although he seemed to be in his early 20s, commanded respect by the men.

Eric's squad comprised of eight privates:

Joseph and his younger brother Reubin, both from Kentucky, had long red beards and spoke with a thick southern drawl that made them hard to understand at first. Both appeared to be in their 20s and were friendly enough.

Robert Frazer, whom Eric had spoken to earlier in the day, also looked to be in his 20s and mostly kept to himself. Eric seemed to remember Robert being court-martialed at Camp Dubois for some mysterious offense, but he wasn't sure what for.

John Newman, a big, strapping guy, was clearly the "alpha" male of the group. Eric immediately knew he was not to be messed with, though he didn't feel threatened by him.

John Thompson appeared to be the cook but didn't talk much either. Eric hoped these men would open up more as the expedition progressed.

Richard Windsor, who Eric knew had gotten very drunk the night before and was still recovering, was the group comedian, cracking jokes throughout the day, especially about the things he'd do when he'd meet the first attractive Native women.

It was a good thing Alexandra wasn't here; she likely would have whacked Richard across the head with an oar for some of his comments.

Lastly, there was Eric's buddy Hugh, who was in his mid-20s and, like George, was from Pennsylvania.

On their first night at camp, Eric found himself chatting mostly with Hugh. It was rainy and cloudy, and most of the men were in their tents or huddled up with other members chatting in their tents.

"You ready for this trip, are you?" Hugh asked Eric as they finished the stew and bread served tonight.

"I am. Been looking forward to this for many months," Eric replied, speaking as George, but feeling it was true for him as well. "You?" Eric asked.

"Aye, I reckon when this is over, I'll have my pick of the ladies who will fancy a night with newly appointed Governor Hugh." Hugh laughed, seemingly convinced he would become governor. He was a good-looking guy, with blond hair, light blue eyes, standing about 6'2" and weighing around 170 to 180 pounds.

"You are mighty confident in yourself, huh?" Eric asked.

"Absolutely, my good man," Hugh said, pulling a small square object from his bag. It didn't seem to be a proper mirror but seemed to generate a reflection "I see my reflection every day, and I know what the ladies appreciate, especially back home." He chuckled.

"Hey, let me look at that, will you?" Eric asked, reaching for the object. He realized that, other than his hands, he hadn't even seen what he looked like. Eric saw his reflection and almost laughed out loud at what stared back.

He was so young—maybe in his early 20s—with light brown eyes, a bit of facial hair, and long sideburns reaching past his ears. His hair was a tannish shade, and curly and ran all the way down past his ears. It looked like he had a scar on his face that ran from just below his ear to right above his eye. He had an uncanny resemblance to Elvis Presley.

Somehow Eric knew that scar was from a small skirmish with Indians in Pennsylvania a few years back.

He still looked far better than the slightly overweight, out-of-shape, and balding man strapped to a chair in Denver.

Eric had struggled with his weight for years, and the stresses of work and life hadn't helped. He hoped this experience would help clear his head, get right with himself again, and use that as a springboard for improving his mental and physical health. If he could paddle up the Missouri River for 183 days, surely he could manage an hour on the treadmill four days a week.

Besides, staying mentally and physically healthy was a requirement for the Anticipation Day program.

"You have competition, my dear sir. I think the ladies will flock to George first," Eric teased as he sifted his fingers through his thick hair.

"In your dreams, mate." Hugh laughed again, stifling a yawn. "Speaking of dreams, I'm pretty exhausted. There is a long day ahead tomorrow for us. I think we're meeting Captain Lewis in St. Charles the day after tomorrow. They'll probably ride us heavily to get there before him." He stood and proceeded to the entrance of George's tent.

"Goodnight, mate," Hugh said, poking his head back in. "Enjoy dreaming of those women you'll never meet." He grinned before disappearing into the rainy night.

Eric lay down on his uncomfortable sleeping area and listened to the soothing sound of rain hitting his tent. If he could sleep, he would have drifted off right then and there.

He lay there for what felt like forever, listening to the rain, closing his eyes, and thinking about… nothing. It felt so fucking *good*.

He could have stayed in this moment forever, just taking in the complete and utter nothingness of this new reality.

Finally, after what must have been an hour, Eric decided to skip ahead to the next morning to see what the rest of this adventure would bring.

▼▼▼

MAY 19. 1804

Eric had underestimated how slowly the expedition would start. The members had to wait in St. Charles for a few days until Captain Lewis arrived from St. Louis before they could proceed with the trip. So, their journey seemed to stall as soon as it started.

The delay wasn't all bad. Eric took advantage of the time by joining the team on small excursions to hunt for game, fish the river, and explore the land beyond the small encampment of St. Charles, in what he believed was present day Missouri.

The captains had instructed everyone to document any plants, bugs, or animals they encountered, just in case it happened to be a new species. Eric found himself cataloging all sorts of bugs and animals that were somewhat recognizable. He saw butterflies, beetles, bees, other flying insects, as well as some unfamiliar animals.

This was a zoologist's wet dream.

Eric also got to know his squad better, particularly Sergeant Floyd, who had extensive knowledge of the outdoors and survival in the wild. The sergeant was from Kentucky and had been recruited by Captain Clark. Apparently, he also had a cousin in one of the other squads.

Eric and Sergeant Floyd spent a lot of time hunting for game along the banks of the Missouri. Either Eric or George turned out to be a damn skilled hunter. Eric brought home close to a dozen kills for the expedition during the few days they were stuck in St. Charles. This earned him popularity among the other members and it made Eric feel good to contribute right away.

The rifles and bows of 1804 were far different from the deer hunting rifles he had used as a boy.

All the time spent outdoors seemed to be therapeutic for Eric as it kept bringing him back to those camping trips with his father and brother.

▼▼▼

There, they would spend most of the day outdoors, hiking, hunting for small game or fishing for trout in Ouzel Lake. The only thing that mattered to the three of them was being together and surviving in the wild, as dangerous as it could be.

On the last trip they made to Rocky Mountain National Park, Eric had a rather frightening encounter with a grizzly bear during one of his morning walks. The bear, which had to be eight feet tall when standing on its hind legs, was easily the largest bear he'd ever seen.

Eric remembered the bear staring at him from 20 or 30 feet away causing him to panic as he realized he didn't have a whistle or mace to scare it off. Eric was pissed at himself, as he usually carried his backpack on his walks, but that morning, he hadn't, assuming the short walk from the tent would be uneventful. Plus, they hadn't encountered any bears on that trip up to that point.

So, he did the only thing he could think of: he screamed. As loud as he could.

He screamed as if his life depended on it, which it probably did. For close to thirty seconds, he screamed at the bear, which was confused at first but then began approaching him slowly.

Eric debated whether to run, curl up in a ball, or keep screaming. He was scared shitless, though, which resulted in him pissing his pants.

Just as he was about to make a run for it, a shot rang out from behind him, causing the bear to dash back into the forest.

Eric turned around and saw his dad standing about 20 feet behind with a shotgun yelling at Eric to run to him.

Eric sprinted to his dad and hugged him tight, so thankful that his had had come to his rescue. At that moment, Eric felt safer than he had ever before.

During his dad's eulogy, Eric recounted this amazing story and thanked his dad once more for always loving and protecting him. He missed his dad greatly.

▼ ▼ ▼

While the hunting was fun in 1804 and gave the crew something to focus on, the time spent in St. Charles was fairly miserable, as it rained most of the time they were there. Eric half-expected a typhoid fever or pneumonia outbreak among the crew.

When the men weren't hunting, fishing, or sleeping, they enjoyed spending time around the fire, drinking wine and bourbon, dancing to the music of fiddle playing, and talking late into the night. Although Eric wasn't familiar with the songs, George knew them well and joined in the dancing and singing enthusiastically, as if he was auditioning for a singing competition on national television.

Eric was determined to keep his promise and not drink during the expedition. Would he have fun with the men if he indulged? Yes, without a doubt. Still, he wanted to prove to himself that he could resist the urge to drink.

During the days, Eric ventured into St. Charles to visit the church for a Catholic mass. It had been years since he last went to mass, and he was curious about how locals celebrated back in 1804.

The service was much more solemn, yet the core messages of faith and God were familiar to him from his church days back in Denver. It was calming to hear the chants of the members and the hymns being read out loud.

Eric assumed that in 1804, everyone was religious, with the concept of God likely central to every part of society. While Eric wanted to interrupt the services and tell the people God wasn't real, he realized it would be pointless to argue with simulated characters in a simulated world. Nothing would come out of it.

The spectacle of the service was interesting and eye-opening for him, so that would have to be enough.

On the last night they were in St. Charles, some of the men were enjoying themselves at the local brothel. Eric couldn't blame them; they were young, single, and had served in the Army before this expedition, which seemed to attract the ladies. While the men were generally civil, enjoying a good piece of meat and a stiff drink, some additional activities were enjoyed afterward and some of those went a little too far, resulting in a brawl at the brothel.

Unfortunately, this earned three of the members a court-martial and a sentence of 25 lashes on their backs.

While Eric had seen lashings in movies before, witnessing it firsthand was very different. Even in a simulation, the sound of the whip striking their backs was unlike anything he had heard before—brutal and awful. The sight of the men's backs, their skin *torn* open, was horrifying.

What made it worse was the collective groan let out by the other men as they watched. After seeing this, Eric was 100% certain he wasn't going to drink because, knowing his dumb ass, he'd sleep with an entire village of women and end up receiving three times the amount of lashes. Nope. He was going to be a good boy this trip.

Finally, on the afternoon of the fifth day, Captain Lewis arrived in St. Charles, accompanied by Army officers, traders, and other distinguished individuals. Eric couldn't hear much as the members corresponded mostly with Captain Clark and the squad leaders, but the newcomers seemed important.

Captain Lewis didn't hang out with the expedition members for too long; quickly heading into town to meet some locals. Eric hoped to interact with Captain Lewis during the trip, but only time would tell if he'd get any one-on-one moments with him.

▼▼▼

MAY 20, 1804

The day after Captain Lewis arrived, the party was ready to launch from St. Charles, this time with all members accounted for.

After another symbolic gun firing and shouting Three Cheers, the full expedition set off into uncharted lands and the unknown. It felt good to get going again, and Eric felt like this was the *true* beginning of the trip.

He was excited and ready for whatever came his way, or so he thought, as the next several days were long, rainy, and generally miserable. Moving west along the Missouri River, the going was tough and slow at times due to unfavorable winds and numerous obstacles they had to maneuver around.

The men were exhausted from the grueling process of dragging the boat up the river to bypass some of these obstacles. Eric was sure he'd excel at any future tug-of-war competition with all the rope-pulling he was doing these days.

Even with the long and hard days, he was continuously amazed by the beauty around them: tree-lined shore banks filled with various animals, fields as far as the eye could see, and countless birds that flew overhead.

With all five senses fully active and engaged, Eric could not believe how real this simulation was.

Visually, it was stunning. Every detail was meticulous—from blades of glass glistening in the sun after a rainstorm to varied insects scattered throughout the forests and fields. Even Captain Lewis' dog, Seaman, who constantly drooled on the members, seemed to be created with no detail forgotten.

One added benefit of the simulation was his perfect 20/20 vision, unlike in Denver, where he had an upcoming appointment with Dr. Kushner to check for early signs of glaucoma.

The sounds were equally impressive, but in a different way. Gone were the noises of cars, planes, music, or television, and screaming kids running around, replaced by the pure sounds of nature.

Eric enjoyed the sweet bird songs and the rhythmic chirping of crickets each morning and evening, the gentle patter of rain on his tent, and the constant soothing sound of the Missouri River as thousands of gallons of simulated water flowed by their campsite. It was all so beautiful and calming to listen to.

He was also fortunate to hear some local Indian dialect when the expedition encountered a local Native American tribe several days after they departed St. Charles. Aside from some movies he had watched, this was an entirely new language to him, and he found it fascinating.

Not all of sounds were calming, however. The simulation nailed the sound of thunder when a lightning bolt crashed nearby. While Eric had heard loud thunderstorms before, especially when camping, the thunder here was the most deafening he had ever heard. He wondered if Patrick was hearing the same type of thunder in his tornado-chasing simulation.

Then there were the natural fragrances of flowers and bushes encountered during his strolls through nearby woods and fields, which reminded him of one of the stores Alexandra used to drag him to when they were younger. He'd never admit it, but he loved the scents in those stores. He wished he could bottle some of these flowers to bring them home for her.

Eric also *loved* the smell of fresh coffee each morning by the campfire. There were no cappuccinos or lattes here; this coffee was pure, hearty, and rich.

▼ ▼ ▼

The smell of coffee always brought Eric back to his childhood, at least before his parents got divorced. He and Richie would wake up every morning to the smell of a fresh coffee pot brewed by their mom. They'd come downstairs to find her sitting at the kitchen table, reading the newspaper or watching the morning news, while breakfast sat warm on the stove for them.

Their dad would join them shortly after, ready for work. He'd chat briefly about their day, kiss their mom, then kiss them both on the head before grabbing a piece of fruit and heading out the door. There was no fighting, no bickering, no crying—just a family together in peace, even if only for a few minutes.

It was a perfect way to start the day, and it always allowed him to leave his house for school in a good mood.

Even after his parents divorced, his mom would still make a pot of coffee to start the morning, as it had become part of their routine by that point.

That all changed the morning after his dad died.

That day, Eric and Richie woke up late and realized there was no waft of coffee. When they went downstairs, their mom wasn't there, no coffee was brewing, and breakfast wasn't waiting. They knew then that their dad was really gone. It was the worst moment of Eric's life.

Even though their parents got divorced, they still remained close and his dad's death had a large impact on Eric's mom.

One morning, Eric asked his mom why she stopped making coffee and she told him that it reminded her too much of his father. Eric understood but told her that Richie and him loved the smell of coffee in the morning so from that point on, the three of them settled into a new routine of preparing coffee and breakfast together.

It marked a new chapter in their lives, with coffee as its comforting constant.

▼ ▼ ▼

Back in 1804, in addition to coffee, the air was often filled with the smell of fresh hickory and cedar usually during the evenings as the expedition set up camp most nights on the shores of the Missouri River, where various trees lined the shore.

Of course, this smell reminded Eric of the camping trips with his dad and brother, where he was in charge of starting the campfire every evening. The three of them would sit around the fire, cooking beans, making s'mores, and talking about whatever came to their minds, usually about what they did during the day.

He hadn't realized how much this journey would stir those memories, as he had suppressed some of them from his brain. He was beginning to understand that they were fond memories for him of a time when his life made sense, and it was all about the future. A time when he was… happy.

Eric needed to get back to that space somehow. Maybe this trip would help.

Now, as for the sensation of taste, he had mixed feelings. He was eating foods typical of the early 1800s: venison, salted pork and other meats, corn, and berries deemed safe by the expedition leaders. That stuff was not enjoyable to taste.

However, he had plenty of his favorite food in the world: beans.

Eric loved beans and couldn't get enough of them. Unfortunately, they came with an embarrassing side effect: farting. Alexandra hated it, which forced him to cut back on his weekly bean intake.

But here, in the simulation, beans were abundant, and he was enjoying every bite, even if they were heartier than he was used to.

The last sense, touch, was the final piece that pulled everything together. Whether it was holding onto the oar while rowing, gripping the gun or arrow he was using to hunt, or scratching his growing stubble, everything felt authentic and natural.

All of this gave Eric the perfect picture of what the members of this expedition saw, ate and did during a normal day of the excursion.

One evening, as Eric sat by the campfire after a long day of rowing upriver, eating beans of course, he swore to take his kids camping more often. He didn't want them to grow up without a father, as he had for much of his childhood.

Eric was alive and wanted to create more experiences for them, so he vowed to take them camping this spring so they could see how he had grown up. At least Corey and Noah could join; Sophia might have to wait a little longer.

This experience was far more grueling than anything he'd done with his dad, but he knew he needed to make special memories with his own kids. One that would help him make a bond with them that would last a lifetime.

▼▼▼

EARLY JUNE 1804

The days had now settled into a routine: rising at dawn for breakfast, loading any newly acquired supplies or meat onto the boat, and heading off by early morning to continue up the river as best they could.

The day would be spent navigating obstacles in the river, stopping to rest and hunt and then continue upriver until evening, when they would find a campsite for the night. Eric would eat whatever meal was prepared by the cook, spend time outside watching the sunset, and chat with his squad members until they retired, usually around 9 p.m. Then, he'd advance to the next day, repeating the cycle.

Though no one complained—especially when the wine and whiskey were flowing—the journey was physically and mentally challenging. Eric considered using the skips granted but kept telling himself to experience as much of this journey as possible to better appreciate his real life.

However, the daily grind was getting exhausting for him, especially when the weather was poor or he wasn't feeling great. They hadn't even reached the peak of summer's heat, and Eric could only imagine how much worse that would be.

For now, the rain was the hardest part of the experience, as it had poured most of the past week, leaving everything muddy and slippery. The expedition members tried to set up camp in covered areas to avoid the worst of the mud, but after torrential downpours, it was impossible not to get mud on their boots.

The uniforms were warm enough, but Eric could have used a dryer now. And a hot shower.

Everyone seemed to understand the task at-hand and were committed to seeing it through, which comforted and uplifted Eric. It was nice to feel part of something again, as it made the long days easier to endure, knowing they were all in it together.

Every once in a while, they would come across local Indian tribes. The captains and sergeants, with the help of a translator, would attempt to communicate with them. Sometimes, they would trade for bison meat or local fruits and vegetables. Eric never really felt threatened by the tribe members—they genuinely seemed more curious about the expedition than anything. It was pretty cool to be able to see these interactions though, even if they were simulated.

The river remained challenging to navigate, with overhanging branches and floating logs from recent storms. After several days of heading up the river, they reached a fork in the river, which Captain Clark identified as the Osages River.

That night, they camped to restock on meat and supplies and to allow Captain Lewis and Clark take the observations they needed on the river.

▼▼▼

JUNE 4, 1804

The morning after they camped on the Osage River began like most others: back on the river, heading north.

After several hours of rowing, a strong westerly wind suddenly blew in, pushing the boat toward the eastern riverbank. The men struggled to regain control as the boat drifted closer to the shoreline.

As the men scrambled, Eric spotted a large hanging tree protruding out over the water along the shoreline. Realizing it was about to collide with the boat, he shouted loudly, just as he had when confronting the grizzly bear.

"We are going to hit a tree! Back away from the center of the boat! Back away! Richard, secure that crate on the side! It has our meat supply. Hurry!"

It was just in time as thirty seconds later, the mast struck the tree, sending it tumbling over the area where the meat supply was being housed and partially splashing into the river below.

After stopping to asses the damage and ensuring everyone was safe, the captains decided to halt the expedition to search for a new mast.

Once they reached the shore, Captain Clark summoned Eric over to the top of the boat. Up until then, only the squad sergeants had interacted with the captains, so Eric hadn't yet spoken with either Captain Lewis or Captain Clark.

Eric had thought he could easily approach either captain—this was a simulation, after all—but after seeing those gentlemen get lashed for what he considered to be a minor offense, he was in no mood to disrupt the way things were supposed to be.

He climbed the stairs to the upper canopy, where Captain Clark was sitting.

"Son, I'm sorry that wood almost hit you. I should have predicted the wind better. Thank you for alerting the crew before it hit. Would you consider joining me? I need to take river measurements here and find a good replacement mast. George, right? From Pennsylvania?"

Eric responded as George, "Yes sir, that's right. I'm from the Philadelphia area, sir. I would be delighted to help you. Thank you." Eric chuckled inwardly at how proper he was being as he knew Alexandra would get an absolute kick at the way he was speaking.

"Wonderful. Gather your gear and head over to the pirogue. I'll have two privates row you to the other side once I stake the surveying chain down." Captain Clark pointed to the iron chain he used to measure the distance of the river as the expedition worked up the Missouri river. Eric had seen him using it but hadn't paid much attention. The thing looked damn heavy, but he did want the good, the bad, and the heavy with this simulation, so bring it on.

Eric headed down to the smaller boat and waited as Captain Clark approached with the chain and handed it to him. And yes, it was heavy and long.

It took about 15 minutes for the privates to row to the other side of the river, where Eric got out and staked the rope along the opposite shoreline so Captain Clark could take measurements. From having season tickets to the Broncos, he would have guessed it was somewhere around four hundred yards across, though the flow of the river made measuring distance a little difficult.

After a few minutes, Captain Clark gave the signal from across the river indicating he had gotten the measurements he needed, so Eric picked up the chain and returned to the boat for the row back to Captain Clark waiting for him.

"380.5 feet, George. It's a quick river today, son, so thank you for your assistance. Please join me as I need a better view of the river, so I would like to ascend that cliff to the right." Captain Clark pointed to a rocky hill on his right, maybe 150 to 200 feet high, overlooking the Missouri River.

Eric figured this would be an easy trek. "Sure, sir, happy to accompany you."

"Wonderful," Captain Clark said. "Let us begin our journey to ensure we have enough light to return."

It was a sunny, but humid afternoon as they set off towards the hill. The worst part of these days was the humidity, but it didn't bother Eric because he wasn't sweating, which was the weirdest, yet best feature of the simulation so far.

Captain Clark, on the other hand, was sweating bullets, which made Eric chuckle when he asked why Eric wasn't sweating.

"Well, sir, I'm not sure. No one in my family is very wet on the skin. Am I lucky or cursed?" Eric said as George.

"That is a good question, son. Many say that sweating helps the body cool itself. However, it also soils clothing and is a reminder of the heat." Captain Clark laughed.

They continued walking through the woods in silence for a few minutes until Captain Clark spoke again. "George, you were an ensign in the army, correct? I believe you served under Captain Thompson briefly? Captain Thompson was a good friend of mine before his unfortunate death."

"Yes, sir. I served mainly in Virginia and Pennsylvania from 1798 to 1802. It was a perfect learning experience for me, sir. Captain Thompson was a great leader, and I was fortunate to learn from him. I understand you retired in 1796?" George knew his history.

"That's right, son. I was 26, but my health was poor, and I needed a break, so I retired to my family's plantation near Louisville. I enjoyed Army life but wanted to do something more. Now, here I am, in the Corps of Discovery, exploring the Louisiana Purchase. I guess I could consider this journey 'something more.'"

Captain Clark smiled and wiped his brow, then turned to Eric. "Why did you decide to join, George?" He seemed genuinely curious.

"Well, sir, after my dad died and my brother moved to Boston, there wasn't much left for me to go home to after the Army. I truly enjoy being in nature and wanted something to be remembered by. When I ran into Captain Lewis in Philadelphia, he asked if I wanted to join, and I knew it was something the Lord called me to do. So, I accepted, and here I am. I am excited to see what the rest of this trip has in store."

"I am sorry for your loss, son. I know what it is like to lose a father. I lost mine five years ago, and it is difficult. I miss him greatly. When I was forced to sell our family's farm two years ago, I felt like I had let him down. When Captain Lewis sent my invitation about a year ago to join this expedition, I took it as a sign from my father to go out and do great things with my life, which is why I am here. I want people to read about my name when I am long gone. I believe they will write about yours as well." Captain Clark smiled and patted Eric on the back, which felt amazing to be acknowledged by one of the great explorers in the United States' history.

Eric couldn't help but realize that George had also lost his father. In a way, it made it easier for him to relate to the character. He wondered if the simulators had done that intentionally.

Captain Clark interrupted his thoughts. "For now, George, let's climb this cliff and see if we can find our next mast." So, they began their ascent.

Thirty minutes later, Eric and Captain Clark stood at the summit, overlooking the Missouri River. The forests and grassy plains stretched as far as he could see in either direction. This is exactly what he thought the middle of the United States would look like in 1804.

In the late afternoon breeze, standing at the top of this hill, Eric felt completely at peace.

In 2032, this area would be developed with farms, highways, strip malls, and buildings that provided services to boats along the river. He wondered if this cliff still existed or if it was demolished to make room for a highway or bridge or to make the river wider for boat traffic.

ANTICIPATION DAY

Either way, to stand here, next to a simulated Captain Clark, and just take in the beauty of what the world looked like was simply amazing and exactly what he sought in this adventure.

For the next hour, Eric's job was to help with some observations on air temperature and wind speed, jotting down notes about the land ahead of them on their trip. They also spotted a suitable tree to cut down for their next mast.

On the walk back to the boat, they discussed Captain Clark's life. It was very interesting. At 19, he had followed his oldest brother George into the Army, eventually becoming a lieutenant by 1792. He participated in several campaigns against local Indian tribes, and by 1794, he was part of the campaign that ended the Northwest Indian War.

When his father died in 1799, the Captain inherited more than 3,300 acres, over twenty slaves, a distillery, and a gristmill, making him part of the landed gentry. He was unsure about his future until the invitation from Captain Lewis in June 1803 set him on this course.

Captain Clark spoke about the enslaved people he owned as if they were merely part of his life. Eric had to set aside any negative feelings about slavery, knowing it was a reality of the world he was in right now. Hell, one of Captain Clark's body slaves had joined the expedition and seemed to be treated exactly like the other men.

Eric felt comfortable with Captain Clark. He was serious, but also had a sense of humor and was very knowledgeable about the world around him. Again, Eric had to resist correcting some of Captain Clark's scientific theories, but he respected the hell out of him for his knowledge and curiosity.

▼▼▼

That evening, after they returned from their bonding experience, Captain Clark invited Eric to dine with him, Captain Lewis, and the Sergeants. Eric assumed it was a big deal to join them for dinner, so he accepted.

The dinner took place in a large tent on the shores of the river, elegantly set with tablecloth, silverware, and proper wine glasses. For 1804, this would have been considered fine dining in Boston, New York, or Philadelphia.

The food wasn't too shabby either: fresh-caught venison, vegetables, and fresh bread the expedition had traded with local Indians earlier in the day. Compared to his usual rice and beans, this was definitely a step-up.

The one downside of this meal was that the captains and sergeants drank. A lot. Normally, when Eric was eating a meal by the campfire with other members of the expedition, he could just pleasantly reject any call for liquor, but this was the first time during the trip he was pressured to take a drink.

Luckily, by the time the Captains and Sergeants began realizing he wasn't drinking much, they were all drunk themselves. So, to get out of drinking, he bluffed needing to go take a piss in the river and threw his drink in the water, before returning to the table.

During the dinner, Eric learned a great deal about both Captains through their stories about their time in the militia and the army. It was striking how different the two men were.

Captain Lewis was an educated man, eventually serving in the militia and being appointed to President Jefferson's Secretary in 1801. He had a deep love of the wilderness and was an expert outdoorsman. He spoke well, was articulate, and was calculated with his thoughts. He had enlisted as a private in the Virginia Volunteer Corps during the Whiskey Rebellion of 1794, where, interestingly enough, George's father had served as well.

Captain Clark was more raw than calculated; he said what he was feeling and also journaled *everything*.

They were both so interesting in their own ways. Captain Lewis shared thoughts and stories about President Jefferson. *President Jefferson!* An American Founding Father had known the man who was talking to Eric—well, not exactly this man, but it was damn close enough!

Late in the evening, Captain Clark and the sergeants took a bathroom reprieve in the nearby river, so Eric found himself alone with Captain Lewis.

"Son, I cannot say whether I knew your father or not, but if he served in the Whiskey Rebellion, he must have been an honorable gentleman," Captain Lewis said. "There were 13,000 of us in that battlefield that were asked to put down that rebellion. I myself missed most of the fun but stayed in Pittsburgh after the rebellion was squashed in case there was another outbreak by the protestors. I quite enjoyed the army life—the camaraderie, the formality of the processes. I took quite a lot from my time in the army to what we do here on this journey of ours. I know you witnessed what happened back in St. Charles and must think me a monster."

"No, sir, I don't," Eric replied. "I served in the army myself and understand that law and order must be followed. It is hard to witness, but I understand the reasons for it."

"Thank you, George," Captain Lewis said gently. "I hold no ill will towards anyone on this journey. All the men are making many sacrifices to be on this expedition, and I do not take those punishments lightly. But they must be done. The men must understand that law and order *has* to rule above all else. Without law and order, what do we have?"

Captain Lewis stared into the distance after asking that question.

"We have nothing, sir," Eric replied.

After a few seconds, Captain Lewis turned his attention back to Eric. "What do you hope to accomplish on this journey, son?"

Eric thought for a moment before replying. "Well, sir, I'm not entirely sure. I love being out in nature and want to experience all it has to offer. My mother died birthing me, my father recently passed away, and my only brother moved to Boston, so there wasn't much waiting for me at home.

I was fortunate to meet you in Philadelphia when you were recruiting. I consider it fate, I imagine, to join you. I want to be remembered as someone who sacrificed part of their life for the greater good, for the benefit of this nation. I hope to make my children proud, should I return to have some, of course." George chuckled at that last statement.

"I don't know, sir. I guess I just wanted my life to mean something. I hope that if we succeed and return, we'll have something to be proud of, something to give hope to others that will be awaiting our return. Plus, I am sure the girls will love me," he added with a laugh.

"Well, son," Captain Lewis said with a chuckle. "That's the best answer I have received to that question. With God on our side, I'm confident we'll return to many, many girls." He laughed, raising his glass of whiskey in a toast.

At that moment, Captain Clark and the sergeants returned from their urination break, and the group conversation continued.

Eric felt uplifted after that conversation. He wasn't sure if he was speaking as himself or George, but saying all that to Captain Lewis felt genuine and relieved a weight from his shoulders. Eric was searching for meaning in his life, and he hoped this journey would be part of it.

After a lively discussion, Eric bid goodnight to the members as the crickets chirped wildly, signaling that nighttime was fully present and the captains and sergeants began to slur their words, indicating they would pass out soon.

▼▼▼

As he walked back to the campground, Eric couldn't help but think that, despite nearly being crushed by a boat mast, this had been a great day. He had met *both* Captain Clark and Captain Lewis, had great conversations about their lives, and enjoyed a stunning view atop the Missouri River.

Even with the amazing day, Eric realized he needed to discover something that he was truly passionate about; something that would get him excited about life again.

He loved Alexandra, but their relationship had felt more like co-parenting roommates than husband and wife for the past decade. They still went out with friends and had occasional date nights, but it wasn't the same as before they had children.

While he was proud of his kids and he loved them very much, he felt disconnected from them. Most of this disconnection likely stemmed from prioritizing his career, which demanded long hours and last-minute meetings or travel, often keeping him away from family time.

This needed to change. He didn't want them to think of him a deadbeat dad more focused on work and drinking than on them. He could make this change, especially with some financial assistance from the government.

However, he knew he needed more than just spending time with the kids outdoors. He considered going back to writing, recalling the few short stories he had penned in college but never had the guts to get them published.

They were fairly outdated now, but maybe he would brush off that creative side of his brain and see what he could turn them into.

Eric liked that idea.

Before advancing to the next day, he promised himself he would start writing again.

▼ ▼ ▼

LATE JUNE 1804

The next several weeks of the expedition were routine as they proceeded north and west along the Missouri. The land became less tree-lined and grassier, as Eric guessed they were somewhere in present-day Kansas by now. The heat and humidity were increasing, and mosquitoes were becoming a major issue. Eric would've killed for some bug repellant.

Various animals roamed the grasslands, providing an abundance of meat to hunt—a skill that Eric had now mastered. They even killed a few rattlesnakes, for good measure, and cooked them over the campfire.

At one point, the expedition caught a wolf pup and brought it back to camp to try to tame the damn thing. However, when mommy wolf came looking for it, the men quickly released the pup back to where it belonged.

Near the end of June, the expedition was banked along the shoreline when two privates were caught stealing whiskey from the sentry and were sentenced to backlashes.

Again, Eric had to witness these lashes being given and couldn't help but wonder if this form of punishment should be brought back to modern day society. He hoped that with Anticipation Day gaining popularity, crime would decrease, but he definitely felt that a punishment of backlashes would deter it even further.

▼ ▼ ▼

JULY 4, 1804

Eric remembered 4th of July celebrations from his childhood: baseball games, fireworks, hanging out with his buddies, and setting off sparklers in parking lots. As he got older, his celebrations shifted to hanging with friends in parks, first in Denver and then in Central Park, New York City.

Now, with his kids older, the celebrations reverted to baseball games and fireworks, though he was usually too drunk from drinking all day to enjoy the fireworks at night.

In July 1804, on the banks of the Missouri River, with 40 members of the expedition, the celebration was very different. This celebration included partying, dancing, feasting on corn, and lots and lots of alcohol.

However, the focus of the celebration was truly on the concept of *freedom* and the ability to do whatever the fuck you want to do. By 2032, the original ideas of the holiday, like independence and freedom had been replaced with hot dog eating contests, spending a day at the pool, escaping to the mountains or a local lake, or simply enjoying a day off from work.

Most people didn't give two shits as far as what the founding generations of this country suffered through to gain their freedom.

But these men *did* give a shit. They celebrated their freedom as if it were the most important thing in the world.

So, they did what any free man enjoys doing. They got loaded.

Instead of joining the drinking, Eric spent a good portion of the holiday taking care of Hugh, who had been bitten by a snake and required bark treatment throughout the night. It was pretty bad, but it felt good to be needed, as the poor lad had a fever and was in a lot of pain.

Back in 2032, Eric generally tried to stay away from the immigration debate with his friends and colleagues. Still, as he tended to Hugh, he wondered if people heard the stories of their ancestors and what drove them to the United States in the first place, would it change their views and make them more empathetic to immigrants? While immigration reform had finally reduced the stem of immigrants coming into the United States illegally in recent years, Eric believed most people would benefit from understanding a little more empathy.

"Maybe this is the goal of this whole experience," Eric said out loud as he placed a damp towel on Hugh's forehead, who was luckily sleeping now. "Maybe we all need to see things through others' eyes. If we realized that we have more in common than we think, the world would be a better place. If so, good on you, simulation folks. You've won me over." Eric laughed, feeling slightly guilty doing so given Hugh's condition.

For the first time in a while, Eric realized how grateful he was for his life back home. He missed Alexandra: how she smelled, how they cuddled at night, and how she laughed when he cracked one of his stupid jokes.

He missed his kids, especially Sophia, who still got excited when he got home from work and was truly his soulmate. He missed the boys too; as loud and obnoxious as they could be, their energy was infectious. Most of all, he missed his bed. His body ached from sleeping on the ground for almost two months.

Listening to the men's stories about their families and what they had to endure to get to this point in their lives made him miss his own family even more.

Eric was quickly learning the meaning of family and home and what it meant to truly love. While his and Alexandra's relationship would never be perfect, they genuinely loved and cared for each other.

There were still more good times than bad, and most of their problems stemmed from his drinking. He hoped that if he could get his drinking under control, their issues might partially resolve themselves.

Would there still be things she did that drove him up the wall? Most likely. But he hoped he could now accept her for her and learn to love her for the imperfect human being she was.

Though he wondered how long he could stand to be away from his family, he kept reminding himself that he wanted to experience as much of this expedition as possible. If things got rough, he got bored, or he wanted to return to his family, he always had the "skip ahead" option.

But boredom wouldn't be in the cards for the coming weeks.

▼▼▼

MID JULY 1804

The next several weeks featured tough sledding up the Missouri River. Eric imagined they were somewhere near Iowa or Nebraska at this point.

These were some of the most exhausting days of the journey so far, with the boats frequently capsizing after running into sandbars along the Missouri River.

The grueling task of moving upriver wasn't something Eric would wish upon anyone. Every muscle in his body ached, but knowing he wasn't alone and the other expedition members were suffering as much as him, only made him feel slightly better. Deep down, he knew this was not real and temporary, so he pushed on, ensuring the expedition continued.

Luckily, by this part of the trip, food was plentiful. Buffalo, elk, horses, and even wolves roamed the nearby prairies they were now fully surrounded by. It reminded Eric of the scene in *Jurassic Park* where all the dinosaurs in the fields coexisted peacefully—yet there was always a threat of a hunter ready to pounce.

Seeing so many animals in their natural habitat was remarkable. His friends who had gone on safari in Africa had sent him videos, but he had to imagine that what he saw in this simulation was right up there with any of those experiences. He had seen wildlife before, especially camping in Rocky Mountain National Park, but nothing compared to this.

The weather was typical of the Midwest in the middle of July: scorching heat and humidity, swarms of mosquitoes, followed by periodic fronts that came through, bringing rain and wind but also cooler and drier air behind them.

The rain was a welcome relief, raising the river level and reducing the risk of hitting sandbars. Although some downpours increased the likelihood of a quick river surge, the men were used to it at this point and knew what to expect with the downpour surges.

The other good thing about the storms is that they kicked up the river, making for great fishing. The men caught several types of fish, including catfish, which was a pleasant change from gamey venison or elk.

By now Eric, as George, was fully bearded. The humidity made the beard uncomfortable and sticky, so one morning in late July, after passing what they determined to be the Platte River, he decided to shave. Using the scissors he found in his gear bag, along with soap and water, he tried to trim his beard. In the process, however, he accidently nicked his neck. Or at least he thought he did. He felt the pain and winced but he was surprised to see no blood.

"What the fuck?" He said out loud to no one. "Of course, that fucking no-liquid thing again." Eric laughed and thought about what else he could do with the scissors.

He pressed the scissors against his stomach, and dug in enough to cause a cut, but again, no blood appeared. He dug a little deeper, revealing a shiny, synthetic material beneath his skin. Still, no blood.

"What the fuck is this?" Eric asked out loud, again, to no one.

"Mr. Right." A man's voice came through the entire world, which he realized was Brian's robotic voice back in Denver. "Please stop cutting yourself. This is considered a form of self-harm and will be grounds for immediate termination from the simulation. Since we don't believe you are doing this to harm yourself, you are receiving a warning. Any perceived intent to self-harm will result in immediate termination from the simulation. Any questions, Mr. Right?"

"Uh, no." Eric was freaking out as the world around him froze. The sounds ceased, the campground fire was no longer burning, and everything looked motionless. "No sir, I apologize. I was just trying to shave this damn beard—it's so sticky."

"I understand, sir" The voice cut off. "Resuming simulation in 5, 4, 3, 2, 1."

And just like that, the simulation continued.

After that Matrix-like experience, Eric continued to hack at his beard with the scissors. The result wasn't the prettiest, and the other privates enjoyed teasing him about it for the next few days, but it did the trick. He'd have to live with it until he could trade for a proper razor blade.

Aside from his half-shaven beard, the next few weeks brought another challenge: several men, including Eric, were developing infections and boils on their skin. He wasn't sure if it was from mosquito bites or drinking contaminated river water, but Eric was in pain. A lot of pain. It reminded him of a bad stomach virus he'd had a few years back when he was shitting and puking every 30 minutes and eventually had to go to the emergency room to get an IV.

Unfortunately, here, there were no IVs, and Eric was genuinely worried that he or one of the men might perish because of this thing. Luckily, he couldn't have diarrhea or puke in the simulation, but the pain was still very real.

One night, Eric had a fever, and his stomach felt like it was in knots. The men brought teas and herbal remedies, but nothing worked. He shivered with chills and had one of the worst headaches of his life. He was sure he was delirious because of the fever, which made him laugh, given he was in a fucking simulation.

Fed up, Eric decided to use one of his skips, advancing the simulation by a few days until they were healthy enough to continue. He was willing to sit through the physical pain of moving the boat up the river, but fever and severe stomach aches were too much. So, he gave in and asked Brian to skip him ahead five days.

▼ ▼ ▼

After skipping ahead, the expedition appeared to be back on track, heading up the river and Eric felt better. It was hard to tell exactly where they were since everything looked the same, but they had to be somewhere around Iowa or Nebraska. There were still endless plains all around them with herds of elk, deer, and the occasional wolf along the riverbanks. Every so often, they would pass by cliffs of different types of beautiful sand and stone, which were unidentifiable to Eric.

Most of the men were still excited, although fatigue was setting in. The days were long but most of the men seemed to be accustomed to such conditions from their time in the army. So, they sucked it up and did their jobs.

Sergeant Floyd, whom Eric now referred to as Charles, was a great leader of the men. He continuously led by example, being the first one out of the barge to grab a rope when it got stuck, the first one up in the morning to go hunting so the men had breakfast waiting for them, and one of the last to sleep, ensuring the team was prepared for the next day.

At the beginning of the expedition, Eric and Charles would rise early every morning to have breakfast before the others, discussing the plan for the day and what obstacles might lay ahead. At day's end, they would briefly discuss their accomplishments and what the next day might bring. Their conversations were never deep, but they both seemed content with leaving it at that.

Over the past few weeks, though, the conversations had become more personal. Charles opened up about the girl he left behind in Kentucky to join the Corps, Charlotte. He missed her, sending mailings whenever he could, hoping that after this journey ended, he would return to Kentucky to marry her and start a family.

He had enlisted in the Corps of Discovery after Captain Clark recruited him and eventually was groomed into a strong soldier. Eric had to keep reminding himself that he was still a kid, being only 22 years old.

Charles also spoke about his family, including his four siblings and many cousins, one of whom was on the expedition. He mentioned that his mother believed they might be related to Captain Clark, but Charles had yet to bring it up with him for fear of retribution from the other expedition members. Charles didn't want anyone to think he was made sergeant because of some favorable connection to the captains.

He was very fond of his mother, and she seemed like a very loving woman who focused on her children until she died of an infection two years earlier.

When Eric heard this, he felt a pang of longing for his own mother. She had been a rock after their dad died, continuing to support the family until she passed away five years ago. He wished she had lived to see Sophia born and grow up; they would have adored each other.

In contrast, George never knew his mother, who died giving birth to him.

"*Creative storytelling*," Eric thought when this detail of George's backstory came up during a recent campfire session.

Eric sincerely liked Sergeant Floyd and knew they would have been good friends in real life if they had actually met in 1804.

▼▼▼

One morning, while hunting together for deer, Charles and George stumbled upon a lake as clear and beautiful as any Eric had ever seen in Colorado.

"Shall we?" Charles asked.

"Reckon we should, mate. Let's do it!" Eric replied as George, already undressing himself down to his underpants.

Charles did the same, and they both ran into the water like a pair of children.

The water was perfect—refreshing and clean. Back in 2032, Alexandra would have warned him about potential parasites or other hazards lurking in the lake. But she wasn't here, and this wasn't 2032, so Eric enjoyed the refreshing feel of the cool water against his fake skin.

After a few minutes of swimming, they were both floating on their backs a few feet from each other when Charles asked: "So, you imagine we will lose anyone?"

Eric thought about that question for a few seconds. He vaguely recalled that one or two members of the actual expedition had died on the journey, but he hadn't put much research into who they were. He had no idea who the unlucky souls were that didn't make it through the entire journey.

"Hugh is probably my guess. Stupid fucking guy gets bit by a damn snake. Thank Jesus, John was there to suck out the poison, else he would have been a goner," Eric replied, chuckling lightly as he looked at the deep blue sky above him.

"Robert is my bet. After what he did at Camp Dubois, he's probably due." Charles laughed.

"Yeah, he really needs to cut back on the drink," Eric said quietly, unsure if that was him or Alexandra talking.

"Well, let's hope no one succumbs to anything," Charles said. "I want to live, return, and receive a governorship of some exotic territory—with gold and jewel mines buried underground. And beautiful women as far as the eye can see. And the best washrooms money can buy."

They both laughed at that.

"Yeah, not being able to wash properly has been the worst part of this trip," Eric said with a grin. "And the bugs. And the sickness. And the food. Oh, and the tree that hit our mast. But I've also gotten on with the captains, and you have become a good friend, Charles. I truly enjoy our conversations and hope we both become governors of exotic lands."

"You got it, my friend. I believe in my heart we will," Charles replied, as they lay there for a few more minutes before dressing and returning to the camp.

That was a nice morning, and Eric continued to appreciate his friendship with Charles.

▼▼▼

Eric was getting tired, though, and wondered how long he could continue this, given it had been several months in the simulation. He missed his family very much, especially his kids. He kept reminding himself that they were safe at home and that he would be away for only about ten hours, depending on how quickly he exited the facility.

However, the journey was starting to wear on him, especially on days when his back ached or he got sunburned from the relentless time in the sun. He wanted to prove to himself that he could survive this expedition and knew that the more he suffered in 1804, the more he would appreciate what he had in 2032.

Things like toothpaste. Down pillows. A good pastrami sandwich—with mustard and cheese. *Pizza*

The expedition eventually made their way to a beautiful, long island, where they decided to camp for a few days. It was the end of July, and the days were so hot and humid that the members needed a break. The island was eventually named Camp White Catfish after the catfish the men had caught nearby.

It was a good time to rest and relax before the worst part of his journey began.

▼▼▼

AUGUST 1804

Eric never forgot the pain of losing his father—the shock, the anger, and mostly the sense of helplessness. Despite knowing there was nothing he could have done to prevent it, the pain never really faded.

So, when Charles died about a month after leaving Camp Whitefish, Eric was devastated by the same sting of grief. Even though he reminded himself it was only a simulation and part of the journey, the loss felt no easier than when his father died.

Initially, when Charles became ill, Eric didn't think much of it. Based on the recent weather, Eric hoped it was merely a temporary sickness that would pass in a few days.

On August 1st, Captain Clark's birthday, the sergeant appeared to be doing just fine, drinking and dancing into the early morning hours. However by August 18th, Captain Lewis' birthday, Charles had taken a hard turn for the worse.

While members of the expedition, including Captain Clark's servants, York and Peter, tried their best to take care of him, there was only so much they could do.

Eric did his best to comfort Charles, but he wasn't eating and seemed to be in constant discomfort and pain, sleeping most of the day. Despite his condition, he still managed to write in his journal until August 18th where Eric helped him relay notes about the expulsion of a member who ran off from the expedition, was eventually caught and made to run the gauntlet five times.

The gauntlet was basically just a beat down by a line of soldiers and was no fucking joke. Given Charles wasn't well enough to see it for himself, Eric had to describe it in pretty good detail so Charles could write it in his journal.

It reminded Eric of when the boys recently tested for black belt in Ju-Jitsu, and they had something called the "Chain of Pain," where the kids essentially got their asses handed to them by a row of black belts for about 15 straight minutes. It was difficult to watch, as some of the other kids in the testing were crying, but his kids made it through and earned their black belts.

However, the gauntlet was different, especially since Eric, as George, got to do some of the beating. He wasn't going to lie; it felt damn good to hit this guy multiple times for running away. At this point, Eric felt like a true member of the expedition, and for anyone to just give up and try to leave was disheartening and angering. So, when Eric participated in this running of the gauntlet, he definitely "participated."

Two days later, that good feeling completely faded as Eric watched his friend—yes, his *friend*—Sergeant Charles Floyd, pass away. Robert was with Eric as they wrapped his body in cloth when Eric began sobbing uncontrollably.

Eric didn't know why. Maybe it was because he was upset about Charles. Perhaps he was letting go of everything he had held inside him over the past decades. Perhaps he just missed his dad. It could have been all those things combined.

Robert put his arm on Eric's shoulder and the tearless crying eventually stopped, leaving Eric feeling unexpectedly lighter and at peace.

It was at this moment that Eric realized he had changed. He was done wasting his life worrying about his career and what would happen at his accounting firm. Sure, he wanted to keep his job and be a partner in the company, but he knew it would be okay if things didn't work out the way he wanted.

Life would go on.

Eric had a wonderful wife who ran a successful business, three exceptional children whom he hoped still loved him, great friends, and an awesome big brother who was always there for him. Deep down, he knew his father would want him to stop wasting so much time worrying about his career and focus more on his kids and his family.

Sitting quietly alone with Sergeant Floyd as Robert went to tell the captains, Eric closed his eyes and proclaimed, "Thank you, sir. Thank you for the chats by the campfire. You gave me a reason to get up in the morning and look forward to the day's end. You taught me to see again. I am eternally grateful. I know you were a good man in real life, and I hope you rest in peace. Amen."

He opened his eyes, covered Sergeant Floyd's body with another blanket, and waited for the captains to arrive.

▼▼▼

AUGUST 20, 1804

Burying Charles on a bluff overlooking the Missouri the following day was an emotional experience. Eric had attended a few funerals before, starting with his father's, but this one was different. The men's grief was raw and real. As they spoke, they expressed their emotions and truly honored the fallen member.

Perhaps it was the fear that their own fate would mirror Charles', or the unsettling thought that someone had died just three months after the launch. Either way, every man on the expedition was given a chance to speak; some spoke longer than others.

Captain Lewis delivered a short speech, proclaiming all honors of War on Sergeant Floyd, then placed a small cedar wood post at the head of his grave, inscribed with the name and date of death.

Eric spoke as George, relaying the hunting and fishing trips they had taken together and the amazing chats they had by the campfire. Eric didn't hold back in expressing how much he would miss Charles and promised to find Charlotte when the expedition was done and personally tell her how much Charles had meant to him. Maybe he would save that for next year's simulation.

After everyone else had returned to the boat, Eric knelt by the gravesite to give his last respects and spend a final few minutes alone with Sergeant Floyd.

As he looked over the Missouri River to see plains as vast as the eye could see, he knew he had gotten what he needed out of this experience and the time to return home was drawing near. The initial thought of sticking it out as long as possible was replaced with a strong desire to return to his life and see his family.

Based on calculations provided by Brian, he could skip ahead another 43 days to October 2, 1804, which would put him at 141 total days for the total simulation, meaning he would be a week away from meeting the 80% threshold to end the simulation early if he wanted to.

So, sitting down by the campfire after paying his final respects to Sergeant Floyd, he took one final look around before asking Brian to advance him.

▼▼▼

OCTOBER 2, 1804

The next thing Eric saw were bright colors. He seemed to be back in the boat, in his usual position, rowing up the Missouri River. The sun was setting in the sky to his right, creating the most vivid array of brilliant reds, oranges, purples, and blues filtering across the sky. It was one of the most beautiful sights he had ever seen.

He glanced down at the colorful foliage on all the trees along the riverbank, extending endlessly in both directions. It was as if he had been transported to another world.

As the sun continued to sink lower in the sky, its rays scattered light across the river's surface creating a reflection equally as impressive as the sky above him. Although he wasn't terribly religious, he imagined this is what heaven would look like if it did exist.

The scene created an almost euphoric sensation of peace and calm that overtook him. His eyes felt like they were tearing up, even though he knew tears wouldn't fall.

If he only had a goddamn camera.

He took a few deep, simulated breaths, taking in the scene's beauty. Then, from above, he heard the booming voice he knew as Captain Clark:

"Gentlemen, pause for a second. Pause your rowing please. I want you to look around and slow your breath for a moment. I want you to breathe in this warm autumn air and observe this beautiful and amazing array of colors all around us. You know what this is, gentlemen? This is God. God who surrounds us and protects us. God who will protect us when we will surely need it later on in this journey. God who will lift us up from the depths of hell when we are in our darkest moments.

Gentlemen, I want you to remember that God is with us.

When you struggle to keep warm in the winter and yearn for a good piece of meat, remember that God is with us.

When you yearn to talk to your mother, father, sister, or wife and long to share everything you see and experience, remember that God is with us.

When you long for a woman's embrace, embrace God.

When you doubt why you are here, remember that there is a greater purpose for you. This is part of your destiny.

With God's help and guidance, we will reach the sea on the far side of this land. Imagine the tales you'll tell and the people that will be eager to hear your story.

So, I beg of you all to take this beauty in and embrace it, gentlemen. With that, I leave you to your thoughts."

Captain Clark fell silent. Lord, that man could stir an emotion or two.

As Eric gazed at the world around him, he knew it wasn't real. He knew his body was lying back in a cold, leather chair in that facility back in Denver, and his wife was, hopefully, enjoying her own simulation. He knew that his life, his *real* life, was not this.

Yet every fiber of his being and his soul told him this was real. It told him he was seeing this beauty in front of him, and it warmed him to the point that he knew the man entering this simulation was not the man who was going to leave it. That much was real.

The man leaving would be more appreciative of life's blessings and prioritize what made him happy: his children, camping, Alexandra.

The one thing he knew didn't make him happy was the bottle. After going many simulated months without drinking, he would try to conquer his demons at home and try sobriety out for a bit. It wouldn't be easy, but he wanted to try. He needed to try. His family needed him to try.

If not for Alexandra, his kids, or himself, then for his dad, who had wanted him to be happy, and that was what Eric wanted to try to do. Be happy.

Would he and Alexandra work out their differences if he stopped drinking? Who knew?

What was certain was that he had a short time left on this planet and he was determined to spend as much of it as he could happily, rather than worrying about the past and things beyond his control.

He would miss this journey. He would miss the sunrises over the eastern plains every morning. He would miss the serene colors in the sky, the solitude, and the overwhelming sense of calmness that came with it. He would miss hiking, hunting, fishing, and sitting by the campfire contemplating life and the nature of the world he was in.

He would miss the campfire conversations with the men, especially Hugh and Charles. The utter stupidity and hilarity of what was said there was something he would not forget. He could now imagine what it was like to live in the 1800s, and he liked it, with a few exceptions.

Eric, as George, had grown close to these men. Hell, they had been through a lot together. This was not an easy journey up the river. It was grueling, backbreaking work at times. But they were all in it together, and that's what made it special.

However, as much as he would miss it, he knew the journey would only get colder and shittier from here. He would likely pick this journey up again next year to experience what it was like to continue through the Rocky Mountains and eventually onto the Pacific Ocean.

As his boat slowly drifted along the Missouri River, with the men taking the picture in with their minds, Eric looked back down to where the trees met the shoreline and then back up at the colors surrounding him in the heavens above. He smiled.

▼▼▼

OCTOBER 8, 1804

Six days later, after continuing a bit further up the river, eating more beans, sleeping outside along the shoreline, and securing a few more kills, Eric was ready to go home. He took his time enjoying the last few days of the journey to get his mind right for what he needed to do when he got back home.

At one point, he considered skipping ahead to the winter camp just to see what it would be like, but he decided that if he continued this journey next year, he would pick up at the end of their time at the camp.

On the evening of the last day he could leave the simulation early, he sat by the riverside, thinking about his experience in this fantastically made-up world.

He was proud of himself for surviving the trip, even if he was ending it a bit sooner than planned.

Eric would miss being George, but he had a feeling he would see him again. Hopefully, next time he would have a decent razor, at least to get rid of this awful beard. Eric was genuinely happy with this experience and looked forward to hearing about Alexandra's journey when she was ready.

So, as he took one final look around at the men around him and everything this world had to offer, he took a deep breath and knew he was ready to go home.

"*What was the phrase, again?*" Eric thought, "*Brian, get me out of there or something?*" No, that wasn't it.

"Brian, I would like to end my simulation, please." Eric said as everything faded to black.

CHAPTER 5

ALEXANDRA - TRIP
TO BRAZIL

MARCH 8, 2032
8:45 A.M.

As Alexandra's car pulled up to the facility, she had only one thought on her mind: "*Get me to a beach!*"

The past few months had been exhausting and stressful with work, the kids, and constant bickering with Eric. It had gotten to the point where she was seriously considering separating from him, even looking to file for divorce.

Divorce. The word terrified her. To her, it meant failure, and she couldn't bear to be viewed as a failure.

But above all else, she needed happiness, peace and control of her life. Right now, finding any of those was hard sometimes.

She wasn't sure what to expect today, but from everything MaryAnne had told her, it would be "life-changing and soul-refreshing."

Refreshing. Alexandra thought about the word. It wasn't so much refreshment she was after as it was clarity—finding herself and what she wanted for the rest of her life.

With that in mind, she hoped to make the most of this experience. She desperately needed something to take her mind off the daily grind of kids' activities, cooking, cleaning, daycare drama, and stress with Eric.

Lately, she had been wound up tighter than usual. Eric's drinking, despite his promises to cut back, was affecting the kids, which was intolerable in her eyes. She hoped his Anticipation Day experience would improve his behavior going forward.

Over the past few months, they had discussed the need for a reset in their lives. While they hadn't agreed on whether they would share their experiences with each other, she hoped they would, sooner rather than later. There was no point in continuing their relationship if they couldn't be honest about what happened in their simulations.

For now, that was out of her control. For now, she was focused on the positive experience she was hopefully about to have.

▼ ▼ ▼

After checking in, Alexandra sat by a window, watching as the sun struggled to pierce through the clouds on this Sunday morning. The waiting room was filled with others waiting for their simulation.

Eric had arrived an hour earlier, aiming to return home in time to relieve the babysitter, assuming he didn't get committed to the facility afterward. They had neighbors on standby just in case the babysitter didn't hear from them when she was expecting to.

About 20 minutes later, a woman called out, "Alexandra Right," from a large door at the front of the waiting room. Alexandra stood and walked over to the nurse, who introduced herself as Debra and shook her hand.

As they walked through the doors, Alexandra noticed hallways branching off in several directions. "This place is huge. I think it used to be a mall or something," she said.

Debra replied, "I'm not sure, actually. I grew up in Wisconsin and moved here with my husband about three years ago. It could've been a mall; it's certainly big enough."

They took the elevator to the fourth floor, eventually arriving at room 469.

"Feel free to put your personal effects in this plastic bag and then into that locker. We'll transfer it to the recovery area after your simulation," Debra said, getting a tablet from the desk.

Alexandra scanned the room. There were several computer screens, a reclining chair that looked mildly comfortable, and wires running across the floor connecting to a large computer-looking thing on the table. An IV stand with a bag was set up beside the chair. The variety of equipment and tools reassured her a little that she'd be safe.

A robotic assistant rolled into the room through a side door, introducing itself as Vivian. Debra explained that Vivian would monitor her vitals before gesturing for Alexandra to sit.

"Ok, so it looks like your simulation will involve being a single female in her early 30s, visiting various cities throughout Brazil for two months, starting on September 1, 2015, and going through the end of October 2015. Is that correct?" Debra asked, glancing at the tablet.

"Yes, that's correct," Alexandra replied.

"Why 2015?" Debra asked, genuinely curious.

Alexandra thought for a moment before answering, "Well, I've always wanted to see coral reefs, and I know they started dying off in the late 2010s, so I chose a year before then to see them while they were still healthy, you know? With climate change, it's hard to find many healthy reefs anymore with all the bleaching that has happened. Plus, 2015 is special to me because I met my husband that year. When I did my intake, I had the option to choose any year, so I picked one that meant something to me. So here we are!"

"Got it." Debra nodded. "Just wanted to make sure everything is accurate. It sounds wonderful. Can you confirm if you've had any changes in medicines, health conditions, both physically and mentally, or significant trauma in your life since you last saw us three months ago?"

"No, nothing that comes to mind," Alexandra said. "Other than consuming more weed than usual because, well, just because. I'm not sure if that counts as a change in medicine, but that's all I can think of."

"Did that cause any change in your health, either physically or mentally?" Debra asked, checking her tablet.

"No, nothing bad; just more relaxed in general," Alexandra said with a smile.

"Perfect, thank you," Debra said, noting something on her tablet. "Now that everything is confirmed, let's review what will happen next. We'll lay you down in the chair and attach a ring over your head while you're sedated. The ring has about 1.5 billion sensors that will make your brain perceive what you're experiencing within the simulation as 'real.' It essentially acts as your brain during the simulation. You'll be administered a sedative to slow down your brain activity while the ring takes over. The sedatives are completely safe and are similar to those used in certain types of surgeries. Any questions?"

"No, my friend did this two years ago and was fine. So I trust it's safe and won't cause any long-term damage," Alexandra said, smiling. Despite feeling the benefits would outweigh whatever perceived risk there was, a small part of her still couldn't fully trust this process.

"I assure you, these sedatives are safe," Debra said confidently. "Vivian will notify us if anything happens, and the medical staff will be right in to review your vitals. Now, just to note that when you wake up in the simulation, you may feel confused for a few minutes as the ring adapts to the environment and learns your neural pathways. That will go away as you get used to your simulation."

"Sounds awesome," Alexandra said with a tinge of nervousness in her voice.

"Great," Debra responded. "Before we start, let's go over a few points. These were covered during your initial intake, but we want to reiterate them. Please hold off any questions until the end."

Debra reviewed the rules, including that Alexandra could skip up to 25 times, but only up to two weeks at a time, or whatever 50% of the remaining simulation period was. She could end the simulation on the 48th day without penalty, which would place her in mid-October.

"*Good to know*," Alexandra thought as Debra wrapped up her speech.

"Okay, that's my spiel." Debra glanced at Alexandra.

"Wow, that's a lot to take in," Alexandra said, laughing. "So, to confirm, I'll have both my memories and those of my simulated character? How does that work?"

"More or less," Debra replied. "You'll intuitively know your simulated character's background, but not consciously. Don't ask me how they did it, but it's programmed into the ring, which then takes over." Debra gestured, palms up, as if to say: *Who knows?*

"Meanwhile, you will still have memories pulled from your brain simultaneously. The designers wanted you to interpret what was happening in the simulation with your own life and tie your emotions to your experience. It's like a real-time therapy session. I've done it, and it helped me come to terms with what made me happy.

Seeing people after their experiences makes me happy. I don't even like calling it a simulation because that implies it's not real. That's why I refer to it as an 'experience.' Hopefully, it does change you for the better. Sorry if I am rambling a bit, but I hope that gives you some comfort."

Alexandra laughed. "It does, and thank you for being so honest; it definitely helped calm me down. Okay, well, I guess let's do this then! I'm ready for Brazil!"

Debra confirmed that Alexandra was not planning on deviating from the planned simulation.

Alexandra thought about the question for a moment. "Well, what if I want to stay longer in any of the places than I planned to? Like, if I wanted to stay an extra day in Fernando de Noronha?"

"Good question." Debra responded with. "So, if you would like to spend an extra day in any one place, please just let Vivian know and she will adjust the simulation accordingly. Unless you say something to Vivian, the simulation will assume that on the 21st day, you will advance to Lençóis Maranhenses. In theory you could spend the entire trip in Fernando de Noronha if you wanted to, as long as you indicate to Vivian that is your choice. Okay?"

Alexandra was less confused now. "Okay, got it—thank you for clarifying. I really want to see all of Brazil though, so don't imagine that happening."

"Ok, great. I am going to start the sedation and fit the ring. The next thing you'll see is a beach. I wish you a pleasant and fun journey. We'll see you on the other side." Debra smiled and walked away.

Alexandra was excited, nervous, and curious about what this adventure would bring. The last thing she saw before blacking out was Vivian's weird robotic face staring down at her.

▼ ▼ ▼

SEPTEMBER 1, 2015

It was dark. Alexandra couldn't see anything.

But she could hear sounds. Were those bird songs she was hearing? Growing up in Colorado, she had heard many bird songs, but these were different—more beautiful, as if the birds were expressing how much they were loving life at the moment.

In the distance, she thought she heard waves crashing in the distance.

She inhaled deeply, taking in the intoxicating scent of salt air mixed with the scent of flowers. It was so unbelievably refreshing.

Slowly, Alexandra was able to see her surroundings. She realized she was in a bed, her head resting on a pink pillow, a light blanket draped over her. Above her, a ceiling fan spun lazily, providing a gentle breeze against the humid air.

"Okay, let's try to sit up," Alexandra said, noticing her voice sounded younger and fresher. Sitting up, she glanced to her right and saw a small desk with a lamp, a sink, and a coffee maker. Above the desk was a small television—something Eric would have scowled at, as he always needed a hotel with a large television. Size mattered greatly to him.

To her left, a large glass door led to a wooden deck with lounge chairs and a table for two.

She closed her eyes, taking in the utter silence of the moment. No children asking for lunchboxes, no husband searching for his dry cleaning, no employees calling saying they would be late, and no parents calling to say their kids couldn't make it to the daycare.

Just pure and complete silence, and already she felt better.

After a few minutes, she got up and stepped onto the cool floor. "Holy shit," she said. "This is fucking incredible." She laughed and cried at the same time, though no tears came. She ran her hands along the walls, amazed at how real they felt.

She walked to the bathroom and felt the soft towels against her skin.

"*How the fuck did they do this?*" She thought.

Looking in the mirror, she saw an unfamiliar face—flawless, unblemished, and wrinkle-free. People her age paid good money for skin like this.

Her eyes were hazel, and her skin had a warm tan, as if she had spent weeks in the Brazilian sun. She looked rested and carefree. Her long, light brown hair was healthy, with no split ends or gray strands.

Alexandra stared at her reflection, marveling at the realistic details, down to a few faint lip hairs growing on the side of her mouth and a pimple on her cheek, for good measure.

She was no longer Alexandra. She was now the person in the mirror and that person was breathtakingly beautiful.

"*Hell, if I'd known I'd look like this, I would've signed up for more than two months,*" she thought. "*Perhaps I'll buy that add-on package after all.*"

Finished admiring herself, she stepped out onto the outdoor patio to take in the first stop in Brazil: the stunning Fernando de Noronha, which was known as one of the most romantic getaways in Brazil.

She planned to spend 20 days here with plans to snorkel, lounge by the beach and pool, enjoy delicious food and cocktails and just… relax.

Next, she intended to visit Lençóis Maranhenses, another romantic spot in the country's north, famous for its white sand beaches and freshwater pools. She would spend five days there before heading to the heart of the Amazon rainforest for two weeks of exploration.

From there, she planned to travel to Iguazu Falls and the area around Foz do Iguaçu. Her friend Catherine had visited years ago and insisted it was a must-stop in Brazil, so Alexandra decided to check it out and spend ten days there.

For the final ten days, she would explore Rio de Janeiro. No trip to Brazil, real or simulated, would be complete without experiencing Rio, especially since the kids were at home.

But for now, she was in Fernando de Noronha, and she wanted to make the most of her time. As she walked outside, the view took her breath away.

"Oh my god," she whispered.

The scene before her was like something out of a movie. Two rows of vibrant pink, red, and yellow flowers stretched before her, unlike anything she had seen before. Between the rows, lush green grass swayed gently. To her left were buildings she assumed housed other simulated characters.

In front of her, she saw the clearest, bluest ocean she had ever seen. It was unlike any ocean she'd encountered in Florida or the Caribbean— pure, crystalline water.

A few hundred yards off the coast were rock formations that seemed to rise hundreds of feet in the air.

"How did they do this?" She asked again in awe. The level of detail was amazing. Blades of grass fluttered in the wind, large bees jumped from flower to flower, and clouds drifted at varying heights in the atmosphere. It was truly phenomenal.

She closed her eyes and took in the air, the smells, and, once again, the quiet. Whatever soul was with her in this place was somehow lifted. She didn't know if she was smiling back in Denver, she certainly felt a smile spread across her face for the first time in a long while.

"*This really was an amazing idea,*" Alexandra thought as she sat on the deck outside her room, gazing at the beach.

After 15 minutes, a buzz at her door startled her.

She grabbed her robe from the chair and opened the front door to find a young man with a cart of food and beverages, ready to be wheeled in.

"Uau, isso parece incrível. Por favor, entre," Alexandra said in Portuguese, staring at the spread that truly looked incredible.

"Bom dia, señiorita Murphy. Eu confio que você dormiu bem," the young man said in Portuguese, asking her if she slept well.

During her intake process, Alexandra was given the option of having her character automatically understand Portuguese or allowing her own knowledge of the language to communicate with the simulated locals. She chose the latter option, seeing it as an opportunity to learn a new language. So, for the past month, she had been studying Portuguese and felt like she would have enough command of the language to engage in some basic conversation.

At this moment, her priority was eating the delicious food in front of her: pastries, biscuits, scrambled eggs, a meat and cheese plate, coffee, juice, and water.

"*My god,*" Alexandra thought. "*If I stay here for 2.5 weeks, I'll gain 15 pounds. Oh, who cares? This isn't my body.*" She laughed, catching the young man's attention.

"Are you okay, Ms. Murphy?" He asked her in English.

Alexandra noted he called her "Ms. Murphy." Interesting last name.

"Yes, sorry," she said. "I was just thinking about all the weight I will gain if I keep eating all this food." She continued laughing at how silly she sounded.

"Well, I think you look just fine, Ms. Murphy. Eating like this is good for you. It wakes your body up and prepares it for the day."

"*Is this kid flirting with me?*" Alexandra thought. He was handsome, with a tall, lean build, dark skin that glistened with a hint of sweat, a lush head of hair, and strikingly light eyes.

She guessed he was in his mid-20's, very fit, and he smelled nice. Alexandra started feeling a tingling in places she hadn't felt for a long time. She couldn't have sex with this kid, could she?

She and Eric hadn't been active in the bedroom lately, and they hadn't discussed the rules about sex in their simulations. They agreed to share their experiences with each other if it helped their relationship but wanted to give each other time to process them first.

Alexandra hadn't planned on having sex in the simulation. She just wanted to return to her *happy place* and enjoy her time in her simulated world, but hadn't considered what the concept of "enjoying" might entail.

Now, seeing this young man, she wasn't entirely against the idea. For now, though, she focused on the food.

"Well, gracias, Javier," Alexandra said.

His name was Javier, apparently. "*Was that because I saw his nametag, or did I just know his name?*" Alexandra thought. She didn't recall seeing a nametag, but she was sure of his name. Weird. That must have been one of those memories Debra mentioned she would have from the character.

"De Nada, Ms. Murphy," Javier replied, heading towards the front door. "Don't forget you have a 10 a.m. snorkeling session with Mr. Carlos at Baía do Sueste Beach. He will meet you in the lobby around 9:50, and you'll walk down together. Please look for a sign with 'Lauren Murphy' on it."

She didn't remember booking that session. Maybe her character was supposed to be forgetful, or the simulators messed up. Either way, she was excited to snorkel.

"Oh, perfecto. Gracias, Javier. Te veré más tarde," Alexandra said, politely trying to get him to leave so she could enjoy her meal.

She showed Javier out and looked at the clock on the wall: 7:45 a.m. Great. That gave her a couple of hours to eat, stroll to the beach, and then meet Mr. Carlos.

Alexandra sat at the table and dove into the food before her. Everything was delicious. The eggs were warm and perfectly fluffy, and the pastries and biscuits were freshly made, accompanied by various jars of jam and butter. She avoided the meats this early, but enjoyed the fresh, warm cheeses. The coffee was exceptional—strong, hot, and spiced in a way she'd never tasted before. It woke her body up like no coffee had before.

As she slowly finished her food, she couldn't ignore the tingling sensation that was still there. She thought, "*Should I rub one out?*" feeling a little hot and bothered between her handsome delivery boy and the delicious meal she just consumed. She looked around and shrugged: *Why not?*

She crawled onto the bed and quickly brought her fingers between her legs and slipped them inside, noting the weird sensation—it didn't quite feel like a real vagina. Debra certainly wasn't kidding about the "no liquids" rule. Still, the feeling was pleasurable, and she came in a matter of minutes, not even having time to think of Robert Mancini, the new star of her favorite romantic reality show.

It was a hard, explosive orgasm, and she wondered if it had woken up the simulated characters who were staying nearby.

"*Oh my god,*" she thought, catching her breath with a laugh. "*What if I had an orgasm back in Colorado?*"

She couldn't stop thinking that multiple people were in the room watching her pleasure herself.

It reminded her of when she gave birth to Sophia and a gaggle of interns walked into the delivery room, gawking at her while offering no real help for the birthing process.

"*Ah, it doesn't matter.*" She exhaled deeply. It was a much-needed release. She felt more relaxed than she had in a long time. Strangely, she wasn't tired; normally, she felt sleepy after an orgasm, but right now, she felt like she could run ten miles.

With some time to spare, Alexandra dressed, slipped on sandals, and headed out the door. Of course, she knew exactly how to get to the beach. As she strolled through the grass path outside her building, she took a wood-planked trail leading directly to the shore and could not get over the realism of the simulation.

The sights, sounds, smells, and breezes made her absolutely feel like she was walking to the beach on a beautiful morning in Fernando de Noronha. Despite being only an hour into simulated time, she was already immensely enjoying this experience.

Once on the beach, she found a warm spot on the sand near the water, sat down, and closed her eyes. The rhythmic crash of the waves on the shore and the warmth of the simulated sun on her skin, coupled with the gentle breeze, soothed her.

She breathed in, catching the smell of seaweed, salt, and iodine. The smells instantly took her back to her and Eric's honeymoon in Hawaii back in 2018.

▼ ▼ ▼

Fourteen years ago really felt like 44, but Alexandra remembered how much fun her and Eric had in Hawaii. They had sex every morning, then walked onto the beautiful beach to sit in the water for hours, talking, drinking, and feeling excited for their future together. They had the most wonderful romantic dinners and usually ended the day with another romp in the Hawaiian hay.

That was before kids, before career stresses, and before Eric's drinking worsened. It truly felt like a lifetime ago.

Now, they barely had the time or energy to go out to dinner by themselves.

It was sad, and while she didn't want to blame all their problems on Eric's drinking and mood swings, the truth was his stress was straining their relationship and affecting the entire family.

Unfortunately, the kids, especially the boys, were beginning to resent their father, and that saddened her the most.

Eric wasn't a bad person and had a wonderful heart, but when he drank, he turned into a completely different person. Alexandra wished she could help him more, but aside from offering him edibles and suggesting he cut back for his health, he had to make the change. So far, he hadn't shown that willingness, and it frustrated her a lot.

Eric loved his kids, especially Sophia, whom he adored and would do anything for. But Alexandra worried that if things continued as they were, Sophia might grow up to hate her father. She was only five and looked up to him, but that would not last forever.

If things didn't improve, Alexandra would have no choice but to get him help or ask him to leave. She didn't want either option and hoped his Anticipation Day experience would help him find the peace he needed.

"*Time will tell*," she thought as a couple walked by, speaking in Portuguese.

"Oh man, speaking of time, what time is it?" She muttered to herself. A quick glance at her watch showed it was 8:55. How long had she been down there daydreaming?

She wasn't sure, but she did want to shower before preparing for her snorkeling experience with Carlos.

With that, Alexandra headed back to her hotel to get ready.

▼▼▼

An hour later, Alexandra walked to the lobby to meet Carlos, feeling amazing—clean, refreshed, reenergized, and still a bit horny. Whatever this simulation was doing, she didn't want it to end.

The hotel's lobby was stunning, filled with lush plants, beautiful paintings, and local arts and crafts. Though Alexandra was seeing it for the first time, it felt familiar, as if Lauren's memories were popping into her head.

Still weird.

Approaching the entrance, she noticed a tall, dark, and ruggedly handsome man holding a sign with "Lauren Murphy" written on it. Yep, that was her.

He was close to 6 feet tall, with dark skin, a chiseled face, blue eyes and short brown hair. He was wearing a tight shirt that accentuated his sculpted body. He reminded Alexandra of Mario Lopez from Saved by The Bell.

This morning just kept getting better.

"Buenos días, soy Lauren Murphy," Alexandra said, walking up to him and shaking his hand.

"Bueno días, Ms. Murphy." Carlos said, showcasing his beautiful smile and dimples. "I'm Carlos, and I'll be guiding you on your snorkeling adventure this morning. How are you doing?"

"Por favor, me chame de Lauren. Eu sou bom. Eu sinto, uh, muito relaxado esta manhã, si?" Alexandra responded in Portuguese, expressing how relaxed she felt. She continued in English, "I've been waiting to snorkel for, like, ten years." She smiled, gazing into his gorgeous, light blue eyes.

"Relajada, look at you, muy bonita," Carlos said with a smile. "Let's keep you relaxada all day with some beautiful snorkeling, sí?"

"Sí, estou pronto, vamos fazer isso." Alexandra replied. She *was* ready to do this. Snorkeling had always been something she enjoyed, dating back to trips to Greece and Italy during high school and spring break in college. She genuinely felt connected to the world underwater and was curious how this experience would compare to real life.

Carlos and Alexandra walked down to the beach, a short five-minute stroll from the hotel lobby, arriving at a spot about 200 yards from where she had been earlier that morning. The ocean, calm and blue, looked as beautiful as it had an hour ago.

They approached a small boat near the shoreline, where flippers and goggles were waiting for them. At the bottom of the boat lay two oars, a small anchor with a rope that appeared to be about 10 to 12 feet long attached to it. Carlos held the boat steady as Alexandra climbed in and sat at the back, facing towards the beach. He pushed the boat into the water and hopped in.

They rowed in silence for a few hundred yards, navigating a few incoming waves until they arrived at a calmer area near a large rock formation rising from the ocean like a giant wall.

Carlos set the oars down and dropped the anchor overboard until it hit the bottom.

"Okay, Ms. Murphy—excuse me, Lauren. Since you have snorkeled before, I assume you know how to use the flippers and goggles, sí? So, let's get them on. As you can see, Miss, the water is calm right now, sí? Sin olas. It should stay this way until this afternoon because we're at low tide. We should see plenty of fish and some beautiful coral reefs today, sí? This coral is very sensitive to the touching." Carlos pointed to his fingers to make sure she understood. That was cute.

"Por favor, do not touch it with your body. Bueno?"

"Eu entendo," Alexandra said, nodding indicating she did understand.

"Okay, the boat will be here, so if you need to take a break, just swim back and you can help yourself. I will be with you in case you get into any trouble."

"What kind of trouble?" Alexandra asked, a hint of worry in her voice.

"Well, sharks swim here, but they usually come out in the morning and evening, so we should be fine now. But they can still come. Você entende?" Carlos asked, pointing at Alexandra to ensure she understood.

"Sí, entendo," Alexandra replied. Ever since she was little, she'd been afraid of sharks—probably because of the *Jaws* movies she used to watch with her dad during their movie nights. Sometimes he picked the movies, sometimes she did. The first time he picked *Jaws*, she enjoyed it, but ended up developing a huge fear of sharks from that movie.

But this wasn't real, so whatever fears she had, they needed to be put aside.

"I'm ready to go in. It looks beautiful," she continued.

"Okay, I think the American phrase is 'Last one in is a rotten goose', si?" Carlos asked before putting in his mouthpiece.

"Close enough." She laughed, inserting her own mouthpiece and jumping into the water. Alexandra immediately felt the ocean's warmth envelop her as she was briefly submerged. Surfacing, she saw Carlos give her a thumbs-up, which she returned to him. He pointed toward the rocks, indicating they would head that way.

As they swam slowly toward the rocks, Alexandra dipped her goggle-covered face into the water to see what lay beneath. Instantly, she was blown away by what she saw under the clear blue water.

The coral reefs were right there, a few feet below, rising above beautiful brown and green rocks. Bright yellow sand covered some of the rocks, shifting slightly with each passing wave. The reefs were *absolutely* stunning and bursting with colors. It was like nothing she had seen before, even in Europe.

The colors spanned the full spectrum of any crayon box she had ever seen: vivid pinks, yellows, blues, greens, reds, oranges, and purples covered corals of every shape and size. It seemed as if the ocean was deliberately careful not to replicate one reef with another.

As the waves moved over them, the corals seemed to move in a harmony similar to any synchronized swim team.

And then there were the fish—unbelievable. It was like a nature documentary come to life: they were *everywhere,* decorated in the brightest blues, greens, purples, reds, oranges, and yellows she had ever seen.

Sure, she'd seen aquariums in various cities her and Eric had traveled to, and some of those fish were colorful, but nothing like this. There had to be hundreds—no, thousands—of fish swimming beneath her. As she reached out to touch some of the larger schools of fish, they all scattered in perfect synchrony, a few brushing against her fingers.

The peace and calmness she experienced while swimming were unmatched with anything in her life to-date. Perhaps it was the warm, calm water surrounding her, the sun on her back, or the stunning fish and coral reefs below her, but she didn't have a care in the world right now.

For the next 90 minutes, Carlos and Alexandra explored the entirety of the coral reef structure, which spanned several hundred yards across. They took breaks as needed, with Carlos explaining the reef's features and the efforts to protect the remaining reefs from bleaching, which was crucial for their local economy.

Alexandra saw several large sea turtles gracefully making their way amongst the reefs. Carlos and her swam amongst the cliffs and under natural arches connecting the various cliffs to each other.

It was one of the most beautiful and serene things Alexandra had ever done.

As their time neared its end, Carlos reminded Alexandra that they needed to head back to the beach.

In the final few minutes, Alexandra closed her eyes and floated on her back, letting the ocean carry her wherever it wanted. She wasn't thinking about anything in particular, still taking in the amazement of the experience so far and how real it felt. MaryAnne's description certainly came close, but didn't give it near the full justice to what she was experiencing.

Alexandra let the waves carry her towards the boat, where she eventually climbed in and they began their trip back to shore.

On the way back, Carlos shared his simulated life story. He was studying to become a teacher, hoping to be a part of the teacher exchange program in the United States. After his dad's death when he was just 13, he had taken on the responsibility of caring for his two younger brothers.

Starting work at the age of 14, Carlos had saved enough from his hotel job to send his brothers to a private school on the mainland. He was single, having broken up with his ex-girlfriend a few months ago.

Alexandra felt a special place in her simulated heart for Carlos. Here was a kid trying to make it in the world who seemed very smart and responsible at the same time. She had started working when she was 15 and hadn't stopped since, so she respected his work ethic.

"Really pulling at my heartstrings, simulators," Alexandra thought as they made their way to the beach.

Once Carlos finished, he asked Lauren about her story, which again came to Alexandra seamlessly. At 32, she was a recent divorcée without kids. Her friends, Stacy and Harmeet, had gifted her this trip, and they planned to meet her in Rio de Janeiro in a month or so.

Lauren, apparently from a wealthy background, had written four successful books on investing wisely, so she had some money and was just looking for some fun while down here.

As they arrived at the shore and walked back toward the hotel, Alexandra quickly found herself asking Carlos out to dinner that night. The impulse was sudden and not something she was planning on at all, but before she could second-guess herself, he had replied.

"I'd love to, Ms. Lauren. While I can't ask guests out to eat, I can certainly accept if asked. How about 9 p.m. at the hotel restaurant?"

"Perfect, Carlos. Thank you for the wonderful experience. It was exactly what I needed. See you later at dinner." What did she just do? Alexandra never had the guts to ask men out like this; she was way too shy. But here, in this place, in this world, she wasn't Alexandra. She was Lauren and apparently Lauren had no problem asking men out.

Smiling broadly, Alexandra returned to her bungalow to enjoy the rest of the day.

▼ ▼ ▼

It was still weird to look in the mirror and see a different face and body, but Alexandra didn't mind what she saw.

The dress she chose for dinner was one of the nicest she'd ever worn. It had an interesting mix of red, yellow, black, white, pink, and orange, cascading from her midsection down the right side of her body.

The left side of the dress rode up her upper thigh, exposing most of her tanned, toned legs.

The top was held up by two thin straps of fabric that wrapped around her neck and back, accentuating her decent cleavage until they joined the rest of the dress near her breasts. It didn't scream *Fuck me,* but it also didn't say, *We're heading home early tonight.*

She wore stunning ocean blue earrings, and her makeup perfectly complemented her skin tone.

If she were a man, she would have sex with her.

Alexandra knew what the potential result of this evening could be. After the day she'd had, she felt goddamn good about herself, even if she wasn't quite "herself."

Having spent the day in a beautiful location, she was honestly a little horny. Could she act on it? Only time would tell, but she also wondered if Carlos felt the same. Maybe he treated every simulated customer this way to make them feel at home so they would tip him more generously. She would soon find out.

Ten minutes later, Alexandra arrived at the hotel restaurant entrance to find Carlos waiting for her. When she went closer, he greeted her with a kiss on her cheek. "*Interesting,*" she thought.

Carlos wore a simple white jacket over a blue and green button-down shirt, paired with brown khaki shorts and polished shoes. Simple, yet elegant.

The restaurant itself was also simple, yet elegant, and it smelled *amazing.* The staff, clearly familiar with Carlos, had hooked them up at the best table: a corner spot on the patio, overlooking the forest below and the Atlantic Ocean 100 yards away.

The night was enchanting, with a full moon, a light breeze, and a clear sky. The distant sound of the ocean added to the ambience, making it one of the most romantic places Alexandra had ever been to.

She had dined in Italy, Spain, and the Philippines, where the settings were beautiful and the food amazing. But this felt... perfect. Maybe it was the company, or maybe it was the lack of concern about Eric's drinking or how the kids' were doing with grandma and grandpa back in the U.S.

Regardless, it was a beautiful and romantic setting for dinner.

They started with drinks: Alexandra ordered a pink Russian, while Carlos opted for local tequila.

The nighttime air grew chilly. Noticing her discomfort, Carlos offered her his jacket, a gesture that struck her as one of the most romantic things anyone had ever done for her, simulated or otherwise.

Alexandra scanned the menu. The appetizers featured fried Brazilian beans, crab meat with bread, fried shrimp, calamari, ceviche, and other local specialties. For mains, the options were predominantly fish—tuna, prawns, octopus, and calamari—alongside meat dishes like filet mignon, pork ribs, and beef tenderloin risotto. Although there were pasta options, she decided against them; she didn't come to Brazil to eat pasta.

Alexandra had always enjoyed this type of food, but this cuisine was not up Eric's alley—he preferred Italian restaurants or local pubs. Quite simply, her palette was more refined, and she often enjoyed dining at Spanish restaurants.

Alexandra decided on the calamari but before she could even let Carlos know, he called the waiter over and ordered for both of them without even asking her what she wanted.

Normally, she would have been irritated by this, but this time, she didn't care. There was a rare trust she felt with Carlos and she knew that whatever he chose would be delicious. And boy was she rewarded.

Fifteen minutes later, the appetizers arrived: octopus carpaccio drizzled with olive oil and curry, peppers, homemade chips, and traditional ceviche with peppers, onions, and orange and citrus juices. Carlos explained that the fish was locally caught tuna and was considered some of the tastiest in the world.

The salad was a mix of local greens, green beans, Brazilian rennet cheese, and prawns with garlic and dried tomato. The freshness and flavor were perfect for her. How did Carlos know her preferences so well?

She couldn't wait to see the main dishes as they enjoyed a second round of drinks.

Between courses, they talked, mostly in English with some Portuguese mixed in, about life, love, heartache, family, and their dreams and aspirations. Their conversation flowed naturally, making it feel like they had been friends for years. She laughed more than she had in ages. It felt so freeing.

Their mains finally came, featuring prawn risotto with turmeric, cherry tomatoes, basil, and a local catfish with delicious rice and potatoes. Although she wasn't usually a huge fan of prawns, these were sweet and mildly flavored with only a hint of saltiness. The risotto was creamy and perfectly seasoned. She never really liked catfish either, but this dish was simple and rustic and did the trick.

By the end of the meal, she felt ready for a nap. Carlos suggested they have dessert, and she agreed, thinking, *"Why not?"* It wasn't her real body, after all. When she and Eric went out to dinner, the few times a year they did, they rarely got dessert because Eric was usually drunk by the end of the meal, and she wanted to go home before things got worse.

Twenty minutes later, their chocolate ganache arrived, the perfect finish to a nearly perfect meal. Made with vodka, coffee, Amarula, vanilla ice cream, and cinnamon, it was rich, but not overwhelming, and erotic at the same time.

As they sipped cappuccinos after rounding out the meal, Alexandra teased, "So, Carlos, how many women have you been with? You must do this with all your snorkeling customers."

Carlos laughed. "I wish, Ms. Lauren."

"Please, just Lauren," she said, smiling. She couldn't help herself with that one.

"Okay, Lauren," he said, smiling back. "To answer your question, I've never done this with a customer before. I'm, how do you say... *tímida*..."

"You're shy?" Alexandra translated, her eyes wide.

"Sí, *tímida*. Shy, you said? Yes, I am usually shy. But there was something about you Lauren. I felt a connection the moment I saw you. Just seeing your happiness when we were in the sea. It was beautiful to see.

I wasn't sure if you were here by yourself. You didn't come with anyone, so I thought either you're alone or... how do you say... *homosexual?*"

"Gay," Alexandra responded with a laugh. "No, I'm not gay—at least, I don't think so. I kissed a girl once in college." She and Lauren apparently had that in common.

"Asombrosa," Carlos responded, clearly enjoying that. "Well, if you're not gay, are you single?"

She paused. Was she single? Right now, she certainly didn't feel like she was married. She felt like a single woman, having dinner with a beautiful, romantic man.

"Sí, I'm single," Alexandra replied, her lips curving into a smile.

"I'm glad I asked you to dinner then," Carlos said, licking his lips. He leaned in and kissed her. The kiss sent a thrill through her body. She wanted more.

"Wow, okay," Alexandra murmured as he pulled away. "I'll be right back." She got up and went to the restroom.

In the bathroom, she stared at her reflection, fully aware of the tingling sensation in her loins. She hadn't been this horny in *decades*. Eric hadn't made her feel like this in a long time.

At this point, she knew she would likely be having sex with Carlos tonight and was okay with it. She needed it. The question of whether it was cheating was for another time.

After freshening up, she returned to Carlos.

"Sorry, I just wanted to freshen up. Look, I like you Carlos. I just want you to know I have been lonely recently. That is why I asked you to dinner. Do you understand the word lonely?" She asked while staring right into his eyes.

"Si, we call it sozinho'. In Brazil, we believe in companhia—I am not sure how you say in English. But we enjoy each being with others and when we find someone beautiful, we hold onto them. Entender?" He asked Alexandra.

"Sim, eu entendo". Alexandra did understand and she leaned over and kissed him again. This time there was no holding back and she wanted him. Badly.

They left the restaurant and arrived at her bungalow 30 minutes later. She barely waited to open the door before grabbing his face and kissing him deeply again. His shirt came off, revealing a finely sculpted body—a literal Brazilian god.

Carlos laid her on the bed, his tongue tracing her ears and neck, eliciting a moan she couldn't control. As he moved down to her breasts and nipples, an overwhelming surge of pleasure overtook her body, intensifying when he reached her groin.

She'd had plenty of orgasms in her life, but the one Carlos gave her with his tongue was *explosive*. Her body shook, and her eyes rolled to the back of her head. She had no idea what was happening back in Colorado, and she didn't care.

Carlos entered her, and she orgasmed almost instantly again, overwhelmed with euphoria. She saw stars.

She rolled him over, taking control. The breeze from the open windows poured into the room, overtaking both of their heated bodies, only serving to enhance the sensation.

Having sex with Carlos was raw, animalistic, and exhilarating. By the time they finished, she had lost count of her orgasms, unable to move as Carlos finished on top of her.

Sweat gathered on his body but not hers, which normally would have been strange, but she didn't care. As they spooned, with him holding her from behind, a profound sense of pure relaxation settled over her.

Did she feel guilty? Yes, a little, but not enough to regret it. Would she tell Eric? Maybe, but that was a problem for another day.

In a few days, she'd be back at work, dealing with crying kids and rude parents, all while trying to run a household. All the problems that seemed so far away would be back soon enough, and she just wanted to enjoy this feeling and take in this experience.

Listening to Carlos snore beside her, she decided to slip out of bed and onto the patio, gazing at the moonlit night. It was a full moon, and the reflection off the ocean was simply perfect.

She closed her eyes, took a deep breath, and asked Vivian to skip to the next day.

▼ ▼ ▼

SEPTEMBER 2, 2015

The next thing Alexandra saw was Carlos walking over with a tray of food towards her bed in the early morning light. She instantly smelled the scent of freshly baked bread.

"This just keeps getting better and better. Good morning," Alexandra said, smiling at Carlos as he kissed her forehead.

"Good morning, Lauren. I trust you slept well?" Carlos asked as he sat on the bed next to her.

"Yeah, I think so," Alexandra said, unsure how to respond to that question.

"That's wonderful. Thank you for last night. I enjoyed myself, and I hope you did too." Carlos kissed her forehead gently again before standing. "I have many snorkeling lessons today and need to visit my brothers back on the mainland. I'll be back in four days. May I see you then?"

Alexandra felt a tinge of sadness. "I leave in a little over two weeks, so I'll be here when you get back. Let's see each other when you return, okay? Have a great time with your brothers."

Carlos kissed her softly on the lips, said goodbye and left the room. Alexandra lay alone and naked, with a mini buffet of delicious food waiting for her. Simulated life could certainly be worse.

She brought her food outside and sat at the table. The morning was cloudy, and the air felt thick with moisture. It looked like it would rain soon as she dove into her breakfast.

The food was again incredible. An assortment of breads, muffins, and pastries, accompanied by jams, spreads, and butters. An array of fruits—some familiar, others not—were joined by French toast and waffles, which completed the meal. Coffee, tea, and juices were available to wash it all down. She would gain 20 pounds if she kept eating like this. Oh well, not her concern.

Alexandra was finally alone in her thoughts for the first time after her romp with Carlos.

That had been one of the best sexual experiences of her life, and it wasn't even with a real man. The programmer behind this simulation had to be a man for the sex to be as good as it was in here. No man she'd been with could do what Carlos did last night.

Alexandra didn't feel guilty about what happened. This was her experience and hers alone. The truth was, she was a very sexual woman, while Eric wasn't, or at least not when he was drunk. In college, she had experimented with women, including MaryAnne, and had enough experience before marrying Eric to consider herself skilled in bed.

But with Eric, the sex had become mundane and routine. When sober, he lasted maybe five to ten minutes, and when he was drunk, he didn't give a shit about her needs, doing whatever he wanted until he either orgasmed or fell asleep on her, both of which were nothing to write home about.

It was sad. Before kids and before the drinking, they were sexually compatible, active two to three times a week. Now it was maybe once or twice a month, which just wasn't enough for her.

Sure, Alexandra could pleasure herself; she had enough toys to open a sex store at this point, and batteries were her most frequent purchase. But it wasn't the same.

She needed connection during sex—whether it was looking into someone's eyes, talking dirty, or making them moan in pleasure. Last night reminded her how much she missed and craved that connection.

Alexandra knew they would have to talk about his drinking, but her needs in the bedroom would also have to be discussed.

For now, she sat outside, finishing her tea as the clouds opened up, releasing heavy tropical rain onto the patio roof and the surrounding trees.

The intermittent crack of thunder mixed in with the rain, while the occasional bird chirped, sounding out to either say *Help!* or *This is awesome!*

Alexandra was happy, and she didn't care if she was alone because the beach was always where she felt most at home.

As she got ready for the day, she couldn't believe how excited she was to explore this beautiful tropical island.

▼▼▼

EXPLORING FERNANDO DE NORONHA

For the next few days, Alexandra enjoyed a blend of relaxing on the beach, swimming in the ocean, visiting one of the two amazing pools on the property, and exploring the island.

She hiked along trails that reminded her of those she and Eric had traversed on their honeymoon, ran along the shore, and snorkeled at various beaches along the island, continuing to be amazed by the diverse fish and coral.

On Saturday, she visited Dolphin Bay and was thrilled to see a large pod of 20 to 30 dolphins swimming and feeding in their natural habitat—her first time seeing dolphins in the wild. It was an exhilarating experience.

She had dinner alone on a restaurant by the beach, this time ordering a beautiful fish dinner for herself. While she was alone, she didn't care one bit. This was her time and she was going to do whatever she wanted to.

Sunday brought her to the Capela de São, a small, stunning white church high up on a cliff overlooking the vast Atlantic Ocean. From the cliff, the ocean seemed like it went on forever and you could really get a sense of how isolated this island was.

For Alexandra, it was a humbling realization of how small and insignificant she was in the grand scheme of things. From up on the cliff, it was hard not to think that.

As she got lost in her thoughts while sitting on a bench outside the church, she knew that she still wanted to live a good life and try to leave the world a better place than when she came into it. She still hoped to pass on positive traits to her children, imagining that one of them, or perhaps one of her grandkids would make a huge impact, like curing cancer or extending the human lifespan to 300 years or more.

In her mind, the goal of humanity should be to improve the world for future generations. It seemed so simple, yet so difficult, as egos, money, and power often took priority. She hoped Anticipation Day would be the first step in correcting past wrongs.

Leaving the bench, she stepped into the small church that could maybe accommodate six or seven people. According to the sign in front, it dated back several centuries.

Inside, the building had two small benches on either side of the building and a pulpit raised just six inches above the floor. A wooden cross hung above the pulpit, and a green statue of Jesus stood in a corner.

Alexandra sat on one of the benches, watching the ocean below, imagining what someone building this church must have known about the world.

No phones, electricity, indoor plumbing, or any sort of connection with the outside world.

The isolation and tranquility must have been surreal for the inhabitants of this island, but also lonely. She would have gone mad without much interaction with the outside world. From her research, she knew the island was about 250 miles from the mainland of Brazil, so it would have been a *long* time before you got help if something went wrong here.

It was amazing how far humanity had come since this church was built, and she could only imagine what the next few hundred years would bring.

For now, she was fully happy embracing this island's overwhelming beauty and extremely friendly people.

▼▼▼

SEPTEMBER 8, 2015

Carlos returned from the mainland, and Alexandra made a point to see him as often as possible, mainly at night. He had a busy schedule of snorkeling sessions and bartending at night at a local restaurant.

The night after he returned, he invited her to hang out with him at the restaurant. Located at the island's far end, the restaurant was part of an exquisite resort with dozens of private bungalows overlooking the ocean. It was one of the prettiest resorts Alexandra had ever seen.

The restaurant had a beautiful wooden deck surrounded by bushes and trees, and the food smelled incredibly delicious and tasted even better. She sat at the bar and talked with Carlos as much as possible, considering he was working.

Later that night, Carlos offered her to stay in one of the bungalows for the rest of her trip, as he could get her a special deal. After some thought, Alexandra accepted, appreciating the gesture and the chance for a change of scenery—especially since she wasn't paying for anything. At least not with her money.

The next morning, after playfully nudging Carlos out of bed, Alexandra packed up and checked into the Garden Suite at the hotel, which was an isolated private suite off to the side of the property, featured a fenced backyard garden with a hot tub, a swing, and lounge chairs arranged around a central firepit.

Inside, the suite was equally lovely: a king-sized bed covered with chocolates and rose petals, a marble bathroom, and a spacious living room area that could easily fit ten people. It was the most luxurious room she had ever stayed in, and she knew Carlos was the reason. Though she planned to thank him later, she first decided to take full advantage of the hotel's pools and her suite's hot tub.

When Carlos arrived after his shift, she thanked him profusely with some more of the most intense sex she had ever had. To the point where she was genuinely curious what she was doing in that chair back in Denver.

From that point on, they were inseparable. And she couldn't have been happier.

On the last day she was scheduled to be on the island, Carlos took off work so they could spend a wonderful day together. They snorkeled, relaxed on the beach, hiked through the island's beautiful mountains, and enjoyed a final delicious dinner at the hotel restaurant, where they had dined on their first night.

At night, they had sex, which, at this point, Alexandra would probably consider making love. She certainly had feelings for Carlos, even though he wasn't actually a person; he felt real to her.

Outside on one of the lounge chairs, their naked bodies glistening in the moonlight, Carlos said, "This is beautiful, sí?"

Having improved her Spanish, Alexandra replied, "Esse é o site mais lindo que eu já vi." It really was the most beautiful site she had ever seen.

Carlos chuckled and said, "Eres la chica más hermosa que he visto," meaning that Alexandra was the most beautiful girl he had ever seen.

Goddamn. Men like him did not exist in real life. Every compliment made her heart flutter, enough to make her not want this journey to end.

"Wow, you are good," Alexandra finally responded in English, laughing. "Carlos, this has been an amazing trip. When I first saw you, I felt a little jolt in my heart. I think it was your dimples. Do you know what a dimple is?" She touched the spots on his cheeks where dimples would form.

"When you smile, you have the cutest dimples. Right here and here," she said, tapping his cheeks lightly. As she did, Carlos smiled, and her finger dipped into the dimple on his cheek.

"It's funny." Alexandra laughed. "Every boy I've ever dated and married had dimples. I fucking love dimples."

▼▼▼

This was true. She immediately flashed back to the first night she met Eric. The first thing she'd noticed about him at the bar in New York City was his dimples.

She was at the same bar she went to every Friday evening in the West Village with her close friends after a long work week. It was the one with the cute bartender and excellent chicken wings. That night, her good friend Rachel brought her boyfriend, Rick, and his friend, Eric, to the bar. Eric was a CPA who had graduated from Penn State a few years ago and was working for a national accounting firm.

The initial conversation was awkward; Eric had made a sarcastic comment about her dress, which she found off-putting. But after he bought her a drink, their conversation flowed better. Four hours later, they found themselves sitting at a diner in downtown Manhattan, talking for an hour about food, movies, music, sports, work, family, friends, life, and the universe. It was the most connected she'd ever felt with someone, and she felt both safe and comfortable with him. He never gave the impression that he was interested in her just to get into her pants. She respected that, and by the time she kissed him on the cheek when leaving the diner that night, she felt a spark similar to what she'd felt with Carlos on their first night together.

She missed that version of Eric—happy, fun, funny.

▼▼▼

Carlos interrupted her trip down memory lane. "Well, now I know what dimples are." He chuckled.

"Lauren, I have met many beautiful women here on this island. I have been asked to go out to dinner by maybe, five or six of them. But you are the first one I said yes to. Something in my heart told me to say yes to you.

"Eu queria que você ficasse aqui comigo. Você vai ficar?" He quietly said in Portuguese asking Alexandra to stay with him.

Could she stay with him? Would she abandon the rest of her trip and stay here on this beautiful island with this beautiful man? Certainly, she would have a blast staying the rest of the time here with him.

Hell, Debra said she could stay the entire time here if she wanted to. It certainly *was* tempting.

Alexandra remembered what MaryAnne said the prior night about not getting too attached to anyone. She was right. Alexandra could easily find herself getting way too attached to Carlos and then being affected in real life. That was something she could not afford as her focus needed to be on her kids, her job and, in theory, her husband.

She could always pick this journey with Carlos back up next year. God only knew where her life would be at that point. For all she knew, she could be a recent divorcee, in which case she could spend a year with Carlos and be just fine.

Alexandra decided to let Carlos down gently. Doing it in Portuguese seemed to be the best way.

"Sei que tenho que partir amanhã, mas queria que soubesse que tornou esta experiência extraordinária. Este lugar era lindo, mas passar um tempo com você o tornou realmente de tirar o fôlego.

Você não tem ideia do quanto vou sentir sua falta. E você não vai entender por que não posso ficar. Mas não posso.

Vou pensar em você todos os dias quando estiver longe de você. E sei em meu coração que nos veremos novamente.

Mas tenho que partir amanhã para continuar minha jornada. Vamos aproveitar ao máximo o tempo que nos resta juntos.

I *do* love you Carlos." She said and kissed him firmly on the lips.

"I believe it was fate that we met, and I believe we'll meet again should fate decide. Te amo." Alexandra wanted to laugh at how cheesy that line was, but she held it in. It was still pretty damn romantic.

Hours later, after one final love making session that knocked Carlos out, she watched him sleep, wondering how she could possibly go back to the real world after having this experience.

Alexandra had no idea what the rest of the experience would bring, but for now, she was so happy with how the past couple of weeks had gone. She knew she would not forget Carlos, and his penis, for a long time.

Most importantly, she felt confident again. She felt beautiful again. She felt like she would now control her destiny. And *that* was something Alexandra was bringing back to the real world.

For now though, she was ready to move on to see the next stop on her journey: Lençóis Maranhenses.

Feeling grateful for this piece of her journey, she kissed Carlos on his forehead and whispered, "I love you, and I will see you again."

"Vivian, advance to 5 p.m. tomorrow, please."

▼ ▼ ▼

SEPTEMBER 21, 2015

Thunder rumbled, followed by the gentle patter of rain against a window.

Slowly, the sight of a yellow floral pillowcase came into focus, which made Alexandra realize she had advanced to whatever hotel she was staying in near Parque Nacional dos Lençóis Maranhenses.

She closed her eyes, aware that Carlos wasn't beside her, and took a few deep breaths of the simulated air. When she opened her eyes again, the pillowcase made her laugh as she imagined how much Eric would hate it.

As she chuckled, she realized it was the first time during her simulation that she missed Eric. As much as he pissed her off at times, the reality was she still loved him. She only slept well with him and never slept well when he was away for work. He always warmed her up at night when she was cold. He took care of her when she was sick. He calmed her down when she had a bad day. There were other things he did that reminded her of why she fell in love with him in the first place.

Alexandra just wanted peace and happiness in her life. She didn't regret her time with Carlos; sure Eric might be hurt by it but he would hopefully focus on the reasons why she did it, rather than the action itself.

Either way, Alexandra hoped Eric was getting the same experience out of his as she was out of hers; well maybe not *everything* she was experiencing. Knowing his dumb ass, he was probably challenging some heavyweight boxer at the height of their prime to prove that he was a man. If that were the case, she hoped the boxer would knock some sense into him.

After lying in bed for a few minutes, she got up and walked outside to a covered area attached to her hotel room. The rain had eased a bit, and the sun began to shine through, making the surrounding area near her room glisten with dew and mist. She inhaled deeply, taking in an array of unfamiliar tropical floral scents.

Alexandra wasn't an expert in fragrances, but she detected hints of vanilla and hibiscus, combined with a few other things she couldn't quite identify.

Alexandra laughed, remembering the time she bought a pricey bottle of perfume in Chicago during a trip with her sister a few years earlier.

Eric had taken the kids for the weekend, allowing her to meet her sister in Chicago for a relaxing weekend they had been planning for a while. They had eaten deep-dish pizza, taken a riverboat tour, and explored Millennium Park. It was a fun getaway.

Yet, the highlight of that trip was the hot salesman who flirted his way into a $750 sale at a store on The Magnificent Mile. He was irresistible—deep blue eyes, tanned skin, sculpted cheekbones, perfect blond hair, and an intoxicating scent.

Alexandra regretted the purchase, not because of the cost or the possibility of Eric finding out, but because she had caved into the attention of a young, attractive salesman.

Despite her regret, she loved how she felt wearing the perfume. It was a blend of oud, jasmine, saffron, and other elusive notes that made her feel sexy whenever she wore it. It was hard not to notice the way the dads at her daycare stared at her when she had it on. She *liked* when they stared.

However, as beautiful as that fragrance was, this fragrance she was experiencing in the simulation was five times more powerful and beautiful than that perfume.

Her euphoria was interrupted by the phone in her room ringing. As she picked it up, a voice on the other end greeted her with, "Buenos días, Señorita Lauren. This is Iara from the front desk. A reminder that the tour of the National Park departs in 45 minutes. The rain is clearing, so it should be a nice day."

"Sí, muchas gracias. Estarei aí em 15 minutos. Gracias." Alexandra hung up, excited about what she was about to see. She had extensively researched this park at the northern tip of Brazil. It had towering sand dunes spread over 600 square miles, with dazzling blue lagoons lying between them like desert oases.

She showered quickly and headed downstairs to grab some fresh pastries from the beautiful breakfast buffet. These breakfasts would set an impossibly high standard for all her future meals. She was going to make a point of trying to bake more pastries and bread with her kids, if only to fill the house with the smell of fresh bread in the morning.

After finishing her meal, she went to the main building to meet the tour group. This time, the sign with "Lauren Murphy" was held by a beautiful girl with dark hair and blue eyes.

"Buenos días, soy Lauren," Alexandra said without missing a beat.

"Buenos días," the girl replied, smiling. "Soy Francisca. ¿Prefieres inglés o español?"

"Inglés, por favor. I know enough Portuguese, but English will be easier."

"No worries, Lauren," Francisca said with a laugh. "I need to practice my English to go to America for school, so this is perfect."

"That's wonderful—good for you. What do you want to go to school for?" Alexandra asked, genuinely interested.

"I want to be a scientist—study the oceans and help protect them. I have always loved the ocean and want to make sure they are protected."

Although Francisca was just a simulated character, Alexandra felt a pang of sympathy for her. The oceans of 2032 were on the brink of a total collapse, with plummeting fish populations, vanishing coral reefs, and rampant algae blooms. Governments were scrambling to develop alternative solutions, from funding the expansion of lab-grown fish to relocating millions of people to urban centers from ocean communities that depended on the ocean for their livelihoods.

It was one of the greatest challenges of the 21st century for humanity, with no easy solution. This was one of the reasons Alexandra wanted to go back in time—to witness these rare and natural environments before they were ruined by the touch of humans.

Still, all she could say to the hopeful Francisca was, "Good for you. I wish you the best of luck and hope you succeed. Which school will you attend?"

"The University of Miami. They government of Brazil will allow me to study there. I am very happy to go." Francisca said, beaming with pride.

"How exciting! So, are we waiting for anyone else?" Alexandra asked, wanting to get this going.

"No, señora, it's just us today. We had another person scheduled, but they canceled."

"Got it. Well, I'm ready to go," Alexandra replied, trying not to sound impatient.

"Very good, señora. There's a Jeep outside for us to use. Please follow me." Francisca pointed to the door, and they headed out.

The drive from the hotel to the park entrance was beautiful. The earlier rain had passed on, and rays of sunlight danced on the ocean's surface off to the right as they rode through some wooded areas.

After about 20 minutes, they arrived at the entrance parking lot. They got out of the Jeep and packed water bottles, snacks, an emergency kit, rain gear, clothes, a small shovel, two hiking sticks, two flare guns, a knife, and a whistle (Alexandra wasn't asking why). All of this, plus some other gear, went into two backpacks that they would both carry.

Alexandra raised an eyebrow. "Okay, why the shovel? Is it for… you know?" She pointed to her butt discreetly.

Francisca laughed. "No, it's for digging a ditch to crouch in case of a thunderstorm. It helps avoid lightning strikes."

"Interesting. Well, let's hope we don't need that," Alexandra said, strapping on her backpack.

She was a little worried about getting struck by lightning but reminded herself it was all just a simulation. While she hoped nothing bad would happen, it didn't really matter. Still, she could picture herself being the first actual death while in the simulation due to a lightning strike.

Other than avoiding death, the plan for the three-day hike was to travel about 20 kilometers to Queimada dos Britos, a remote village in the middle of the park with a few small buildings to stay in, a snack bar, and a rustic inn that sounded more like a hut than anything.

Francisca explained it usually took around six to seven hours to reach the village, as most people stopped to swim in the various lagoons. After spending the night there, they would continue about another 25 kilometers to the town of Travosa at the northern tip of the national park. The next day, they would make their way to Campo Novo, where someone from the tour group would meet them and take them to the village of Santo Amaro do Maranhão for a proper meal, followed by a jeep ride back to the hotel across the dunes and lagoons.

Alexandra was excited about this part, as it was said to be an amazing experience.

As they left the parking lot and began the trek into the park, the dunes very quickly came into view. Some appeared to be 40 or 50 feet tall, and they were *everywhere*. In the distance to the right, she could hear the ocean crashing against the shoreline.

As they walked, Francisca explained that the wind constantly moved the dunes, preventing the sand from heating up, so it stayed relatively cool. This allowed people to walk on it barefoot. She also mentioned that the best time to visit was July and August when there was no rain and the lagoons were full, as it typically rained from December through June.

From what Alexandra could understand, the dunes were formed as sediment from two rivers was carried towards the ocean and deposited.

The dunes were simply stunning. Bright white, and extending as far as the eye could see, it felt like they were on another planet. They soon came across their first lagoon, which was small but beautiful, calm, and serene. It was the bluest and clearest water she had ever seen—like something out of a movie.

They continued west towards the village, encountering lagoons every half mile or so. Alexandra was amazed that every single lagoon they saw was slightly different in size and shape, yet each was equally inviting.

After about two hours of hiking, Francisca suggested they take a dip to refresh and relax for a bit. The sun was getting high in the sky, making it a much-needed respite from the heat.

Alexandra headed to the nearest lagoon, sitting on the sand for a few minutes and soaking in the view. She thought, "*I wish the kids were here to see this.*"

She missed her kids. Though to them, she had only been gone a few hours, at this point it felt like she had been without them for weeks. She had never been away from all three of them for more than a few days so it was getting challenging to be without them.

Her kids were her life. Corey was just like Eric—feisty and competitive but with a deep, warm heart. He was also very handsome. She always had a soft spot for her firstborn.

Noah was her twin in every way, a goofball who could make her laugh whenever he wanted.

Sophia was her little princess. Once a daddy's girl, Eric's attitude had recently drawn her closer to Alexandra. She spoiled Sophia with dresses, toys, and their special Sunday morning breakfasts, where it was just mommy and daughter.

She missed Sophia the most; they had never been apart for more than a few nights and it was getting harder and harder to be without her.

As she stared into the blue lagoon, surrounded by beautiful white sand, she closed her eyes and listened to the sound of nothingness. What a magical and soul-cleansing place to visit.

At that moment, sitting in this place, feeling as relaxed as she was, she came to the decision that she would skip ahead in her trip in order to get home quicker. Alexandra still wanted to see Iguazu Falls, as she heard it was breathtaking.

She had also been *dying* to go to Rio de Janeiro, so she would likely experience the full time there, but she would cut short her time here in Lençóis Maranhenses and skip the Amazon rainforest altogether, as it excited her the least.

It felt like a good compromise; she could always revisit this experience next year if she wanted to. Initially, she thought two months away from her kids was doable, but now, sitting here amongst this beautiful scenery, imagining how much her kids would absolutely love this place, she realized there was no way she would be able to last the full time.

With her revised plan set, she removed a few layers of clothing and waded into the water. As she dipped her toes, legs, and then her whole body into the water, she could only think one thing: "*It's perfect.*"

It was like the freshest and warmest bath water she had ever been in. She floated with her eyes closed for a few moments, letting the water embrace her.

For the next half hour, Alexandra and Francisca swam and chatted. They talked about Lauren's life back in the United States, her recent divorce, and Francisca's career aspirations. It was a pleasant conversation between two simulated characters.

Although Alexandra could have stayed there for another two hours, Francisca insisted they continue their hike in order to reach the town by sunset. So, they dried off and trekked toward the village of

Queimada dos Britos, arriving about four simulated hours later after a rather uneventful hike.

They approached the village as a stunning sunset unfolded around them, casting a magical blend of oranges, blues, and yellows over the lagoons and sand. Alexandra wished she could capture the beauty of the moment and show it to Eric and the kids.

The village was quite simple, as one would expect in the middle of nowhere with a few hundred people scattered throughout. Francisca explained that there were somewhere between 50 and 70 regulars and the remaining people were likely tourists and visitors from outside of the park.

There were several huts and small buildings surrounded by sand and water. Francisca explained that the village was named after Manoel Brito, who had wandered onto the dunes during a drought in his home state of Ceará. His descendants continued to live and intermarry in the village, raising cattle and goats and fishing in the ocean. In the winter, they bred fish, mainly Bicudo, in the lagoons filled by the rainwater. The locals were all descendants and relatives of Mr. Brito.

Francisco and Alexandra were dog-tired from the hike and spent the evening quietly talking with a few locals. Francisca translated, as the locals spoke a dialect of Portuguese unfamiliar to Alexandra.

Alexandra learned about their daily routines: Mornings were spent fishing, feeding livestock, and tending to other chores. The adults socialized in the afternoon while the children wandered around the village, generally alone to explore. In the evening, people relaxed and ate their meals around Kerosene lamps before retiring for the night.

It was an eye-opening conversation for Alexandra. These people just knew how to live. They had no sense of what a mortgage was or what it was like to wait two hours for a refrigerator repairman to arrive, and they had likely never seen a phone or computer. Yet they seemed so happy and connected with the earth and the natural resources around them. It was refreshing to see.

After everyone said goodnight, Alexandra walked outside, settled on a tree log, and looked up at the dark, star-filled sky. She had never seen so many stars; it was like the entire universe was at her fingertips. While she never considered herself religious, seeing this sky was something she could only consider to be divine.

"Was this how this place looked back then?" She thought. While she would never truly know, the sight she was seeing was absolutely breathtaking. After spotting her fifth shooting star, she asked Vivian to advance to the next day.

▼▼▼

SEPTEMBER 22, 2015

After saying goodbye to the locals and having a breakfast of some provisions that Francisca had brought with them, Alexandra and Francisca made their way northwest toward the town of Travosa, roughly 27 kilometers away. Most of the walk there was across similar dunes and lagoons as the day before, some more inviting than others.

In the heat of the day, they stopped for another swim in one of the lagoons and had lunch. Luckily, the weather cooperated, and no life-threatening storms came through, for which Alexandra silently thanked the simulators.

They arrived in Travosa by evening. The village was tiny, and there were only a couple of places to get something to eat, which consisted of establishments that served fish, fish, and more fish.

With how much she was starving, it didn't matter what type of fish it was; she was eating it. Apparently, walking 17 miles in the Brazilian heat would do that to a person. Once again, the food was simple, fresh, and delicious.

That night, her and Francisca sat in one of the small huts they were staying in and spoke about their lives.

"Do you want to have kids one day?" Francisca asked her as they sat by the fire, drinking a local drink called Guaraná Jesus, which was a delicious pink soft drink that was unlike anything Alexandra had ever had before.

"Interesting question." Alexandra responded, trying to figure out how to answer it. "Well, my sister has kids and I think they are wonderful. It's awesome to watch them learn and grow up but they can also be exhausting."

Francisca nodded and laughed. "Yes, yes. My brother has two young children and they are fun to play with but I am happy to give them back to him at the end of the day. I am so tired after playing with them!"

"Well, that is what makes them beautiful I guess. To have some of my own would be fun so maybe one day." Alexandra responded slowly, thinking about her kids again.

"Would you want boys or girls?" Francisca asked her.

"I would want one boy and one girl I think." Alexandra responded, chuckling. "I have always wanted one of each. Anything more than two might be a little crazy, right?"

"Yes, yes. I agree!" Francisca exclaimed. "My parents had eight children and I do not know how they did that. I am the youngest and growing up, our house was, how do you say…crazy? Noise everywhere. But it was also fun. My parents loved noise and loved having family around. It was beautiful. Loud, but beautiful". Francisca laughed as she looked down at the fire. "I miss my parents—they both died a few years ago."

"Oh, I am so sorry." Alexandra replied, putting a hand on Francisca's shoulder.

"It is okay, obrigado. They had a wonderful life and we loved each other very much. I want to have a big, happy family just like them." Francisca said, tearing up now.

"Well, I hope you do. Anyone would be lucky to have a big happy family with you." Alexandra replied, smiling at Francisca.

"Thank you Lauren. I hope you find some happiness in your life too." Francisca noted as she took a last gulp of her drink. "Well, I am tired and we have another long hike tomorrow, so I am going to sleep now. Boa noite."

"Boa Noite." Alexandra responded as Francisca left the hut.

"I hope I find some happiness in my life too", Alexandra thought. While she always complained about how messy the house was and how loud the kids were, she always knew she would miss those days when they were older and moved out of the house. Hearing Francisca say those things about how much her parents loved having all their kids around really made Alexandra appreciate her kids and the energy they brought to the house. She knew she would miss them when they were older and out of the house.

She promised herself she would appreciate them more from now on as she laid down in her hut, stared at the ceiling and asked Vivian to advance to the next day.

SEPTEMBER 23, 2015

The next morning, they started what would be a beautiful but tough hike through the forest and wetlands of the western part of the park. The area was lush with thick vegetation and teeming with wildlife— monkeys, lots of colorful birds, and enough spiders to last Alexandra a lifetime.

Alexandra *hated* spiders. She wasn't sure if she had full-blown arachnophobia, but these spiders were far from the normal ones back in Denver—they were the size of small pizzas and looked like they were the creation of some evil and dark being.

She caught herself repeatedly screaming, *"Oh fuck, that is disgusting,"* *"What the fuck is that on me?"* and *"Holy shit, that's the biggest thing I've ever seen!"*

Though she considered herself a nature lover, the wildlife on this leg of the trip was a little too much for her. She was unprepared for spiders as big as her head or snakes that can kill with a single bite.

Still, it was a beautiful hike through the remaining parts of the park. Fortunately, Francisca was knowledgeable about what to do when they did encounter wildlife (usually the answer was just *'Keep walking'*).

They got through the hike and arrived at Campo Novo later in the day, just as Alexandra realized skipping the Amazon part of her experience was the right move. While she had wanted to see the natural wildlife that existed decades earlier, the thought of being surrounded by bugs and other creepy crawlies was enough to make her shit her pants. It would also be sweltering and humid in the Amazon, along with the risk of getting sick from bad water or weather. As such, she didn't think it would be as good an experience as she had initially anticipated it to be. Maybe next year.

Sure enough, one of Francisca's colleagues was waiting for them at Campo Novo and drove them to a cute town called Santo Amoro do Maranhão, where they ate some delicious local barbecue, explored a few local shops, and then returned to the hotel a few hours later.

On the jeep ride back, Alexandra felt she had achieved what she wanted from this simulation—rediscovering herself and finding what made her happy. No more wasting time on people who didn't love her or want to make her happy. Life was too short for that. She went into this simulation looking for something to refresh her and give her a break from her life, and she felt she had gotten that.

While time would tell if Eric achieved the same result, she was ready to return to her real life to figure out what her real future would bring.

Alexandra genuinely enjoyed Francisca's company. She reminded her of a younger version of herself—fun, full of life, funny, and easy to talk to. Though she wished she could keep Fransisca in real life, she knew this journey was ending. When they parted, Alexandra wished her well, hugged her and retreated to her room, where she collapsed on the bed, exhausted.

▼▼▼

OCTOBER 10, 2015

Alexandra skipped to her first day at Iguazu Falls, which was in southern Brazil on the border with Paraguay and Argentina. The waterfalls there were said to be some of the most amazing in the world and Alexandra was excited to see them.

While there were rainforests surrounding the falls that she had initially planned on exploring, she had already experienced the rainforests of Lençóis Maranhenses. As such, she decided to advance the simulation to just before her arrival at the falls, giving herself a moment to take in the surroundings before getting to the area where she'd get her first glimpse of the massive waterfall structure.

The first thing she saw was a big old boat speeding down the middle of a mostly brown river. She turned around to see about 25 to 30 people on board, with the driver standing behind her on a raised platform.

The riverbanks were lined with trees above rocky beaches. A warm, moist breeze tousled her hair, occasionally mixed with spritzes of water from the boat's spray. The motor hummed softly as she overheard people's conversations around her.

From her vantage point, she spotted a fork in the river ahead, with one path going straight and another curving right. As they rode closer to the bend, a distant roar slowly grew louder and louder—like a freight train and a heavy rainstorm combined.

Excitement bubbled within her to finally see what this place was all about.

The boat sped along for a few more minutes before they reached the bend, where the driver veered right. That's when she saw it in the distance: her first waterfall.

It wasn't that large, but it felt like a precursor to what was coming.

Sure enough, as they approached the smaller waterfall, a much larger and expansive one appeared on the left, with multiple cascades spilling from the cliffs above. It had to span 800 or 900 feet across, and it was *spectacular*.

As they drew closer, the roar became louder, and the mist of the falls spread wider. Multiple rainbows arched through the waterfalls as the sun's rays mixed with the mist of the waterfalls to produce beautiful and vibrant rainbows.

Or, in this case, mistbows.

It was loud, but Alexandra didn't care. The sheer power and energy of the waterfalls were overwhelming, as if the earth itself shook from the weight of the water crashing down into it.

After a few minutes of hanging out, the boat turned back towards the bend, where it made a right turn, revealing a longer stretch of the river with additional waterfalls crashing from cliffs hundreds of feet above. The amount of water coming down off the cliffs was staggering, creating a mist that extended across the 200-yard-wide river.

The boat sped towards a larger waterfall on the right—massive, like the previous ones, but much closer this time. The driver steered the boat close enough for Alexandra's side to get soaked.

The passengers screamed with joy as the boat drove through the water. It was warm, and it felt quite nice on her simulated body. She hesitated but decided the water was probably no worse than tap water at home, so she let a little flow into her mouth. It tasted clean and pure, which was a pleasant surprise.

The driver continued down the river, navigating past waterfall after waterfall, with some cascading above others.

Eventually, they approached the largest waterfall she had ever seen in front of them. It formed a large semicircle spanning at least a mile across the top. It was also pretty tall—maybe 200 to 300 feet from the riverbed. Given the pure volume of water coming down, it was hard to tell, but the size was undeniable. Plus, it was loud.

Hearing someone speak was impossible over the roar, not that Alexandra wanted to talk. She just wanted to take it all in, as it was simply stunning. Similar to Lençóis Maranhenses, she wished she could take a picture or video of this to share with her kids and Eric later.

Unfortunately, she'd have to rely on her memory until she could visit this place for real. She hoped it would be the same in the 2030s as it was in the simulation.

For the 15 minutes the boat lingered near the waterfall, Alexandra absorbed the energy of the place. She couldn't describe it, but she felt connected to the earth in a way she had never felt.

Though she had never considered herself an environmentalist by any stretch, this place inspired her to become more active in environmental causes. The raw power, energy, and beauty of Mother Nature moved something in her.

There were plenty of local environmental causes she could get involved in where she could try to make a difference. She promised herself that, upon returning to reality, she would get more involved in environmental initiatives.

As the boat slowly turned and headed back upriver, it docked near a small beach to the right, adjacent to the road. A small bus picked them up, bringing them to a lookout point about half a mile away.

At the lookout, Alexandra wandered around, taking in the magnificent view. From this vantage point, she could see the waterfalls stretching across both the Brazilian and Argentinian borders, seeming endless.

For the next hour, she followed the guide along various paths leading to various viewpoints of the waterfalls. Each path offered a new way to appreciate how large and expansive this area was.

The final path led her to the highest point on the Brazilian side of the falls, where she could see the entire system of waterfalls.

"*This was so worth it,*" she thought, staring into the distance.

It was a perfect way to end this part of her trip—however, she had her fill of nature and was ready for some nice restaurants, amazing beaches, museums, and everything else Rio had to offer. She was also eager to finally meet her friends, so she asked Vivian to skip ahead to Rio de Janeiro.

▼▼▼

RIO DE JANEIRO - OCTOBER 2015

Alexandra used to roll her eyes when people said their vacations felt like a *blur*, always retorting, "Well, why didn't you take time to relax and enjoy?"

She never understood why people needed to run around seeing everything they could see while not taking the time to unwind. But after ten days in Rio de Janeiro with her friends Stacy and Harmeet, she found herself thinking the same thing—it had all been a blur.

They had a blast visiting all the iconic spots: the Christ the Redeemer statue and Sugarloaf Mountain, Tijuca National Park, the lush botanical gardens, and Escadaria Selarón with its 250-step staircase. They also explored the local aquarium and were amazed at the wall art featured along Boulevard Olimpico.

They saw dozens of other local gems, like Mauá Square, where they watched a stunning sunset; the Carioca Aqueduct, showcasing the arch design from the 18th century; and Morro da Urca, which offered beautiful views of the city.

And then there were the beaches. They were extraordinary. From Grumari Beach, nestled against mountain views, to Macumba Beach, near the Pontal Stone Nature Preserve, which was a beautiful day trip itself.

Her favorite was Arpoador Beach, at the eastern end of the strip. From the rocks accessible from the beach, Alexandra and countless other simulated people could take in a panoramic view of the city. She was able to sit above the ocean and admire the landscape, with cloud-covered mountains off in the distance.

She visited this beach twice, once with Stacy and Harmeet and once alone. On her solo visit, she sat on the rocks for hours, gazing into the distance, listening to the ocean, and pondering what her life would be like after this simulation.

The experience was exactly what she needed: not a ton of excitement, drama, or partying. Just peace, calm, and lots of fun. It was perfect.

Speaking of fun, Stacy and Harmeet were just a hoot. They shopped in the most amazing stores, enjoyed each other's company at dinner, and even placed bets on who would be the first to cave in and sleep with a Brazilian man. Alexandra, like Lauren, kept quiet about her fling with Carlos, not wanting to be judged—even by simulated people. That secret would stay with her until she decided to tell Eric.

As Lauren, Alexandra knew everything about her friends, making it feel like three friends just hanging out in Rio for a week and a half. It was enjoyable, and she couldn't have asked for a better way to end the trip.

The food in Rio was, of course, delicious. Alexandra ate Feijoada, which consisted of stewed beans in pork gravy, potatoes, and some other things she couldn't identify. She also tried several different types of barbecued meats, local cheese snacks, and her favorite dessert of all time, a Brigadeiro, which was a small hot chocolate cake.

She felt like she had some quality *girl time*, even though she would likely never see these "girls" again.

Alexandra realized that she needed more girl time back in the real world. Though she often saw MaryAnne and Clarise, there were other friends she didn't connect with as frequently. She wanted to make more of an effort to see them and have time without Eric. It was healthy and necessary, at least on her end.

On her last night in Rio, Alexandra was more-than-ready to go home. She ventured to Urca, a quaint neighborhood on the city's far edge, for a quiet dinner alone with some wine followed by a stroll by the beach.

She used this time to mentally prepare for her return to reality and the conversations that were waiting for her.

Alexandra was ready for those conversations to happen and whatever result would come from them. She had to come to terms with what needed to happen.

Walking along the shoreline, enjoying a small pack of truffle-flavored Brigadeiros, she found a spot on the sea wall to watch the sunset to the west, over the bay, with the Christ the Redeemer statue silhouetted against the evening sky.

Several boats sat in the bay filled with people dancing and partying, enjoying the sunset just as she was.

It was the perfect end to a perfect trip. She took another Brigadeiros and shoved the whole thing in her mouth. Who gave a fuck at this point? It was delicious.

Alexandra was going to miss Brazil and all that it had given her in this brief experience. She would miss Stacy and Harmeet. And Carlos.

But she knew she would return one day, either in real life with her family or in a future simulation.

Right now, she felt ready to face whatever life brought on next. Most importantly, she knew she would be okay.

As Alexandra asked Vivian to end her simulation, she knew it was time to go home.

PART 3

CHAPTER 1

GETTING READY, AGAIN

AUGUST 14, 2032
8:30 A.M.

Though it had only been eight days since she heard the news, Alexandra didn't feel prepared for today. She opened the door to her closet and surveyed her options.

Some outfits were now too big due to her recent weight loss, while others seemed inappropriate for the occasion.

As she scanned her choices, a dress she had bought on a whim about 15 years ago caught her eye. It seemed as close to acceptable as anything else, so she grabbed the hanger and headed to the bathroom to try it on.

Eric was downstairs with the kids, allowing her to take her time to examine her reflection in the bathroom mirror. The past few months had been kind to her. After her simulation experience, she had decided to get back into running the way she did in college and dedicated herself to a diet plan that appeared to be working. At 41, she would never resemble her college self, but she felt she was in better shape than the average 41-year-old mother of three.

Slipping into the dress, she couldn't help but feel grateful for the positive changes in her life since Eric and her simulations.

She was happier with herself and her life. She was more at peace with her job and enjoyed being around the kids more. Eric had cut down on his drinking substantially, with only the occasional glass of wine on the weekend. He seemed happier, taking the kids camping one weekend in Rocky Mountain National Park.

All-in-all, she was seeing positives from their experiences. Her and Eric still weren't really having sex though; maybe in time.

About a month earlier, she had met with MaryAnne to discuss their individual experiences. Alexandra was candid about her journey, including the time with Carlos. As understanding and non-judgmental as MaryAnne was, she didn't blame Alexandra given her lack of a sex life, but she also advised her to ensure it didn't translate into anything more in real life. Although Alexandra felt a twinge of guilt over her romantic ventures, she knew she had used what she had learned about herself to improve her mental and physical health in real life.

MaryAnne had shared her own experience reliving the day with her dad and how seeing her dad like that was such an amazing time. She was impressed by the simulation's ability to reconstruct the day based on her memories, even if it may not have been fully accurate.

For Alexandra, it was nice to see MaryAnne happy again; she seemed more at peace with where she was in life.

Her and Eric had agreed that couples therapy with an independent therapist would be the best way to share their experiences with each other. Their first session was next Thursday, which she was looking forward to.

Their required quarterly mental health checkup went by smoothly, but these sessions focused more on whether a participant was thinking of harming themselves or others. She did discuss her marriage in those sessions but framed any issues her and Eric were having as typical marital strife—something everyone could relate to.

Sure, there were days when she felt like punching, kicking, or mutilating Eric's balls, but she knew that was as far as she would go.

Since Anticipation Day, Eric and Alexandra had seen little of their other friends. Clarise and David, who had done their experience around the time Alexandra met up with MaryAnne a month earlier, were still too emotional to meet up. Today would be her first time seeing them since their experiences.

They had seen Mike and his girlfriend a couple of times, once at their house for Memorial Day and then a month ago at the hospital after Mike's daughter was born. Eric had met Mike a few times, including a couple of weekends earlier, but, according to Eric, Mike didn't mention too much about his experience, other than they held for him for a couple of weeks afterwards because he woke up pissed off.

Mike had seemed fine when Alexandra saw him in the hospital.

Patrick, on the other hand, had been spending more time with his kids since Anticipation Day, which seemed to have made him happier. However, they had not really seen him either.

So, today would be a reunion, of sorts.

"Alexandra!" Eric's voice downstairs interrupted her thoughts.

"What's up?" She called back from her bedroom.

"What time do we need to leave?" He replied, his voice lower this time.

"Can we aim to get out of here in 30? The babysitter is coming in 15 minutes, and I want to show her around before we go."

"Okay," he said, as she heard him slowly walk away from the bottom of the stairs.

After putting on her dress, she focused on her makeup, applying a touch of mascara, rouge, and lip gloss—nothing too over-the-top.

"Let's get through today," she told herself out loud as she put the finishing touches on her concealer—enough to hide the bags under her eyes from the lack of sleep the night before.

She took a deep breath. "You got this, Alexandra. Everything will be okay today."

She headed downstairs and saw Eric with Noah and Corey. Sophia was at her painting desk, creating some sort of concoction she'd want to hang in her bedroom.

"Where are you going, Mama?" Sophia asked quietly as she painted a green dinosaur—her favorite.

"Daddy and I have to see our friends for a bit, so you'll stay with Anya and the babysitter for a few hours."

"Okay, Mama. I hope you have fun. Can we get pizza for dinner?" She looked up with an expression that said: *Pretty please.*

"Sure, honey. We can order pizza and some soup for dinner, but only if you behave for Anya."

"She always behaves, Ms. Alexandra," Anya said from the other room.

"I know she does, Anya, and that's why we love her so much," she said, smiling at Sophia and hugging her.

The doorbell rang, and Alexandra went to get the babysitter.

"Alright, kiddos, we gotta get going soon," Eric said. "Please be good for Anya and the babysitter. We'll be back in a few hours." He looked at Corey and Noah. "Remember, we're going hiking tomorrow near Boulder, okay?"

"Okay, Dad," they said in harmony, though Eric wasn't sure they heard a word as they were both immersed in some game on their virtual glasses.

Alexandra returned with the babysitter, Christy, and explained the house rules and what the kids could and couldn't do. Normally, they would leave the kids alone with Anya, but since they would be gone for at least four hours and would be an hour away, they felt more comfortable with another human being in the house.

Ten minutes later, Alexandra finished giving Christy the house tour, grabbed her virtual glasses, and went to grab a jacket.

"Ready?" She asked Eric in the kitchen.

"As I'll ever be, I guess," Eric responded.

Hugs and kisses were exchanged, and they were on their way.

CHAPTER 2

THE CALL

AUGUST 6, 2032
7:40 A.M.

Eric had hated flying since his parents took him and his brother on a trip from New York to Paris when he was around eight. During the flight, they experienced horrific turbulence that caused the plane to nosedive for what felt like an eternity, though, in reality, it was probably only about ten seconds. The experience rattled him and his fear of flying stayed with him through adulthood.

Though Eric loved taking his family on vacations, he usually stuck to destinations within reasonable driving distance. When he did have to fly for family trips or business, he relied on strong prescription medicine to calm him down. He still dreaded flying, despite knowing the risk of anything bad happening was extremely low.

This morning, he was on a flight to Dallas for a lunch meeting with a long-time client who was looking to sell a major retail business in the Dallas/Ft. Worth area. The client had asked Eric to join him for a meeting with his lawyers and investment bankers. About 40 minutes into the flight, as Eric tried to doze off, he received an in-flight call from a number he thought he recognized but couldn't immediately place. He decided to answer.

"Hello?" Eric said, trying to shake the cobwebs off.

"Hi, Eric. This is Stacy Chambers. Can you speak?" It was Mike's on-again, off-again girlfriend and the mother of their baby girl, Isla Megan. Something in her voice sent a chill down Eric's spine.

Given he had only met her twice, he wasn't sure why she would be calling him early on a Thursday morning.

"Uh, yeah, hi Stacy. How are you? I'm on a flight to Dallas and was dozing off. Everything okay?"

She whispered, "Mike died last night. The police think it was an accidental overdose, but I'm not sure. He had started drinking again, and I don't know what he could have mixed it with, but… he's *gone.*"

The phone went quiet, and Eric heard Stacy sniffling but Eric was in shock and couldn't form any words. After a moment, she continued "I wanted to let you know as I know you two were good friends. He also left an envelope with your name on it. I haven't opened it yet; I assume he wanted you to read it."

Eric was listening and comprehending what Stacy was saying, but he still couldn't speak.

She tried to catch her breath. "Can you stop by to pick it up and make a statement to the police? They want your statement since I know you met up with him last weekend. I'm sorry to tell you this way, but I didn't know what else to do."

A thousand thoughts raced through Eric's mind, and Stacy's voice faded into the background.

▼▼▼

Accidental overdose? Drinking? When did he start again? Eric just saw him last weekend at a coffee shop, and he seemed fine. A little out of it, but Mike said he was tired from not sleeping, so Eric hadn't thought anything of it. He had just become a dad, for Christ's sake!

Did this have something to do with his Anticipation Day experience? Mike had complained to Eric about the simulation, saying they gave him a character with a bunch of injuries but he hadn't shared much about the experience, saying he would get into it at a later point.

Eric knew Mike was held for a couple of weeks after his experience, but they had released him and Mike swore he was fine and was just pissed they didn't give him a healthy body. He had passed his recent monthly mental health checkup. Wouldn't they have noticed any issues?

Was it something Eric said last weekend? They talked about many things, including Mike's lack of sleep because of Isla, but other than that, he seemed okay. There was no sign he was suicidal.

Why did Mike leave him a note? What did it say?

Should he tell Alexandra? What about the others?

How the fuck could he be gone???

▼▼▼

He snapped back to reality, hearing Stacy crying on the phone. Finally, he spoke. "Oh my god, Stacy, I am so sorry. I'm speechless." Eric was numb, his throat dry, and his eyes filled with tears. He struggled to remain composed and calm, unsure of what to say.

Eric had lost his father, Sergeant Floyd, and now Mike. He instantly saw flashbacks of memories with Mike racing through his mind.

▼▼▼

The time in ninth grade they missed the bus back from Elitch Gardens amusement park and kept riding the rides until the park closed, and their parents had to pick them up.

Sneaking into a Tool concert at 16, getting wasted with college girls in their van and making out with them until their parents picked them up.

Going to Florida to visit Eric's family, where Mike hooked up with Eric's cousin, resulting in Eric punching Mike in the face.

The night Mike tore his ACL and Eric rode with him to the hospital, reassuring him everything would be okay.

Their first college party at the University of Denver the summer they turned 18, when they both hooked up with sorority sisters.

Checking Mike into a rehab facility after Mike begged Eric to take him there.

Mike holding Isla in his arms and kissing her forehead just a few weeks earlier.

▼ ▼ ▼

Stacy's voice pulled him back again. "The police found empty liquor bottles, empty bottles of sleeping pills, and painkillers. They're sure it was an accident, but he left me a note… under my pillow. It said, '*For Eric. Do not show the police.*'" Stacy paused again. "Can you stop by?"

"Holy shit Stacy. Ok, as soon as I land in Dallas, I'll get a ticket back to Denver and can come by. Are you okay? Is anyone with you?" Eric asked, tears streaming down his face at this point.

"My mom is here, but that's it. I haven't told anyone else. Isla is sick, so I've been careful about having people over. But I could use some company. You have our address, right?" Stacy sounded like she was about to pass out.

"Um, yes, yes, I have it. I'll be there as soon as I can, but it likely won't be until this evening. Stacy, I am so sorry. I had no idea he was thinking this way. I wish I could have done something," Eric said.

Stacy sniffled. "Eric, it's not your fault. I didn't pick up on anything, and I *lived* with him. Please don't blame yourself. We'll talk more when you get here, okay?"

"Okay, Stacy. I'll be there tonight. I am so, so sorry." Eric disconnected and broke down, crying openly at 35,000 feet somewhere above New Mexico.

▼ ▼ ▼

Roughly 12 hours later, he was sitting outside of Mike and Stacy's townhouse in the southern suburbs of Denver, trying to collect his emotions. The police had just taken his statement and left, leaving him alone on the stairs.

It had been a long day. After getting up at 4:30 a.m. to catch a 7 a.m. flight to Dallas, landing at 10 a.m. local time, and waiting in the Dallas airport until the first flight out at 3:30 pm, he spent that time at the Dallas airport speaking with Alexandra about what happened. She reassured him, saying he couldn't have done anything. He made some work calls to colleagues to let them know what was happening and ensure he had proper client coverage.

He walked a lot. It was the only thing that calmed his emotions—a mix of sadness, anger, confusion, and exhaustion.

By the time he got home around 7 p.m. local, he was mentally and physically drained. After a quick shower and hugs from Alexandra, he left for Mike and Stacy's townhouse, arriving around 8:30 p.m.

There were still so many questions that he knew might never be answered. He had lost friends before, but those were due to long-term health issues, allowing him to prepare mentally for the loss.

This was different. Mike was his friend for over 25 years, who, after a lifetime of both physical and mental pain, finally seemed to have peace in his life, only to have it abruptly end.

Eric knew he had to see what the letter said and if it gave any insight into what happened.

He stood slowly off the pavement and walked up to the front door, knocking softly, unsure if the baby was sleeping. It was a hot night, and even after the shower at home, he was still sweating a lot.

After a few seconds, Stacy opened the door and immediately hugged him. Eric hugged her back as she cried on his shoulder. He closed his eyes and let a few tears fall, both of them letting the emotions of the past 24 hours fall on each other's shoulders.

After a minute or so, Stacy lifted her head from his shoulders and said, "I'm sorry. I don't know why I did that—I just had to hug someone, and you're the first person I've seen since it happened who knew him." Her gaze dropped to the floor.

Eric gently held her arms and lowered his head to meet her eyes, before saying sternly, "No, no. Listen to me. There is absolutely nothing to apologize for. I needed that as much as you did. Okay? Come here." He hugged her again, briefly this time.

Stacy sniffled and wiped away some tears before walking inside the townhouse, with Eric following.

The apartment was messy, with papers and clothes strewn everywhere, like a hurricane had recently hit. The television was on, but muted. Stacy's mom sat on a couch to his left, with Isla fast asleep on her shoulder.

Her mom welcomed him with a finger to her lips and a quiet, "*Shh.*"

Eric waved, acknowledging her as Stacy said, "Sorry for the mess. I was angry and threw some stuff off the dining room table. Half this shit is Mike's anyway; he always left his things lying around." He believed her—Mike wasn't known for his neatness.

"Please, come in and sit," Stacy said, moving toward the kitchen and taking a seat on a stool.

The kitchen was no better than the living room, with unwashed pots, pans, dishes, and glasses piled in the sink. Bread, peanut butter, and jelly, with two knives, cluttered the counter, along with half-full bottles of beer and vodka sitting next to the sink. A few lemons and limes, half-cut, lay next to them.

Noticing Eric glancing at the counter, Stacy sighed. "I think he got wasted and made himself a peanut butter and jelly sandwich in the middle of the night. He loved peanut butter and jelly sandwiches." She chuckled. "I hate them. You should take some home to your kids; I'm sure they love it."

"Yeah, of course, thank you. Stacy, I swear I didn't know he was drinking again," Eric said, sitting on a stool beside Stacy and taking a good look at her.

She was in her early 30s, with dark brown hair in a ponytail, fair skin, and hazel eyes under a pair of glasses. Eric could see why Mike was attracted to her, though she looked like she hadn't slept in a week. Under her glasses, her eyes were red, presumably from lack of sleep and crying. She wore a gray robe and brown bunny slippers, which seemed out of place given the circumstances.

She didn't seem to hear his response, but continued, "I woke up around 4 a.m., thinking I heard Isla crying, even though she wasn't. But when I woke up, I noticed Mike wasn't in the bed beside me, which wasn't terribly weird because he usually gets up in the middle of the night to pee, especially recently. I had to pee, so I went to the bathroom and he wasn't there, which *was* weird. I thought he might be checking on Isla, but she was asleep, and he wasn't in her room either.

So, I went downstairs and saw the kitchen lights on, with liquor and beer bottles fucking everywhere. His pain medicine bottle was completely open with pills spilled all over the damn floor. I freaked out, not knowing where the fuck he was. I ran to the bathroom downstairs and then the TV room—still no Mike.

Suddenly, I noticed the back door open with an empty wine bottle in the doorway. Then I saw him. First, his legs, then the rest of him, sprawled out on the back porch, belly up, shirt off, pants down by his socks, not breathing. I called 911 and tried CPR, but nothing worked. The paramedics arrived maybe ten minutes later, but it was too late.

They can't conclude anything until an autopsy, but it must have been the combination of liquor, painkillers, and whatever the fuck else he took. Knowing him, he was probably jerking off and ended up having a heart attack. Stupid, selfish fucking asshole. Always thinking of himself.

They took him away around 6 a.m. as Isla woke up. I called my mom, and she came over, then I called you. I was in shock, and I didn't know who else to call, especially after I found the note in our bedroom with your name on it. The fucker didn't even have the courage to leave me one. I can't *believe* he did this!"

Stacy was visibly upset now. She stood from the kitchen stool and walked toward the stairs. Stopping at the foot of the stairs, she screamed, "How could this fucker leave me alone with a month-old baby? What kind of selfish asshole does that? Was his life so fucking horrible that he had to end it? Why? I didn't do shit to that motherfucker except support him after he came out of that fucking Anticipation Day experience all depressed. Did he tell you what happened?

The rage was pouring out of her now, and Eric could only stand and respond with: "No, he never told me what happened."

"That experience fucked him up, that's what happened. He lost the game because he got hurt or some shit on the last play of the game. He wasn't the same coming out of that. I should sue the motherfuckers who came up with that simulation shit. He was so weak."

She sat on the stairs, hands over her head, and cried. After a few moments, she tried to compose herself.

A little calmer, she continued, "Like, who cares if you fail in a simulation? It's not fucking real. Why wasn't he strong enough to realize that? Why did he do this? We were supposed to be a family; did he not love us enough?"

She looked up at Eric, tears in her eyes, silently asking: *Why?*

Eric knelt on the step in front of her. "I don't know Stacy. I can't answer that for him. Maybe that experience triggered something from his past, from when his dreams were destroyed in high school. I know that hurt him deeply. Even though he got back on the ice, he was never the same. And he knew it. Playing hockey gave his life meaning, and he was amazing at it.

I know that's what led to his drinking and depression. Even though I thought he was doing better recently, I guess he wasn't. I missed it too. Shit, I saw him last weekend for coffee, and while he told me he was pissed about the experience, I had no idea he had started drinking again. I feel so blindsided. Maybe I wasn't paying attention because I was so focused on getting my own drinking under control."

Eric wiped his eyes, took a deep breath, and looked around. Stacy sat on the steps, crying quietly.

"You know the last thing he asked me when I left the hospital after Isla was born? He said, 'Eric, I can't believe this is my life now. I love everything about my life. I love this new little girl that is somehow mine, this new little being that I have to take care of. And I love Stacy so much; she has stood by me for so long, even though I don't think I deserve it. Do you think I deserve it?'

I told him, 'Dude, out of anyone in my life, you deserve this the most. Don't ever forget that.' I hugged him and left. Deep down, maybe I didn't think he believed that. But never in a million years did I think he would do something like this. I know you didn't either, so please don't blame yourself. He loved you, and Isla was the love of his life.

We may never know why he did this, but I hope something in that letter helps us understand. Do you have it?"

Stacy slowly got up, and a few seconds later, Eric did the same.

"Thank you. I needed that. Follow me," she said quietly as she walked upstairs. Eric followed her to their bedroom, with clothes and baby products cluttering all parts of the room.

Stacy pointed to the nightstand on Mike's side of the bed. "I found it under my pillow. He must have slipped it there after I passed out in the middle of the night. I hid it until you got here. I haven't touched it; I figured there was a reason he addressed it to you, not me."

Eric placed a hand on her shoulder and walked over to the letter that just said:

FOR ERIC

DO NOT SHARE WITH POLICE.

Opening the flap, he pulled out a typed, double-sided letter folded into threes.

He took a seat on the bed. "I'll read it aloud. You deserve to hear this."

In the corner, Stacy sat in the baby rocking chair and said, "Go ahead."

Eric took a deep breath and looked down at the letter.

"Dear Eric,

Well, If you're reading this, I guess I've done the unthinkable. I've probably imagined writing this letter a thousand times over the years, but this is the first time I've actually done it. Well, maybe the second; the first was when I tried to off myself back in New York City.

You know what I've been through in my life—the ups, the downs, and everything in between. I don't need to rehash it.

It wasn't until that bastard killed my mom over two years ago that I knew I had to change.

And I did. I stopped drinking and using. It was the hardest thing I had ever done.

Every day was a struggle, especially passing bar after bar after bar on my way home from work. Stopping in for a drink was my routine for so long, and it took everything I had not to walk in for a bourbon or a beer.

But I didn't. One day at a time, I just didn't go in. Eventually I got my mind and body back on track, and I felt normal again.

AA helped me get through my days and my weeks and a little closer to feeling happy. Dating normal women helped me regain my confidence.

I reconnected with you and your family, and then I met Stacy. We fell in love, or so I thought. I just didn't want kids.

So, when she told me she wanted to have children, I did what I thought was right and let her go. I wanted her to find someone who could give her what she wanted before we got too serious.

Then, BAM! She got pregnant. It felt like the universe was trying to find a way for us to be together. At first, I was furious. How could she not tell me? Was she lying about the father? I always jumped to the worst conclusions, didn't I?

But after thinking about it for a while, I realized that this was a chance for me to finally do right by someone. I had punished myself for so long that I'd forgotten what happiness felt like.

When I realized that being a dad was a blessing, I felt happy for the first time in a long time. Genuinely happy.

Then March 8th happened. My simulation.

The feeling I had when I ended that goddamn simulation after losing the game they way I did—with my selfishness costing my team a chance at a win--brought me right back to 2007, when I found out my ACL was torn again and my dream of playing in the NHL was gone. Just absolutely crushed. Even though I knew the experience wasn't real, the feelings I had certainly were and it was like all the good feelings I had built up over the years were instantly wiped out.

After leaving the simulation, those fuckers kept me in that facility for two weeks to 'monitor' me. I knew what I needed to say to get out; I had been down that road before. If they were smart, they would have kept me there for much longer, but they probably needed the bed for some other poor soul.

Then Isla was born. I thought seeing her would give me the clarity and purpose I needed to move past the simulation. But it didn't.

Holding her, all I could think about was how I would just end up disappointing her. I just knew it.

I stayed with her as much as I could that first night, talking and holding her, hoping to feel something good. Some cloud of positivity that would embrace me. But it didn't. All I felt was sadness and disappointment with my life.

The next day, after saying goodbye to Isla and Stacy in the hospital, I left for work but didn't go. Instead, I stopped by a liquor store, bought a bottle of bourbon, and drank it all that night.

Since then, I've been drinking almost every night when Stacy passes out with Isla. She didn't know, so please don't hold anything against her. I kept my stash hidden and always went to a liquor store far away, where no one knew me. No one knew but me."

Eric glanced at Stacy, who was crying again. After a few moments, she calmed down and said quietly, "I knew. The dumbfuck smelled like alcohol when he came to bed. I'm not stupid. I was just too tired to deal with it. I should have spoken up sooner, but I knew he'd deny it and it would lead to a fight."

Eric stood silent, unsure of how to respond. Then he continued:

"I wish I had more control over my decisions, but I don't, and I don't think I ever did. As I write this, I know what my life path will be if I continue on. If the thought of being a family with Stacy and Isla isn't enough to stop me from hitting the bottle again, then nothing will.

I don't want Isla to remember me as a drunk, deadbeat dad who hit her mother for no reason or, god forbid, hit her for no reason. I don't want history to repeat itself or be known as that kind of husband and father.

The reality is I am a drunk. I am a failure. You might see me as weak, cowardly, and selfish for doing this. That's fine. I've considered myself weak for a long time. I'll leave it to others to judge what kind of man I am.

In my heart and soul, I know where this was heading, and I don't believe any therapy, medicine, or future simulation would change it.

So, here we are, Eric. You're the one reading this. I'm sorry, man, really.

I have one request, or rather, many requests, but here's the first:

Let's keep this between us. If they classify it as suicide, I'll lose my government benefits. If they suspect it was an accident— just a lot of alcohol and some sleeping pills—Stacy and Isla can keep their benefits.

So, please, as a friend, tear this up.

I assume Stacy is with you, so please keep reading."

Eric checked if Stacy wanted him to keep going, which she did.

"To Stacy: Words cannot express how much you've meant to me. You brought me back to life long before I found out you were pregnant. I love you and never wanted to let you down or hurt you, which I knew I would have in the long run. Isla is a blessing, and it also brought me the gift of your love. Thank you for being that gift, and please take care of our baby for me. I know she's in good hands. I'm sorry you had to find me as you did. I hope I was at least clothed and had a rocking hard-on. Please remember me for my hard-ons."

Stacy burst out laughing through her tears. "Oh, you bastard."

Eric walked over to her, and gently touched her shoulder. She eventually regained her composure and said, "Please, keep reading."

He sat back down and continued:

"I trust you will make the best decision for you and her, including bringing another man (or woman—I remember what you told me about college) into her life. Thank you for everything you did for me and everything you will do for Isla.

To Eric: Thank you for always being there for me. You and I have shared so much together—from supporting me through my injuries to that high school threesome (You know I had to throw that in there—hope you're blushing) to watching your kids being born. I've seen you grow from a boy to a man to the best father I know. I hope you find happiness for the rest of your life with whatever you choose to do. You deserve it. Maybe next year you can relive a day back in college for Anticipation Day. Make it that time in senior year at that frat party—holy hell.

My second request is for you to always be there for Isla. Treat her as a daughter. A daughter you don't have to change dirty diapers for or get up in the middle of the night for. When she starts bringing boys over to Stacy's house in 15 years, be there to greet them on my behalf and let them know that if they hurt her, either you'll kill them or I'll haunt them. You're her acting father now—please guide her through her life so she becomes more successful and happier than I ever was.

I love you, brother.

To Isla: Oh, my dear Isla, I'm so sorry I won't be there to see you grow up. To take your first steps. To hear your first words. To laugh and play with you. To cuddle with you. To watch you learn about the world around you. I wish I could. I know you'll become a beautiful little girl, a rambunctious teenager, a successful woman, a wonderful mother, and an amazing grandmother. Live the best life possible and find happiness in whatever you do and whomever you choose to spend it with. Please do not hate me for what I have done. Remember that I will always be with you—in spirit, soul, and in your heart. I love you, baby girl."

Eric choked up and took a moment to collect himself before finishing the last line through tears.

"My third request, Eric, is to take care of my will. It's in the Denver National Bank's safety deposit box. I recently amended

it so that all my financial assets go to Stacy and Isla. Help them make good decisions and do their damn taxes for free please.

My final request is for you to take $200 from my sock drawer and go to a nice strip club in town. Don't say I never did anything for you, buddy.

With love forever,
Mike (Mikey) Stanza."

Eric flipped the last page over, looked up at Stacy, and said, "That's it. That's the letter."

"Wow, that motherfucker. I should hate him for this, but... I just miss him so much. How am I supposed to do this without him?" Stacy asked with a mix of anger and sadness in her voice.

Eric looked up, cheeks wet with tears. "Well, you heard him. I'm Isla's acting father now. Alexandra, the kids, and I are here for you. Always. Whatever you need, we're your family now. Please don't forget that."

She let out a strained laugh. "Thank you. Mike was lucky to have you as a friend and brother, Eric."

He hugged her, leaning in so that his forehead touched hers and said, "You're welcome." Backing away, he stood up and added, "I'm sorry. I should have been there more for him. I wish I could have said or done something different to prevent this. All I can say right now is that I'm sorry."

Stacy took his hand gently. "You couldn't have known, Eric. He hid his drinking well and knew what he was doing. You heard the letter. I'm not sure you, or anyone, could have stopped this."

"Yeah, I don't know what to think right now. I just need time to process all of this. It's too much right now." Eric paused, trying to steady himself. "Look, um, I'm exhausted, so I'm gonna head home. Thank you for letting me read this. Let's talk tomorrow about the arrangements. We'll take care of everything, so you don't have to worry, okay? Consider us family now."

"Thank you. I need to fucking sleep, and I'm sure Isla will wake up for her bottle in two hours. Thank you for being his friend. He always spoke highly of you and admired how successful you were, for what it's worth." Stacy yawned.

"Well, if he only knew." Eric responded. "Things aren't always as rosy as they appear. But thank you for telling me. He was a good friend, and that's how I will remember him."

Stacy smiled softly. "I know that would mean a lot to him, wherever he is."

"I'm sure wherever he is, he's scoring that Game 7 winning goal this time," Eric said, glancing at the bedroom ceiling.

"God, that was cheesy, but I hope you're right," Stacy replied with a small laugh. They hugged again before Eric went downstairs and out the door. Moments later, he drove off into the Denver night, finally heading home.

CHAPTER 3

THE CAR RIDE

AUGUST 14. 2032
9:15 A.M.

It was a lengthy drive to the service, held in Niwot, about an hour or so north of their home.

The day was beautiful, and Eric and Alexandra had the windows slightly open for some fresh air.

After about fifteen minutes of sitting silently in their self-driving Fisker electric car, Alexandra broke the silence with the phrase that sends chills down any man's spine. "Can we talk?"

Eric slowly looked over, his expression asking: *What now?*

"Well, if you're going to look at me like that, I won't bother," Alexandra said coldly.

"I'm sorry, but no man wants to hear that. It usually means you're breaking up with me, someone is sick, or I'm going to be a dad. Which one is it?" He asked, curious.

"No, no, it's not any of those. I wanted to talk about our simulations. I knew we planned to wait to talk to the therapist, but with everyone at the funeral, I don't want anything slipping out, especially with MaryAnne being such a loudmouth. Is that okay? I know today is

tough, and the timing might not be great, but I think it's important."
She took his hand, imploring him to have this conversation.

Eric looked down and then out the window. "Uh, yeah, sure. I
guess we can. Why not? I'll be getting some things out in the open
today anyway, so why not this too? What the hell? Who goes first?"
He glanced at Alexandra.

"I'd like you to go first, if that's okay," she said firmly.

"Alright, gentlemen first, apparently." Eric chuckled, shifting in his
seat slightly. "How much detail do you want me to get into?"

"As much as you're comfortable with, but I'd like to know as much
as you're willing to share," she replied.

"Alrighty then. Well…I guess I'll just start by asking if you
remember me mentioning how I was in school when I found out my
dad died?" Eric paused to look at Alexandra.

"I do." Alexandra responded.

"Well, what I didn't mention is that when I got the news, I was in
history class learning about the Lewis and Clark expedition. I always
thought it was weird that, while I don't remember much else from that
day, I remember that.

I guess, as a kid, I thought it would've been cool to be on that
expedition, seeing all these new lands, people, and animals, you know?
You'd possibly be the first person on the planet to see some of these
places. How fucking cool would that have been?

Plus, you know I've always loved nature. Or at least I used to. It's
always given me peace and calmed me down. I guess that comes from
those trips with Richie and my dad that I used to talk about. We'd
camp out in Rocky Mountain National Park for a week, shoot the shit,
and be ourselves. It was fucking amazing. Those were some of my best
memories growing up.

At some point, I lost that love of the outdoors and wanted to get
it back.

So, with all that said, I decided to do the Lewis and Clark
expedition as my experience. Initially, I was going to do the full year,
but I realized a good portion of the last few months would be spent

in their winter camp, which just sounded *miserable*. So, I decided to go from May 1804 through November 1804, from where they launched near St. Louis to where they settled into their camp for the winter.

What? What's the smile for?" Eric narrowed his eyes as Alexandra smiled at him.

"Sorry, that's really sweet. I didn't know what happened the day your dad died. You don't talk about it much, but that's a great way to honor him. So, how was it?" She asked curiously.

Eric laughed. "Well, to be honest, it was amazing, surreal, emotional, funny, painful, scary. It was just...*real*. It's the only way to describe it.

The days were an absolute pain in the ass. We had to drag this huge boat up the river, sometimes with ropes, because the damn thing kept getting stuck in the river. Most of the guys with me were in their 20s, but so was I. But man, it was such a pain. And, of course, I got sick. But this was *way* worse than anything I've ever had. The weird part was that I didn't have to vomit or have diarrhea; there was that 'no liquids coming out of you' thing. It was so strange. I still felt like shit though, but it eventually passed.

So yeah, it was hard work. And tough. And raw.

But in the early morning and evening, it was so fucking peaceful, especially when it wasn't pouring. We'd be by the river at our campfire, shooting the shit, and just being in nature. There were birds in the morning and evening and bugs pretty much all of the time—you would have *hated* it. But the sound of the river calmed me the most, especially when it was all whipped up after a storm.

No kids screaming, clients calling, things breaking, or laundry needing to be done. And you weren't yelling at me for anything.

So yeah, we were just a bunch of young, horny men out in the wilderness together." He chuckled.

"We spent most days rowing, hunting, fishing, and talking. Everything I did with my dad when we were younger. It was awesome. I was a really good hunter in this simulation.

But seriously, how the fuck did they do that? It was so realistic. I don't know how they did it, but I genuinely felt like I was there. I'm sure you did too.

Everything felt real, you know? The characters were real—their accents, the way they dressed, the way they reacted to everything I said and did. The weather was definitely real—I almost got struck by lightning several times." They both laughed.

"The food was certainly real. Rough, but real. I got to eat more beans than I ever imagined. And the coffee—wow, that coffee! It definitely put CoffeeHut to shame. Although, I have to say I missed a good pastrami sandwich. And my toothbrush."

Alexandra laughed at that.

"You know the coolest part? I actually got to talk to Captain Lewis and Captain Clark—not much, since I was just a lowly private, but I had one-on-one conversations with both of them. It was so weird. I kept wondering if that was how they really talked back then; it seemed accurate, but who knows.

You know the worst part? The guy I got closest to, one of the Sergeants named Charles, died. I talked to him almost every day. He was awesome and I genuinely became friendly with him. We would talk about all sorts of things, but mostly about hunting, fishing and being in nature.

I knew one of the guys on the expedition died, but I never checked who. Maybe I did that on purpose, who knows. I researched it afterward, and I guess he died of appendicitis, but man was that tough to watch. He was in a *lot* of pain, and there wasn't much me, or anyone, could do about it.

The worst part about his death was that it brought me right back to that day in school when I heard about my dad. I felt helpless and small, like there was nothing I could do to change anything.

I knew this guy wasn't real, but man, it sure as hell felt real. I'm not sure if you dealt with death in yours, but this was rough." Eric looked out the window, trying to hold back tears.

After a few seconds, he continued. "You know what's funny? I cried. I cried like I've never cried before. But there were no tears! Did you have tears in yours?"

"No, it was the weirdest fucking thing," Alexandra confirmed. "And I did some crying, believe me."

"I'm sure you did, and we'll get into that. But before I finish, I want to let you know that I'm proud of myself. And I think you'll be proud of me too. I didn't drink at all for the whole trip. I literally woke up with a hangover in the simulation and at that point I was like, 'You drink in real life, time to take a fucking break.'

So I did. I wanted to prove to myself that I could go without liquor to function and be happy. And I could.

I think you've noticed I haven't been drinking as much since my experience—maybe a few on the weekend, but that's it." Eric paused, looking at Alexandra.

"Oh, was that a question? Yes, I noticed… I didn't ask because I assumed you were still grabbing drinks at work or on work trips."

"No, not really. I just wanted to rely on it less. I guess I was using it as a crutch to deal with my unhappiness. I didn't like how I felt, but that was all I knew. So, I've been trying. It hasn't been easy. There are days when I want one, but I've learned to punch myself in the balls or something to change my mindset.

I have to say I'm proud of myself. I know I'm not there yet, but I want to continue drinking less for you and the kids. And myself too.

In the simulation, I realized that I was focusing too much on the past and what I didn't have instead of what I did have: You, the kids, my health, my life.

I realized that the kids are growing up without a dad who's *actually* there for them. I don't want them to grow up without a dad like I did. It sucks.

That's why I've taken the boys camping. I want them to have that sense of belonging to something bigger than themselves. I want them to have that sense of being out in nature and learning to survive.

I hope they enjoyed it; they seemed to have fun. They kept asking me about my trips with my dad: what we did, what we ate, and what animals we ran into. It was great. They were so curious."

"I know. They've been telling me how much fun they had and that they want to go again," Alexandra said, smiling.

"That's awesome to hear. So, that's it. I'm not sure what else to say. I can get into some weird details about the simulation if you want. Let's just say I appreciate my bathroom more than ever…" Eric paused as she was looking at him, smiling.

"I'm happy for you, Eric. I was half expecting you to say you went to some college and just lived as a college kid for a few years, getting ass and drinking as much as you wanted." She laughed.

"Why would I need to simulate that?" He smiled at her, before realizing it maybe wasn't the best time for a joke.

"I'm going to ignore that, asshole. But thank you for telling me. It means a lot to me and I'm happy for you and hope you can keep doing what you're doing. I have noticed a change in you, and I know what happened with Mike hurt. A lot.

But I hope you know you can talk to me if you want to. About whatever happened in your simulation too. Okay?"

"Okay, I appreciate that. I will." Eric leaned over and kissed her.

Alexandra paused for a moment, gathering her thoughts.

"So, speaking about whatever happened in our simulations, I wanted to tell you about mine—"

"Interesting way to start," Eric interrupted.

"Let me tell my story, please. You know my happy place is by the beach. I've always loved the sun, the sand, the wind, and the water. It's where I've always felt at peace.

So, for *my* experience, I decided to go to Brazil for two months back in 2015. It wasn't six months like you did since I would miss the kids *way* too much if I did anything longer than two months. I wanted to see how I felt this first year before trying a longer time period. I figured I could always do a longer one next year if I wanted to.

I started in Fernando de Noronha, an island off the coast of northeastern Brazil. It was gorgeous, Eric. So peaceful and beautiful. The food, the people, and the lifestyle—it was all perfect. I hiked, ate, and relaxed by the pool and beach. I went snorkeling and saw amazing fish and coral reefs. That's been a dream of mine for so many years.

It was just what I needed to relax my brain.

Then I went to Lençóis Maranhenses—I'm probably not pronouncing that right, but it's a big beach on the north coast full of these amazing and beautiful blue lagoons. It was breathtaking. I was so at peace there. I swam in a few of the lagoons, and it was like heaven. I'm pretty sure I had an orgasm. We met these local people in the villages that were totally isolated from the rest of the world. They just seemed so…at peace, you know? Like they didn't have a care in the fucking world. It was amazing. We went hiking and saw some insects that were bigger than my face—I was *losing my mind* Eric. "Alexandra chuckled thinking about how ugly some of those insects were.

Eric just stared at her as if to say "*Go on…*"

"Anyway, next, I went to Iguazu Falls, which I had read were some of the most amazing waterfalls in the world. The absolute power and sound of the water coming down off of these cliffs was just unbelievable. They drove the boat under some of them, and I almost fell over. You know me." She laughed at herself again.

"For the first time in a long time, I felt connected to the Earth. It made me realize I needed to do more for the environment, you know? That's why I got involved in the local Sierra Club chapter here. I wanted to contribute more. I wasn't doing enough of that before.

In Rio, I hung out with two amazing simulated friends named Stacey and Harmeet. I had so much fun with them. The food, culture, beaches, and beautiful people were unforgettable.

I planned to see the Amazon, but honestly, the jungles in Lençóis Maranhenses trip were enough wildlife for me.

The trip was such an amazing adventure. Like you said, everything felt so entirely real. I felt like I was absolutely there.

The beaches were so beautiful. You would be proud of me—I speared a fish! In Fernando de Noronha, I was like Tom Hanks in *Cast Away*. I threw a metal spear right through a tuna. It was huge. I never thought I'd do that.

It was just what I needed to take my mind off the past few years. Your work stress and my daycare stress have been exhausting, you know? I don't think you noticed how tired I am constantly. Sure, having Anya helps a bit, but I still don't trust that technology, and I need to be involved with the kids pretty much everyday.

I've tried to take that off your plate so you can deal with your shit at work, but it's hard. Sometimes, I'm at work from 6:30 a.m. to 7 p.m., and I come home to the kids' homework undone or they haven't eaten. And it's just like, 'What the fuck? What have you done to help all day?'

You've been better since Anticipation Day. More empathetic and helpful. I hope therapy continues to help us improve. But there's one thing I need to tell you."

"Oh boy, here we go." Eric sighed.

"Well, if you're going to act like that, I'm not sure I want to have this discussion now. I need you to be open-minded." She furrowed her eyebrows at him.

"Damn, you throw that on me, huh? Okay, let's hear it," he said, irritation clear in his voice.

"Fine. When I was in Fernando de Noronha, I went snorkeling. My instructor, Carlos, asked me out to dinner. We talked, ate, drank, and laughed. It felt so natural, so wonderful. I hadn't had that much fun at dinner in years."

She glanced out the window before continuing. "After dinner, we went back to my bungalow and... had sex." She looked back at Eric, gauging his reaction.

He sat silently, his hand on his chin. Finally, he looked at her and asked slowly, "Is that it? Or is there more?"

"Well, we did spend more time together, and, yes, we had more sex."

Alexandra hesitated before speaking again. "He made me feel amazing and wanted again. I haven't felt that way in a long time. When I was with him, I didn't give a shit about anything else—not you, the kids, my business, my sister, nothing. Just being there with him in that moment."

Her eyes started glistening, and she paused to collect herself.

"I won't say I shouldn't have done it. I wasn't trying to get even with you. I'm not going to get into how long it took me to get over the shit you did in the past. I told you I'd try my best to move on and not bring up the past, and I think I have.

That's not what this was about. Before our simulations, I hadn't felt wanted by you in a long time. We never went out to dinner; we rarely had sex. When we did, it was routine and, honestly, quite boring. Most of the time, you were drunk and passed out after five minutes.

We rarely talked. Whenever I would try to start a conversation, you would push me away or tell me we would discuss it later, but we never did. So, I started giving up. I shut down. I reached a point where I didn't want to be around you. Before the simulation, I told myself I would see how your experience went first, and if you hadn't changed, I'd ask for a divorce."

"Okay… good to know, I guess," Eric said slowly, now looking out the window.

"I'm trying to be honest with you. That's where I was when I went into this experience, and that's why I did what I did. Do I regret it? No, I don't. I needed that for myself.

But the experience gave me clarity on what I want and need to make me happy. I can't go back to the way we were. I just can't—I won't survive. I know you have been trying these past few months, and I've seen a difference. You seem happier and more content with your life now.

But I have no idea if that will continue. I truly want to believe you can, and you'll stay sober and be happier for it."

Tears streamed down her face. "I love you so much and can't picture my life without you. But I won't tolerate the behavior you showed in the past—no more lying, cheating, fighting, or bickering. It has to stop, for both me and the kids.

If you want to be a father to them, show them what a father should be—loving, kind, respectful, and stern when needed. I know you are all those things when you're happy. I need you to be happy. And if you're not, tell me so we can work together.

Nothing is worth sacrificing your happiness, certainly not your career; it will be fine either way. You're the smartest and hardest-working person I know. We'll figure it out. Together. That's what I need from you. Can you do that for me? For our family?"

Silence fell over the car. Eric took deep breaths, trying to calm down, while he clenched his fists against the steering wheel.

"Wow. Okay. Sorry, that's a lot to take in. Give me a second to collect my thoughts." He rubbed his temple before looking at her.

"First off, thank you for telling me. I appreciate the honesty. That couldn't have been easy for you. Secondly, I don't know what to say about your Brazilian boyfriend. I'm in no position to get mad at you for having sex with someone else, even if they were simulated. I'm certainly not the pillar of fidelity over here.

But it still stings and hurts, and I feel a bit sick to my stomach. I'm sure you felt the same when you found out about me."

He sighed and glanced at Alexandra. "I need time with this. I'm not mad, just trying to wrap my head around what it means. When you cheat with someone in real life, you can see them again and cheat again. But here, you can't see him again unless you choose to next year for your simulation." He looked away. "Do you miss him? Be honest."

Alexandra slowly looked at him and said, "I don't know. I miss the feeling of having fun, going out, enjoying life with someone who enjoys your company. Yes, having sex that lasted more than five minutes was nice too, I am not gonna lie. He made me feel alive. I need to feel alive again, Eric. I want to feel that with you. It won't be every day—we both know that's not realistic." Tears welled up in her eyes.

"I want us to appreciate life everyday. So many people have it much worse than we do, and we are lucky to have each other, to have the kids, our beautiful family, and for now, our jobs.

If we can't find that happiness together, I'm okay with moving on and separating. I'm sorry if that hurts or if that's different than what you thought it would be, but it's the truth. I'm not the same person I was before, and I can't deal with our bullshit anymore."

Eric, on the verge of tears himself, took a deep breath.

"Woah, okay. Well, I will need some time with this but I do want us to be a family. I really do. I'm also not the same person I was before I went into Anticipation Day. I want to be here and be happy with you and the kids. If that ever changes, I promise I'll let you know. It's not fair to them or you.

But you will need to give me some fucking time to work through this. I'll get there, but it won't be tomorrow or next week. But in some time, I'll be okay with it. Between Mike's service today and my speech, seeing everyone for the first time—plus thinking about this—it's a lot. Let me get through today, and I'll process this."

"I love you, Eric. Please always remember that. I will always love you, regardless of what happens. You were always my home, and I hope you can be again." Alexandra smiled through her tears.

He pulled her close and kissed her. He hadn't kissed her like that in years. Passionately. Lovingly. Deeply.

Alexandra felt a familiar sensation in her loins and knew what it meant: Eric was getting lucky tonight.

As they pulled away, he said slowly, "At least you know I couldn't have done anything like you did in my simulation. I was with a bunch of single men for five and a half months."

"Weren't there women where you stopped along the way?" Alexandra asked.

"There were a few, but they didn't quite match up to the women you probably saw in Rio. I can't even imagine what they looked like down there—no razors or anything. No thanks. I'm good." Eric cracked a small smile.

"Well, we'll have to talk about our policy next year. I doubt I was the only one who did that in their simulation. I bet 90% of the guys did, maybe even more." She chuckled. "Maybe next year you could continue the journey, meet a nice native, have some babies, and hunt wolves together." She laughed again; she was on a roll.

"We'll see what I do next year. What about you? Have you thought about it?" Eric asked.

"Somewhat. I wanted to have this conversation first and see where my head was after it. We have another three months to submit for next year's experience, so I want to give it more time. I might use the go-back-in-your-past option that MaryAnne and Clarise did. We'll see."

Alexandra paused, then added, "I know this is a tough day, and this week has been rough. Thank you for how you handled that. I was expecting much worse, to be honest. I want you to know that I'm here for you today, and we'll get through this together. Okay?"

She took his hand, and they stayed that way until they reached the church 20 minutes later.

CHAPTER 4

THE CHURCH

AUGUST 14, 2032
10:30 A.M.

Alexandra first pointed out the television trucks, with their small satellite dishes towering ten feet above the road. A dozen or so were scattered in the road before the church, all marked with their TV station logos—mostly local or regional—from across the state.

Eric knew regional news outlets had picked up on Mike's story as authorities had begun investigating possible links between overdoses and Anticipation Day experiences.

Even before Mike's death, Eric had heard some talking heads on the news opining about the potential negative consequences of the experience. He generally ignored them.

The consensus he saw when doing some digging was that more monitoring and data were needed before making any sort of correlation.

Rumors and conspiracy theories circulated about the government using Anticipation Day to "thin the herd," but Eric didn't have it in him to buy into those rumors—at least not yet.

As reporters and camera operators surrounded their car, shouting questions, traffic police had to step in and push them out of the way to clear a path to the parking lot.

"What the fuck?" Eric muttered as he took over the auto drive to maneuver through the sea of trucks, reporters, and camera people. "Fucking vultures." Most of the questions were about whether Mike's death was connected to Anticipation Day.

He fought the urge to roll down the window to yell "Fuck off," and run over a foot or two on the way to the church entrance for good measure.

The car finally pulled in the church lot.

"Jesus, I knew it was on the news locally, but I didn't expect this many news stations here. Guess it's a big story around here, huh? Are you sure you're ready for this?" Alexandra asked, rubbing his hand.

Eric took a deep breath. "No. But I need to tell Mike's story and make sure people knew who he was." He took a few more deep breaths and added softly, "I'm ready. Let's go."

"I have your back. Remember that, okay?" Alexandra said, as they both opened their doors stepped outside to look at the modest church before them. It stood against the backdrop of a clear blue sky, with the partially snow-covered Twin Sisters and Longs Peak mountains in the distance.

"Beautiful day, huh?" Alexandra said, putting on her jacket and waiting by the car. On any other day, she would have loved to take advantage of being up here and go hiking in Rocky Mountain National Park, stopping in Nederland on the way back, and spending the night in Boulder to enjoy that community's amazing culture and food. Not today, though.

"Yeah, Mikey hated days like this," Eric said with a chuckle. "He always preferred cloudy, gloomy days to stay in, watch sports, and play video games. I don't blame him; that sounds wonderful." Hand in hand, they walked toward the church, ready to confront the task ahead.

▼▼▼

As they approached the entrance to the church, they spotted Patrick first. At 6'2", he was the tallest in their friend group and had a distinctive head of hair, making him easy to identify.

Standing beside him was a pretty young lady who couldn't have been more than 30. She was holding his hand as they approached them from behind.

"Hey, Patrick," Eric said as he touched Patrick's shoulder from behind.

Patrick turned around and, seeing Eric, immediately hugged him. They patted each other's backs before separating.

"Hey buddy, good to see you," Patrick said. "Been way too long, dude. I'm so sorry I didn't reach out to you after I said I would. I really am. I feel like a prick for not getting back to you. I sincerely apologize for that."

"I know, man, I know," Eric replied as he gave Patrick another pat on the shoulder. "We all needed time to process what we went through. I certainly needed time to process mine. I just wanted to make sure you were okay, that's all. So, are you?"

Patrick took a deep breath. "I think I am. I needed time, like you said. It was an amazing and surreal experience—I can't really compare it to anything else, you know? And I guess I needed time to understand how it changed me. It was just *so* real—I am sure you both know. It was hard to come to grips with the fact that it wasn't real.

But I saw stuff that I was hoping not to see. I knew tornado chasing would be dangerous, and I might see people get hurt, but I never expected to see families and little kids lying dead in their houses..." Patrick's voice faltered as he got emotional.

"Look, even now, I can't talk about it without getting choked up." Patrick composed himself before continuing. "But despite all the awful shit I saw, I had some incredible experiences and made amazing connections. I did see an insane tornado, which I wanted, I guess. But it was just a whole range of emotions that I had in there."

Maybe that's what they wanted?" Alexandra asked. "For us to feel emotions we haven't felt in a long time. Good emotions, bad emotions, and everything in between. Maybe this whole thing was meant to remind us of what's important in life and to re-examine our priorities. I'm so sorry you had to see some bad stuff though."

"Yeah, I hadn't really thought about it like that, but you might be right. I also had a thing with a girl that I was traveling with. I know it sounds weird, but I did care about her and was sad to leave her. But it made me realize that I'm ready to love again and *be* loved—as stupid as that sounds, you know?" Patrick chuckled.

But now, I appreciate everything I have at home much more, especially time with the kids. Honestly, it's been great spending some more time with them." He was tearing up a little.

"Speaking of being loved, I want to introduce my girlfriend, Emily. She knows all about my simulation since she was the one watching it in the simulation facility. Emily, this is Eric and his wife, Alexandra. Alexandra, I'm so sorry I didn't greet you earlier. Come here." Patrick leaned in to kiss her on the cheek.

Eric extended his hand to Emily. She was an attractive blonde with beautiful blue eyes and a warm sun-kissed complexion. And perfect teeth.

"Nice to meet you, Emily. I appreciate you being here with Patrick today. It means a lot to both him and us," he said.

Emily gave a light smile. "Of course. I'm so sorry about your friend. I know he has a little daughter—I can't even imagine what you're all going through. My condolences."

"Thank you, Emily," Alexandra replied, shaking her hand. "We look forward to getting to know you better."

Patrick turned to Eric and said calmly, "So yeah, she was my nurse during my experience. Can you believe that? I threw everything I had at her until she finally gave in." He smiled and kissed Emily. "I think she was impressed by my heroics in the simulation, where I saved a little girl trapped under debris."

Emily chuckled. "When he came out of it, he was so cute. He was telling me about what happened in there, and he genuinely seemed like a good guy. So when he asked me for coffee, I finally gave in and said yes. No regrets—it's been wonderful so far. And yes, I know all about his little fling in the simulation."

"That's so sweet. I didn't realize you were dating anyone, Patrick, but I'm happy for you both," Alexandra said, giving Patrick's arm a reassuring rub.

Patrick smiled and turned to Eric. "So, man, are you ready for today? It's just so fucking awful what happened to Mike. I know he was like a brother to you. I'm really sorry. Did you see all that chaos outside? The press is everywhere. Like, what the fuck? Are they even allowed to be here?"

"I think they can stay as long as they don't enter the church's property," Alexandra said. "I'm not sure about all the rules, but the cops are around, so I guess that makes it okay. I'm surprised this has become such a huge story. They're trying to tie his death to other overdoses in the state, I think."

"Honestly, I haven't followed the news much over the past few days, but I guess I'm ready," Eric said, taking a deep breath. "I don't really have a choice. I have to tell his story. I know he would have wanted that."

"Yeah man, he seemed like a nice guy the few times I met him. I wasn't close with him like you were, but I'm here for you if you need anything. We can catch up more after the funeral. You wanna head to our seats?" Patrick pointed towards the clergy, who was ushering everyone inside the church.

Once inside, Alexandra glanced around at the 20 rows of pews holding ten to twelve people on each side. So, basic math led her to estimate a total capacity of around four to five hundred people.

Niwot was a small town, but with its large Catholic community, the church's size was no surprise.

Scanning the room, Alexandra didn't recognize anyone she knew. Suddenly, a voice called out from behind, "Hey you," and she felt an arm wrap around her waist.

She knew it was MaryAnne right away. She turned around and hugged MaryAnne, saying, "Hey you." As they stepped back, Alexandra continued, "Thank you for coming, MaryAnne. We appreciate it."

"Hey, MaryAnne," Eric said, hugging her. "Thank you so much for being here. Mike always said you were way funnier than I was."

MaryAnne hugged Patrick and shook Emily's hand and introduced herself before turning back to Eric.

"He was a good man. I'm really sorry. I know you two were close, and he just had a daughter—so fucking sad. It's hard to know how these experiences are going to impact people. I was an emotional mess after mine two years ago, but I was also still furious at Kevin for what he did so I'm probably not the best person to compare to."

"Thank you. I appreciate that. He *was* a good man," Eric said, looking down at the ground. "Hey, speaking of good men, where is Mr. AI?" He asked, referring to Opie, MaryAnne's new official boyfriend.

"Oh, sorry. He really wanted to come but wasn't feeling well and didn't want to get anyone sick. He sends his condolences." MaryAnne responded.

"No problem. Hope he feels better," Eric said. "I heard you guys are doing well, so congrats. We can catch up after the service. How was your experience reliving your day with your dad? Alexandra said you seemed happy."

MaryAnne smiled. "It was… amazing, yet also somewhat depressing, if that makes any sense? It felt so real and brought back so many feelings, especially towards Kevin, ones that I thought I had gotten past. But, I tried to look past that prick and focus on my dad and mom and my brothers' families, which brought back a lot of good memories.

Don't get me wrong, there were times when I wanted to grab a steak knife and ram it through Kevin's beautiful hazel eyes, but I didn't. Mostly because I couldn't!" MaryAnne chuckled. "I think if I could have, I would have! But seriously, it was a great experience, and I'm glad I did it. It was fun and weird to relive a day without being able to change anything about what you were doing. You were just kind of stuck, moving based on how your memory remembered it. I'm not sure I'd do it again next year, but it was nice to see my dad happy and in good spirits."

"How is your dad doing?" Eric asked.

"I don't think he has much time left, maybe a few months. This Alzheimer's shit just sucks, you know?" She said, tearing up. "I'm sorry."

She composed herself. "Thank you for asking, Eric. I'll be okay. I've been able to prepare for what's coming, especially after helping move him to long-term care. I'm emotionally ready. I'm happy I could see him again like I remembered him—happy, funny, and full of life."

MaryAnne smiled. "I know Clarise and David were going to be here. It's the first time since their experience with Charlie, right? Any idea how they're doing?"

Alexandra responded first. "Well, when I spoke to Clarise last week about what happened to Mike, she sounded better than a few weeks earlier. She said we'd catch up more here, so I didn't push her. I'm sure it was raw and emotional for both of them. I just wanted to give them space and be there if she reached out, you know? I'm sure they'll tell us when they're ready."

Eric continued, "Yeah, I spoke to David briefly but haven't heard from him much, other than a couple of stupid things about fantasy football. I'm sure we'll talk later."

"So, Patrick, how was your experience? And how did you two meet?" MaryAnne asked, turning to Patrick and Emily.

"We met at the facility actually; she was the intake nurse," Patrick said as he smiled.

"Wow, a simulation couple. Pretty cool. Patrick's a great guy, so hold onto him," MaryAnne said, winking at Patrick. "So, how did you do? Mr. Tornado Chaser. Was it crazy?"

"I was just telling Eric and Alexandra a little about it. It was raw, real, awful, and amazing all at the same time. Let's talk more after the service. It made me realize how much I missed my kids, and I've been trying to spend more time with them since.

I am happy that you enjoyed your experience too, MaryAnne. I also want to hear about your guys' experience, but maybe next time," Patrick said, looking at Eric and Alexandra.

"Yeah, thanks; next time we see you," Eric replied. "Well, we better get to the front before they start. See you guys after, okay?"

"Sure man, good luck," Patrick said.

Eric and Alexandra turned and walked towards the front of the church, leaving MaryAnne, Emily, and Patrick to find their seats.

As they walked to the front, they finally saw the table where the coffin would be placed once the hearse arrived.

Eric and Alexandra sat in the front right pew and waited a few minutes for the service to start.

▼ ▼ ▼

A couple of minutes later, a priest emerged from a side door.

Mike's family had taken the lead in organizing the funeral and had designated his brothers and cousins as pallbearers. Eric didn't argue; he was giving one of the two eulogies today, so that was his contribution to the service.

He noticed that Mike's family had organized three bagpipers to play the service, who were dressed in traditional garb and lined up at the church entrance. While Irish Lutherans were rare, they did exist, but Mike wasn't one of them. He was as Italian as they come.

"Oh my god," Eric said, laughing.

"What's so funny?" Alexandra asked, looking like she might slap him.

Eric, still chuckling, lowered his voice. "I just remembered when Mike tore his second ACL, he was so depressed it took me two weeks to drag his butt out of the house. Finally, I convinced him to get drunk with me. We bought some Jack Daniels with fake IDs and went to a local rooftop where kids would throw rocks at passing cars.

"What?" Alexandra asked earnestly.

"What?" Eric repeated, shrugging. "We were young, drunk, and stupid. It's what teenagers do."

Alexandra gave him a look that said they would discuss this topic later.

Eric continued, "Anyway, I remember us up there on the roof, talking about deep topics like death, women, and the universe. I remember him telling me that when he died, he wanted bagpipes at his funeral. The most Italian guy in the world asking for bagpipes? It was so random and weird."

Suddenly, his eyes started tearing up and he chuckled. "But that's who Mike was. He did things his way, right until the end."

"I know," Alexandra replied, squeezing his hand. "Make sure people remember that."

As the bagpipes began playing "Amazing Grace," their heavenly sounds immediately overtook the church. Eric closed his eyes, instantly transported back to his simulation at the cliff where Sergeant Floyd was buried. An expedition member had played this same tune on the bagpipes he'd brought along. Under the scorching sun, Eric clearly remembered the look of despair on the faces of the men gathered around, mourning their friend and colleague.

Though the simulation version didn't sound as good as the current rendition in the church, Eric felt the same sadness, hopelessness, and anger.

As Eric waited for Mike to be brought into the church for his final goodbye, he couldn't help wondering if that experience had been a prelude to what happened with Mike.

At the same time, he considered whether the simulation had made him stronger in the face of death. In some ways, seeing the determination of the men to keep going on the journey despite Sergeant Floyd's death was an inspiration to Eric. Instead of focusing on the pain, he realized he needed to ensure that Mike's death was not in vain and that something positive came from it.

As the bagpipers walked down the pews, continuing their rendition of "Amazing Grace," Eric saw Mike's brothers, Danny and Bobby, and his cousins, four on each side, carrying Mike's coffin up the stairs to the church entrance.

They stopped at the top of the stairs as the bagpipers transitioned to what Eric believed was the "Skye Boat Song."

The pallbearers moved slowly down the center of the church, finally putting the coffin on the table in front of Eric and Alexandra.

Behind them were Mike's sister, Janet, and her husband, Sebastian, with their two young children, Melani and Robyn. Behind them, Stacy walked down the aisle with Isla in a stroller, along with Stacy's mom. They all took seats on the first pew to Eric's left.

The pastor got up and began the service.

"I invite the congregation to rise if you can, and we will begin our service. Welcome, in the name of Jesus, the Savior of the World. We are gathered here to worship, proclaim Christ Crucified and Risen, and remember our brother Mike before God. To give thanks for his life, commend him to our Merciful Redeemer, and comfort one another in our grief.

When we are baptized in Christ Jesus, we are baptized into his death. We were buried, therefore, with Him, by baptism into death, so that, as Christ was raised from the dead by the glory of the Father, we too might live a new life. If we have been united with Him in a death like His, we shall certainly be united with Him in a resurrection like His. Eternal God, maker of Heaven and earth, who formed us from the dust of the earth, who by Your breath gave us life, we glorify You."

The congregation responded, "We glorify You," before the pastor continued:

"Jesus Christ, the resurrection and the life, who suffered death for all humanity, who rose from the grave to open the way to eternal life, we praise You."

The congregation replied, "We praise You."

As the pastor continued praying, Eric felt a surge of nervousness. Mike's brother would speak first, then Eric would give the final tribute.

Eric had done plenty of public speaking, mostly for work, and he was usually fine, but today would be very different. And he knew it.

He took a deep breath as the pastor announced, "At this time, I call on Mike's brother, Danny, for a time of family remembrance."

Eric had met Danny a few times but was never close with him. He was about eight years younger than Mike and Eric and seemed like a nice enough guy.

Danny stepped up to the podium, adjusted the microphone, and unfolded a sheet of paper.

"Hi everyone. I'm Danny, Mike's youngest brother. On behalf of my brother, Bobby, and the rest of our family, we want to thank you all for coming to help us say goodbye to Mikey. I was eight or nine when Mikey tore his ACL for the first time but I vividly remember him coming home from the doctor's offices on crutches and how upset he was. He went straight to his room and cried himself to sleep.

Even as a kid, I knew something was wrong. As it turned out, his ACL was torn, and he needed surgery and months of rehab.

The next few months were tough for my brother, but he was determined to keep playing. And eventually he did, making a comeback in his senior season of high school. Everything was going great, and he was playing well until he tore his other ACL in the last game of the season. The doctors said continuing his professional career would be nearly impossible.

This was a low point for Mikey. Unfortunately, he turned to drugs and alcohol and wasn't himself for several years, as he left for New York City before returning to Denver years later.

It took him a while, but he got his life together. He worked for a technology business, then later helped run a construction company. He got sober, met Stacy, learned he would be a dad, and was trying to live a normal life.

We may never know why this happened. Maybe he couldn't handle the pressure of being a dad, or maybe the weight of his lost hockey career drove him too far. What I want everyone to remember is my brother was a kind, good-hearted, and welcoming person.

Mikey was the first to show up at the hospital when my wife and I welcomed our son, Russell, three years ago.

He was also the one to drive two hours in a snowstorm to pick me up when my car broke down two years ago.

When I was nine, he took care of me when I fell out of our treehouse and broke my leg, carrying me a quarter of a mile up to our house to call an ambulance."

Danny paused, visibly emotional.

A few seconds later, he continued, "*This is the Mikey I remember, and I want you all to as well. Yes, he had his problems. Who here doesn't? But he was a loving, caring, and dedicated brother and uncle and we will all keep those warm memories of him in our heart.*

Rest in peace, Mikey. I hope you're with Mom and Dad, playing hockey and living your dream. I know we will see you again. We love you.

Love,

Danny, Bobby, Janet, Nicky, Jamie, Russell, Catherine, Sebastian, Melani, Robyn, and Terri. Our dog Luna misses you too."

Danny stopped reading, crumbled up the paper, and walked away from the microphone. On his way down, he paused and placed a hand on Mike's coffin. After a moment, he returned to his seat.

The pastor continued, "Thank you, Danny. That was beautiful and helps us remember the man Mike was. Now, we welcome Mike's friend Eric to continue the remembrance. Eric?"

Okay, he was up. He looked at Alexandra, who smiled and let go of his hand.

As he climbed the small step to the pulpit and unfolded his speech, a sudden calm washed over him. He had been anxious all day, but now the nerves had disappeared.

Looking at the crowd of roughly 200 people, he noticed Clarise and David had finally arrived and were sitting in the back row. They waved at him.

Eric took a deep breath and began.

"*Hi, thank you all for coming. I apologize for the length of my speech, but I know Mike would want his story told.*

I'm Eric Right. I grew up around here, in Gunbarrel. I live in Denver now, but I always loved coming back here. It's so beautiful. Mike and I knew each other for many years, going all the way back to our days in the High Plains Hockey League and then to the same high school. We were teammates before we became great friends. Playing hockey together was magical. I was nowhere as skilled as Mike, but we always looked to get each other the puck so the other could score. We were selfless like that I guess. Our line was one of the league's top-rated.

In our junior year, Mike decided to transfer to Boulder for better college exposure and a potential scholarship.

He was so incredibly talented—fast, strong, with a great sense for the puck, and was competitive as all hell. He wanted to attend college and get into the NHL. His dream was to say he played in the NHL, even if it was just one game.

It was what drove him through his junior and senior years. Because of his drive, we lost touch a bit, as I gave up on hockey for other passions and hobbies, and he continued with his ice time. I went to his games to support him as much as I could and we would always hang out after the game and talk about life, but his sole focus was hockey.

I attended the game during his junior year when he tore his ACL in his right knee on a fluke play. I was crushed for him. ACL injuries are tough to recover from, especially with college scouts making decisions on scholarships towards the end of the junior season.

As Danny said earlier, Mike was devastated but remained optimistic. After his surgery, we sat down and talked about our futures. I told him I wanted to go to a big college and experience college life—get away from the West and head East to a college like Penn State or Virginia."

Eric started tearing up a bit, so he took a moment.

"But Mike—Mikey wasn't even thinking about college. All he was thinking about was rehabbing his knee, getting back into playing shape, and staying local to hone his skills and work his way up the minors.

By senior year, he got in a few games before the end of the senior season, and he felt good about his career prospects. He had secured an NHL summer developmental league spot and felt strong—until he tore his other ACL in the last game of the season.

It was the worst thing that could have happened to him. After that game, I called him every week for a month before he was willing to talk. When we finally connected, we spent an hour on the phone. I tried to keep him positive, telling him everything would be okay.

However, something in his voice had changed. He sounded like he had given up inside. I felt horrible for him, but there wasn't much I could do.

We hung out and partied that summer after his second surgery, and I tried to show him some fun to help him forget about his dream being crushed.

Unfortunately, we lost touch over the next few years. I went to Penn State, and he stayed here. I would reach out occasionally to check on him, but we never spoke again during college.

At first, I was devastated. He had been my best friend for years, and now he was out of my life. My mom wisely told me to make peace with it. I hadn't done anything wrong, and if he wanted to, he would reach out.

After graduation, I heard from a mutual friend that he had nearly overdosed on a bad combination of drugs and ended up in the ER. Again, I tried reaching out, but got nothing.

At that point, I thought, 'What the hell did I do to this guy to deserve this treatment?'

I had to move on with my life, and I did. I met Alexandra in New York, started a family with her, and eventually moved back to Denver to raise our children and advance our careers.

Then, roughly four years ago, I got a call from a number I didn't recognize. I decided to pick it up. I never do that. I always send those calls to voicemail. But for some strange reason, I answered this call.

All I heard was, 'Hey man, what's up?'. It took me a second, but even after twenty years, I recognized the voice almost immediately. It was Mike.

We spoke for three hours that night. He poured his heart out, telling me how his life took a complete nosedive for years after his second injury. He was depressed and turned to drugs and alcohol to dull the pain, eventually becoming addicted.

He moved to New York to try to get his life in order, ironically at the same time I was there.

Side story, but there was one time I was on the PATH train, which connects New York to New Jersey, and I was getting off at a station in New York when a guy with long hair and a beard got on at the same time who somehow looked very familiar to me. I had to do a double take, but to this day, I am pretty sure it was Mike.

Anyway, he told me his girlfriend had been cheating on him in New York. When he found out, it sent him into a tailspin. He fell back into the cycle of booze, drugs, and depression that he was, unfortunately, familiar with.

This led to his overdose, and he was admitted to a hospital in New York. When his mom found out, she came to visit him, and he swore to her he would get better.

Eric paused as several members of Mike's family cried loudly. He felt bad but knew he had to tell the story—the good, the bad, and the ugly.

"I'm sorry if this is hard to hear. But this is Mike's story, and he would want me to tell it.

After everything Mike had been through, seeing his mother like that was the point where he decided to try to change his life and clean himself up. He wanted to go home, help his mother, and become a better person.

And he did try, but it wasn't easy. He returned to Denver, attempted to quit drugs and alcohol, got a local sales job, and joined AA to work on his sobriety. However, it didn't quite work, and he continued struggling with alcohol and drugs.

Losing his mom in the car accident two years ago was the thing that drove him to complete sobriety. He was devastated and asked me to take him to a recovery center, which I did. He swore he wasn't leaving until he was clean. Three months later, he left and didn't look back.

For the first time in a long time, Mike seemed to be in a good place. He met Stacy. She got pregnant, and he was heading into his Anticipation Day experience with his head held high. He was what I would consider to be a happy person.

I say this because the Mike who went into his Anticipation Day experience was very different from the one who came out.

I couldn't imagine his experience would push him back to alcohol and drugs after two years clean.

For those who don't know, Mike's simulation was him playing Game 7 of the Stanley Cup Finals for the New York Rangers. He finally got to live his dream of playing in the National Hockey League. It didn't go well, and he came out of the simulation with a bad mindset. Apparently, a very bad mindset.

In the simulation, his character had several injuries, one in particular which affected the game's outcome as Mike's character was injured with seconds left in the game that led to the Rangers losing.

How could the simulators, knowing Mike's history of injuries, give his character multiple injuries in the simulation? They had to know it would impact his performance and result in negative feelings both within the simulation and afterwards if those injuries impacted the result.

Personally, I find it completely irresponsible not to factor someone's physical and mental history into the facts and circumstances of the simulation itself.

What happened to Mike should never happen to others. The only question is: How could this have happened? There is only one answer that makes sense. The systems and processes that were put in place to prevent something like this failed. Quite simply, the individuals who created this simulation in the first place and those responsible for monitoring Mike's mental state after his experience failed, especially given his history of substance abuse.

That's the only logical conclusion I could come to.

In a way, I feel like I failed Mike for the second time. I should have noticed he was not himself, just like the first time I heard his voice in the hospital after he tore his second ACL. Unfortunately, I was so wrapped up in my own experience that I probably missed some subtleties in his behavior that would have clued me to the fact that something was happening with him.

The few times we met after our experiences, he told me he wasn't ready to talk about what happened yet. So, we talked about my experience instead.

It was great to talk to someone about how I was feeling. He was so helpful and was a good friend, just listening and talking me through my feelings. I will always appreciate that and will always remember him for the good man he was.

After Isla was born, he was so happy to welcome a new life into the world that I didn't think anything negative from his experience would spill over into his real life. Isla was his pride and joy, and I know he would have been a phenomenal father.

I want to apologize to Mike's family—Stacy, Isla, Mike's brothers Danny and Bobby, his sister Janet, and all his cousins and family members here today. I apologize for being so wrapped up in all of my crap that I didn't pick up on Mike's state of mind. Would it have changed anything? I don't know, but maybe."

Eric became emotional again. He took a swig from the bottled water next to him and caught his breath.

"I want to make this right. I want to fight for answers about why the system failed him and how we can prevent this from happening in the future. If this could happen to Mike, it can, and will, happen to others. If I can help prevent just one person from drifting back into a negative place because of their experiences, I will have done Mike proud, and his death would not have been in vain.

Mike, I will miss you everyday for the rest of my life. I promise to take care of Isla and treat her as my daughter as I know you would have wanted. I hope you rest in peace and I know we will see each other soon."

He looked out over the congregation. Most people were crying or sitting quietly. He looked down at Stacy, who looked back and him and mouthed, "Thank you."

"So, that was the end of my official speech. I had no idea there would be news vans here today. I was going to reach out to some local news outlets and contacts after today, but given the news is here, my plans changed a bit.

Out of respect to Mike's family, I want to let you know that after the service, I will go to the news vans and make a public request for further investigation into Mike's death and other deaths that may be somehow related to their Anticipation Day experience.

These incidents cannot continue. The government must spend additional resources to ensure high-risk individuals are mentally and emotionally fit to participate in the simulations and reintegrate into society after their experience is complete.

Anyone who wants to join me for support is welcome, but there is no pressure. This is the fight I am taking on for Mike. I think it was George Washington who said, 'It is better to be alone than to be in bad company,' so I will gladly accept any company, good or bad."

A few smiles spread through the crowd.

"Mike was a good man. One of the best I ever knew. I want to honor his memory and do him justice. So, that's it. Rest in Peace, Mikey."

It took Eric a moment to compose himself before he walked off the stage, paused by Mike's coffin to say a quick prayer and returned to his seat, where Alexandra greeted him with a hug and kiss.

"Mike would have been proud," Alexandra said, tears in her eyes.

"Let's see how I do in front of the cameras," Eric said quietly.

▼ ▼ ▼

Thirty minutes later, as the service ended and people began to funnel out of the church, Eric stepped outside into the bright, sunny day.

He looked up at the sky, put on his sunglasses, and murmured, "You better have my back, buddy. I can set anyone up for a one-timer, but I could use some help putting an accurate shot on the net. I hope you're with me."

Alexandra, noticing his expression, asked, "You okay? What are you thinking?"

He paused before answering. "Honestly, I'm just thinking, don't piss your pants in front of the cameras.' Who knows how many people are going to see this? I forgot to trim my nose and ears."

She smiled and took his hand. "Eric, you're fine. No nose hairs, no ear hairs. This isn't about you though. It's about Mike. Be real, be yourself, and you'll be fine. Okay?"

Her words seemed to calm him down. "You're right. Thank you. This is about Mike. He'd probably want me to have a big hair hanging out of my nose. It would go viral." He laughed nervously. "Okay, okay. I'm good. Thank you."

Eric kissed Alexandra and started walking over to the news vans, about 20 feet away. Reporters were gathering at the entrance of the driveway behind police tape, already shouting questions without order.

He would have to control this. Make a statement, then take on a few questions.

As he approached the reporters, their voices grew louder. He paused, took a deep breath, and raised his hands to silence them. The reporters finally shut the fuck up as Eric put his hands down.

Just as he was about to speak, he turned around and was somewhat surprised to see what looked like the entire service, including the priest, standing behind him. Clarise, David, Patrick, Emily, and MaryAnne were right there, supporting him proudly. They all looked at him with smiles, encouraging him to do what he came to do.

"Guess the speech worked, huh?" Eric turned to Alexandra, who smiled.

"They want you to do what needs to be done. To make Mike proud, as you said," she replied, squeezing his hand.

Over the next 30 minutes, Eric did just that. Mike would have loved every second of it.

TO BE CONTINUED... MAYBE.

THE END

Made in the USA
Middletown, DE
24 March 2025

73170864R00298